Praise for **Trust No One**

"A gripping thriller. *Trust No One* draws us into a world where truth blends with delusion. This story of a writer losing his memory and bearings pulls us into a maze where fiction blurs into murder. I couldn't put it down."

—Meg Gardiner, Edgar Award–winning author of *Phantom Instinct*

"On almost every page, this outstanding psychological thriller forces the reader to reconsider what is real."

—*Publishers Weekly* (starred review)

"With an unexpected ending, this thriller is one to remember."

—*New York Journal of Books*

"This powerhouse novel plays with the subtexts at the core of the mystery genre."

—*Booklist*

"A vivid, jangled exploration of mental illness, dark imagination, and the nowhere territory in between . . . Cleave spins one nightmare scenario after another out of Jerry's homely malady, leaping with such fiendish élan between past and present tense and first-person, second-person, and third-person narration that you may wonder if you've killed someone yourself."

—*Kirkus Reviews*

"This one will keep you guessing until the end."

—*The Strand Magazine*

Praise for
Five Minutes Alone

"[A] fiendishly twisted thriller . . . Cleave's masterful plotting skills are matched with superior pacing and characterization."

—*Publishers Weekly* (starred review)

"*Breaking Bad* reworked by the Coen Brothers."

—*Kirkus Reviews* (starred review)

"[A] powerhouse of a tale . . . A gripping thriller from beginning to end."

—*Booklist* (starred review)

Praise for
Joe Victim

"Cleave pulls out all the stops in his seventh Christchurch noir. . . . [He] juggles all the elements with impressive ease. Darkly humorous references to horrific violence will resonate with Dexter fans."

—*Publishers Weekly* (starred review)

"Cleave does his usual great job of threading two ongoing stories from two different serials into a single, closely knit unit and as usual, keeps the reader eager for more. It's hard not to empathize with Joe, even cheering for the bad guy is allowed, if for no other reason, we need to know what he will do next."

—*Suspense Magazine*

Praise for
The Laughterhouse

"An intense adrenaline rush from start to finish, I read *The Laughterhouse* in one sitting. It'll have you up all night. Fantastic!"

—S. J. Watson, *New York Times* bestselling author
of *Before I Go to Sleep*

"Piano wire–taut plotting, Tate's heart-wrenching losses and forlorn hopes, and Cleave's unusually perceptive gaze into the maw of a killer's madness make this a standout chapter in his detective's rocky road to redemption."

—*Publishers Weekly* (starred review)

"A wonderful book . . . The final effect is that tingling in the neck hairs that tells us an artist is at work."

—*Booklist* (starred review)

ALSO BY PAUL CLEAVE

TRUST
NO ONE

A THRILLER

PAUL CLEAVE

ATRIA PAPERBACK
New York   London   Toronto   Sydney   New Delhi

ATRIA PAPERBACK
An Imprint of Simon & Schuster, Inc.
1230 Avenue of the Americas
New York, NY 10020

First Atria Paperback edition June 2016

ATRIA PAPERBACK and colophon are trademarks of Simon & Schuster, Inc.

For information about special discounts for bulk purchases, please contact Simon & Schuster Special Sales at 1-866-506-1949 or business@simonandschuster.com.

The Simon & Schuster Speakers Bureau can bring authors to your live event. For more information, or to book an event, contact the Simon & Schuster Speakers Bureau at 1-866-248-3049 or visit our website at www.simonspeakers.com.

Manufactured in the United States of America

10 9 8 7 6 5 4

The Library of Congress has cataloged the hardcover edition as follows:

Cleave, Paul, date.
    Trust no one : a thriller / Paul Cleave. — First Atria Books hardcover edition.
       pages ; cm
1. Novelists—Fiction. 2. Alzheimer's disease—Patients—Fiction. 3. Psychological fiction. I. Title.
PR9639.4.C54T78   2015
823'.92—dc23
                                                                                      2015022805

ISBN 978-1-4767-7917-1
ISBN 978-1-5011-0367-4 (pbk)
ISBN 978-1-4767-7918-8 (ebook)

To Miss Roberts—my favorite teacher. Bees?

"The devil is in the details," Jerry says, and back then the devil was him, and these days those details are hard to hang on to. He can remember the woman's face, the way her mouth opened when all she could manage was an *oh*. Of course people never know what they're going to say when their time is up. Oscar Wilde said something about curtains when he was on his deathbed, about how ugly they were and either they must go or he would. But Jerry also remembers reading that nobody knows for sure if Wilde really said that. Certainly he wouldn't have said something pithy if Jerry had snuck into his house and used a knife to pin him to the wall. Maybe a *hurts more than I'd thought*, but nothing to go down in the history books.

His mind is wandering, it's doing that thing it does that he hates, that he oh so hates.

The policewoman staring at him has a look on her face one would reserve for a wounded cat. In her midtwenties, she has features that make him think he'd like to be the devil around her too. Nice long legs, blond hair down to her shoulders, athletic curves and tones. She has a set of blue eyes that keep pulling him in. She's in a tight, black skirt and a snug-fitting dark blue top that he'd like to see on the floor. She keeps rubbing her thumb against the pad of her ring finger, where she's sporting the type of callus he's seen on guitar players. Leaning against the wall with his thick forearms folded is a policeman in uniform, an 80s, TV-cop moustache on his lip and a utility belt full of citizen-restraining tools around his waist. He looks bored.

Jerry carries on with the interview. "The woman was thirty, give or take a year, and her name was Susan, only she spelled it with a *z*. People spell things all sorts of weird ways these days. I blame cell phones," he says, and he waits for her to nod and agree, but she doesn't, nor does the cop holding up the wall. He realizes his mind has once again gone wandering.

He takes a deep breath and tightens his grip on the arms of the chair and repositions himself to try and get more comfortable. He closes his eyes and he focuses, focuses, and he takes himself back to Suzan with a *z*, Suzan with her black hair tied into a ponytail, Suzan with a sexy smile and a great tan and an unlocked door at three in the morning. That's the kind of neighborhood Jerry lived in back then. A lot has changed in thirty years. Hell, he's changed. But back before texting and the Internet butchered the English language, people weren't as suspicious. Or perhaps they were just lazier. He doesn't know. What he does know is he was surprised to find her house so easy to get into. He was nineteen years old and Suzan was the girl of his dreams.

"I can still feel the moment," Jerry says. "I mean, nobody is ever going to forget the first time they take a life. But before that I stood in her backyard and I held my arms out wide as if I could embrace the moon. It was a few days before Christmas. In fact it was the longest day of the year. I remember the clear sky and the way the stars from a million miles away made the night feel timeless." He closes his eyes and takes himself back to the moment. He can almost taste the air. "I remember thinking on this night people would be born and people would die," he says, his eyes still closed, "and that the stars didn't care, that even the stars weren't forever and life was fleeting. I was feeling pretty damn philosophical. I also remember the urgent need to take a piss, and taking one behind her garage."

He opens his eyes. His throat is getting a little sore from all the talking and his arm keeps itching. There's a glass of water in front of him. He sips at it, and looks at the man against the wall, the man who is staring at Jerry impassively, as if he'd rather be getting shot in the line of duty than listening to a man telling his tales. Jerry has always known this day was coming, the day of confession. He just hopes it comes with absolution. After all, that's why he's here. Absolution will lead to a cure.

"Do you know who I am?" the woman asks, and suddenly he gets the idea she's about to tell him she's not a cop at all, but the daughter of one of his victims. Or a sister. His eyes are undressing her, they're putting her into a home-alone scenario, an alone-in-a-parking-garage scenario, a deserted-street-at-night scenario. "Jerry?"

He could strangle her with her own hair. He could shape her long legs in all directions.

"Jerry, do you know who I am?"

"Of course I know," he says, staring at her. "Now would you kindly let me finish? That is why you're here, isn't it? For the details?"

"I'm here because—"

He puts his hand up. "Enough," he tells her, the word forceful, and she sighs and slumps back into her chair as if she's heard that word a hundred times already. "Let the monster have a voice," he says. He has forgotten her name. Detective . . . somebody, he thinks, then decides to settle on Detective Scenario. "Who knows what I will remember tomorrow?" He taps the side of his head as he asks the question, almost expecting it to make a wooden sound, like the table his parents used to have that was thick wood around the edges but hollow in the middle. He'd tap it, expecting one sound and getting another. He wonders where that table is and wonders if his father sold it so he could buy a few more beers.

"Please, you need to calm down," Detective Scenario says, and she's wrong. He doesn't need to calm down. If anything he might have to start yelling just to get his point across.

"I am calm," he tells her, and he taps the side of his head and it reminds him of a table his parents used to have. "What is wrong with you?" he asks. "Are you stupid? This case will make your career," he tells her, "and you sit there like a useless whore."

Her face turns red. Tears form in her eyes, but don't fall. He takes another sip of water. It's cool and helps his throat. The room is silent. The officer against the wall shifts his position by crossing his arms the other way. Jerry thinks about what he just said and figures out where he went wrong. "Look, I'm sorry I said that. Sometimes I say things I shouldn't."

She wipes the palms of her hands at her eyes, removing the tears before they fall.

"Can I carry on now?" he asks.

"If that will make you happy," she says.

Happy? No. He's not doing this to be happy. He's doing this so he can get better. He thinks back to that night thirty years ago. "I thought

I was going to have to pick the lock. I'd been practicing on the one at home. I still lived with my parents back then. When they were out I'd practice picking the lock on the back door. I'd been shown how by a friend from university. He said knowing how to pick a lock is like having a key to the world. It made me think about Suzan. It took me two months to figure out how to do it, and I was nervous because I knew once I got to her house the lock might be all kinds of different. It was all for nothing, because when I got there her door was unlocked. It was a product of the day, I guess, though that day really was just as violent as this day."

He takes a sip of water. Nobody says anything. He carries on.

"I never even had doubts. The door being unlocked, that was a sign and I took it. I had a small flashlight with me so I wouldn't bump into any walls. Suzan used to live with her boyfriend, but he'd moved out a few months earlier. They used to fight all the time. I could hear it from my house almost opposite, so I was pretty sure no matter what happened to Suzan with a ʒ, he would be blamed for it. I used to think about her all the time. I imagined how she would look naked. I just had to know, you know? I had to know how her skin would feel, how her hair would smell, how her mouth would taste. It was like an itch. That's about the best way to describe it. An itch that was driving me insane," he says, scratching at the itch on his arm that is also driving him insane. An insect bite, maybe a mosquito or a spider. "So that night on the longest day of the year I went into her house at three o'clock in the morning with a knife so I could scratch it."

Which is exactly what he did. He walked down her hallway and found her bedroom, and then stood in the doorway the same way he'd stood outside, but this time instead of embracing the stars he was embracing the darkness. He's been embracing the darkness ever since.

"She didn't even wake up. I mean, not right away. My eyes were adjusting to the dark. Part of the room was lit up by an alarm clock, part was lit up because the curtains were thin and there was a streetlamp outside. I moved over to her bed and I crouched next to it and I just waited. I'd always had this theory that if you did that, the person would wake up, and that's what happened. It took thirty seconds. I put the knife against her throat," he tells them, and Detective Scenario flinches a little and looks ready to cry again, and the officer still looks like he'd rather be anywhere else. "I could feel her breath on my hand, and her eyes . . . her eyes were wide and terrified and made me feel—"

"I know all about Suzan with a *z*," Detective Scenario says.

Jerry can't help it, but he feels embarrassed. That's one of the cruel side effects—he's told her all this before and can't remember. It's the details—those damn details that are hard to hang on to.

"It's okay, Jerry," she says.

"What do you mean it's okay? I killed that woman and now I'm being punished for what I did to her, to all of them, because she was the first of many, and the monster needs to confess, the monster needs to find redemption because if he can, then the Universe will stop punishing him and he can get better."

The detective lifts a handbag off the floor and rests it on her lap. She pulls out a book. She hands it to him. "Do you recognize it?"

"Should I?"

"Read the back cover."

The book is called *A Christmas Murder*. He turns it over. The first line is "Suzan with a *z* was going to change his life."

"What in the hell is this?"

"You don't recognize me, do you," she says.

"I—" he says, but adds nothing more. There is something there— something coming to the surface. He looks at the way her thumb rubs against the callus on her finger, and there's something familiar about that. Somebody he knows used to do that. "Should I?" he asks, and the answer is yes, he should.

"I'm Eva. Your daughter."

"I don't have a daughter. You're a cop, and you're trying to trick me," he says, doing his best not to sound angry.

"I'm not a cop, Jerry."

"No! No, if I had a daughter I would know about it!" he says, and he slams his hand down on the table. The officer leaning against the wall takes a few steps forward until Eva looks at him and asks him to wait.

"Jerry, please, look at the book."

He doesn't look at the book. He doesn't do anything but stare at her, and then he closes his eyes and he wonders how life has gotten this way. Eighteen months ago things were fine, weren't they? What is real and what isn't?

"Jerry?"

"Eva?"

"That's right, Jerry. It's Eva."

He opens his eyes and looks at the book. He's seen this cover before, but if he's read this book he doesn't remember. He looks at the name of the author. It's familiar. It's . . . but he can't get there.

"Henry Cutter," he says, reading the name out loud.

"It's a pen name," his daughter says, his beautiful daughter, his lovely daughter with a monster of a father, a disgusting old man who moments ago wondered how she would feel beneath him. He feels sick.

"I don't . . . is this . . . is this you? Did you write this?" he asks. "Did you write this after I told you what happened?"

She looks concerned. Patient but concerned. "It's you," she tells him. "This is your pen name."

"I don't understand."

"You wrote this book, and a dozen more just like it. You started writing when you were a teenager. You always used the name Henry Cutter."

He's confused. "What do you mean I wrote this? Why would I confess to the world what I had done?" Then it comes to him, something he's forgotten. "Did I go to jail? Did I write this when I came out? But then . . . how would . . . the timeline doesn't . . . I don't get it. Are you really my daughter?" he asks, and he thinks about his daughter, his Eva, but now that he's thinking about it, Eva is ten years old, not twenty-something, and his daughter would be calling him Dad, not Jerry.

"You're a crime writer," she says.

He doesn't believe her—why would he? She's just a stranger. Still . . . the crime writer label seems to fit, like putting on a comfortable glove, and he knows what she's saying is true. Of course it's true. He wrote thirteen books. An unlucky number—at least if you believe in that kind of thing, and he has been very unlucky, hasn't he? He's writing another book too. A diary. No, not a diary, a journal. His Madness Journal. He looks around, but it's not here with him. Maybe he lost it. He flicks through the pages of the book Eva handed him, but not looking at any of the words. "This was one of the early ones."

"Your first," she says.

"You were only twelve when it came out," he tells her, but hang on now, how can that be if Eva is only ten?

"I was at school," she says.

He looks at her hand and sees there's a wedding ring, then looks at his own. There's one on his hand too. He wants to ask about his wife, but doesn't want to look a bigger fool for doing so. Dignity is only one of the things the Alzheimer's has been taking away from him. "Do I always forget you?"

"You have good days and bad," she says, in the way of an answer.

He looks around the room. "Where are we? Am I here because of what I did to Suzan?"

"There is no Suzan," the officer says. "We found you in town. You were lost and confused. We called your daughter."

"There is no Suzan?"

"No Suzan," Eva says, reaching back into her handbag. She pulls out a photograph. "That's us," she says. "It was taken just over a year ago."

He looks at the picture. The woman in the photograph is the same woman talking to him. In the photograph she's sitting on a couch holding a guitar, a big smile on her face, and the man in the photograph sitting next to her is Jerry, it's Jerry a year ago, back when all he was forgetting were his keys and the occasional name, back when he was writing books and living life. The last year has been stolen from him. His personality stolen. His thoughts and memories twisted and decayed. He turns the photograph over. Written on the back is *Proudest dad in the world.*

"It was taken the day I told you I'd sold my first song," she says.

"I remember it," he tells her, but he doesn't.

"Good," she says, and smiles, and in that smile is a lot of sadness and it breaks his heart that his daughter has to see him like this.

"I really want to go home now," he says.

She looks at the officer. "Is that okay?" she asks, and the officer tells them that it is.

"You'll need to speak to the nursing home," the officer says, "tell them this kind of thing can't keep happening."

"Nursing home?" Jerry asks.

Eva looks at him. "That's where you live now."

"I thought we were going home?"

"That is your home," she says.

He starts to cry, because he remembers it then—his room, the nurses, the gardens, sitting in the sun with only his sense of loss as company. He's not aware he's crying until his tears hit the top of the table, enough of them to make the officer look away and to make his daughter come around and put her arms around him.

"It's going to be okay, Jerry. I promise."

But he's still thinking about Suzan with a z, about how it felt back when he killed her, back before he wrote about it. Back when he embraced the darkness.

DAY ONE

Some basic facts. Today is a Friday. Today you are sane, albeit somewhat in shock. Your name is Jerry Grey, and you are scared. You're sitting in your study writing this while your wife, Sandra, is on the phone with her sister, no doubt in tears because this future of yours, well, buddy, nobody saw it coming. Sandra will look after you—that's what she's promised, but these are the promises of a woman who has known for only eight hours that the man you are is going to fade away, to be replaced by a stranger. She hasn't processed it, and right now she'll be telling Katie that it's going to be hard, all too terribly hard, but she'll hang in there, of course she will, because she loves you—but you don't want that from her. At least that's what you're thinking now. Your wife is forty-eight years old and even though you don't have a future, she still does. So maybe over the next few months if the disease doesn't push her away, you should push her away. The thing to focus on is that this isn't about me, you, us—it's about family. Your family. We have to do what's best for them. Of course you know that's a gut reaction, and you may very well, and probably will, feel differently tomorrow.

At the moment you are very much in control. Yes, it's true you lost your phone yesterday, and last week you lost your car, and recently you forgot Sandra's name, and yes, the diagnosis means it's true the best years are now behind you and there will not be too many good ones ahead, but at the moment you know exactly who you are. You know you have an amazing wife named Sandra and an incredible daughter called Eva.

This journal is for you, Jerry of the future, Future Jerry. At the time of this writing, you have hope there's a cure on its way. The rate medical technology is advancing . . . well, at some point there will be a pill, won't there? A pill to make the Alzheimer's go away. A pill to bring the memories back, and this journal is to help you if those memories tend to have fuzzy edges. If there is no pill, you will still be able to look back through these pages and know who you were before the early onset dementia, before the Big A came along and took away the good things.

From these pages you will learn about your family, how much you love them, how sometimes Sandra can smile at you from across the room and it makes your heart race, how Eva can laugh at one of your small jokes and go *Dad!* before shaking her head in embarrassment. You need to know, Future Jerry, that you love and that you are loved.

So this is day one in your journal. Not day one where things started to change—that started a year or two back—but day one of the diagnosis. Your name is Jerry Grey and eight hours ago you sat in Doctor Goodstory's office holding your wife's hand while he gave you the news. It has, and let's be honest since we're among friends here—scared the absolute hell out of you. You wanted to tell Doctor Goodstory to either change his profession or change his last name, because the two couldn't be any further apart. On the way home, you told Sandra that the diagnosis reminded you of a quote from Ray Bradbury's *Fahrenheit 451*, and when you got home you looked it up so you could tell her. Bradbury said, "It took some man a lifetime maybe to put some of his thoughts down, looking around at the world and life, and then I came along in two minutes and boom! It's all over." The quote, of course, is from one book-burning fireman to another, but it perfectly sums up your own future. You've spent your lifetime putting your thoughts down on paper, Future Jerry, and in this case it's not the pages going up in flames, but the mind that created them. Funny how you could remember that sentiment from a book you read more than ten years ago, but can't find your car keys.

Writing in this journal is the first time in years you've handwritten anything longer than a grocery list. The computer's word processor has been your medium ever since the day you wrote the words *Chapter One* of your first book, but using the computer for this . . . well, it feels too impersonal, for one, and too impractical for another. The journal is more authentic, and much easier to carry around than a laptop. It's actually a journal Eva gave you for Christmas back when she was eleven. She drew a big smiley face on the cover and glued a pair of googly eyes to it. From the face she drew a thought bubble, and inside that she wrote *Dad's coolest ideas*. The pages have always remained blank, because your ideas tend to get scribbled down on Post-it notes and stuck around the sides of the computer monitor, but the notebook (now to be a journal) has always remained in the top drawer of your desk, and every now and then you'll take it out and run your thumb over the cover and remember when she gave it to you. Hopefully your handwriting is better than when you get an idea during the night and scrawl it down only to find you can't read your own words the following morning.

There is so much to tell you, but let me begin by being blunt. You're heading into Batshit County. "We're all batshit crazy in Batshit County"—that's a line from your latest work. You're a crime writer—now's as good a time as any to mention that. You write under a pen name, that of Henry Cutter, and over the years have been given the nickname The Cutting Man by fans and the media, not just because of your pen name, but because many of your bad guys use knives. You've written twelve books, and number thirteen, *The Man Goes Burning*, is with your editor at the moment. She's struggling with it. She struggled with number twelve too—and that should have been a warning flag there, right? Here's what you should do—get this put on a T-shirt: *People with Dementia Don't Make Great Authors*. When you're losing your marbles a plot is hard to construct. There were bits that made no sense and bits that made even less sense, but you got there, and you felt embarrassed and you apologized a dozen times and put it down to stress. After all, you'd been touring a lot that year so it made sense you were going to make some mistakes. But *The Man Goes Burning* is a mess. Tomorrow or the next day, you'll call your editor and tell her about the Big A. Every author eventually has a last book—you just didn't think you were there yet, and you didn't think it would be a journal.

Your last book, this journal, will be your descent into madness. Wait—better make that the *journey* into madness. Don't mix that up. Sure, you're going to forget your wife's name, but let's not forget what we're calling this—it's a journey, not a descent. And yes, that's a joke. An angry joke because, let's face it, Future Jerry, you are exceptionally angry. This is a journey into madness because you are mad. What isn't there to be mad about? You are only forty-nine years old, my friend, and you are staring down the barrel of insanity. *Madness Journal* is the perfect name. . . .

But no, that's not what this is about. This isn't about writing up a
memorial for your anger, this is a journal to let you know about your
life before the disease dug in its claws and ripped your memories to
shreds. This journal is about your life, about how blessed you've been.
You, Future Jerry, you got to be the very thing you'd always dreamed of
becoming—a writer. You got the amazing wife, a woman who can put
her hand in yours and make you feel whatever it is you need to feel,
whether it's comfort or warmth or excitement or lust, the woman who
you wake up to every morning knowing you get to fall asleep with her
that night, the woman who can always see the other side of the argument, the woman who teaches you more about life every day. You have
the daughter with an old soul, the traveler, the girl who wants people to
be happy, the girl taking on the world. You have the nice house on the
nice street, you sold a lot of books and you entertained a lot of people.
Truthfully, F.J., you always thought there would be a trade-off, that the
Universe would somehow balance things out. It turns out you were
right. Most of all, this journal is a map to the person you used to be. It
will help you get back to the times you can't remember, and when there
is a cure, this journal will help restore anything you have lost.

The best thing to do first is explain how we got here. Thankfully,
you'll still have all your memories tomorrow and you'll still be you, and
the next day, and the next, but those next days are running out the
same way authors have a final book. We all have a last thought, a last
hope, a last breath, and it's important to get all this down for you, Jerry.

You've got the badly written book this year and, spoiler alert, Jerry,
last year's novel didn't review that well. But hey—you still read the
reviews, is that another effect of the dementia? You told yourself years
ago not to read them, but you do anyway. You usually don't because of
the occasional blogger calling you a *This is Henry Cutter's most disappointing novel yet* hack. It's the way of the world, my friend, and just
part of the job. But perhaps one you don't have to worry about where
you are now. It's hard to pinpoint when it started. You forgot Sandra's
birthday last year. That was tough. But there's more. However, right
now . . . right now exhaustion is setting in, you're feeling a little too all
over the place, and . . . well, you're actually drinking a gin and tonic as
you're writing this. It's your first of the evening. Okay, that's another

---

joke, it's your second, and the world is starting to lose its sharp edges. What you really want to do now is just sleep.

You're a good news, bad news kind of guy, F.J. You like good news, and you don't like bad news. Hah—thanks G&T number three for giving you Captain Obvious as another narrative point of view. The bad news is that you're dying. Not dying in the traditional sense—you might still have a lot of years ahead of you—but you're going to be a shell of a man and the Jerry you were. The Jerry I am right now, that you are as of this writing, is going to leave, sorry to tell you. The good news is—soon you're not even going to know. There'll be moments—of course there will be. You can already imagine Sandra sitting beside you and you won't recognize her, and maybe you'll have just wet yourself and maybe you'll be telling her to leave you the hell alone, but there'll be these moments—these patches of blue sky on a dark day where you'll know what's going on, and it will break your heart.

It will break your fucking heart.

The officer leads Jerry and Eva through the fourth floor of the police department. Most people stop what they're doing to look over. Jerry wonders if he knows any of them. He seems to remember there was somebody he'd used for the books—a cop, maybe, who he could ask how does this work or how does that work, would a bullet do this, would a cop do that, talk me through the loopholes. If he's here Jerry doesn't recognize him, then remembers that it's not a police officer he got help from, but a friend of his, a guy by the name of Hans. He still has the photograph Eva gave him in his hand, and he can remember when it was taken. Things are coming back to him, but not everything.

Eva has to sign something and then speaks to the officer again while Jerry stares at one of the walls where there's a flyer for the police rugby team that has six names on it, the last one being Uncle Bad Touch. The officer walks over with Eva and wishes Jerry a nice day, and Jerry wishes for the same thing—he wishes for a lot of nice days, and then they're riding the elevator down and heading outside.

He has no idea what day it is, let alone the date, but there are daffodils along the riverbank of the Avon, the river that runs through the heart of the city and appeared in some of his books—beautiful in reality, but in his books normally a murder weapon or a person is being thrown into it. The daffodils mean it's spring, putting the day in early September. People on the street look happy, the way they always do when climbing out of the winter months, though in his books, if he's remembering correctly, people were always miserable no matter what time of the year. His version of Christchurch was one where the Devil had come to town—no smiles, no pretty flowers, no sunsets, just hell in every direction. He's wearing a sweater, which is great because it's not really that warm, and great because it means he must have had an attack of common sense earlier that told him to dress for the conditions. Eva stops next to a car ten yards short of a guy sitting on the sidewalk sniffing glue. She unlocks it.

"New car?" he asks, which is a dumb thing to say, because the moment the words are out of his mouth he knows he's set himself up for disappointment.

"Something like that," she says, and she's probably had it for a few years or more. Maybe Jerry even bought it for her.

They climb inside, and when she puts her hand on the steering wheel he notices again her wedding ring. The guy sniffing glue has approached the car and starts tapping on the side of the window. He has *Uncle Bad Touch* written on his T-shirt, and Jerry wonders if he's going to play rugby for the cops, or if he was the inspiration for the comedian who wrote the name on the form upstairs. Eva starts the car and they pull away from the curb just as Uncle Bad Touch asks if they'd like to buy a used sandwich from him. They get twenty yards before having to stop at a red light. Jerry pictures the day being split into three parts; the sun is out towards the west and looks like it'll be gone in a few hours, making him decide they're nearing the end of the second act. He's trying to think about Eva's husband and is getting close to picturing him when Eva starts talking.

"You were found in the town library," she says. "You walked in and went to sleep on the floor. When one of the staff woke you up, you started shouting. They called the police."

"I was asleep?"

"Apparently so," she says. "How much can you remember?"

"The library, but just a little. I don't remember walking there. I remember last night. I remember watching TV. And I remember the police station. I kind of . . . switched on, I guess, during what I thought was an interview. I thought I was there because the police figured out what I'd done back when—"

"There is no Suzan," she says, interrupting him.

The light turns green. He thinks about Suzan and how she doesn't exist outside the pages of a book he can barely remember writing. He feels tired. He stares out at the buildings that look familiar, and is starting to get an idea of where they are. There is a guy arguing with a parking attendant on the sidewalk, poking his finger into the attendant's chest. There's a woman jogging while pushing a stroller and talking on her cell phone. There's a guy carrying a bunch of flowers with a big smile on his face. He sees a young boy, probably fifteen or sixteen, help an old lady pick up her bag of groceries that has split open.

"Do we have to go back to the nursing home? I want to go home instead. To my real home."

"There is no real home," Eva says. "Not anymore."

"I want to see Sandra," he says, his wife's name coming out without any effort, and perhaps that's the key to tricking the disease—just keep talking and eventually you'll get there. He turns to Eva. "Please."

She slows the car a little so she can look over at him. "I'm sorry, Jerry, but I have to take you back. You're not allowed to be out."

"Allowed? You make it sound like I should be under lock and key. Please, Eva, I want to go home. I want to see Sandra. Whatever it is I've done to be put into a home, I promise I'll be better. I promise. I won't be a—"

"The house was sold, Jerry. Nine months ago," she says, staring ahead at the road. Her bottom lip is quivering.

"Then where's Sandra?"

"Mom has . . . Mom has moved on."

"Moved on? Jesus, is she dead?"

She looks over at him, and because of that she nearly rear-ends a car that comes to a quick stop ahead of her. "She's not dead, but she's . . . she's not your wife anymore. I mean, you're still married, but not for much longer—it's just a matter of paperwork now."

"Paperwork? What paperwork?"

"The divorce," she says, and they start moving forward again. There's a young girl of six or seven looking out the back window of the car ahead, waving and pulling faces.

"She's leaving me?"

"Let's not talk about this now, Jerry. How about I take you to the beach for a bit? You always liked the beach. I have Rick's jacket in the back, you can put that on—it'll be cold out there."

"Is Sandra seeing somebody else? Is she seeing this Rick guy?"

"Rick's my husband."

"Is there another guy? Is that why Sandra is leaving me?"

"There is no other guy," Eva says. "Please, I really don't want to talk about this now. Maybe later."

"Why? Because by then I'll have forgotten?"

"Let's go to the beach," she says, "and we'll discuss it there. The fresh air will do you good. I promise."

"Okay," he says, because if he behaves, then maybe Eva will take him back to his home instead. Maybe he can carry on with the life he had and work on getting Sandra back.

"Was the house really sold?" he asks.

"Yes."

"Why do you call me Jerry? Why don't you call me Dad?"

She shrugs and doesn't look at him. He lets it go.

They head for the beach. He watches the people and the traffic and stares at the buildings, Christchurch City on a spring day and if there's a more beautiful city in the world he hasn't seen it, and he has seen a lot of cities—that's one thing the writing has given him, it's given him freedom and . . .

"There was traveling," he says. "Book tours. Sometimes Sandra came along, and sometimes you came too. I've seen a lot of countries. What happened to me? To Sandra?"

"The beach, Dad, let's wait for the beach."

He wants to wait for the beach, but more is coming back to him now, things he would much rather forget. "I remember the wedding. And Rick. I remember him now. I'm . . . I'm so sorry," he tells her. "I'm sorry about what I did."

"It wasn't your fault."

The shame and the humiliation come rushing back. "Is that why you stopped calling me Dad?"

She doesn't look at him. She doesn't answer. She swipes a finger beneath each of her eyes and wipes away the tears before they fall. He goes back to looking out the window, feelings of shame and embarrassment flooding his thoughts. Up ahead cars are coming to a stop for a family of ducks crossing the road. A camper van pulls over and a pair of young children climb out the side and start taking photos.

"I hate the nursing home," he says. "I must still have some money. Why can't I buy myself a home and some private care?"

"It doesn't work that way."

"Why doesn't it work that way?"

"It just doesn't, Jerry," she says, using a tone that lets him know she doesn't want to discuss it.

They keep driving. It's crazy that he feels uncomfortable with his own daughter, but he does, this giant wall between them feels unbreakable, this wall he put up by being a bad father and an even worse husband. They get through town and head east, out towards Sumner beach, and when they arrive they find a parking spot near the sand, the ocean ahead of them, a line of cafés and shops and then the hills behind. They get out of the car. He watches a dog rolling itself over a seagull that's been squashed by a car. Eva gets Rick's jacket out of the trunk, but he tells her he doesn't need it. It's a cool wind, but it's like she said—it's refreshing. The sand is golden, but there are lots of pieces of driftwood and seaweed and shells. There are maybe two dozen people, but that's all, most of them young. He takes his shoes and socks off and carries them. They walk along the waterline, seagulls chirping overhead, people playing, and this—this right now, feels like a normal day. This feels like a normal life.

"What are you thinking about?" Eva asks.

"About when I used to bring you here as a kid," he tells her. "The seagulls used to scare you. What happened with your mother?"

She sighs, then turns towards him. "It wasn't really one thing," she says, "but a combination of things."

"The wedding?"

"That was a big part of it. She couldn't forgive you. You also couldn't forgive yourself."

"So she left me."

"Come on," she says. "It's a beautiful spring day. Let's not waste it on sad memories. Let's walk for another half an hour and then I'll take you back, okay? I told them I'd have you back by dinner."

"Will you stay for dinner?"

"I can't," she says. "I'm sorry."

They walk along the beach, they walk and talk, and Jerry looks out over the water, and he wonders how far his body could swim, how far he would make it before the dementia kicked in and he lost all rhythm. Maybe he'd get ten yards out there and drown. Just sink to the bottom and let his lungs fill with water. Maybe that wouldn't be such a bad thing.

DAY FOUR

No, you haven't lost day two and day three—in fact you can remember them clearly (though you did misplace your coffee and Sandra found it out by the pool, which is weird because you don't even have a pool).

Eva came over on the weekend, and there's big news. She's getting married. You've known for a while it was probably going to happen, but that didn't make it any less of a surprise. It's hard to sum up what you felt in that moment. You were excited, of course you were, but you felt a sense of loss, one that's hard to explain, a sense Eva was moving on with her life and out of yours, and there's a sense of loss because there will be grandchildren you may not get to meet, or if you do, you may end up forgetting them.

She came over on Sunday morning and popped the news. She and What's His Name got engaged on Saturday night. There was no way you and Sandra could tell her about the Big A, not then, but you will soon, of course you will. You'll need *some* explanation as to why you keep putting your pants on backwards and trying to speak Klingon. Just kidding. Speaking of kidding, you *do* have a pool, but you sure don't remember walking down to it, because it's winter, but hey, there you go.

So day two and three went by, and you're not really dealing with the news any better. Before we get into what happened on the Day at the Doctor, first let me do what I said I would do on Day One, and that's tell you how it all began.

It was at Matt's Christmas party two years ago. Christ, you probably don't even remember Matt. He's what you would call a background character, somebody who pops into your life every few months or so, mostly after you've run into him at the mall, but he does throw a pretty good Christmas shindig. You and Sandra went along, you socialized, you mingled, it's what you do, and then it happened—Matt's brother and sister-in-law showed up and introduced themselves, *Hi, I'm James and this is Karen*, and then you, *Hi, I'm Jerry and this is my wife* . . . and that was it. This is your wife. Sandra, of course, filled in the blank. This is your wife, *Sandra*. She didn't know it was a blank—she thought it was you trying to be funny. But no, Mr. Memory Banks, from which you'd withdrawn her name thousands of times over the nearly thirty years you've loved her, had blocked your account. The moment was so quick, and what was it you put it down to? The alcohol. And why not? Your dad had been a raging drunk back in his day, and it only made sense that was rubbing off on you a little—and after all you were standing there with a G&T in your hand, your third for the night.

Actually, just for the record, your honor, don't go getting the wrong impression about your past self. You only drink a couple of times a year—your dad used to imbibe more in a day than you would in a year. He drank himself to death—literally. It was awful, and one memory that seems unlikely to ever fade is the one of your mother calling you, sounding so hysterical you couldn't make out what she was saying down the phone, yet not needing to as her tone was telling you everything you needed to know. It wouldn't be until you got to their house you found out he had been drinking by the pool. He rolled into it to cool down and couldn't get himself back out.

So you forgot your wife's name and why wouldn't you think it was anything other than the booze? Sure, you were always losing your keys, but if society threw around the Big A label to anybody who didn't know where their keys were then the whole world would be suffering from Alzheimer's. Yes—there was the car keys getting lost, but they would get found too, wouldn't they? Be it in the fridge, or in the pantry, or once (hello, irony) by the pool. Sure, you lost your dad in a pool, you left your coffee there, and your keys, but that's just carelessness—after all, you do have a world full of people living inside your head looking for a voice, remember? All those characters? Serial killers and rapists and bank robbers, and of course then there's the bad guys too (that's a joke). With all that going on inside, of course you're going to lose your keys. And your wallet. And your jacket. And even your car—well you didn't lose it, not really—which is a story that had you calling *This Is My Wife . . . Sandra, Is It?* from the mall and, thankfully, not the police to report it stolen. She came and picked you up, and she spotted it on the way out of the parking lot exactly where you had left it, and you, well, you'd been looking for the car you used to own five years prior to that. You both had a good laugh about it. A concerned kind of laugh. And it reminded you of the time you *had* forgotten her name, and it reminded you of when you used to renovate houses before the crime writing took off, back when you would paint rooms and put in new kitchens, lay tiles and put in new bathrooms, and through it all you would lose the screwdriver or the hammer (and there was no pool back then to look around). And just where. The hell. Were they? Well sometimes you never *did* find them.

Sandra thought the solution was to have A *Place for Everything*. She emptied a shelf near the front door, and when you came inside you would empty your pockets, putting your phone and keys and wallet and watch there—at least that was the plan. The shelf didn't work for one very simple reason. It wasn't so much that you couldn't remember where you were putting these things, it was that you had *no* memory of even putting them down. It was like when you reach your destination and can't remember the drive. You can't use A *Place for Everything* when you're not aware of even taking your keys out of your pocket. Then you would forget birthdays. You would forget important dates. So that and that and all that other stuff—then you forgot Sandra's name again. Just. Like. That. You were filling in passport forms. You were sitting beside each other, and Sandra was filling hers in and you said . . . get this, this will make you laugh or cry, but you said to her *Why are you writing down Sandra in the name box?* Because that's what she was doing—of course that's what she was doing—it's what any Sandra would do, but you asked because, in that moment, you had no clue. Your wife's name was . . . what? You didn't know. You didn't know you didn't know that—you just knew it wasn't Sandra, of course not, it was . . .

It was Sandra. It was the moment. When things changed.

That's how it started—or at least that's when it started showing up. Who knows when it started? Birth? In utero? That concussion you got when you were sixteen and you stumbled down a flight of stairs at school? How about twenty years ago when you took Sandra and Eva camping? You were chasing Eva around the campsite, pretending to be a grizzly bear and she was giggling and you were going *roar, roar,* and your throat was getting raw and your hands were forming claws and you ran right into a branch and knocked yourself out cold. Or maybe it was that time you were fourteen and your dad punched you for the first and only time in his life (he was normally a happy drunk) because he was angry, he was mad, he was what he got sometimes when the *normally* wasn't in play and the darkness was creeping in. Kind of like the darkness you've got coming and, thinking about it, maybe he wasn't as drunk as it seemed—maybe your disease was his disease. It could be one of those things, or none of them, or, as you thought in the beginning, just the Universe balancing the scales for giving you the life you wanted.

Soon you won't remember your favorite TV show, your favorite food. Soon you're going to start slurring your speech and forgetting people, only you're not going to know most of this. Your Brain the Vault is going to turn into Your Brain the Sieve, and all those people, all those characters you've created, their world and their futures are going to drain away, and soon . . . well, hey, in a hundred years you would have been dead anyway.

That moment when things changed, well, Sandra said you had to go and see Doctor Goodstory. Which led to more doctors. Which led to news of the Big A on Big F—that's how you think of that Friday now, as the Big F, the Day at the Doctor, and really you think that's a pretty appropriate name for it, right? You'd been hoping for something simple, something changing your diet and spending more time outside soaking up vitamin D could fix. Instead the Big F brought the exact news you were hoping you wouldn't hear.

What do you want to know about that day? Do you want to know you cried that night in Sandra's arms when you got home? Not the Big F day—that was the result day. But the first time, back when all Doctor Goodstory said was *We're going to have to run some tests*. Sure, we'll get to the bottom of it. No, don't worry about it, Jerry—these were things he didn't say. He asked if you were depressed. You said sure, what author isn't after reading some of his reviews? He asked you to be serious, so then you were, and no, you weren't depressed. How was your appetite? It was good. Were you sleeping much? Not a lot but enough. Diet? How was your diet? It was good, you were getting your vitamins, you were staying healthy and hitting the gym a couple of times a week. Were you drinking much? Maybe the odd gin and tonic or two. He said he'd run some tests, and that's what he did. Tests, and a referral to a specialist.

Then came the trips to the hospital. There was the MRI scan, there were blood tests, memory tests, there were forms to fill in, not just for you, but for Sandra—she was to observe you, and still you kept this from Eva. Then the Big F, Doctor Goodstory had the results and would you please come in and speak to him, so you did . . . well, you know the news. Just take a look in the mirror. Early onset dementia. Alzheimer's. Maybe in the future there's a cure, because there sure as hell isn't one now, and maybe this journal can be inspiration for your next book— maybe you've written fifty books by now and this was just that time in your life, Jerry Grey with his Dark Period, the same way Picasso had his Blue Period and The Beatles had their White.

You have slowly progressive dementia. The Big A. Dementia in peo- ple under sixty-five is not common, Goodstory said, which makes you a statistic. There are drugs to take for the anxiety and the depression that is, he assured you, on its way—but there aren't drugs you can take for the disease itself.

We can't accurately map the rate at which things are going to change for you, Doctor Goodstory said. *The thing is, the brain—the brain still has a lot of mysteries. As your doctor, and as your friend, I'm telling you there might be five or ten okay years ahead for you, or you could be full-blown crazy by Christmas. My advice is to use that gun of yours and blow your brains out while you still know how.*

Okay, he didn't say that, that's just you reading between the lines. You spent half an hour talking about the future with him. Soon a stranger is going to be living inside your body. You, Future Jerry, may even be that stranger. Bad days are coming, days when you will wander from the house and get lost at the mall, days where you will forget what your parents looked like, days where you'll no longer be able to drive. Other than the journal, your writing days are over. And that's only the beginning. The days will get so dark that in the end you won't know who Sandra is, or that you have a daughter. You may not even know your own name. There will be things you can't remember, and there will be things you can remember that never actually happened. There will be simple things that no longer make any sense. The day is coming when your world will be without logic, without any kind of sense, without any awareness. You won't be able to hold Sandra's hand and watch her smile. You won't be able to chase Eva and pretend you're a grizzly bear. That day . . . Doctor Goodstory couldn't tell you when it would be. Not tomorrow. That's the good news here. All you have to do is make sure that day will never be tomorrow.

The nursing home is fifteen miles north of the city. It's set on five acres of land, gardens flowing out into the neighboring woods, a view of the mountains to the west, no power lines to interrupt the view, far enough off the main road to avoid the sound of passing trucks. It's secluded. Peaceful. Though Jerry doesn't see it that way. He sees the nursing home as being out of the way so people can shovel their parents and sick relatives into them then slip into the *out of sight out of mind* phase of their life.

Eva has the car radio on as they drive there. The five o'clock news comes on just as they hit the driveway leading up to the home. The driveway is close to a hundred yards long, the trees lining it mostly skeletal looking, a handful of them with tiny buds starting to grow. A report comes on the radio of a homicide. A woman's body was found an hour ago, and like always when Jerry hears these type of reports it makes him sad to be a human being. Ashamed to be a man. It means while he was walking along the beach with Eva enjoying the breeze, this poor woman was living the last few seconds of her life. It's news like this, Jerry remembers, that has always put his own problems into perspective.

Eva brings the car to a stop. The nursing home is forty years old, fifty at the most, two stories of gray brick stretching fifty yards from left to right, and another fifty yards from front to back, a black roof, some wooden windowsills stained dark brown, not a lot of color other than the gardens where spring is working its magic, bulbs planted in the past now coming back to life. There's a large door at the front of the nursing home made of oak that reminds Jerry of a church door. It all looks familiar to him, but doesn't *feel* familiar, as if he hasn't lived here but saw it once in a movie. He can't even remember what the name of this place is. This life that is now his isn't his at all, but belongs to a man from the same movie this nursing home is from, a man who confesses to murders of women who never existed, a man whose wife hates him, this man becoming less and less of the Jerry he used to be.

"Don't make me go in there."

"Please, Jerry, you have to," Eva says, taking off her seat belt. When he doesn't move, she reaches across and takes his off too. "I'll come and visit you again tomorrow, okay?"

He wants to tell her no, that tomorrow isn't good enough, that he's her father, that she wouldn't exist if it weren't for him, that when she was a baby he once tweaked his back while bathing her and could barely walk for a week, that he once dropped a jar of baby food and cut his finger picking up the pieces, that he once thought about calling an exorcist after undoing her diaper and seeing the mess she had made. He wants to tell her he put Band-Aids on her knees and tweezed out splinters and bee stings, that he brought back teddy bears from faraway countries and then, when she was older, brought back fashion from those same places. These things he can remember. He can't remember his parents. He can't remember his books. He can't remember this morning. The least Eva can do, he wants to tell her, is not make him go in there. And the very least she can do is come in with him. But he says none of this. It's the way of the world, the natural cycle, and he's thirty years ahead of schedule, but that's not her fault, it's his, and he can't punish her for that. He takes her hand and he smiles, and he says, "You promise?"

The big front door of the home opens. Nurse . . . Hamilton, her name comes to him as she walks towards them, stops halfway between the big oak door and the car and smiles at them. She's a big woman who looks like she could bear-hug a bear. Her hair is a fifty-fifty mix of black and gray, and looks like it was last styled in the sixties. In her late fifties or early sixties, she has the exact kind of smile you want to see on a nurse, the kind of smile your grandmother would have. She's wearing a nurse's uniform with a gray cardigan over top that has a name badge pinned to it.

"Do you promise?" he asks again.

"I'll do my best," Eva says, looking down for a moment, and that doesn't sound like a promise at all. He keeps smiling as she carries on. "You have to do your best to stay put, Jerry. How you made it into the city from here I don't know," she says, and nobody knows, least of all him. It's a fifteen-mile walk to the edge of the town, but it's another five on top of that to where he was found. He also can't think why he went to the library. Maybe to see his books, maybe to see other books, maybe to fall asleep and get kind of arrested. They get out of the car just as Nurse Hamilton reaches it.

"Jerry," Nurse Hamilton says, and she's smiling and shaking her head just a little, in a *Well, we've all been very amused at your antics* way. "We've missed you all day." She puts an arm around his shoulders and starts walking him to the door. "How you keep sneaking out is a mystery."

"Can I have a word with you?" Eva asks the nurse once they get inside, and the nurse nods and Jerry imagines it will be more than one word, and that those words are going to be about him finding his way into town, and that none of those words are going to be friendly. He's left standing in a foyer near a reception desk with another nurse behind it while Eva and Nurse Hamilton disappear. The nurse from behind the desk smiles at him and starts chatting, asking him if he enjoyed his time at the beach. He tells her he did, which is no doubt what she was expecting to hear. When Nurse Hamilton and Eva come back, Eva tells him to be well, and he tells her he'll do his best. When he goes to hug her, she pulls back a little at first, but then puts her arms around him. He doesn't want to let her go when she pulls away a few seconds later, but more than that he doesn't want to cause the kind of scene that proves Eva and Sandra made the right decision to put him in this place. He watches her go, then stands in the doorway and watches her car disappear through the trees.

"Come on, Jerry," Nurse Hamilton says, and she puts her arm around him again. It's warm and heavy and comforting. He can smell coffee and cinnamon. He wants to smile back at her, but finds he can't. "Let's get you some dinner. You must be hungry."

She leads him down to the dining room. They walk past people and Jerry looks at them, these people with other problems, and the way they've all been left here by their families makes him think of them as the rejected and the unwanted, and then he thinks of himself as their king, then he thinks he's being too harsh in thinking that, that everybody here has a story and he doesn't know what it is, but then he thinks that maybe he does know those stories but has forgotten them. He sits at a table by himself and puts his appetite to good use. Jerry is the youngest person in here except for one other guy whose skull is caved in on one side. A nurse is feeding him.

When dinner is over he heads back to his room. It's the same size as the bedroom he shared with Sandra. There's a single bed with a striped duvet cover, alternating blacks and whites, the same goes for the pillow, and he finds it a bit of an eyesore. There's a small flat-screen TV on the wall, a small stereo, and a small fridge that he's hoping contains alcohol, but when he opens it he sees only bottles of water and cans of diet soda. On one wall is a small bookcase stacked with copies of his books, probably to remind him of who he is. The whole room is miniaturized, a reflection on just how scaled back his life has become. There's a small private bathroom off to the side, and there's the window that looks out over the garden that is now getting the last of the sun, the flowers closing up for the day. There are framed photos of Eva and Sandra, one of the three of them taken in London, the bright lights of the city behind them, a double-decker bus coming into view, a telephone box on the side of the street—all very quintessentially British. Eva is only a teenager in the picture. He picks it up, and suddenly he can remember that trip, can remember the flight there, the turbulence twenty minutes short of Heathrow that made Sandra throw up. He can remember the taxi ride into the city, but he can't remember what book he was promoting, where they went after London, how long they were away. He still has the photograph Eva gave him earlier. He places it on the dresser next to the London photo.

He moves to the bed where there's a copy of A Christmas Murder on the pillow. He must have been reading it last night, and that's where his confusion started. He remembers the way he looked at his daughter in the police station, the way he pictured her naked, and the feeling of disgust sends him rushing to the bathroom where he throws up into the toilet. He feels like a creepy old man who drills holes into school fences so he can add kids to his mental spank bank. What kind of man looks at his own daughter that way?

The answer, of course, is obvious. A sick one. One who doesn't know who his daughter is, one who even forgets who he is. He can feel them coming now, the dark thoughts, an army of them marching in his direction and, like always, he wonders how he got here. What he did in life to deserve this.

He cleans himself up. He goes back into the room. He puts A Christ-

mas Murder back into the bookcase. He starts to undress. When he slips his hands into his pockets to empty them, his finger presses against something buried near the bottom. He pulls it out. It's a gold chain with a gold four-leaf clover hanging from it. He turns it over and studies it from different angles, but no amount of studying makes it familiar or suggests who it might belong to. Then he thinks that he wouldn't be much of a crime writer if he weren't able to connect the dots—he's stolen it from either one of the staff, or from one of the other residents. Great, so now he's going to be labeled not just the crazy man, but the crazy thief too. Just one more thing to add to the growing list of bad things he's done in his life but can't remember. Tomorrow he'll drop it somewhere on the grounds for somebody else to find, but for tonight he needs to put it somewhere safe. And hidden. Last thing he needs is a nurse to walk in and see it on his bedside table.

He opens the sock drawer and reaches into the back to hide it, but there's something already back there—an envelope the size of a greeting card. It's thin near the ends and a little bulky in the middle. There's nothing written on it. He doesn't recognize it. He sits on the bed and opens it.

Inside is a necklace. And a pair of earrings. And a locket.

You know what that is, don't you?

The words aren't his, but those of Henry Cutter, and Henry is the real deal. Jerry might be able to connect the dots, but Henry's the guy who makes the puzzles.

"No," he says.

Yes you do.

Jerry shakes his head.

They're mementos, Henry says.

"I've been stealing from people?"

That's not all you've been doing.

"Then what?"

But Henry has gone and Jerry is left sitting on the edge of the bed alone, confused, frightened, sitting with an envelope full of memories he can't remember.

DAY FIVE

"My name is Jerry Grey and it's been five days since I was
diagnosed with Alzheimer's."

"Hi, Jerry."

"And it's been two days since I last forgot something."

"Well done, Jerry."

That's how Henry would write about the support group that Sandra
wants you to go to, if he were writing this journal. You still need updating on Henry, and on support groups, and that will happen soon.
Support groups are for other people, the same way car accidents are for
other people. Sandra thinks it will be good for you. You fought about it,
actually—though *fought* is probably too strong a word—but before you
read all about the fight, or about Henry, here's what you need to know
about Sandra. You love Sandra. Of course you do. Everybody does. She
is the absolute best thing that has ever happened to you. She's beautiful, smart, caring, she always knows the right thing to say. When things
are going badly, she is there to talk some sense into you. When the
reviews are bad, she's there to tell you the reviewers don't know what
they're talking about; when the reviews are good, she's there to tell you
that reviewer is the smartest guy in the world. You bounce ideas off her,
sometimes you go to the gym with her, you run with her, you used to
hike when you were younger, you'd go camping and skiing and once
you went skydiving together because you wanted to be able to write
what you know. Your wife can't walk past a cat without wanting to
give it a cuddle, she can't walk past a dog without a *Howzzit going boy*,
can't watch a chick flick without crying at the end, can't walk into a
mall without buying a pair of shoes, and she can't imagine what you're
going through even though she gets you, and you can't imagine a life
without her.

You've been married for twenty-four years and, if you do the math, you'll see that Eva is twenty-five years old. You dated for five years before the wedding, which included three years of living together. You met back in university. You were getting yourself one of those fandangled English degrees that were popular back in the day, and you were doing a psych class too—psych 101. And why were you doing these things? Because you wanted to be a writer. Ever since you were a kid, telling stories is what you wanted to do. An English degree would help you tell those stories, and a psych degree would help you understand the characters. That's where you met Sandra—in a room of people all wanting to learn what makes the mind tick. Your opening line to her was *We need crazy people to make a living doing this*. She laughed, it was a warm wonderful laugh that made you feel warm and wonderful inside, it was a smile that made the world melt away except for her. You can even remember what she was wearing—tight blue jeans with in-fashion holes in the legs and hems that looked like hedgehogs had fooled around on them, a sleeveless red top that matched the shade of her lipstick, and her blond hair was flowing down to her shoulders the way you've always liked it. But for the last ten years or so it's always been in a ponytail, even at the dinner party where you said *This is my wife*—please fill in the blank. You went to the cinema that Friday night. Seeing a film may be a cliché for a first date, but it's a good cliché. You went to see a Star Trek movie. She was a fan, and you told her you were a closet Trekkie, and she asked what else you were keeping in the closet. You told her your last girlfriend.

Back then, of course, in your university days, you weren't really a writer. You always suspected that the university education you were getting is what you would fall back on as your house filled up with rejection slips from the publishers. You wanted to be a writer from day one, but it was your mother who encouraged you to continue your education, her scoring point being what an English degree would do for your creativity. By the time you met Sandra, you had written a couple dozen short stories, but you didn't dare show Sandra any of them until you'd been dating for a few months—and even then it was only after she assured you that she knew they were going to be just great, because you were just great. You were convinced if she read any of your stuff she would tell you it was good in a very vague *Oh yeah, it's good, I mean, sure . . . I'm sure people will like this, and by the way I can't see you Friday night as I have to wash my hair / pick up a cousin from the airport / I'm getting a cold, don't call me I'll call you* kind of way. What she did tell you was that your stories needed work. She told you that every character had to be perfectly flawed. She was the one who over the years convinced you to write a novel. *THE* novel. And that's what you did. You wrote *THE* novel, and *THE* novel was awful and Sandra was kind enough to tell you. So then you wrote *THE NEXT* novel, and that was awful too—but not as awful, she told you, and you tried again. And again. It would be years later you finally put that university degree to good use and got it right, but during those years of study Sandra was tiring of psychology and was thinking of switching to law when she found out she was pregnant.

Life changed then. A few days later you asked her to marry you, and at first she said no, that she didn't want to marry you just because she was pregnant, but you convinced her that wasn't why you were asking. Having her in your life was the most amazing thing, and any day without her would be full of heartache and despair. She said yes. You didn't get married until after Eva was born—Eva was eighteen months old when you walked down the aisle. By then you were also no longer studying, but were renovating houses. Sandra was a stay-at-home mother until Eva started school, at which time she then went back to university and got her law degree, focusing on civil rights. By then you had written *A Christmas Murder*, which a year later would go on to become a bestseller and open up the world for you. Sandra got a job at a law firm, and then all these years later you got Alzheimer's and had a big fight with her.

Sandra is concerned, of course, because you spent yesterday moping around in your office, but you told her you weren't moping, but working on next year's book that your editor has just sent the notes for. Of course there were no notes—but you did call your editor this morning and she made the mistake of saying *Nice to hear from you, Jerry. I trust you are well?* which was like trusting politicians to have your best interests at heart. So you laid it out for her. Not like the journal, mind you— just the CliffsNotes. Actually, Mandy, no, you weren't all right—you were five days into becoming somebody else, and your current project was a madness journal. She was very upset when you told her, and you were upset too, and why not? It's something worth being upset about.

That would explain all the mistakes in the manuscript, Mandy said, and you pretended that didn't hit a nerve. *I should've known. . . . I should have*.

Instead you just thought I'd become a horrible writer, you told her, and you laughed to let her know it was a joke, and she laughed too, but it wasn't very funny.

Day five and Sandra is mad at you. The truth is if you were counting the days she had ever been mad at you, you'd be up somewhere around five thousand by now (that's a joke, Jerry—I hope you're laughing!). The truth is you never fight. Never, ever! Of course you *argue* a little, but what couple doesn't?

So here's the thing—you just can't face a support group. Meeting all these folks who are going to forget you at the same rate you forget them—the rate of forgetting twice as fast in reality, like two trains speeding in opposite directions. You're actually scared that any new fact is going to push out an old one to make room. What if you meet these people and forget your family? This is Blair—now who is Sandra again?

You didn't explain it like that to Sandra because she wouldn't get it even though she gets you. Nobody gets it, unless they're like you, but it's not as if you can just go and find a bunch of people who . . .

Ha—looks like you may have to apologize to Sandra after all! But whether you go along is another matter. You've never been a social person at the best of times, and this is not the best of times. Hell, it's not even the worst—that's on its way. This is somewhere near the beginning. A certain kind of limbo with a touch of hope and a touch of madness, all balanced just so.

You're still trying to get used to the idea of what's happening. You have another appointment later in the week, not with Doctor Goodstory, but with a counselor who is going to give you an idea of what to expect. They'll no doubt tell you about the seven stages of grief—wait, no, it's seven deadly sins, seven dwarfs, seven reindeer—grief only has five stages. Denial, Anger, Blitzen, Dopey, and Bargaining. The last few days you've mostly been in shock, to tell you the truth. You still can't believe any of this is happening. Shock, plus some good old-fashioned anger. And . . . some pretty strong gin and tonics. If nothing else, mixing the G&Ts is one skill you have to hang on to, Future Jerry. That's probably why you fought with Sandra. Not the G&Ts, but the rest of it, the nitty-gritty-shitty as your grandfather used to say, back when . . .

Ah, hell. Back when he was navigating his way into Batshit County.

Your grandfather was old school—he took the sickness and twisted it into something cruel and bitter. He'd mutter things like how women shouldn't be allowed to work and those who did were stealing all the men's jobs, or how "the gays" were the reason for earthquakes and floods in this world. Alzheimer's gave him the freedom to become an uncensored version of himself. He would pat the nurses on the ass in the nursing home and ask them to fix him a sandwich. He seemed like the kind of guy to pour himself a neat glass of scotch, sit in a leather chair, adjust his tie, and blow out his brains with a pistol rather than die slowly, but ultimately he rode the Alzheimer's train too long, passing the station where that option had been available to him.

The same option is available to you.

Sandra doesn't know about the gun. You knew she would never approve. You bought it for research. Writers are always saying write what you know, and now you know what to expect when you pull a trigger. You know the sound that will tear into your eardrums if you're not wearing ear protection. You know the weight and the feel, and the smell. You fired it at a range years ago, and since then it's been under a floorboard under the desk, waiting in the dark maybe just for this very thing. You bought it illegally from Hans. You remember Hans? You'll get the update on him later when I tell you about Henry, but if a guy covered in tattoos comes to see you saying you owe him money, that'll be Hans. You don't really owe him money, but it'd be such a Hans thing to try. You'll know that if you remember him.

Eva still hasn't been told about the Big A. She was over again this morning. She's taking a couple of days off work, and Sandra is taking a few weeks off for me, and today they spent their time talking nonstop about the wedding. Dancing, cakes, flowers, dresses, bridesmaids—that's the future. But for you it may now all be in the past. Eva is marrying a guy called Rick. You like him. You fired up the barbecue when Eva was over and the three of you had a nice lunch together and you're glad you didn't tell her. Soon, though.

Let me tell you about Eva. She is, without a doubt, the best thing that has ever happened in your life. The day you found out Sandra was pregnant, you almost collapsed. In fact, you didn't ask Sandra immediately to marry you because you spent two days on the couch barely able to function. You were going to be a dad, and that scared the hell out of you. You used to think children didn't come with manuals, but the fact is they do. There are a million books out there, and Sandra would buy them then hardly read them. The bookcase would be stacked full of parenting books that didn't even have the spine cracked because you didn't read them either, you didn't need to, because everything just happened naturally. Everything you've done in your life, nothing comes close to those days when you would spend hours putting together a brand-new toy for Eva. That look on her face when she would see it, that smile, Jesus, that smile and those big blue eyes of her mother's . . . that sense of wonder at something new . . . if the Big A left you with one memory, pray that it's one of those. You kept thinking the magic would disappear as she got older, but no, it only got better. The day she broke her arm . . . she was seven years old. She used to love watching reruns of the shows you grew up with, and she ran up to the car and tried to slide across the hood like they do in *The Dukes of Hazzard*, and slid right off the other side into the driveway and twisted her arm beneath her. You were calm and collected and got her to the hospital, but that night neither you nor Sandra could sleep, and you knew, each of you knew, if anything bad ever happened, if you ever lost Eva, the world would end. You still feel that way. But this . . . this is telling you more about you, not about her. How to sum up Eva? She's warm. She's empathetic. She's intelligent. At school she was a straight-A student, she excelled in volleyball, on the track, in the pool. By the time she was nine she could sing along to any Rolling Stones song you had playing on the stereo. When she was ten she dressed up for Halloween as a police officer from the TV show *CHiPs* because she knew you used to watch it when you were a kid. When she was eleven she would visit your mother and read to her during those final few months. She used to chase after the neighbor's cat every time she saw it catch a bird, free the bird, and bring it home to try and nurse it back to health. Sometimes it'd work, sometimes it wouldn't, and when it wouldn't she'd make you dig a hole and stand with her as she held a small funeral. She begged you to buy her a guitar for her thirteenth birthday, then taught herself to play. She lived at home when she started university. She studied art, and politics, and law. But it was travel . . . there was something about travel that pulled her away from her studies. At nineteen she went to Europe by herself for a year. She learned French. She lived in Paris for a while. One year turned into two. She learned Spanish. She backpacked her way across a dozen countries. She was gone almost three years, but you'd see her when you were in Europe promoting the books. Travel made her want to show the world to people. When she came home she became a travel consultant. She met Rick. She's in love, Future Jerry. She's happy. That's Eva. Your daughter. And if the Big A is the balance for this amazing life, then so be it. It might take away your memories, but it cannot take away the fact that you have an amazing daughter. A daughter, who at this moment, has no idea her father is sick.

Rick, by the way, does something involving software. He writes code or designs websites or plays computer games all day long—something like that. You and Sandra are going to tell them next weekend, after the appointment with the counselor who is going to, in a friendly way, prepare you for what is to come. If she mentions the words *adult diaper* then you're going to pry up that floorboard.

Good news—you are still sane. You are still you in every way. You lost your watch this morning and it's not on the A *Place for Everything* shelf. But more good news—soon you're not going to need a watch. Bad news—you fought with Sandra, and you hate that. You'll make it up to her. You'll buy her some flowers when you find your credit card. Oh yeah, that's the other bad news. Your Visa is floating around the house somewhere, God knows where. Good news—at least it'll be a low bill this month.

❖

It's the thought of a buffet breakfast that gets Jerry's stomach grumbling. He sits on the edge of his bed and he rubs his eyes and stretches his legs and stretches his back and hears something click into place. There's a copy of *Vault* on the bed. It's a novel about a bank robbery that goes horribly wrong, the twist at the end is that it all actually went horribly right. It's one of his earlier books, though he can't remember reading from it last night, and he's not sure what it's even doing here. He usually travels light.

He heads into the shower, and when he comes out he switches on the TV. He leaves it on the first channel that comes on, which is the news, and he guesses the last person who stayed here must have been English because it's on an English channel, or perhaps it's just the default setting of the hotel. His stomach kicks into overdrive. One of the best things about traveling for writers festivals and book signings are the nice hotels and big breakfasts. Suddenly he's very keen to see what this hotel has available. He can't remember the details of his schedule, but it normally involves a train in the morning as they travel from one part of the country to the other. And Jerry loves being in Germany, even if he does only know a couple of phrases—*Mein name ist Henry*, because Henry is who they think he is. Henry Cutter. He looks around the hotel room for his watch but can't find it. No matter. He's a morning person and has never slept past ten o'clock in his life. It can't be much later than ten o'clock now. If it were, his German editor, who he's traveling with, would have pounded on his door already. But not knowing where his watch is is somewhat of a worry. He had his wallet stolen once while in Germany, so these days he tends to lock his wallet and passport in the safe—which is probably where his watch is too. Though, for the life of him, he can't remember the pin code for the safe and, come to think of it, where is the safe? A quick look around the room doesn't reveal one, which must mean he's left everything down in reception.

The hotel is a little drab, he thinks, as he steps into the corridor. He rounds the corner where two old people are standing outside a door, each of them wearing robes, and as he passes one of them nods and calls him by name. Probably somebody he met in the bar last night, or somebody he signed a book for. The man just says *Jerry*, which means it must be somebody he liked enough to have given his real name to, but with just the one word he can't tell how good the man's English is. He can't find the elevator, but he does find the dining room, which probably means he's on the ground floor anyway. In the dining room is a mishmash of people, most of them elderly, some of them staring into the distance, some wearing pajamas, some with food all over their mouths, making him wonder exactly what kind of hotel this is. In fact one person is being spoon-fed by another. His editor isn't here—he's either still asleep or out having a cigarette. He finds a table and waits for one of the waitresses to come over—they normally do with coffee, and to check your room number—but nobody shows up, which is okay, because he can't actually think what his room number is, and, come to think of it, he must have locked his key card in the room. He starts checking out the buffet selection, which is, he thinks, not what he was hoping for. He grabs some soft-boiled eggs, toast, and a bowl of cereal, and makes his way back to his table.

He's halfway through his cereal and has just spilled some when he realizes he's still wearing the robe he put on when he got out of the shower. He pulls it aside and sees he's wearing nothing under it. An intense feeling of embarrassment comes over him—this is exactly the sort of shit Sandra said would happen if he drank too much while on tour, and who the hell forgets to get dressed in the morning? He stands so suddenly that he knocks the table and tips over his glass of orange juice. It's an effort not to swear, but he manages it. It's an effort not to look out at all the people who are now staring at him, but he manages that too. There is something strange happening here, he can feel that, but he can't quite figure out what. He keeps his head down and walks out of the dining room, and once he's in the corridor he starts to run. He wants to get the hell out of here—next city please—and tonight, cross his heart and hope to die, he promises he'll leave the gin and tonics alone. This is just like one of those dreams where you show up at work naked. He reaches his room and puts his fingers on the handle, hoping the door will be unlocked.

"Jerry, hey, Jerry, are you okay?"

A man is walking down the corridor towards him. He's in a white uniform—he looks more like a chef than a doorman or concierge or whatever his title is at Hotel Wherever. He's a big guy—the kind of guy who might have been a rugby player back in the day—whenever that was. He can't be much older than forty. He has the kind of hairline that Jerry has always been frightened of getting, where there's hair around the sides but nothing else. He has a pair of wire-rimmed glasses that need a wipe, and a thick set of eyebrows hanging over them. His jaw protrudes further than his nose, it's big and square and well shaved.

"I forgot my key," Jerry says, and decides not to point out he also forgot his clothes. The guy talking to him won't point it out either if he wants a decent tip.

"The door isn't locked," the man says, and Jerry tries it out. Sure enough, the door pops open.

"It doesn't lock automatically?"

"No."

"What the hell kind of place is this?" Then suddenly it all comes to him. Things that didn't make sense do now, and Jerry can feel himself getting angry. "This is why my watch is missing! And my wallet and passport—I can't find them either. Seriously," he says, "I don't really like giving feedback, but you should do something about the security around here." Then he flushes, because he knows what the man's response is going to be. *What, this from a guy who can't remember to pull on a pair of pants?* He decides to stay committed to the cause. To stay on the attack. "I'm going to call the police," he says.

"It's okay, Jerry. You haven't lost anything. How about we get you into your room and sit down for a bit."

"Where are my things?"

"I'll explain it to you."

Jerry shakes his head. "There's no time. I have a train to catch."

"Come on, let's just sit down for a moment," the man says, and he reminds Jerry of a car salesman, the *Come on, just take her for a spin, see how she feels, get her out onto the open road and open her up* kind.

"I don't want to buy a goddamn car!" Jerry yells.

"Come on, Jerry, please, let's just sit down."

They head into the room. There's a bookcase with all his books on it, which is pretty weird, he thinks, but then decides it's not weird at all, but very sweet. The hotel staff must figure he travels a lot, and they're trying to make his stay here feel a little more like home. He appreciates the gesture, but not at the expense of security. Then he sees a photograph of him and Eva leaning up against another photograph. Eva is holding a guitar. They really have gone all out here.

There are two armchairs in the room near the window. The view beyond is a partly cloudy sky with plenty of trees trailing out of sight. Jerry wonders what the collective noun for the trees would be, and decides on *shitload*. He smiles at the thought. He'll have to put that into a book. Then he realizes that the collective noun for trees is probably *forest*. Or *woods*, or *copse*, or an *orchard*, or plenty of other things. They sit down. The TV is on, and the news is on, and the news anchors are talking about a woman who was murdered yesterday, a really beautiful woman with long blond hair that reminds him a little of Sandra. There's a gold four-leaf clover hanging on a chain around her neck, which isn't something Sandra would wear. He feels sad for this woman. Sad for her family. Sad for the human race.

"Jerry, do you remember where you are?"

Hell, he'd almost forgotten he wasn't in here alone. He turns towards the man sitting opposite. "I'm just tired, that's all."

"Would you like to take a nap, Jerry?"

"What time is the train?"

"There's time if you want to take a nap, and I'm thinking you'll feel better once you've woken up."

"And my stuff? My wallet and passport and watch?"

"Safe. All of them safe."

"I have a hangover," Jerry tells the man, though it feels more just like a headache than a hangover. He rubs his fingers against the side of his head. Suddenly the man looks a little familiar to him. "Is your name Derek?"

"It's Eric," Eric says.

"Are you sure?"

"Positive."

"Do you know where my wallet and watch are, Derek? They're missing."

"I'll go and find them, Jerry, I promise," he says, and he stands up. "How about you just lie down here and rest while I'm gone? I'll come back and check on you in an hour or so, okay?"

"Okay," Jerry says, and it does seem like a good idea. He can't believe how tired he's suddenly feeling. "But I don't want to miss the train."

"You won't, I promise, okay?"

"I'll hold you to that."

"It's all going to be okay, Jerry."

"It will be, as long as you come back with my things."

"I will. How about you lie down first, and then I'll leave."

"Fine, if that will get you out of here quicker," Jerry says, moving over to the bed.

"It will."

The man switches off the TV. "Get some rest, Jerry. Yesterday was a big day and no doubt you're tired," he says. "I'll be back soon," he adds, and then slips out of the room.

Jerry knows he's right. Yesterday was a big day—so big he can't even remember it.

DAY TEN

Hey stranger! Remember me? I'm that guy you used to know, what's his name, the writer dude, the one with the funny-sounding disease. This is day ten of the Madness Journal. Sorry it's not so regular, but life and the things that go along with it (that you'll soon start to forget) keep getting in the way.

Actually, enough joking around. How are you? Seriously, Jerry, you doing okay? Hopefully things aren't too messed up. Hopefully the journal isn't having a negative effect on you. It may be a map back to the person you once were, but it's also serving as a reminder to what you've lost.

Day ten and you feel like you've always felt. Fit. Healthy. A little tired, maybe, but that's all. You actually went out to dinner last night with Sandra—in all your years since being married, you've always had at least one date night every month—and you both spoke about books, and movies, what was happening in the news, what some of your friends were up to. It was really nice to just talk about something other than the insanity bomb waiting to detonate at some point in the future. Wherever you are, hopefully you're coping.

The counselor came around this afternoon. Her name is Beverly, and her breasts were so huge they were resting on her knees when she sat down, and were almost resting on her knees even when she was standing. She's in her fifties now, but by the time she's sixty they'll surely have snapped her spine in half. Sandra told me afterwards that she reminded her of one of our professors back at university, a Miss Malady, who she used to call Miss Catlady, and as soon as she said it you saw the resemblance. You'd like Beverly—she's pretty funny, for the most part, but serious when she needs to be. She came around and we were right, buddy—out came the five stages of dementia, or grief. Stage one—denial. She pointed out you had been in denial since the first time you forgot Sandra's name and put it down to the drinks. She said you're still going to be in a stage of denial for a while—it's the shock, you see. Of course where you are, denial was way back, along with the other four. You probably reached acceptance a long time ago—or did you? Are you reading this now, still refusing to believe what's happened? It's hard to know how to feel about that. Sad, in some ways, but in others it's comforting to think of you staying strong, of staying steadfast and refusing to allow the Dark Tomorrow that is on its way to arrive.

Stage two—anger. She said anger was something you were going to be prone to as the disease becomes more pronounced. She said there will be mood swings ahead, that you're going to get pissed off at the disease, at life, at those trying to help. You're going to be snapping at people and saying mean things. You thought earlier it might be useful to push Sandra away—useful for her—but after today, after listening to Beverly, well, you're as scared as ever. There are drugs to make you more comfortable—us more comfortable—and she said this journal was a good idea and asked if Sandra could read it because it might help chart the progression. You said you'd think about it, but you should have just said no. This is for your eyes only, buddy. Remember that.

So denial and anger are the two things you're going through now. Bargaining is next. Not sure who to bargain with, really. Who do you have to sell your soul to around here to get a clean bill of health? It's possible within the next few weeks you'll end up telling Doctor Goodstory there must be something, begging for anything that money can buy, just get you into the next clinical trial that is showing some kind of promise, doesn't have to be the next sure thing—at this point you'd take the next *maybe* thing. You'd sell the house and use the money to bribe your way into any kind of trial at this point—who wouldn't?

You told Beverly it felt like The Very Hungry Caterpillar was about to make its way through your mind, leaving holes everywhere it went as it gorged itself on memories before turning into a butterfly and taking flight. You told her you were starting to think of the man you're going to become as The Jerry Replacement, a version of you that would function on different levels, and you were worried about the kind of person he would be. A kind man? Short tempered? How many of the same qualities would you share with him?

She said there would be good days and there would be bad. Take from that what you will, Future Jerry.

You can't remember what the fourth stage of grief is. You were going to look it up online earlier, but, *eye-roll*, you can't remember the password on your computer. It'll come to you soon, no doubt, and if not Sandra will know it. She knows everything—you just don't want her to know you can't remember it.

Beverly was here for three hours. It was a long day, and she gave you both some worst-case scenarios and some best-case scenarios. It's possible you could be in a nursing home within the next few months. Can you believe that? A few months! She stressed that was the worst case, but the fact that at forty-nine you got Alzheimer's, well, isn't that already worst case? You shook her hand when she left, and Sandra exchanged hugs with her. When she was gone, you sat down with Sandra and between you decided it was time to tell Eva. She's coming over for dinner tomorrow night. She'll ask to pass the salt, and you'll say sure, and by the way I'm dying. Jesus . . . there's no way to tell her in a way that isn't going to devastate her. You can imagine her sitting the same way she did with your mother, reading *To Kill a Mockingbird* to you, pouring a glass of water and asking you every now and then if you're okay.

So it's good news, bad news time. Good news—you're still sane and you still know your name! Perhaps all good news can be rhymed in the future. And you found your credit card—it was in the yard. See? A perfect rhyme. Except it wasn't in the yard. You'd used it to buy cat food the other day from the supermarket and left it there by accident. They called the following day to let you know.

Bad news—you don't have a cat. It died six years ago.

He wakes up thinking about the money. Large bundles of cash stuffed into duffle bags, two security guards tied up and left in the vault, the bank manager with a hell of a concussion, and a future of beaches and pussy and maybe he'll even get a tattoo to celebrate. After all, it's not every day a job like this can be pulled off—they've gotten away with 3.4 million in cash, divided up three ways—he can retire on a million dollars and blow the leftover on partying.

He sits up on the edge of his bed and looks at his wrist where there is no watch and he wonders what the time is, where they've stopped, and all he wants to do is get back to the cash, which they buried beneath the farmhouse, which will stay buried until things die down. The key is to be patient. There is a book on the bed next to him. *Vault*. It's written by a guy named Henry Cutter, and the name is familiar, but he can't place how, even though it feels like it ought to be important. He stands up and stretches, then takes off his robe and pulls on a T-shirt and . . .

And his name is Jerry Grey. He is fifty years old and an Alzheimer's patient. He is an author and not a bank robber. *Vault* is one of his books. This is a nursing home. This is his life.

The news is so sudden he has to sit back down on the bed. There is no farmhouse. No cash. No security guards. Just madness. He looks to the bedside table, but his journal isn't there, nor is it on the bookshelf where there are other copies of his books. He moves to the chair by the window and looks out at the gardens and watches the sun turn shade into light one degree at a time. He can remember pieces of this morning, just small snippets. He was in Crazy Jerry Mode, which is what he sometimes calls it. He finishes getting dressed then heads out to the dining room, desperate for some lunch. Eric sees him and comes over, a big smile on his face.

"How are you feeling?" Eric asks.

"I feel . . ." Jerry says, then thinks of the best way to sum it up. With the truth, he decides. "I feel embarrassed."

"That's the last thing you need to feel," Eric says.

There are people everywhere, murmuring voices, clinking cutlery. A guy with a chunk of his skull caved in is being wheeled towards a window. He thinks the wheelchair guy's name is Glen and he used to be a prison guard until his own private destiny landed him in here with the rest of them.

"Then why do I feel it?"

Eric tells him he has a doctor's appointment this afternoon, and he *had* forgotten—it's the kind of thing he'd have forgotten even before he picked up his hitchhiker, a guy by the name of Dementia with a big fat capital *D*.

"I've remembered," Jerry says.

Eric smiles at him, an all-knowing smile, and if Eric can read his mind then he's forgotten all about it. "Do you remember sneaking out yesterday?"

"What about yesterday?"

"You wandered into town."

Jerry laughs. Then he stops laughing, because it's no joke. It's coming back to him.

"It's the third time over the last few months," Eric says.

"The third time?"

"Yes," Eric says.

Jerry shakes his head. "I'm not sure about the other times, but I remember yesterday. Not all of it. Not the wandering, but I remember meeting Eva at the police station. I remember walking along the beach before being brought back here. I wanted to go home. I still want to go home."

"I'm sorry, Jerry, but this is your home now."

"Until I get better," Jerry says.

"Until then," Eric says, and smiles. "Let's get some lunch into you."

Jerry eats his lunch by the window, where he can look out at the trees bordering the ground. They go for miles in most directions. There are lots of roses and daffodils everywhere, and some of the folks who wander the corridors of the nursing home are pulling weeds and soaking up the spring sun. When he's finished eating, he goes back to his room. He picks up *A Christmas Murder*. He knows it's his first book, but it's been so long since he's read it that he can't remember the details. He sits in the chair with his feet up on the chair opposite and starts reading, and realizes it's not just the details he's forgotten, but most of the entire story. He's thirty pages in when Eric comes and gets him, telling him his doctor has arrived, then leads him to an examination room.

He recognizes the doctor but can't remember his name. The doctor is a good ten years older than him with teeth so perfect Jerry suspects he may actually be a dentist, then realizes it'd make more sense that the doctor trades medical services with a dentist, swapping the painkillers and the occasional backyard surgery for fillings and root canals. The doctor asks how he's doing, and Jerry isn't sure what the doctor is really expecting to hear, so he tells him he's doing fine.

"Do you remember who I am?"

"My doctor," Jerry says.

"Can you remember my name?"

"No."

"It's Doctor Goodstory."

"Why couldn't it be Doctor Goodnews?" Jerry asks.

Doctor Goodstory smiles, then goes about taking Jerry's blood pressure before running some memory tests with him, some things Jerry can answer and some things he can't, then Goodstory asks him some logic questions, and again he can answer some and not others.

Finally Goodstory packs his things, sits back down and crosses his legs. "I hear you had quite the adventure yesterday," he says.

"I can remember bits and pieces," Jerry says. "I remember Eva took me to the beach."

"We've been charting the progression of the disease, Jerry," Goodstory says. "It can vary from day to day, some days you are extremely lucid, other days you're never fully aware of where you are, or even who you are. Like I say, things vary, but there are consistent themes to your overall state. One of those themes is that often, when you wake up, you wake up believing you're back in your old life. The sense that everything is as it used to be stays with you sometimes only for a few minutes, sometimes for a few hours. It's as though you regress to a certain time in your life. This morning, for example, I'm told you woke up believing you were on tour. Mostly you revert back to a time over the last few years, though on occasion back to when you were much younger. There are days where you have absolutely no idea what is going on, where you can't even feed yourself. These days are rare, but they do happen and, sadly, will begin to happen even more."

Jerry looks at his hands as Goodstory talks to him. He feels so silly.

"Even at your best now there are still so many things you've forgotten," Goodstory says. "There are memories you've repressed."

"What kind of memories?"

"Just memories. We'll ask you something that you'll have no idea about. Some things will come back to you, but there are things that refuse to. Mornings are the hardest. Once you become aware, then often you become very lucid, very aware, just like now. I've had conversations where I'm talking to you and I can see the words just falling off you, and I've had conversations where you're almost like the man you used to be. The theme of struggling in the morning after waking up also extends to naps. Often you'll take an afternoon nap, and when you wake up you'll be confused, yet that tends to only last a few minutes. Sometimes much less than that, fifteen minutes at the most, then you become alert again."

"Am I able to function in these other states?"

"Sometimes quite well. You just don't seem to develop the memories. You don't remember any of this morning, do you, about believing you were on tour."

"Little bits and pieces, but not really," Jerry says.

"But you can remember being on tour years ago?"

"Yes," Jerry says. "Sometimes quite clearly. Other times hardly at all."

"Well, you're definitely functioning when you're making your way into town. It's almost twenty miles between here and the library, and that's a lot of ground to cover. You could have walked, or you could have hitchhiked, but the mere fact you were able to means on some level you're very much aware of what's going on."

"But I don't keep the memories. It's almost as though I'm sleepwalking."

"That's as good an analogy as any," Goodstory says. "It's what Alzheimer's does, Jerry. It erases things, it creates, it rewrites."

"Will I remember this conversation?"

"I imagine you will, right up until the moment you won't. That could be twenty-four hours. It could be a week. You might not think about it for twenty years, then it will just seem like yesterday."

"Is there a crueler disease, Doctor?"

"Sometimes I'm not so sure there is. They really should be keeping a better eye on you here," Goodstory adds. "It's one of the conditions."

When he's gone Jerry heads out into the sun with *A Christmas Murder*. For the next few hours all he does is read, caught up in the momentum of a killer and a cop. The book has a theme running through it that he recalls being in some of the others—a theme about balance. The world in his books is out of balance, it's out of whack, and sometimes his characters—the good guys at least—try to fix that. He has the feeling that theme carries over into his life as well. He must have done something terrible for the Universe to treat him this way.

He is a third of the way through when he starts to have a very uncomfortable feeling that whatever that something is, it's to do with Suzan, the woman in this book. She is somebody he used to know. An actual person. He can't remember her real name, but she was a neighbor when he was a teenager, until she was no longer his neighbor because her ex-boyfriend killed her. He used to have a huge crush on her—she was ten years older than him, but he fell in love with her that summer—fell in love from the opposite side of the street, too young and too nervous to ever talk to her. He based this book on what happened to her. He used her story to write one of his own, a story he then went on to sell, a story that helped pay his mortgage, that helped give Eva a good education, a story that gave them the chance to travel the world—all things that couldn't have been any further from Suzan's mind when her ex-boyfriend's hands were around her throat. Jerry remembers coming home from university that day, the police cars on his street, his parents telling him what had happened. Suzan was gone and it didn't make sense how life could end so easily.

That's the balance, he realizes. He took advantage of the bad thing that happened to her. This is why he is being punished.

He decides he doesn't want to finish reading the book.

He decides he doesn't ever want to read any of his books ever again, because there's something more than just the memory of coming home and finding the police cars. There's something else hidden in the darkness—best he stops looking. Best he heads back inside and lets the dementia carry on doing its work.

DAY FIFTEEN

A lot has been happening, and there's a lot to catch up on, the most pressing of which is another fight with Sandra. You always feel sick to your stomach when you and Sandra have fought, and today is no different. Strike that—today you actually feel worse. It was a real doozy. Things are a little more stressful now that the wedding has been bumped up—that was something decided a few days ago, but first you need to be updated on today. This is, remember, a journal—it maps the journey. It's not a diary—you're not going to add something every day just because it's another day. Otherwise it'd be *Day fourteen, ate breakfast, went for a walk, and read the newspaper at the kitchen table*. The long gap (would that make a good book title? *The Long Gap*? No, probably not) happened because you've been so busy, and because—now this is *supposedly so*, because Sandra read the journal. She asked for it, and you said sure, honey, knock yourself out. Or something along those lines. Here's your memory of it. . . .

That's right—that blank page and a half represent exactly what you remember, which is to say none of it. But Sandra says you had the conversation, and how can a man losing his mind and his memory argue with that? It turns out quite easily, because you're adamant that the discussion just never happened. If somebody tells you two plus two equals five, you're going to argue it's not true because you know, you absolutely know the truth. That's how this feels. If Sandra had asked to read the journal, you'd have said no. Absolutely. However, she says you said yes, and you love her and trust her, and the truth is, buddy, you're going to have to start trusting her more than you can trust yourself. You can no doubt imagine what happened after you found out she was reading it, and don't need it explained to you—but here to explain it to you is Henry Cutter, author of novels such as *Dead Man Stalking* and *Dying Made Easy*. But before Henry takes over the reins, here's a little history on who exactly Henry is.

Henry Cutter is your pseudonym. Only it's a little more intimate than that. *Henry Cutter* isn't just the name you put on the cover of your books, he's the person you try to become when you're writing. All those things going on in your head, all those dark things, you try to keep those in Henry Cutter's head and not yours. When you're in your office and some guy is having his arms torn off by gangsters, that's Henry Cutter's world. When you're having dinner with Sandra or watching a movie with Eva, that's Jerry Grey's world. You keep the two worlds separate. Don't worry—you're not suffering from any kind of delusion where you really think you're a different person, and the distinction may be subtle, but when you switch your computer off at the end of the day, you also need to be able to switch yourself off too. It didn't used to be that way. In fact, the reason you do it is for your family. Sandra would often say you were distant, that often you weren't there because your mind was chasing down loose ends, and she was right. You were always trying to figure out how Character A was going to survive what Character B had planned, and that made it very easy to slip out of the real world to pursue what was happening in the imaginary, made it easy to tune out of a conversation you were having with Sandra to make some mental notes. When you got published, Sandra helped come up with the pseudonym, and it was shortly after that she said, *I just wish*

Henry could live his life in your office and we could have Jerry the rest of the time. That was when she explained to you what you were like. You can still remember that day, that hug you gave her when you promised her you were going to try what she just suggested, and guess what, F.J.? It's worked. Henry Cutter is who you become when you're wearing your "author hat." There aren't many professions where you spend all day imagining you're somebody else. And right now you're going to put that hat on, and let Henry take over.

Over to you, Henry.

It was a Tuesday when Sandra borrowed the diary. A Tuesday like any other for most people, but not for Sandra—this was her second Tuesday since learning her husband was leaving her, and she was going to spend it reading his inner thoughts. He was scared, she was pretty sure of that—hell, she was scared. By the end of next year she would be alone, perhaps even by the end of this one. She couldn't help it, but already she was thinking of what she would do—would she move on? Would there be a mourning period for a man who was still alive but in many ways so far gone? Would she meet somebody else and start a new life? She didn't know. And what if she did start that new life, and in five years' time there was a cure and Jerry became Jerry again?

Coffee and a muffin. That was breakfast—not the healthiest, but she never had been the healthiest when it came to eating, which is why she hit the gym three days a week before work—four, if there was time—and time, she thought, was something she wouldn't have much of while Jerry was sick. She would have to take time off work, which would be tough, as there were some cases ready to go to trial, but she would do it. She would do anything for Jerry. She was already taking time off to help Eva plan the wedding. She carried the diary and her breakfast outside. She sat at the table on the deck and sipped her coffee and started to read. Day One, the opening words, and there was Jerry talking to himself, Jerry sounding just like . . . well, just like Jerry. The neighbor's cat had jumped the fence and was sitting on the edge of the deck, pausing from cleaning itself every now and then to stare at her. The coffee was too hot, so she let it cool, and soon it was forgotten. She carried on reading. And as she read, she found herself feeling sad for Jerry. And then she saw something that made her storm into the house. Jerry was still asleep. These last few days he'd been sleeping in every morning.

"Just what the hell is this?" she asked, waking him up. She was angry. She shouldn't have been, but she couldn't help herself.

Jerry looked tired and confused. "What? What's going on?" he asked.

"This," she said, and she tossed the journal onto the bed next to him, and the eyes, the two puppet eyes glued to the cover rattled in their shells.

"You're reading my journal?"

"You asked me to."

"Like hell I did."

She paused for a moment, looking for the deception, but no, he wasn't lying, he had woken with no memory of it. Is this how it was going to be from now on? Lost conversations where Jerry argues everything she says? "You asked me last night," she says, wanting to get to the real issue here. "But what's more important is that we have a gun in the house. How could you! And you think that what, one day you may use it on yourself?"

"You had no right to read any of it!"

"I have every right because you're my husband and I love you, and I hate that this thing is happening to you, but it is, and I need to know what's going on in here so I can help you," she said, and she tapped the side of her head, but really she should have been tapping the side of his. It made her look like the crazy one. He looked distraught. He looked like a cornered animal. She needed to back down. "I'm worried about you."

"Doesn't sound like it," he said. "Sounds more like you're spying on me."

"I'm not, and you asked me to read it," she said.

"I would have remembered something like that. You're using the disease against me. Is this what you're always going to do now to get your way? Lie to me and tell me I said something when I didn't?"

"I would never—"

"Get out," he yelled, and threw the journal at her. It missed and hit the wall behind her. She had never seen him like that, and it frightened her. It worried her. She knew even before Jerry was diagnosed that no matter what the problem was, she would stay by his side. For always. That journal hitting the wall next to her—in that moment there was a flicker of doubt. She picked it up and ran out of the room.

By the time she got out to the deck, she was crying. Twenty seconds later Jerry was behind her. She turned towards him, but it wasn't the Jerry from the bedroom, it was the Jerry she fell in love with, the one she met in university, the one who was in the Star Trek closet, the one whose side she would never leave. Beverly, the grief counselor, had warned them he could get like this. It was all part of the Alzheimer's package. It was going to take time to adapt, but adapt she would. For him. For herself. For Eva.

"Jesus, I'm so sorry," he said, and he put his arms out, and the one percent of her that wanted to push him away was drowned out by the ninety-nine percent that opened her arms to receive him. The flicker of doubt that had already disappeared was now well buried. "I'm just so . . . so messed up," he said.

"It's going to be okay," she said, and they were words she'd heard herself using over the last few weeks, as if her saying them enough would make them come true.

"I want you to read the rest of the journal," he said.

"Are you sure?"

"I'm sure."

He disappeared inside to make breakfast while she stayed on the deck. When she finished she went back inside and found him in the kitchen eating a piece of toast and staring out the window.

"I want you to get rid of the gun," she said, staying calm.

He turned towards her. "I'm not going to kill myself."

"Jerry, please, I would feel better if it was out of the house."

He nodded. He didn't look like he was going to argue. "It's under the desk in my office."

"I know. You mentioned it in the diary."

"It's a journal. Not a diary."

They walked together to the office, and she stood aside as he pushed the desk towards the window. He took a screwdriver out of his desk drawer and used it to pry up a loose floorboard. When he reached into the cavity he went right to his shoulder. Then he started to move it around, searching.

"It's gone," he said, and he sounded confused.

"What do you mean *gone*?"

He pulled his arm back out. There was nothing in his hand. "It was here, and it's always here, but now it isn't." He looked rattled. "I don't . . . I don't know where it is," he said. It looked like Jerry from the bedroom might be on his way back.

"Well it has to be somewhere," she said.

"I know, goddamn it, I know!"

"Well, check again."

He checked again and got the same result.

"Where else would you hide it?"

"Nowhere. This is the place."

"If this is the place then it would still be there," she said, still sounding calm. At least calmer than she felt. "When did you last see it?"

"I don't know."

"Why did you even have one?" she asked.

"For research. I wanted to know how it felt to fire one. I went to the range a few times."

"Without telling me. Is there anything else you're not telling me?"

"No."

"Then when was the last time you used it at the range?"

"It was . . . I . . . . I can't remember."

"When was the last time you saw it?"

"I don't know."

"And you're sure that's where you keep it?" she asked.

"Of course I'm sure."

"So where is it, then? Where in the hell is the gun?"

And . . . scene.

Thanks, Henry, for the recap.

Needless to say, you feel ashamed for yelling at Sandra, and embarrassed because you have no idea where the gun is. It's possible you never even bought one. Actually, you know what? There's a character in one of the books—*he* bought a gun and hid it beneath a loose floorboard in *his* office. He was planning a murder, he was the one who wanted to know how it felt, how it sounded. Is it possible that's what you've been thinking of? Yes. Absolutely. You found the loose floorboard when you moved into the house, and at the time thought it'd be a good place to hide a gun, so gave that to the character you were writing about at the time. You thought it was you, but it wasn't—it was just one of those people living in your head!

Sandra will be relieved when you tell her. But you—you're terrified. To have made a mistake like that . . . what does that mean for your future?

All that stuff—that was today. There's no time now to update you on the other night when Eva came over, as it's date night tonight and you're heading out soon with Sandra. You're off to dinner, then off to see a movie that one of your author buddies wrote. The blanks will be filled in soon, but basically Eva and Rick have set an earlier date for the wedding to make sure you're able to participate.

Good news—Sandra has forgiven you for the fight and will forgive you even more when you're at dinner and you tell her there's no gun in the house. You and me, buddy, we have a lot to make up for after our fight with her, and a lot to make up for for the days that are coming. Also, her birthday is coming up next month—she's going to be joining you at forty-nine. You'll get her something special.

Good news—if you can't remember how your books go, you can read them as if they're new. For the first time you can read them and not know about the twist that's coming. It would be great if you could tap the dementia patient market—they buy your books, forget they've read them, and buy them again.

Bad news—one of the puppet eyes glued to the journal got crushed against the wall when you threw it. It looks foggy now, like a cataract.

❖

Good news—Sandra has her own way for the right mind will to give you even more when we've decided and you tell her there's no point she knows you and that unless we have what remains at least one eye sight with her, and I have to make up to keep—all of that an occupation. Also, her probably running no new month is spoke to be looking

It's been a couple of days since Jerry's doctor came to see him, days which he hasn't gone wandering, days which, as far as he's aware, he has been mostly in control. The daffodils that were in full force in the spring gardens are now limp and wilted. Some rhododendrons are blossoming, others already so heavy with flowers they're breaking off and landing with a thud on the lawn. Trees are budding in every direction. Jerry knows it's that time of the year when things happen quickly, that back at his house he'd have gone from mowing the lawns once every two months during winter to once a week during summer. At the moment he's sitting among it, sitting on a bench under a silk tree whose branches are still mostly bare, the sun touching his face. He's reading a newspaper, on the front page of which is a woman he recognizes. The woman's name is Laura Hunt, and Laura was murdered inside her house. The article says her body was found Monday. Today, according to the paper, is Thursday. The article says her body was found in the afternoon. He remembers hearing that on the radio, and thinking that while he was at the beach enjoying the crisp air this woman was being murdered. He realizes now that he was wrong—her body was found in the afternoon, but the article says she was killed in the morning. There is the mention of a stolen necklace, of the woman being stabbed to death, and that means something to Jerry, and he closes his eyes and tries to figure it out, and—

"Are you okay, Jerry?"

He looks up. Nurse Hamilton is standing in front of him. She has a big smile that becomes a small smile then completely disappears. She sits down and puts her hands on his arm. "Jerry?"

He shakes his head. He's not okay. He folds the newspaper in half so he can no longer see the woman's picture. He is starting to remember.

"I killed somebody," he says, and there—the words are in the open for Nurse Hamilton to do with them what she shall. Call the police would be his bet. He hopes she does. In fact, they might even execute him. The death penalty was abolished over fifty years ago, but with all the violence that's been happening in New Zealand these past few years people have been asking for its return. There was even a referendum. The public voted to bring it back. He remembers it was close, but can't remember when that was. Last year? Two years ago? He also isn't sure if it's been put into effect yet, but perhaps he can be the first. If so, he doesn't want Sandra or Eva there when they hang him. He would like Nurse Hamilton there. He can imagine her sad smile might make things feel a little less scary as the rope gets tightened.

"I know," Nurse Hamilton says, a painful expression on her face, and he wonders how she knows, then comes to the conclusion he must have told her already. She carries on. "And I'm sorry, Jerry. I really am, but you do know it wasn't your fault."

"Of course it was my fault," he says. "I chose Suzan because I had fallen in love with her. I snuck into her house and hurt her and later the police arrested the wrong man."

Her sorrow melts away. Her concern turns to relief. He thinks maybe she didn't like Suzan.

"It's okay," she says.

He shakes his head. It's never going to be okay.

"Do you remember your name?" she asks.

"Of course I remember. It's Henry Cutter," he says, but that doesn't feel quite right. Close but not close enough. Plus she called him Jerry.

"Henry is your pen name," she says.

"Pen name?"

"Jerry Grey is your real name. You're an author."

He searches his memory, trying to form a connection. "I don't think so."

"You used to write crime novels," she says. "Sometimes you get confused about what is real and what you made up. Do you know where you are?"

"A nursing home," he tells her, and as he tells her he starts to look around the grounds, at the trees and flowers, and there are other people here too, people wandering around, some looking happy, some looking sad, some looking lost. He is, he remembers, and somewhat ironically too, he thinks, one of the lost. "I have dementia."

"The dementia has an awful way of rewriting your past, Jerry. It's making the stories from your novels feel like real life to you. Suzan doesn't exist. She never existed."

He thinks about that. Writing books . . . it does feel familiar. And of course his name is Jerry Grey. Not Henry Cutter. Henry Cutter is who he would become when he wrote, because that way he could be Henry for the bad times and Jerry for the good.

"So I didn't kill anybody," he says.

Nurse Hamilton gives him one of the saddest smiles he's ever seen, the kind of smile that makes his chest tighten. This woman pities him. Even he pities him. "There was no Suzan," she says. "She was just a figment of your imagination."

"But she seems . . . seems so real."

"I know. Come on, let's get you inside. It's almost dinnertime."

She leads him inside and he tells her he wants to rest for a bit in his room. She walks him there, and tells him everything is going to be okay, then tells him not to be too long. It's not until he's in his room and alone and sitting by the window that he thinks back over the conversation and picks up on what he missed.

She said *I know.*

"*So I didn't kill anybody.* That's what I asked you," he says, the words going into an empty room—empty except for Forgetful Jerry, and Forgetful Jerry doesn't seem to mind him talking to himself. In fact he encourages it and, come to think of it, it actually feels familiar. When he talks again, he looks at the empty chair opposite as if Nurse Hamilton was there. "Then you said I didn't kill Suzan. You didn't say I didn't kill anybody."

He replays the conversation over again.

He didn't kill Suzan.

You killed somebody. The words aren't his, but he knows who they belong to. Henry Cutter, his pen name, wants to be heard. *You killed somebody, and Nurse Hamilton knew.*

But if it wasn't Suzan, then just who in the hell was it?

DAY TWENTY

The days are racing past and you haven't been able to write as much as you'd have liked. Life, just like it often does when you're writing, gets in the way. There is still day eleven to catch up on, which is when Eva came around for dinner. Of course she's been around a lot since then, and a lot has happened. First of all, let me tell you that Sandra has removed all the alcohol from the house. It's a real shame because at night the G&Ts actually help. They calm you, and a guy in your condition deserves to be calm. Other people get sick, and other people die at much younger ages, but this is you me us we. You're allowed to be upset for yourself—that's your right, and you have to admit you're a little angry at Sandra for getting rid of the one thing that can bring you comfort when nothing else can. She has also taken away your credit card after the whole cat food thing. You've lost count how many times she's said over the last week *You can't do that, Jerry*, or *You should be doing that, Jerry*.

The good news is that you called Hans. Hans has been a pretty big help to you over the years. He's what you would call . . . source material. You met him in university. He was the first out of all your friends to start losing his hair, and he decided early to shave it completely off, which made him the only bald twenty-year-old on campus. He was taking a whole bunch of classes, including the same psychology class as you and Sandra, but for him it was more like he was trying to find the key to unlock not just the mind, but the world. He likes knowing how things tick. You used to go to his flat to study, and often the TV or the computer or the toaster would be in pieces, and once he figured out how all that stuff ticked, he moved on to bigger things, like the car. He's a little like Rain Man when it comes to numbers too. He can't look at a spilled jar of toothpicks on the floor and tell you how many there are, but he can perform all sorts of complex arithmetic in his head. He also has this trick where he can guess somebody's age and weight, though he'd always deduct between twenty-five and thirty-five percent for women over twenty, more if he was attracted to them. Sometimes you'd take a break from studying and sit out on the back porch and he'd be smoking a joint and you'd be drinking a beer, and you'd have a Rubik's Cube he was always fiddling with, using the layer method to solve it in a few minutes, trying to learn a way to solve it in under a minute, which he eventually did, before cutting it down to thirty seconds. He taught himself to speak three languages, and once he spent two weeks doing nothing but origami, making swans and roses and panda bears before moving on and trying to figure out how to make the perfect paper plane. When he was nineteen, he read a dozen books on how to fly a Cessna, then snuck onto an airstrip at night and stole one. He put everything he had learned to the test, flying a mile radius around the runway before returning safely. Once you were at his flat studying and he was practicing how to pick a lock, not because he needed to break into a house, but to see if he could, then he spent hours trying to teach you what he had learned, not for your benefit, but just to see if teaching was another one of his abilities.

The problem, with Hans, was the weed. He probably smoked it just to quiet his brain. Then he started growing it, just to see if he could. Then he started selling it. When he was twenty-one he did four months in jail, and when he came out he wasn't the same Hans that went in—though by then something was changing inside him anyway, and prison just helped advance it, as it would when he served three more years for distribution when he was twenty-five. The friendship became tenuous after his first prison visit, but Christchurch being a small place meant you would always run into him every now and then, and your relationship was based on who he used to be. We all have friends like that, Future Jerry, where it's hard to know whether you'd be friends with them now if you met for the first time (I have to be honest here and tell you I wonder this about you, about whether I'd like the person you are in the future, just as I have no idea whether you will like the person you used to be).

Hans got more heavily into drugs after that first prison stint. He started hitting the gym and he bulked up. He got tattoos. Yet whenever you ran into him, he was the warmest guy. When the first book came out, he came around to see you. He was so excited. The friendship started to grow again—though Sandra always makes herself scarce whenever he drops by, then after he leaves asks you what in the hell you're doing spending time with a guy like that. You've never based any characters on him, but if you wanted to know how to smuggle a baby out of the country or buy a pound of cocaine, he's the guy you'd ask. People often think that crime writers would know how to get away with murder, but you've always thought if anybody could, it'd be Hans. Some of the bad shit in your books, that's all you, Jerry; but the way some of that bad shit unfolds, the little details, some of that is his. From how to create a stolen identity to putting the living fear of God into somebody, Hans is an all-sorts kind of guy in the sense that he can do all sorts of things. Bad things. You probably should know he scares you a little. In fact, he's the guy you thought you bought the gun from.

On day seventeen you rang him and told him about the dementia. He said he would come over. You told him not to worry, but he did worry, and Sandra worried herself into work to catch up on some things that needed looking in on, just so she wouldn't have to face him. You sat on the deck outside and drank one of the beers he brought over while he smoked his joint and you talked about how unfair the world was. He asked you to explain the Alzheimer's to him, he wanted every detail, and he kept asking questions, as if it were a problem for which he could provide a solution. If he thought it would have helped, he probably would have taken you apart on that deck and tried to make right all the bits he thought were defective.

When you told him Sandra had gotten rid of all the gin, he got into his car and disappeared for twenty minutes, and when he returned he had five bottles, all of which you have hidden, and he told you to call him in a week when you'd run out. A week! You weren't sure if he was kidding, but you told him it'd be more like a month. Maybe even two. You miss the way Hans used to be, but the old Hans wouldn't have driven off and returned with all that Bombay Sapphire.

By the way, you have a hiding place in your office—no, not under the desk—and that's not a hiding place anymore since Sandra knows about it, but there's another one at the back of the cupboard. There's a false wall in there. You used those renovation skills of yours to build one when you moved in—it's where you hide your writing backups.

Far easier than moving a desk out of the way every day. Some of the things you've written way back in the past, you'd die of embarrassment if anybody ever found them. You could only fit three bottles in there, and the other two you hid in the garage. Sandra didn't object to the tonic staying in the house.

That's day seventeen summed up. Let's give you a good news and bad news summation. Bad news first. You ran out of alcohol. Good news next. You're restocked with alcohol. More good news—Hans confirmed you never bought a gun. When asked, he said, *So the demen-tia, that means you're going to start saying all sorts of shit to people, right?* You told him that was so.

I never gave you a gun. I've never given anybody a gun.

Now back to day eleven. Hard to believe that was over a week ago now. In fact, why don't you go ahead and add that to your *I can't believe it* list, F.J., a list that is getting pretty full if you must know. Things are moving quickly now. Not the Big A (though that time bomb is still tick, tick, ticking—actually, strike that, the Big A is a bomb that's already gone off, and this is the fallout we're dealing with). You had visited your lawyer during the week, and your accountant—all these preparations for the future—it's like you're taking a trip to the moon and never coming back. They each shook your hand at the appoint-ments and said how sorry they were, but they weren't really sorry. Why would they be? You're dying and they're buying new cars and boats and it's billable hours, baby, billable all the way.

You cooked dinner on day eleven. Eva brought Rick over. You're actually a pretty good cook. It's one of your things—and you don't have many things. You can write, you can play pool, you know some card tricks, you can catch Alzheimer's like catching a cold, and you can cook. What you cooked that day has slipped your mind, but if you really need to know, then send a letter and address it Jerry Grey, care of the past, and I'll get back to you.

They showed up, and they were all smiles, and Eva brought her guitar and you all sat in the lounge and she explained how she's been writing music and, get this, she's just sold her first song! She said she started writing during her three years in Europe. She traveled with a journal and she'd see things that would inspire her—people, sunsets, landscapes—

and she'd write. She never said anything. She said it was something she wanted to do on her own, that if you knew you'd probably try to give her advice, or try to help with her lyrics. The singer who bought her song is planning on recording and releasing it soon. Eva played it, and it was beautiful, but it made the discussion that was coming up so much harder. You sat in the lounge with your arm around Sandra and listened to Eva sing, and Rick sat watching her and he was mesmerized, and you don't think you've ever seen a guy as in love as good ol' Rick.

The song is called "The Broken Man," and is about a guy who breaks the hearts of every woman who falls in love with him, until one day his own heart is broken by the woman he can never have because she's already married. You asked her to play it again, and she did, and Sandra asked for a third time and she said no, maybe later, and smiled as if she were a little embarrassed at how proud you and Sandra were. Sandra took a photograph of you sitting next to Eva with a big smile on your face. (She had the photograph printed the following day, and on the back she wrote *Proudest dad in the world*. The photo is now on the fridge door.)

Later in the evening came dinner. You and Sandra gave them the news as soon as dinner was over. Eva cried, and Rick put his arm around her and she asked the same question over and over, the *How long do you have* question that nobody can rightly put their finger on, and you kept thinking, you kept thinking, if Eva's music is in the world, no matter what happens you're going to be okay.

Eva cried, and she hugged you to make you feel better, but for her own comfort she turned to Rick. You can't quite put into words how you felt then. It wasn't jealousy, but more of a sense of redundancy. You were the person who used to check under her bed for dragons. You were there for her when she thought her world was falling apart after she backed the car into the garage wall. You hugged her until her tears dried up after the cat died. Now you're the Broken Man, not the broken man of Eva's song, but broken nonetheless. Eva has Rick now, and she is going to need him. And really, you should be thankful for that.

It was Rick's idea to bring the wedding forward. Rick, who you didn't like so much when you first met him because he pulled up in his car with that god-awful hip-hop music playing, which reminds me, J-Man

(that's my hip-hop name for you, and my hip-hop name for the Madness Journal is Maddy J.), reminds me that you hate, absolutely hate
hip-hop music and if you're listening to it in the future with your jeans
halfway down your ass then you really are too far gone to be helped.
You're a Springsteen kind of guy. And the Stones. The Doors. You once
wrote a whole novel listening to nothing but Pink Floyd. The music
you listen to is immortal.

Rick. Rick and his damn hip-hop, blaring from the stereo like he
was DJing the whole neighborhood. Eva in the passenger seat making
goo-goo eyes at him, and you did good, J-Man, you didn't tell him to
turn it off otherwise you'd get your gun (nonexistent, mind you) and
put a bullet into his stereo. He did not make a great first impression,
and all you could think was that if this guy married your daughter and
they had kids, that's where your estate was going. Things got better
after that—either the hip-hop was a phase, or Eva said something to
him, because he kept the music low and started pulling up his jeans,
and now—well, now you like him. He's a good guy. They've been living together for the last two years, and now the wedding. Maybe it was
Eva's music that changed him.

Bringing the wedding forward is for you. Hard to walk Eva down the
aisle and give her away if you can't even remember her name. So your
daughter, the most amazing girl, is shifting the biggest day of her life so
you can enjoy it. It was going to be in a year or so, but now it's going to
be in a few months. A man more suspicious than you might think Rick
wants to get a ring on her before your trip to the moon so he gets a cut
of what you leave behind. He may as well—in a year's time you're not
going to care either way.

So there you have it—already your wife and daughter are spending
their evenings planning things, sometimes with Rick, sometimes without him, and sometimes Rick will come over and the two of you will
watch whatever game is on TV, or play darts in the garage, just shooting the breeze. They're struggling to find somewhere on short notice for
the ceremony but are still hopeful.

Good news—Eva is getting married. You can't believe how grown
up she is now. Walking her down the aisle is going to be one of the
proudest days of your life.

Bad news—Sandra mentioned selling the house. She's trying to be practical. She wants to find somewhere smaller. You've added it to the *I can't believe it* list. You told her no, that you want to stay here as long as you can. You told her you don't want to go into a home, that there's enough money and enough insurance to hire home care. She said okay, and that these things would be reassessed further down the line. You know what further down the line means—it's going to be just like when she read the journal. She's going to tell you that you've agreed all along to selling the place and that you've forgotten.

You will have to keep an eye on her.

❦

By the time Saturday has rolled around, Jerry has come to understand the fundamentals behind his disease. His conversation with Nurse Hamilton is proof he killed somebody, and reading passages from his books over the last few days have shown him the way the world works. It's about balance. There is, he believes, a reason he has Alzheimer's, and understanding that reason is the first step on the path to being cured.

He steps into the hallway. He's been told he woke up this morning a little confused, but this afternoon he knows who he is—fifty-year-old Jerry Grey, killer of one, at least one. He heads to the more common areas of the home, where others are watching TV or playing cards or comparing stories about grandchildren. TV has lost interest for him. It's impossible to follow a show when you don't know what happened the week before. There are couches and coffee tables and some people are talking, some are reading books, others are just staring ahead, lost in a thought either real or imagined, confused or not, chasing down a memory they can't quite grab. There are wheelchairs parked against walls and crutches parked against couches. The TV is muted. There's a show on about auctions and antiques, only they aren't really antiques to the core demographic of this show, but items they grew up with.

Eric is busy, so Jerry waits. On a couch. By a window. *Fifty-year-old Jerry Grey, killer of one*, those words going around in his mind like a skipping record, until Eric is free and comes over.

"I need your help," Jerry tells him.

"Whatever you need."

"I need to get out of here."

Eric doesn't answer. He just gives Jerry one of those sad smiles everybody who works here knows how to deliver, a smile Jerry is getting pretty sick of seeing.

"Please, it's important."

"It doesn't seem like you need my help to get out of here, Jerry— you've done it three times by yourself now."

Three times, Jerry thinks, where he's functioned enough to walk twenty miles but not functioned well enough to create the memory. Three times where he's essentially been sleepwalking. Only it should be called *wake-walking*. He is Jerry Grey, fifty-year-old crime writer, killer of one. He is the resident wake-walker. Maybe more than three times, he thinks, if he's snuck his way back in.

"What do you need to get out for?" Eric asks.

He's been wondering how much to reveal, and has decided the best way forward is to tell Eric everything. There is no shame in needing help.

"I know why I have Alzheimer's. It's because the Universe is punishing me for the bad things I've done. I hurt somebody, maybe even more than just one person. The only hope I have of the Universe returning my memories is if I confess to my crimes. I have to go to the police."

Eric's smile has turned into a frown. Jerry remembers somebody telling him once that a frown uses more muscles. The guy who told him that got shot in the back of the head during a drug deal in the back room of a furniture factory. Jerry can remember his face going through all kinds of frowning as he knelt there as a gunman stood over him, telling him he had a number in mind that he was counting to, and when he got there he was going to pull the trigger. The number was twenty-nine, only the gunman didn't say that, he just counted silently as the guy knelt in front of him shaking. Then there was the gunshot. The echo. There was little blood. How does Jerry know this? Is that who he killed?

"Is this about Suzan?" Eric asks.

Suzan. She was the first. "How do you know about Suzan?"

"We've had this conversation before, do you remember?"

Jerry shakes his head. If he remembered, he wouldn't be here.

"It never happened," Eric says, and he leans forward and puts his hand on Jerry's arm. "These people you think you killed, it just didn't happen. Nobody in your street was murdered. You never snuck into anybody's house and killed them. There is no Suzan with a *z*."

"How can you be so sure?"

"Because we checked. Where you grew up, nobody was murdered. Not in your neighborhood, hell, not even in your suburb."

Jerry knows the words are true, they feel true, and his body floods with relief. The fear inside him settles. The same way learning he was a crime writer fit like a glove, so does learning he's not a killer. There is no Suzan. There was no drug deal where he watched some guy get shot in the back of the head after the shooter counted to twenty-nine. They were in his books. He may not remember the details, but he knows he created these people.

Then it hits him. If he's been a good guy all these years, then why the disease? If he didn't kill anybody, then how can he repent? His future is as bleak as ever. "Then why am I being punished?"

"There is no *why*," Eric says. "It's just bad luck."

"So I never killed anybody?"

"The thing is, Jerry, it's all in the way you created these worlds—they all seem so real. People would read your books and they would become the main characters, they would see the world through their eyes, they would feel their thoughts. It's no wonder it all seems real to you—it sure seems real to those who read you. It sure seemed real to me. Your books are amazing," he says. "I've been a huge fan since book one."

"It can't just be bad luck," Jerry says. "The Universe is balancing the scales for something."

"Jerry—"

"I need to think about it," he says. He stands up. "I think I'll go rest a while."

Eric stands up too. They start walking back towards Jerry's room.

"Do you remember me telling you that I wanted to be a writer?" Eric asks.

Jerry shakes his head.

"I asked you for one piece of advice, and you said write what you know. I said that wasn't always possible. Do you remember what you said?"

"No."

"You said fake it. You said, did I really think Gene Roddenberry had been to Mars? Did I really think that Stephen King had been spooked by a vampire when he was a kid? Did I really think Bill and Ted knew how to travel in time? You said write what you know and fake the rest. You said throw some research in there too."

"And how's that working out for you?" Jerry asks.

"I'm still working here, aren't I?" Eric says, then laughs. "The thing about Suzan is exactly that. You didn't kill her, you just faked it, but she feels as real to you as she does to your readers. Now, you're not going to try and sneak out again today, are you?"

"No."

When Jerry gets into his room he sits down by the window. If he isn't being punished, then what is it? A memory comes to him then, one so strong it could have happened yesterday. He's sixteen years old, he's at school and it's career day and they're all trying to figure what they want to do with their lives, as if a sixteen-year-old can possibly know. Only he did know. He's having a conversation with a teacher, telling her he wants to be a writer. The teacher is telling him he needs to plan for a real future first, and to consider writing as a hobby. Jerry says he will do whatever it takes to make it happen. Is that what this is? The Universe taking his remaining years because it gave him the ones he wanted? Did he sell his soul?

"That's not it," he says, as much to himself as to the boy from nearly thirty-five years ago. It's about Suzan with a *z*. Perhaps not her specifically, but somebody just like her. The sense he has killed somebody is just far too real to ignore.

DAY THIRTY

Hey, Future Jerry. How you been? Sorry you haven't been in touch. You've been busy. You know how it is. Things to do. Places to be. People to forget. It's been ten days since you last wrote. This whole thing, this whole Alzheimer's hoopla, has been getting to you. Of course it has. You want to be super optimistic, and make light of it when you can, and fall into line with all the *Everything is going to be fine* ideology everybody is preaching, but you just can't, so rather than face the world, you've been sleeping in every day, hardly ever getting up before lunchtime. It's been a *Who gives a fuck* kind of week, whereas it should be a *Let's do everything you can while you still can* kind of week. You should be out there hang gliding and visiting Egypt and going to rock concerts and bucket-listing your way through your final days, not sleeping in. Also, you've been drinking more. Don't get the wrong idea—you're not getting hammered every night—two or three drinks, enough to take the edge of. Sometimes four. Never more than five. Enough to help you sleep. You also like to take naps during the day too. There's a couch in the office. The Thinking Couch. You'll lie there sometimes and come up with ideas for the books, work on solutions, lie there and listen to Springsteen cranked so loud the pens will roll off the desk. The Thinking Couch has become your Napping Couch and the desk a coaster and the stereo hasn't been on in over a week. Sandra keeps saying you shouldn't mope so much, but hey, if you want to mope then you'll mope. Grant a dying man his final wish, right? Because you're dying. Of course you are. The mind will be gone ten or twenty or even thirty years before the body—and if that isn't death, then what is? These days you also use the couch to hide the Madness Journal. You're sure Sandra sneaks in here at night and looks for it, but you have no proof of that.

It hasn't been all just lying on the couch in the office, though. You got the edit notes back from your editor a week ago. She's a real sweetheart. What you want in an editor is the ability to give you bad news in a good way. It's always in there, hidden in praise—if there was no praise you'd have given up long ago. But this one—this one was an effort for her, no doubt there. She's suggested some changes, and wants you to fill in more of the blanks, some character background, stuff a few years ago you would have been chomping at the bit to change because, after all, editing is your favorite phase, partner. Why wouldn't it be? You've built the house, and editing is picking the color scheme.

So yeah—that's what you've been up to. Napping. Drinking. Editing. You finished the last of the three bottles of gin that Hans brought around. When you rang him he told you he brought around five, but you can't find the other two. Sandra rang Doctor Goodstory today—you don't know what she said to him, and don't really care, to be honest, but she's off picking up a prescription right now. She asked if you wanted to come along, as if you were her pet, and you just shook your head and lay down on the couch in the office instead. When she gets back she'll try to cheer you up somehow, and you'll do your best to pretend that it's working. You'll fake it. That's something you tell people when they ask for advice on writing—people ask you all the time, you know, so be prepared for that. Even in your condition people will go rattling around in that brain of yours for some last nugget of hope, something that will make the difference between their manuscript hitting the bookshops or hitting the shredder. You usually say *Write what you know and fake the rest*. You might want to look out for people trying to pinch your ideas too—not that you're going to care about that, but you should. After all, you wrote all those books and it made you crazy. All those worlds—all those people—the Universe is always expanding, that's what the physicists say, all those worlds upon worlds as new ones are born, but one day all of that is going to change. One day the Universe will be as big as it can be, and then it will shrink. It will collapse. That's what is happening to you. Your mind—those ideas—got as big as it could get, and now it's collapsing.

Oh yeah, and your favorite nosy neighbor—Mrs. You Know Who (but in case you don't, it's Mrs. Smith—I'm not kidding, that really is her name)—came over yesterday. Sandra wasn't home. She was out with Eva going *ooh* and *ahh* at napkins, and you were lying in your office staring at the ceiling. The house has a wireless doorbell that flashes a light that sits on your desk in your office, on account of you having the stereo dialed so loud you'd never hear the bell ring. In fact, because you always write with the stereo turned up, you had to have extra insulation installed in the walls so the music wouldn't annoy Sandra or the neighbors. The entire room is soundproofed. You could shoot yourself in here and nobody would hear. So the doorbell light went off, and you went to the door in your robe and pajama bottoms and there she was, Mrs. Smith, and really have you ever seen her wearing something not saturated in pastel? Her clothes were in fashion sixty years ago and again thirty years ago, but are currently in the out-of-fashion stage of the cycle. Her lips were painted bright red in an attempt to distract from the many wrinkles lining her face, wrinkles deep enough to swallow a penny. She smells like cheap perfume, mixed in with a little bit of earth, as if she's always out planting flowers in the garden or toiling through her husband's grave.

She came over and she just wanted to have a quiet word, you know, just a brief in-your-ear mention that *some* of the neighbors—not her, mind you, not her at all, although she would have to agree with them, but *some* of the neighbors—have been talking. You live in a nice house, Jerry—and hopefully you're still there now—a nice house on a nice street, an expensive street where people have expensive tastes and expensive cars and expensive lives, most of them working less than you or not at all, their working days behind them, retirement homes on the horizon. She came over to be polite, just to let you know *that some, that some people are, well, a little—not angry, no, not angry, or upset—more worried, yes, Jerry, I would say worried, worried that your garden has gotten a little out of shape*. And she did have a point—the lawn hasn't been mowed in three weeks, the garden is full of stinging nettle, the roses need trimming back, and the yard is starting to look like jungle animals could be hiding in there. Mrs. Smith hasn't been the only one to mention it. Sandra has mentioned it too. She's been so busy with the wedding that she's had no time to do any weeding, and anyway, taking care of the garden is your thing. Sandra has mentioned hiring a gardener, but every time she does you tell her no, that you'll get onto it tomorrow. You've been very insistent on the matter, and Sandra understood when you explained it was important because hiring a gardener felt like it was opening Pandora's box. First the gardener, then a maid, then a nurse, then somebody to shower you, somebody to clean your teeth. Hiring a gardener is bringing that Dark Tomorrow you've been fighting to put off one day closer.

I know things have been . . . difficult for you lately, Mrs. Smith said, and doesn't that really just sum up the dementia beautifully? *Difficult for you.* Yeah, lady, really fucking difficult. Between Sandra being obsessed with the wedding and you being obsessed with the need to mope (gotta mope while you can still remember why life is worth moping about), the gardening has taken a backseat. She suggested you get a gardener. You wanted to suggest she mind her own business. You knew your house was letting down the street, this beautiful little *Stepford Wives* street where everything is *just so,* everything except your garden and your Big A. You told her you would take care of it. She said she was sure that you would.

That sums up day thirty. Sums up the first month.

It's time for another nap. The gardening can wait.

Good news, bad news—you know what? I don't really feel like doing that today.

His name is Jerry Cutter Henry Cutter, his name is Cutter Grey and he is an author and this is a nursing home and this is the real deal and he didn't kill anybody even though he knows he did.

His name is Jerry Henry Cutter and he is an author and none of this is real.

His name is Jerry Jerry and he writes crime novels and none of this is real.

"Jerry?"

"My name is Jerry Cutter and I am—"

"Jerry, do you know who I am?"

He is sitting by the window looking out at the gardens. It's sunny. There's a rabbit out there, twenty yards away, hiding in the bushes, but he can see it, oh yes he can, hiding there watching him, watching him, stealing his thoughts, using its tiny little rabbit brain to steal Jerry's thoughts to try and make its own brain bigger, stealing Jerry's thoughts to write a novel of its own, a rabbit novel about rabbits.

"Jerry?"

Jerry turns towards the voice. Nurse Hamilton is standing over him. "He's going to have to fake it," Jerry says, because a rabbit can't really know what he's thinking.

"Jerry?"

"Yes I know who you are, goddamn it," he says. "You're the nurse who won't shut up. Surely you have something better to do."

She smiles at him, and why would she smile? "Jerry, there are a couple of policemen here who want to talk to you, is that okay?"

"Policemen from the books?"

"Policemen from real life," she says.

He looks back towards the window. He's not interested in the policemen. They can't be as much fun as fictional ones. He can't see the rabbit anymore, but he knows it's still in the same bush, still watching him. *It's undercover!* "Is the rabbit a policeman? Where's Mom and Dad?"

The nurse doesn't answer him. Instead she turns towards two men who are standing behind her who he hadn't really noticed, and doesn't really make much of an effort to notice them now. "I don't think this is a good idea," she says to them. "There are bad days and there are okay days. This is one of the bad ones," she says, and Jerry has no idea what she means.

"It's important," one of the men says.

"Rabbit," Jerry says.

"Look at him," Nurse Hamilton says. "Anything he says can't be trusted, not like this. He's going to confess to a dozen crimes. Two dozen."

"We're only interested in one," the man says.

"I know that, but he's not going anywhere."

"Isn't he? He has before."

"I had a rabbit when I was a kid," Jerry says, and they all look at him and he feels the need to explain. "I owned it for two days before it escaped and ran away. It wasn't my fault. I was seven years old and what seven-year-old is going to remember to shut the door on the rabbit hutch?" He stands up and puts his hands against the window. "That's him!" He turns towards the nurse and the two men with her. "That's Wally! Where's Mom and Dad? They can help me catch him! Quick, we have to get out there!"

The nurse puts her hands on his shoulders. "Sit back down, Jerry, please, we'll deal with the rabbit soon."

"But—"

"Please, Jerry. Just do what I ask, okay?"

He looks out the window, then at the men behind the nurse. The way they are looking at him . . . he doesn't like it. He sits down but keeps looking outside.

"We'll keep a close eye on him," Nurse Hamilton says to the men. "Perhaps you can come back tomorrow?"

"Hey, hey, Jerry, are you in there?" one of the men asks, and leans forward and taps Jerry on his forehead hard enough to hurt.

"Don't," Jerry says, and swipes at the man's hand. Jerry doesn't like him. Not at all.

"Hey, come on now, enough of that," Nurse Hamilton says, and she reaches out and pulls the man's hand away, then steps between him and Jerry, so all Jerry can see is the back of her cardigan.

"How do we know he's not faking it?" that same man asks. "Faking the whole thing to get away with murdering—"

"Don't say that around him," Nurse Hamilton says, interrupting him.

"I didn't murder Wally," Jerry says, then looks back out the window. He doesn't want to look at the men anymore. Just wants to find Wally. The rabbit is all he wants to think about.

"Now I'm going to have to ask you both to leave," Nurse Hamilton says.

"Ring us if he gets any better today," the first man says, and Jerry sees movement from their direction and turns to see that man handing a card to the nurse. He wonders if that man is a rabbit salesman. "If we don't hear from you, we'll come back tomorrow morning and try again."

They watch the two men go, Jerry's back to the window, and he can feel warmth from the sun as it comes through. He wants to go outside, but not while the two men are here. They may be rabbit salesmen, but that doesn't make them good people. He decides he will wait for ten minutes. That's a good amount of time for people to disappear. He thinks that some people can disappear off the face of the earth in less time than that, and he's not sure why he would know something like that, let alone think it.

"Who were they?" he asks, once they've gone beyond the doors to the room.

"Just a couple of people who came to see how you are doing."

"Rabbit salesmen?"

"No."

"Friends?"

"Not exactly."

"They don't seem like friends," he says. "I didn't like them."

"I didn't like them either, Jerry."

He turns back towards the window. "I want to go outside. I want to find Wally."

"Let's get you cleaned up first," Nurse Hamilton says.

"Cleaned up? Why?"

"You've had an accident," she says, and when he looks down he sees that he's pissed himself, and when he looks back up he sees Wally running away, disappearing into the trees.

DAY THIRTY-ONE

Holeeee shit!

Hey Grumpy Smurf! How you doing, Grumpy Smurf?

All better? Yes. Yes, you are!

God you feel good. Goooooooood!

The last few weeks—they were stage four. STAGE FOUR! You're really ripping through them now. Can you imagine going along to a support group with people treating it like a competition, people going *No, I got depressed quicker, No, I got angrier than you did,* or *I accepted it first and you denied it longer.*

Sandra came home yesterday with these little blue pills to make you feel better. To balance out your mood, and to be honest you didn't want to take them, and then you thought, you know what? You should take *all* of them. So that's what you decided to do, only Sandra wouldn't give you *all* of them, instead she handed them out like clockwork, two every four hours, and then she made sure you were taking them too, she even made you open your mouth and go *ahh* so she could check you weren't storing them up to take in one shot. By this morning you felt better, and by this afternoon better*er*, and this evening even better*erer*! You are on the mend! In fact, you are so on the mend that it's looking like this Alzheimer's thing can be kicked. People with dementia can't feel this good, can they?

Time for a quick good news, bad news summation. Good news—you're pretty sure the diagnosis is wrong, and that there is nothing wrong with you. So that's not good news—that's great news! That is the best news you could give yourself, which is exactly what is happening here. You're no longer Grumpy Smurf. No longer Drinky Smurf.

Bad news—there is no bad news.

Eva came around today.

She left Hip-Hop Rick at HOME.

And she came ALONE.

Yo.

And she came with wedding magazines and photographs of dresses she had printed from the Internet, and she was buzzing with good news—oh yeah, more good news—none of the places she approached had any cancellations, but there is a church that has a spare date ahead and, get this: they are getting married in six weeks! That's going to put it somewhere around day seventy in the Madness Journal. That gives you me us we something to look forward to. Even though your suit is only six years old, you need a new one, according to Eva. And according to Sandra.

You started working again today on *The Man Goes Burning*. You've had the house to yourself, as Sandra has been busy heading into work on and off this week. She's defending a teacher who was fired from his job after photographs posted online showed him kissing another man—his partner. Enough parents complained about their children being taught science by a gay teacher that the school ended up terminating his contract. Homophobia doesn't run very deep at all in this country, but it still pops its ugly head up every now and then. You've never understood homophobia. Gay guys tend to be better groomed and better dressed and more sophisticated than the rest of us—if they were straight, they'd be stealing all the women. You'd never have met Sandra. With Sandra at work, and you on the mend, the day has felt like one of the classics, just you and your stereo cranked up, that feeling you get from editing when you can feel the magic happening, and there's no way you'd feel that way if you weren't beating the disease. It's quite possible you were misdiagnosed.

Good news—the other two bottles of gin showed up. You'd hidden them in the garage, and that came to you just this morning. You might have a celebratory drink later on. You shouldn't, because of the pills, but you will, because you want to. More good news—if you can't shake, shake, shake the Big A, then the Big Bill from the wedding won't worry you so much.

Bad news—you get the idea Sandra thinks you need a good suit not just for the wedding. Every dying man needs a good suit in the end, don't they?

"You don't remember any of yesterday?" Eric asks him.

The two of them are outside, walking past a group of people being sung to by an entertainer who comes to the nursing home twice a week. The guy is playing a guitar, he's playing a bunch of old-school songs, the kind of music Jerry loves, only he loves it on his stereo, with loud lyrics and drums and electric guitars and saxophones blaring. He loves the way it used to get his creative juices flowing. This guy is playing the songs as if this were a cruise boat for hundred-year-olds. There's a van parked near the front door, a maintenance worker messing around with the outside lights, and Jerry wonders how hard it would be to stow away in the back of that van and go for a ride. Quite difficult, he imagines, because there's a dog sitting in the front seat. The sun is out but not hot yet, however it'll get there soon, and most of the residents are in short-sleeved tops. It's ten in the morning and he's only just gotten up. He hasn't had breakfast yet. Eric's question makes him realize he hasn't even thought about yesterday. Hasn't realized there should be something to remember. Whenever somebody points out to him that he's forgotten a period of time, there's a sense of disorientation. They keep walking. He runs through a small checklist that, when he remembers to use it, he finds useful. Where is he? Well, a hotel is a hotel is a hotel, but this isn't that. This isn't him on tour. This is a care facility. His name is Jerry Grey. He is a man without a future becoming a man forgetting his past. He is a man whose wife doesn't come and visit because she filed for divorce because all of this was too difficult for her.

Jerry nods. "Sure," he says, then realizes he doesn't remember it at all. "Was it memorable?"

"What about the day before?"

This time he shakes his head.

"The name Belinda Murray," Eric says, "does that mean anything to you?"

"Belinda Murray?" Jerry thinks about it, letting the name filter though his memory banks. It goes through his mind without catching. "Should it?"

Eric claps him on the shoulder and smiles. "Possibly not," Eric says. "How are you feeling this morning?"

"I feel good," Jerry says, which he knows is a stock-standard answer, which must mean at the very least he's still remembering how human beings act in society. He also knows half an hour ago when he woke up, he was confused for a little while. He realizes he hasn't asked how Eric is, so maybe he has forgotten a few of the social going-along-to-get-along rules. He does that now.

"I'm good, buddy," Eric answers.

Then Jerry remembers something else. "How's the writing?"

"Good," Eric says, looking thrilled to have been asked, and Jerry is equally as thrilled to have remembered. "I've been inspired by something. In fact, I can have you to thank for that. You and your advice of writing what you know."

Jerry wonders what that advice might be. "You're writing about an orderly?"

"Ha," Eric says, and slaps him on the back. "That's closer to the truth than you'd know. I better go and get some work done, and you need to go and have some breakfast and get ready soon too, as you've got visitors on their way."

"Sandra and Eva?"

"Sadly not, buddy."

The visitors end up arriving just before noon, and it turns out to be a pair of policemen, which is disappointing, he thinks, but not as disappointing as being visited by your accountant. The first cop introduces himself. He's a guy by the name of Dennis Mayor who looks nothing like any Dennis that Jerry has ever known, and the second guy is Chris Jacobson, who looks more like a Dennis than a Chris. They tell Jerry they came out yesterday to see him, and he almost calls them liars, because they weren't here yesterday . . . but then he thinks it's possible they were. Plus now that he thinks about it, they *do* look vaguely familiar. The introductions are made in a bedroom that is currently unoccupied, the previous patient dead, Jerry imagines, since nobody here really ever gets better. There are five of them—the two cops, Eric, Nurse Hamilton, and there's him, Jerry Grey, crime writer.

When they're all sitting down he realizes this isn't just an unoccupied bedroom but an interrogation room. The two cops are sitting opposite him, and Eric is to his left and Nurse Hamilton to his right. He feels concerned. He feels like he should be asking for a lawyer.

Before he can ask what this is about, Mayor leans forward and starts the proceedings. "Does the name Belinda Murray mean anything to you?"

Belinda Murray. Jerry compares the name to faces from the past, scanning through them the way fingerprints are scanned on TV shows, image after image flicking by. He doesn't get a hit. Yet . . . there is something familiar about it. "I know the name."

"You want to tell us about her?" Mayor asks.

He wants to, but . . . "I . . . can't."

"And why is that?"

"I don't know who she is."

"You just said you know the name," Jacobson says.

"I know, but . . ." He runs the name against the faces again. "I just don't know from where."

"That could be my fault," Eric says, and everybody looks at Eric, except Jerry, because he's looking at the two cops who look annoyed with Eric. Eric follows it up. "I asked him earlier this morning if he knew the name. I'm sorry, probably—"

"Shouldn't have?" Mayor asks.

Eric shrugs. "That might be where he's remembering it from."

"You're right, you really shouldn't have done that," Mayor says.

"And why not?" Nurse Hamilton asks, glaring at Mayor. "Jerry was the one who told the name to us, and we're the ones who gave that news to you. Don't sit there trying to make out we've done something wrong here when all we're doing is trying to uncover the truth."

"You're right," Mayor says. "I'm sorry, and we're grateful for your help. However, we're here because he did tell you her name two days ago, so where was he remembering her from then?"

Jerry doesn't like being talked about as if he's not in the room. It makes him feel like an object. A subject. "Who is Belinda Murray?" he asks.

They all look back towards him.

"I don't know who she is," he says.

"Perhaps show him the photograph," Nurse Hamilton says.

Jacobson nods, and opens up a folder that's resting on his knee. He pulls out a photograph and hands it over to Jerry. It's an eight-by-ten glossy of a blond woman with blue eyes and a beautiful smile, a girl-next-door smile, a midtwenties girl with all sorts of hopes and promises who would have had all sorts of men queuing across all sorts of miles for the chance to date her. Jerry already knows where this is going. Of course he does.

"You think I killed her," he says.

"And why would you say that?" Mayor asks.

"Look, detectives, I may be losing my mind, but not enough to miss the obvious. This," he says, and spreads his arms to indicate the room and all that is in it, "is an interrogation. You're here because this girl is dead, and I'm sorry about that, I really am, but I don't know her and I didn't hurt her."

"It's because—" Mayor says, but then stops when Nurse Hamilton holds her hand up to him.

"Let me explain it to him," she says.

Mayor looks at his partner, and his partner gives him a small *why not* shrug.

Nurse Hamilton angles the chair so she can face Jerry almost full on, and she takes his hand in both of hers and leans forward. He can smell coffee on her breath and she's wearing the same perfume his sister-in-law wears. He can't remember his sister-in-law's name, or the last time he ever thought about her, but he can remember how she looks, and can imagine she had a hand in Sandra's decision to leave him. He pictures the two of them slumped on couches, their feet up, drinking wine and listening to music and his wife saying it's all too tough, her sister telling her she's young enough to start over, to cut Jerry loose and find some guy half her age. Suddenly he wishes it were a picture of the sister-in-law they were showing him, not a complete stranger.

"Jerry, are you feeling okay?"

"What?"

"You left us for a little bit there," Nurse Hamilton says.

"I'm fine," he tells her.

"You sure?"

He thinks about it for a few seconds. "I've been better."

"Tell me if things become too stressful, okay?" she says.

"Are you going to get to the point or not?" Mayor asks.

She ignores him. "Okay, Jerry?"

"Tell you if things become stressful. I've got it," he says, Sandra and her sister fading from his thoughts.

"Do you remember where you are?"

He doesn't need to look around. It's a simple question and they must really think he's a special kind of stupid to be asking him this, but he still looks around anyway, just to make sure. "Of course I do. I know who I am and where I am. I'm in a nursing home because I have dementia. I was placed here because my wife decided to divorce me rather than let me stay at home. I'm here because Captain A takes over sometimes and I wander."

"Who the hell is Captain A?" Mayor asks.

"It's what he calls the Alzheimer's," Nurse Hamilton says. She turns back towards Jerry. She still has his hand between hers. "Do you remember what you did for a living?"

He nods.

"Tell me."

"I used to write books," he says. "I wrote ten of them."

"You wrote thirteen. Do you remember two days ago, when you were sitting in the garden?"

"Thirteen? Are you sure?"

"The garden, Jerry."

He's spent a lot of time in the garden. He was there today. Probably yesterday and the day before, but when every day is the same, how can you tell one apart from the other?

"Not really," he says.

Without even looking at the two detectives, Nurse Hamilton puts her arm out to the side and slightly behind her, her index finger raised in a *Don't say a word* gesture. "You were in the garden and you were pulling out the roses, remember? You said you were helping. You said you used to help your neighbor the same way."

"I did?" he asks, unable to remember the neighbor, unable to remember two days ago, unable to remember he wrote thirteen books and not ten.

"I took you by the hand and we sat down in the shade and I gave you a drink of water, and we talked for a while. Do you remember what we talked about?"

"Roses?" he asks, but really it's just an educated guess. Then he thinks about what she's saying, about what he does for a living. "It was about the books."

"He doesn't remember a damn thing," Mayor says, loosening the top of his tie. He sounds frustrated. Jerry thinks he's probably had a lot of frustrated cops in his novels. These guys probably drink a lot of coffee and have a lot of ex-wives and eventually they snap. The room is getting warmer, no doubt the five of them helping to raise the temperature, and he wants to get out of here. Not just out of this room, but out of the care facility. He wants to go back home.

Nurse Hamilton looks back to Jerry after having thrown Mayor another of her angry looks. Jerry doesn't want to be on the receiving end of one of those. "Jerry, do you remember Suzan?"

Jerry frowns and tilts his head a little, gritting his teeth at the same time. Of course he remembers Suzan. She was his first. He remembers finding her door unlocked and walking through her house, trying his hardest to not make any noises, and not making them. "How do you know about her?"

"It's okay, Jerry," she says, and tightens his hand. "Tell us about Suzan."

He shakes his head.

"Trust me, Jerry. Please, you need to trust me."

"With a z," he says.

"That's right."

He lowers his voice. "In front of the detectives?"

"They're here to help you."

He looks over at them, these two men staring at him, one with his tie askew, the other not wearing one, both of them in need of a shave. Neither of these men look like they want to help. "Do I have to?"

"Yes," she says, and so it is said and so it is law. That's the thing about Nurse Hamilton—he can imagine even if he did completely forget about her, he would still follow her orders.

He starts talking normally again. "Suzan with a z is somebody I used

to know when I was younger. She used to live on my street, and I—"
He looks back at Nurse Hamilton. "Do I have to carry on?"

"No, Jerry, you don't, because Suzan with a *z* doesn't exist. She's a character in one of your books."

"She's a . . ." he says, then stops midsentence. Suzan with a *z*. From a book. A couple of synapses fire off somewhere in the Jerry gray matter and there he is, sitting at his computer, trying to come up with a name for the character, and he wanted something relatable but also a little different. When it came to the main characters those names could be tough because you had to get them right, the name had to match the character, a good name would make a character feel far more genuine.

He remembers writing the scene, getting to the end and then going back over it, adding some and deleting some. He remembers every single detail, as if it were only yesterday he labored over the keyboard. He remembers writing a scene from Suzan's point of view, and then deleting it, the book moving forward, going through editing, cover design, then the big day when it was set free into the world, and by then he was already working on the next book. He understands exactly what Nurse Hamilton is saying. He made up Suzan. She is a combination of words on paper, born from his need to write, his need to entertain, his need to pay the mortgage.

"Jerry?"

He looks back at Nurse Hamilton. She's staring at him. "She's a character," he says. "Sometimes I get her mixed up with the real world." He directs that last bit to the cops, and then gives a small appropriate laugh to prove they're all friends here, nothing going on, just a lighthearted misunderstanding. But it doesn't work. If anything, it makes him sound like a madman. And he knows what madmen sound like—he's created enough of them.

"Belinda Murray is in the real world," Mayor says.

"Jerry," Nurse Hamilton says, her hands still on Jerry's, "two days ago when we were sitting in the garden, do you remember telling me about Belinda?"

"Belinda from the books," he says, trying to sound confident, sure that's where she's from but unable to remember her.

"I just said—" Mayor says, but then stops talking when Nurse Hamilton throws him another Nurse Hamilton look.

"No, not from the books," she says to Jerry. "Belinda is a real person. You spoke to me about her."

He runs the name against the Jerry Grey database. No match. "Are you sure?"

"This is useless," Mayor says. "I say we just take him down to the station and talk to him there. We'll get in somebody more qualified." Nurse Hamilton looks towards him, and this time he doesn't back down. "Come on, even you can see this is a waste of time," he says.

"What's happening?" Jerry asks.

She turns back towards him. "Jerry, Suzan with a *z*, you know she doesn't exist, you see that, right?"

"Of course," he says, feeling embarrassed he ever made that mistake, and promising himself never to make it again.

"She isn't the only one," Nurse Hamilton says. "Over the last year that you've been here, you—"

"Wait, wait, hold up a second," Jerry says, shaking his head. "There's some kind of mistake. I haven't been here a year. I've been here . . ." He looks at Eric and gives him a shrug. "What? Two months at the most?"

"It's been a year," Eric says. "Eleven months to be exact."

"No," Jerry says, and starts to stand up, but Nurse Hamilton keeps hold of his hand and pulls him back down. "You're lying to me," he says.

"It's okay, Jerry. Calm down, please."

"Calm down? How can I be calm when all of you are making these things up about me."

"You have been here for a year, Jerry," she says, quite forcefully too.

"But—"

You're Jerry Grey, the man with Alzheimer's as his sidekick, how can you argue this? How can you argue with Nurse Hamilton? Her word is law.

"Are you sure?" he asks.

"Yes," she says. "And in the eleven months you've been here, you've confessed to a lot of crimes."

"The first time you did it, buddy, it was quite a shock," Eric says. "Nurse Hamilton here was getting ready to call the police, but there was something about what you were saying that was familiar. I'm a big fan of your books, and I quickly figured out you were describing a scene from one of them."

"Since your time with us, you've confessed to a lot of make-believe crimes that you remember doing," Nurse Hamilton says.

"They seem so real to you," Eric says.

"Two days ago we were in the garden and you told me a story," Nurse Hamilton says, and she glances at the photo, and Jerry knows what she's about to say—the same way he always used to be able to predict how TV shows and movies would end one quarter of the way through. Is that where they are now? One quarter of the way through his madness? And the Madness Journal? Just where in the hell is it?

"You told me about a girl you had killed. You said you knew her, but you didn't say how. Do you remember this?"

He doesn't remember that at all, and he tries to remember. Hard. He knows that's a thing people probably tell him, to try and think harder or try and remember better, as if he can tighten his brain muscles and put in the extra effort. But it is what it is, and in this case what it is is a whole lot of nothing. "I remember the garden," he says. "And . . . there was a rabbit. Wally."

"You stabbed her," Mayor says.

"The rabbit?"

"Belinda Murray. You murdered her in cold blood."

Nurse Hamilton puts a hand on Jerry's knee when he goes to stand. "Wait, Jerry, please. Despite the fact Detective Mayor here is behaving in extremely poor taste, it's what you told me. You said you knocked on her door in the middle of the night, and when she answered it you . . . you struck her. Then you . . ." she says, and she looks away from him, and he knows what it is she doesn't want to say, and he wonders how she is going to say it, and she says, "had your way with her. Then you stabbed her. You told me all about it."

"But if I've been here for the last year then—"

"It was just before you were sentenced here," Mayor says. "A few days before the shooting."

"What shooting?"

"That's enough, Detective," Nurse Hamilton says, then she looks back at Jerry. "Think about the girl, Jerry."

But he doesn't want to think about the girl because there is no girl. This Belinda Murray is only as real as the other characters he's written about. "What shooting?"

"There was no shooting, Jerry," Nurse Hamilton says, and she sounds calm. "The girl. Do you remember her? Belinda. Do you remember seeing her before you came here? It was a year ago. Look at the photograph again."

He doesn't look at the photograph. "There's something you're not telling me," he says, the statement directed at everybody in the room.

"Please, Jerry, answer the questions so these two men can be on their way."

He looks at the photograph again. The blond girl. The attractive girl. The dead girl. The stranger. And yet . . . "When I think of Suzan, it's like I know her, but this girl . . ." He lets the sentence peter out. "The thing is she does look familiar. Doesn't *feel* familiar, but I do recognize her. And the name—I've heard the name before. When did I hear it?"

The cops are staring at him. He thinks about what he just said and wishes he hadn't said any of it. He wishes Sandra were here. She'd be on his side.

"We think he should come with us," Mayor says to Nurse Hamilton.

"Is that really necessary?" she asks.

"At this point I'm afraid it's the next step," Mayor says, but Jerry doesn't think he sounds afraid.

They all stand up then. "Am I going to be put into handcuffs?" Jerry asks.

"That won't be necessary," Mayor says.

"Can I play with the siren?"

"No," Mayor says.

They start to walk out of the room. "Are you coming with me?" he asks Nurse Hamilton.

"I'll meet you there," she says, "and I'll call your lawyer along the way."

He thinks about that for a few seconds. "Can you ask the detectives if I can play with the siren?"

"Don't make us put you in handcuffs," Mayor says.

"Detective—" Nurse Hamilton says.

Mayor shrugs. "I'm just kidding. Come on, let's get out of here—this place gives me the creeps."

DAY FORTY

This entry isn't going to start with good news or bad news, but with weird news. Two pages have been torn out from this journal, the two pages after the last entry. You didn't do it, and you didn't write in them either because you me us we are still sane. Two blank pages gone. However, it's possible Sandra tore them out for one of two possibilities. She wants you to think you wrote an entry and can't remember it, for which there seems no motive. Or she found the journal, was reading it, and spilled something on those pages and had to tear them out. It means being more careful now about leaving the journal out.

Eva took you to lunch yesterday. It was just the two of you, which is something you hardly ever get to do. She took you to a restaurant that has a view of the Avon river out one side, and the hills out the other. Her friend is a chef there, and she prepared a special lunch that wasn't on the menu, one she was working on to add within the coming weeks. She'd come over and asked what you thought, never taking up too much of your time, so many smiles and so much happiness that even if you and Eva hadn't liked the meal, neither of you would have been able to say anything. You didn't talk much about the future with Eva, or about the wedding, instead you chatted about her music, she told you some more stories of her big trip overseas, she told you that one of her friends from school was having a baby, and that having a family is something she and Rick have been talking about. You asked if she was pregnant, and she laughed, and said no, not yet, but maybe in a couple of years. She told you that before she started writing song lyrics, she had been thinking of trying to write fiction. Just short stories. Not the kind of stuff that Henry Cutter comes up with, but stories based on slice-of-life moments she had seen when traveling, moments that eventually got turned into music. She asked if you would look over some of her work. She said she'd love some feedback, and you know she's doing this for you, not for her, but to be asked was such a thrill.

Then she asked what you were planning for Sandra's birthday. Sandra's birthday, of course, is something you had forgotten about, had remembered again a few days ago, and ultimately had landed on the side of forgetting. You're not sure whether Eva would have decided that was an Alzheimer's thing, or a Jerry thing, but it's a moot point because you have been thinking about it, but at that stage you hadn't decided on either the perfect gift, or the how to spend the day.

"How about a surprise party?" Eva suggested.

You agreed it was a fantastic idea, but what you didn't say was she should have arranged a surprise party without your knowledge. You see one of two things happening—either forgetting about the party, or forgetting that it's meant to be a secret. When Eva drove you back home, she handed you a folder from the backseat with a dozen songs in it. You sat out on the deck in the sun reading the lyrics, putting them to the music in your head, so excited for her, for her future, for the people who will one day get to hear them.

Your own writing, by the way, is going well. You sent the revised edition of *The Man Goes Burning* to your editor this morning. It was, it turned out, a lot of work. The book is about a firefighter who is also an arsonist who falls in love with a fellow firefighter, and burns down buildings just so he can work with her, with the ultimate goal of being able to save her life. You ended up introducing a new character, which has really helped—a guy by the name of Nicholas, and Nicholas brings a whole new element to the story, some heart and depth that was lacking before. Nicholas is a punk teenager accused of an armed robbery, and while in a holding cell at the police station he is severely beaten and raped and almost dies, and of course Nicholas never committed the robbery at all. He uses what little money he is given in compensation to put himself through law school—so all of that is in the past, and now your main character, the arsonist, uses a lawyer when he becomes a suspect after the woman he loves disappears. Nicholas is the kind of lawyer willing to go to the end of the world for a client he truly believes in.

The book isn't the only thing going well. The wedding preparations are racing along, all the pieces of the big day falling into place. It's *wedding* this and *wedding* that, *Let's talk about flowers*, *Let's talk about place settings*, *Do you like the dress*, *Do you like the cake*, *You're the writer, Jerry, so tell us what font do you think looks best on these dinner menus? That one? Are you sure? How sure?*

Thank God you've had all this work to do because really you've just been able to stay out of the way, which is probably the best gift you can give your family. The wedding is less than five weeks away and you can't wait until it's in the rearview mirror. In five weeks you'll have shaken off the dementia too, and maybe you can get a good chunk of book fourteen written before going on tour with book thirteen. You're enough of a realist to know that even though you're dodging the dementia bullet now, that doesn't mean it still hasn't got your name on it. It could be twenty years away, or it could be ten. You need to keep writing for you, for your fans, for your family.

Getting caught up in the rewrite has been a lot of work as well as a lot of fun, but it has kept you away from this journal. In saying that, there is definitely less of a need to keep writing here—why would anybody clearly not mad need to keep a Madness Journal? You barely read from it anymore anyway.

Before signing off for the day, here's a little something from a few mornings ago, a weird incident that's hardly worth mentioning, but here goes . . .

Sandra was at work, and your neighbor, Mrs. Smith, comes over. She comes over and she is pissed off. Somebody tore all of her flowers up, and Mrs. Smith wants to know if you know anything about it. You don't know—of course you don't—but then she says one of the neighbors said they *saw* you doing it—or at least somebody who looked like you. You tell her no, it wasn't you, you're a forty-nine-year-old crime writer who has been inside writing crime all week and who, you assure her, has far better things to do than wipe out rows and rows of her roses.

I just find it strange that Mrs. Blatch says she was sure it was you, and that she thought you were doing some gardening.

Now, Mrs. Blatch, to put things into perspective, Future Jerry, is of an age that can only be prefaced by a seven again if she reaches seven hundred. She wears glasses so heavy her eventual cause of death will be from a broken neck.

Then Mrs. Blatch is wrong, which can't be much of a surprise, can it? She is almost two hundred years old.

Be that as it may, Jerry, she is sure it was you and, well, there's no real delicate way of putting this, but after our conversation the other day, it seems like you're paying me back.

What conversation?

I asked you to tidy up your yard. Your garden is a disgrace.

I'm working on it, and it wasn't me that dug up your roses.

How can you be so sure it wasn't? A man in your condition—really, how can you be so sure?

If you're going to accuse me of having a grudge against your garden, then next time try to have a witness who wasn't around when fire was invented.

You wished her *good day*—you actually used those very words, straight out of a Victorian drama, then closed the door on her.

Good news—Nicholas is going to save your manuscript. You're sure of it, and the book will be out next year. Good news—Replacement Jerry is no longer knocking on the door. You're beating this thing.

Bad news—last night you took a leak in one of the bedrooms. You were halfway through when you suddenly realized you were pissing in the corner of the guest bedroom rather than the bathroom. You did manage to stop midflow (good news), and you did manage to clean it up without Sandra knowing (also good news).

So this is it, Future Jerry. No real time to stay in touch now and not much point either. You're going to dedicate your time to the wedding and to the next book. You actually have an idea for a new novel—about a crime writer who has dementia. Not quite based on you, because this guy actually has the Big A. *Write what you know,* remember? *And fake the rest.*

Jerry doesn't get to play with the sirens on the way. He doesn't get to do anything except sit in the backseat and stare out the side window. He is starting to feel a little like his old self. Could be the motion of the car is stirring up the brain chemistry, stirring up the memories like silt from the bottom of a river. Could be the smell of fast food and coffee that has soaked into the pores of the upholstery, taking him back to times overseas where he's eaten in takeaway joints while pressed for time. It could be the change of environment, it could be the fresh air he got between the nursing home and the car. There are bits and pieces of his past floating to the surface. He remembers his dad drowning in the pool, he remembers meeting Sandra at university, he remembers taking his family to cities so big they made Christchurch look like a drop in a bucket. Of course there are things he can't remember. He has no idea what he ate for breakfast. He can't remember what he did yesterday, whether he watched TV or walked in the garden. He can't remember the last time he looked at a newspaper, the last time he held his wife, the last time he made a phone call or typed an email. The memories shift, they stir, some of them settle, some of them disappear.

He says nothing to the policemen—Nurse Hamilton was very specific about that. *Say nothing. Ask for a drink if you're thirsty, ask for the bathroom if you need to go, but that's all. Now say it back to me.* He said it back to her. They spoke in front of the two detectives, Detective Mayor and Detective Something Else, and then she told them not to engage Jerry in conversation until his lawyer arrived.

We know our jobs, Mayor said, but Jerry knew their jobs too. He knew they would try.

That trying begins five miles closer to town, Mayor adjusting himself in the passenger seat and tilting the mirror so he can look at Jerry. "So you're a writer, huh?"

Jerry doesn't answer. He's thinking about Sandra, and whether Nurse Hamilton has called her already. No doubt Sandra will want to come down, either to support him, or to prove divorcing him was the best decision she's made of late.

"Must be a pretty good gig," Mayor says.

He can see Mayor's eyes and nose in the mirror, but nothing else. There's nothing between the front and the backseat to stop Jerry from tousling the man's hair. Or trying to strangle him.

"Come on, this is us just shooting the breeze," Mayor says, "ain't that right, Chris?"

"Gotta do something on the ride back," Chris says, "otherwise it's a pretty boring trip."

"We're just chitchatting here," Mayor says. "Think of it like we're meeting for the first time at a barbecue and we're having a couple of beers. You must get that all the time, right? Mr. Bigshot writer? You must love talking about it. So pretend we're at that barbecue. You write crime fiction, right? You written anything I would have read?"

"Maybe," Jerry says.

"Maybe. I like a good crime novel, you know? I like a good mystery. I like unlocking a puzzle. Your novels, are they like that?"

"I'm not . . . I'm not sure," Jerry says, and he isn't sure.

"He's not sure, you hear that, Chris?"

"I heard it. It's the dementia. Guy can't even remember his own stories."

"But you remember the characters, right?" Mayor asks. "You remember killing them. Is that why you write? You write about these things because it's an outlet for you, you figure writing is better than doing the actual crimes? I've always wondered that about you guys."

Jerry doesn't answer him.

"The way I see it, I've always figured a guy who writes the kind of books you write, well, there must be something wrong with him, something sick and twisted inside. Why else come up with all that stuff?"

Jerry doesn't answer him.

"The shit we see every day, and we see a lot of shit, don't we, Chris?"

"Sure we do," Chris says.

"We wade through it," Mayor says.

"It's deep," Chris says, "and it's never going away."

"It's never going away," Mayor agrees. "If you saw what we saw, I mean, how does a guy like you take what slowly kills us on the inside and turn it into entertainment? Do you turn on the radio and hear about some poor kid tossed into a dumpster with her throat and panties all torn and you think to yourself, well now, that'll make a good story?"

Jerry wants to say nothing, but he can't help himself. "It's not like that," he says, getting angry. He knows writing isn't like that. He knows it because of the moving car, the swirling brain chemistry, like silt in a stream.

Mayor twists around in his seat so he can look right at him. "Do you get off on it? You're just sitting by the TV, waiting for the news to come on every day, sitting with your notepad waiting to be inspired by somebody else's tragedy?"

"Of course not."

"Do the messier ones give you better ideas?"

Jerry doesn't answer him. There's nothing you can say to somebody who already has their mind made up.

"You make your money by selling crime," Mayor says. "Make more than we do by solving it."

"And without crime you'd be out of a job," Jerry says. "The suit you're wearing, the house you live in, the food you give your children, all of that is bought and paid for on the back of other people's suffering."

"Ooh, you hear that, Chris?" Mayor asks, and he keeps looking at Jerry. "Our buddy here is making a point."

"It's social commentary," Chris says.

"So tell us, Jerry," Mayor says. "Tell us how much real-life sad stories inspire you."

Jerry looks between the two men at the road ahead, staring out at a logging truck they're following, the load swaying side to side as it races down the motorway at sixty miles an hour. "Like I said, it's not like that."

"No? Then what is it like?"

"You wouldn't understand."

"You hear that, Chris?" Mayor asks, and Jerry hates how he keeps doing that, how he keeps running everything past his partner. "He doesn't think I can understand."

"I think you can understand," Chris says. "Our friend back there just needs to give you a chance."

"I think you're right," Mayor says. "What do you say, Jerry? Want to give me a chance? I'm no crime writer, and I hear the cops in your books don't do much other than scratch their asses and sniff their fingers, but how about you explain it to me?"

It's something he used to get a lot. He remembers that—it was a question journalists always used to throw his way. *So you're fascinated by crime.* No, he's not—he likes crime writing, but not crime, and how many times has he pointed out the two are very different animals? It's like thinking people who watch war movies must love war. Over the years he's turned down interviews for TV and radio where reporters have wanted his perspective on a current homicide, always feeling how inappropriate it would be, how hurtful it would be for the family, having an author throw in his two cents just for some publicity.

"They're just stories," he tells them. "Stories have been around forever, and without them the human race never would have evolved."

"Crime has been around forever too," Mayor says.

"But I've never used a real crime in any of my books," he says, and he can hear himself getting closer to whining. "The things I come up with—they are all make-believe. All of it. I've never used a real person's tragedy. I make a real point of that."

"You don't think what you write inspires people to kill? You don't think there are people out there who read about one of your killers and think to themselves, *I can do better?*"

"It doesn't work that way, and people who think it does don't know what the hell they're talking about," Jerry says, and right now he is very switched on. Right now he feels like the man he used to be. Not all the details are there, and he still can't figure out what he did to make Sandra divorce him, but there's more there than what there's been of late, he's sure of that.

"Then tell me how it works," Mayor says.

"People don't read my books and think, *Hey, that's a great idea, let me try that,*" he says, and then he realizes that Mayor probably knows all this already and is just trying to bait him into slipping up. Or Mayor doesn't know this, in which case he's never going to convince him of anything different. He should shut up, he knows that, but he carries on. "People don't wake up and become killers because of a piece of fiction. People have to be messed up first. By the time our books come along there's already something seriously wrong with them."

"So you don't mind your books lighting that fuse?"

Jerry takes a deep breath the same way he used to when people would ask this during an interview. Then he stares at Mayor. "Let's blame the writer. Let's not blame society, the justice system, the mental health system, the economy, let's not try to shorten the gap between the rich and the poor, let's not blame education and people slipping through the cracks, and minimum wage not covering the cost of living and forcing people to do things they normally wouldn't, let's not blame the twenty-four-hour news cycle instilling fear into everybody, or how easy it is to get a gun, let's blame the author, it's his fault, lock all the authors up and there's your world peace," he says, and he can feel his heart rate climbing, can feel something pulsing in his forehead, can feel the old Jerry returning.

Mayor doesn't answer. Jerry can't tell if he's scored a point or if Mayor's just thinking about his next question. Then it comes. "Let me ask you something else," Mayor says, and his tone is the same, just casually shooting the breeze. "You ever think that a crime writer could outsmart the police? You ever think to yourself if anybody could kill somebody and get away with it, it would be you?"

He's been asked that before as well. People always tend to think crime writers could get away with murder. When he doesn't answer, Mayor carries on.

"A guy like you, I bet you think you could do it, huh? I bet you think you could contaminate a crime scene in a way so nobody would even know you were there."

Jerry doesn't say anything.

"Your characters ever cover up crime scenes?" Mayor asks.

"Sometimes."

"Sometimes," Mayor says. "So how would you go about it? How would one of your characters go about it?"

"I don't know."

"You don't know. Come on, Grey, you're the writer here. Would you wipe away the fingerprints?"

"I guess."

"Of course you would. That's one-oh-one stuff. What else? You'd use bleach, right? You'd pour bleach all over the body?"

"Something like that."

"Maybe set fire to the place?"

"Something like that."

"Hide the body somewhere?"

"Maybe."

"All the books you've written, all the research, all the movies you've watched—I bet you have quite a knowledge of police forensics."

Jerry says nothing.

"So tell me, what would it take?" Mayor asks. "What would it take, do you think, to get away with murder?"

Instead of answering, Jerry stares at the logging truck, willing the logs to fall off the back and . . . and what? He doesn't know. Something. Not crush their car, but something.

"See, this girl we were asking you about earlier, Belinda Murray," Mayor says, "her murder is still unsolved. So somebody pretty clever got away with it, don't you think?"

"Maybe they were just lucky," Jerry says.

"You ever have characters who commit a crime and then can't remember doing it?"

"I don't want to talk anymore," Jerry tells him. It's what Nurse Hamilton said to do—say nothing. He's already said too much as it is.

"Come on, we're just getting warmed up here."

"Making barbecue talk," Jerry says, and he knows he shouldn't even have said that. But there is something inside him that knows if he can just talk to these people, if he can get them to relate to him and see he's not a bad person, then all of this can get cleared up. They'll know he's not a killer.

"Exactly. Barbecue talk. I like that. You should use that in one of your books," Mayor says. "Let's say you've got a character who says he can't remember killing somebody. How does that go?" he asks, and when Jerry doesn't answer, Mayor answers for him. "They're usually lying, right?"

"I didn't kill that girl," Jerry says.

"But two days ago you said you did."

"I don't remember saying that."

"Let me ask you this," Mayor says.

"No more questions."

"Last one," Mayor says. "If you had killed her, would you know? Would you feel it? I don't mean remember it, but feel it . . . in your bones somehow?"

Jerry thinks about it, and it doesn't take long to come up with an answer. "Of course I would. I might not remember it, but I would know it, and that's how I know I didn't hurt that woman."

Mayor twists around a little further. There's a look on his face, something between a smirk and a smile. "That's interesting. Really interesting. You want to know why?"

"You said no more questions."

"But you're a curious guy, right? All authors must be. So let's carry on, for the sake of learning. You ever killed anybody, Jerry? I don't mean in the books, I mean in real life."

Jerry doesn't answer.

"I'll take that as a no, because you'd remember it, right? And if you didn't remember, you'd feel it in your bones."

"I don't want to talk anymore until my lawyer arrives."

"What about your wife?" Mayor asks.

"I'll wait until she arrives too," Jerry says.

Mayor shakes his head. "That's not what I mean. I mean do you remember killing your wife?"

The question is confusing, and makes Jerry feel like he's just missed part of the conversation. Did he zone out? Is his memory retreating? Then he gets it. "You're talking about one of my books."

"No, Jerry, in real life."

Jerry shakes his head. "Of course not. How could I? She's still alive."

"She's dead, Jerry," Mayor says. "You killed her."

"Don't say that."

"You shot her."

"I said don't say that."

"Why not? It's true."

"That's not funny," Jerry says, and it's not funny, not funny, not

funny, and it's not true either, not true, and the silt is shifting, it's shifting, and it can't be true because he doesn't even own a gun, and it's like
he's been saying—he would feel it.

"It was almost a year ago. You murdered your own wife," Mayor says,
that smug look on his face, that all-knowing, *I'm smarter than you* look
that is making Jerry start to shake with anger. If he did own a gun, and
if he had it on him, he would shoot Mayor for saying what he's saying.
"You know you did," Mayor says, carrying on, ignoring his partner who
has taken his eyes off the road to frown at him. "After all, you would
feel it, right? That's what you're saying. That's what I would call a plot
hole, Jerry. You can't say you didn't kill Belinda Murray because you'd
have felt it if you did, then say you can't remember shooting your wife
when we know for a *fact* that you did."

"My wife isn't dead."

"Dennis . . ." his partner says.

"What? It's true," Mayor says, looking at his partner before focusing
his attention back on Jerry. "She's dead thanks to you, Jerry. That's why
you're in a nursing home. If it'd been up to me, I'd have put you in jail,
but you were deemed non compos mentis."

"Don't say that," he says, and he starts slapping the sides of his face,
gently, not enough to hurt, not in the beginning, then just a little
harder, and a little harder again. "She's not dead, she's not dead," he
says, and he knows that right now he must look like the very mental
patient they think he's been pretending to be, but he doesn't care.

"I think that's enough, Mayor," Chris says.

"Sandra isn't dead," Jerry says, still slapping himself.

"You shot her," Mayor says, speaking louder to be heard over Jerry,
and he points his top two fingers at Jerry and cocks his thumb back,
turning his hand into a gun. He reaches into the backseat and points it
to within an inch of Jerry's chest. "Bang. Right in the heart."

"Take that back! You take that back!"

"Bang."

*His name is Jerry Henry Grey Cutter and he is an author and he makes
things up and he's making this up. This isn't real. These people aren't real.*

"Bang," Mayor says.

Jerry grabs that finger gun and twists the barrel backwards until both of the fingers snap. Mayor starts to yell, and Jerry lets go and grabs two fistfuls of Mayor's hair and start pulling.

"Get off me, you crazy prick," Mayor screams, and buries the fingers of his good hand into Jerry's forearms, but Jerry keeps a tight hold, all while Chris swerves the car to the side of the road and brings it to a stop.

"My wife isn't dead," Jerry says, and the thought of it is overwhelming. "Say she isn't dead! Say it!"

Chris leans over and tries to get Jerry to let go, then Mayor lashes out with a fist and gets Jerry in the side of the face. The blow pushes him back into his seat, but a handful of Mayor's hair goes with him.

"You crazy son of a bitch," Mayor says, and he starts to lean over to get another shot in when his partner pulls him back.

"Don't," Chris says.

He doesn't need to say it again. Mayor stops coming for him, and instead reaches to the fresh bald spot where there are patches of blood too. "You asshole," he says, then starts cradling his broken fingers.

Jerry opens his hand and lets the hair fall onto the seat next to him. "Say she isn't dead," he says, much quieter now.

"We're going to have to cuff you now, Jerry, okay?" Chris says, keeping his voice calm while his partner sucks in deep lungfuls of air.

"He said Sandra is dead."

"He shouldn't have said that," Chris says.

"No, he shouldn't have. It's not funny."

Chris gets out of the car. He opens the back door and tells Jerry to climb out. When he's out, Chris tells him to turn around, then he slips a pair of handcuffs on him. Jerry has the feeling he's been handcuffed before.

"Is she though?" he asks.

"Is she what?" Chris says.

"Dead."

Silence for a few seconds, then Chris starts nodding. "She is, Jerry. I'm sorry," he says, and Jerry can't even make it back into the car. Instead he falls down on the side of the road, his knees banging heavily into it, his hands cuffed behind him, and he tips onto his side and starts sobbing into the asphalt.

DAY FIFTY

You actually started the Day Fifty entry earlier today, got two paragraphs into it and tore those pages out and tossed them into the trash because your thoughts were too jumbled, your spelling too messy, you couldn't figure out what you were trying to say because you were too upset. Tearing out the pages and starting from scratch seemed the way to go, as if by doing so, you could delete the events of the day. If only it were so simple (yet in a way it is. If I don't write it down, it will become easy for you to forget. Not now, but when the Dark Tomorrow comes). There are, it turns out, some speed bumps. You were, it turns out, premature in your decision to part ways with the Madness Journal. You need the journal to help remember who you are, because this disease you're pretending you don't have, well, you have it. You can't kid yourself anymore.

The speed bumps.

Let's start with Nicholas, the lawyer you came up with for the novel number unlucky for some. Nicholas—the no-good son of a bitch who you trusted, who you gave life to, who let you down because Mandy, your editor, didn't like him. What happened? Why didn't she like him?

Mandy said that for the first time you've taken an edit backwards. They were hard words to hear. Bloody hard. So for the last week you've been taking Nicholas back out of the story. Mandy said to take your time, but doesn't she get there is no time? If Captain A has his way, you won't be able to write your own goddamn name let alone rewrite a novel. Captain A, by the way, is the new name you've given the disease, because when that Dark Tomorrow arrives, it'll be Captain A steering the ship. You're really all at sea with this manuscript, partner. You sent the revised manuscript to Mandy two days ago, and she rang this morning and said maybe it was time to look at getting a ghostwriter. A ghostwriter! One more thing to add to the *I can't believe it* list.

That's Nicholas and Mandy for you. You do know that Mandy is looking out for your best interests. *You know that*. It just, well, it's just the entire thing. You've let her down, and you've let yourself down.

Mrs. Smith, on the other hand, is a different story. Mrs. Smith isn't just your neighbor, but also the mayor of Batshit County. She has her own Captain A steering her own ship. A while ago she complained about your garden (though good ol' Hip-Hop Rick did spend a day in the yard a week ago, mowing and weeding and pruning and making things look nice before Sandra's upcoming surprise birthday party), and now she seems to think you tore the roses out of *her* garden, but come on, you're a forty-nine-year-old crime writer who has better things to drink than rip out her damn roses. Ha—not *drink*. *Do*. Better things to *do*. Yesterday, however, the police got involved, and now Sandra is angry because she took You Know Who's side of the argument.

Basically here's what happened—yesterday you all woke up to see the word *CUNT* had been spray-painted onto the front wall of Mrs. Smith's house, the *C* on the front wall, the *U* covering the width of the door, the *N* on the wall next to that, and the *T* on the window. Nobody saw anything happen because it probably happened at night, and Mrs. Smith didn't hear a thing because years of nagging her husband to death have perforated her eardrums. Naturally she came over and banged on your door. Of course she did. You're the go-to guy when people have had obscenities painted on their walls. Somebody spray-painted the word *asshole* on your door? Go see Jerry. *Fucktard* on your letterbox? Go see Jerry. *Shitburger* on the car? Go see Jerry. So she came and saw Jerry while Sandra was at work, and Jerry told her he had no idea what in the hell she was talking about, and she pointed out that Jerry had the same goddamn color spray-paint on his fingers, which Jerry pointed out wasn't paint, but ink, because he'd written one hundred and ten goddamn names on one hundred and ten goddamn place cards the previous night for the wedding, and he'd been using a felt, so stop accusing him of spray-painting on her wall when, obviously, she was a cunt and everybody in the street knew it, giving everybody in the street a motive.

The words were barely out of your mouth before you regretted them. Mrs. Smith, though she is nosy and annoying, didn't deserve to be spoken to like that, especially after what was done to her house. There was a time when you were very neighborly with her. In fact, back in the day of book tours, when your family would go with you, it was Mrs. Smith who would look after your house and fetch your mail and feed the cat while you were gone. You and Sandra went to her husband's funeral, and she always popped over with muffins on Sandra's birthday. So of course you regretted saying those things, you regretted that somebody had done this mean thing to her, and most of all you regretted that Captain A had changed you into the type of person who could be blamed for anything wrong on the street.

You slammed the door on her.

It was an hour later when the police arrived. They asked to look at your fingers, but by then you'd cleaned up, of course you had—you do shower, you try to stay clean, and hygiene isn't a crime. They asked if they could look around. Of course by then you had phoned Sandra, and she had come home, and she told them no. She said she wouldn't allow them to treat you as suspect, but if there was evidence to suggest otherwise, then she would gladly allow them to search the house once they obtained a warrant. They asked if they provided you with a can of spray-paint, if you could paint the same word that appeared on the neighbor's house so they could see if there was a match in technique. You actually thought they were kidding, and laughed, but they actually did want a handwriting sample on a scale where the letters were five feet high. Sandra told them no. She told them she was sorry for what had happened to Mrs. Smith's house, but that neither her nor you had anything to do with it.

Is it possible you did this without being aware of it? one of the officers asked.

No, you said. And it wasn't possible. You'd know if you had done it.

They said they would talk to others in the neighborhood, and would get back to you. As soon as they were gone Sandra asked if you had done it. You said no.

Are you sure?

Of course I'm sure.

Show me the hiding place, she said.

What hiding place?

The one beneath the desk.

How the hell do you know about that?

Just show me.

So you showed her. After all, you had nothing to hide. You hadn't spray-painted Mrs. Smith's house. You pushed the desk aside and got out the screwdriver and pried up the loose floorboard.

Want to take a guess as to what was under there?

Nothing. That's right. Nothing.

You found the spray can later that night. It was where you hide the writing backups, next to the gin and the gun.

They drive to the hospital without any more barbecue conversation. Mayor sits cradling his hand and Jerry stares out the window, his mind tense, his anger hot, his pain deep. His face is wet with tears. Being told you've done something and having no memory is like being told black is white and up is down. They've told him Sandra is dead, but she can't be dead because he'd know it. Even if he doesn't remember killing her, he would at least sense her absence from the world. They *have* been married twenty-five years. He can clearly remember his conversation with Eva last week on the beach. She said Sandra had left him. Things had gotten too difficult. Sandra wasn't dead—the weight of Jerry's sickness had been too much for her, and she had left rather than let it crush her.

At the hospital Mayor gets out of the car and throws angry looks at Jerry as he makes his way inside, and Jerry guesses he can't blame him. He walks with his hand held against his chest, protecting it as if it were a small bird. Then it's just Jerry and Chris, and Jerry says nothing as they make the five-minute drive from the hospital to the police station parking lot. They take an elevator up to the fourth floor. It all looks vaguely familiar, and Jerry suspects he's been here before, that at some point in his career he must have been curious enough about the police station to ask for a tour. *Write what you know, and fake the rest.* He wonders how many books he faked this place in, then he remembers he was here last week, that it's from here Eva came and picked him up. He's led to an interrogation room. Chris undoes the handcuffs and Jerry starts massaging his wrists.

"You want something to drink?" Chris asks.

"A gin and tonic would be great."

"Sure thing, Jerry. I'll bring you one right away. Would you like anything else? You want a small umbrella in it?"

Jerry thinks about it. "Sure, if you've got them."

Chris places the photograph of Belinda Murray on the table, then leaves the room. Jerry knows what's going on—he's put enough fictional people into this situation before to know they'll let him sweat in here for a while, before hitting him with a round of good cop, bad cop. Fifteen minutes later he's still alone and sitting down. Maybe they're waiting for Mayor to have his fingers set. Maybe they're going to wait for the bone to knit back together and for Easter to roll around. His lawyer hasn't arrived. His gin and tonic hasn't arrived. He tries the door and finds that it's locked. He paces the room a few times then sits back down and stares at the photograph of a woman he's never seen before until today, and he wonders why it is they think he killed her, and if she was involved with his daughter's wedding then of course he wouldn't know her—all that stuff was taken care of by Sandra and Eva.

Then the door opens up and a man Jerry has never seen before comes in and sits opposite and says his name is Tim Anderson and that he's his lawyer. They shake hands. Tim is in his midfifties with silver hair slicked back on the sides and flattened on top. He's wearing glasses that make his eyes look smaller, like looking backwards though a pair of binoculars, and has a summer tan even though it's spring, which means it's either paid for or he's just back from an overseas holiday. He has a nice suit and a nice watch, and Jerry figures that means he gets paid well, and that probably means he's good at his job.

"What happened to your eye?" Tim asks.

"I was hoping for my usual lawyer."

Tim has his briefcase open and is pulling out a pad when Jerry says that. He stops in midmovement and stares at him. He looks concerned. "I am your usual lawyer," he says. "That answers my question as to whether you recognize me."

Jerry shrugs. "Don't take it personally."

Tim puts the pad on the table. He puts a pen next to it. Then he puts the briefcase on the floor and interlocks his fingers and leans his elbows on the desk and his chin on his knuckles. "I've been your lawyer for fifteen years."

"I'm sorry," Jerry says, shaking his head a little. "I don't know why I'm here."

"That's why I'm here, Jerry, to get things cleared up," Tim says, and he shifts the pad a little closer and picks up the pen. "Tell me everything you remember, starting with that lump under your eye. Who hit you?"

Jerry tells him everything he can about the two policemen, how they think he killed the girl in the photograph. He tells him about the car ride, getting handcuffed and punched along the way. He tells him they're trying to convince him Sandra is dead, and then stares silently at the lawyer, waiting for a confirmation he doesn't want, and that confirmation comes in the way his lawyer drops his pen, sighs, and looks down at his hands for a few seconds.

"I'm afraid that it's true, Jerry. Did they tell you how?"

This time the news isn't as big a shock, but it is just as hard to hear. He opens his mouth only to find he can't answer.

Tim carries on. "She was shot. You . . . you didn't know what you were doing," he says. "It's why you're in a nursing home and not in jail. You weren't of sound mind enough to stand trial. It was an awful, awful thing, and nobody is to blame."

Jerry thinks that's a stupid thing to say. Nobody to blame? So what, the gun just magically appeared in the house, just magically pointed itself at Sandra and went off? He knows who is to blame. It was Captain A. These people have known about Sandra's death for a year, but for him the news is fresh. For him she's only been dead half an hour. He puts his hands over his face and cries into them. The world goes dark. He thinks about Sandra, the good times, and there are no bad times— there never were. All those smiles, all the times they've laughed, made love, held hands. His chest feels tight. The world without Sandra is a world he doesn't want to be in. He doesn't know how he can cope without her, even though he has for the last year, though that wasn't coping. That was forgetting. He pushes away from the table and throws up on the floor, the vomit splashing and hitting his shoes. His lawyer stays where he is, probably figuring he can't charge any more than he already is so there's no point in patting Jerry on the back and telling him everything is going to be okay. No point in risking getting anything gooey on his suit. When Jerry's done he wipes his arm over his mouth and straightens back up.

"The disease is to blame, not you," Tim says. "I'm sorry about Sandra, I really am, and I'm sorry about what happened to you, but we have to talk about today. We have to talk about Belinda Murray. Go over again everything that happened today," he says, and he picks the pen back up and positions it over the notepad.

Jerry shakes his head. The smell of vomit is strong. "First tell me about Sandra."

"I'm not so sure that's going to be helpful."

"Please."

Tim puts the pen back down and leans back. "We don't know, not exactly. Do you remember the wedding?"

"No. I mean . . . yes," he says, and the wedding he can remember, but not what happened to Sandra. He ruined the wedding. "Is that why I killed her? Because of that?"

"Nobody knows. The disease was progressing quickly by that point. By the time the alarms were installed all through the house, you—"

"What alarms?"

"Sometimes you would wander," he says. "Sandra hid your car keys so at least you couldn't drive, but you would sneak out of the house and you would disappear, so she had to get them in."

"Really? I would sneak out?"

"The alarms were for your protection. If you tried to leave, she had a bracelet that would notify her. If Sandra went out, she would take you with her, or she would call somebody to come over. By then she was taking time off work to look after you. You didn't like how it made you feel."

"I would have felt babied," Jerry says.

"The problem is you used to sneak out the window. Alarms were going to be put on those too after Sandra found out, but then . . . well, they were scheduled to go in the same day she died. The problem now, Jerry, is that it shows a pattern of escape. The police are going to think that you killed this woman, then killed Sandra because she figured it out."

"I . . . I couldn't have done it. Any of it."

"The police don't know exactly what happened. They didn't even find the gun. You were tested for gunshot residue and none was found, but you showered several times over the days between her death and you calling the police."

"How long?"

"Four days," he says. "Because your office was soundproofed, nobody heard the gunshot. The other forensics were hazy. If there was blood splatter on your shirt, it was hidden by the fact you sat in your wife's blood for considerable stretches of time, holding her. When you did call the police, you confessed. We don't know why you shot Sandra, Jerry, we just know that you did."

Jerry wonders how many times over the last year this news has been broken to him, then he thinks of Eva telling him that Sandra left and was filing for divorce, not wanting to tell him the truth, wanting to spare him unnecessary pain. It hits him then as to why his daughter calls him *Jerry*, and not *Dad*. Not because he messed up the wedding, but because he killed her mother. He imagines sitting on the floor of his office, a smoking gun in one hand, holding his dead wife in the other. He imagines it the same way he's imagined dozens of other deaths over the years, deaths that have made it between the make-believe pages of his books. What he wouldn't give to have Sandra's death be make-believe.

"Why can't I remember killing her?"

"The doctors believe you've repressed the memory because it's too traumatic for you. Bits of your life are going to come and go, but they believe it's unlikely that will be one of them. Your doctor thinks you just may never remember it. I'm sorry, Jerry, I really am, and I don't want this to sound awful, but we really need to focus on why we're here. Tell me what you told the police."

Jerry buries his face in his arms as he thinks about Sandra, and if it's true, if he did hurt her, then what does anything else matter? He should pick up the lawyer's pen and, if the door is unlocked, run among the desks threatening to stab somebody until they put him down and end this nightmare.

"Jerry, come on, we need to work on this, okay? I'm sorry about Sandra, but now we need to concentrate on you. You need to work with me if we're to get you out of here."

"I don't care if I get out," Jerry says, talking into the table.

"Well you should, because if you didn't kill this girl, and the police believe you did, then the real killer is going to get away with it. Is that what you want?"

Jerry looks back up at him. He hadn't thought of that. The smell of vomit seems to be getting stronger. He shifts in his seat for a better angle, trying to block the smell somehow.

"Wait here a minute," Tim says, and he steps out of the room. He's back thirty seconds later with a janitor. The janitor brings in a mop and bucket and takes care of the mess, and a minute later Jerry is alone again with his lawyer and the room smells a little better. "Tell me everything," Tim says.

"Okay, okay. Let me think," Jerry says, and he takes a few deep breaths and he tries to push thoughts of Sandra aside and focus on today. He sniffs and wipes his eyes then runs through everything. He doesn't think anything in his story changes, but how can he possibly know? He's the man who can't even trust himself. He starts talking. Tim takes notes along the way.

When Jerry's done, Tim says, "I spoke to Nurse Hamilton before I came in. She says it's common for you to get confused between reality and fiction. She says there are days where you think things in your books are real and you've done them. She says you sometimes confess to killing your neighbor when you were at university. She says you were so adamant about it that they looked through old news reports and they spoke to Eva about it, but it just didn't happen."

"I remember her," Jerry says. "Suzan."

"She doesn't exist, Jerry."

"I know. I mean I remember her in the books."

"And Belinda Murray? Do you remember her too?"

Jerry takes another look at Belinda Murray, but no matter how hard he tries, he can't picture her in any context other than this photograph. She seems far less real than Suzan. "I don't know. I don't think so. Do the police have any evidence I hurt her?" he asks. "Any DNA?"

Tim shakes his head. "Doubtful. They already have your prints and DNA after Sandra's death. If there'd been a match in the system it would have come up eleven months ago. Could be your confession is the only lead they've had, that they weren't able to get anything from the scene."

Jerry thinks about that. He remembers Mayor asking him in the car if he thought he could outsmart the police, whether crime writers thought they could get away with murder. Is that the theory here? "I didn't do it. That's why they're not finding any evidence of me at the scene."

"Was there a history back then of you doing other things you don't remember?"

"You mean other than killing Sandra?"

"There was a report last year of your neighbor having an obscenity spray-painted across the front of her house. Do you remember that?"

"What neighbor?"

"Mrs. Smith."

Jerry shakes his head. He can remember the neighbor, but not what Tim is talking about. "I remember somebody pulled her flowers out."

"I don't know anything about that," Tim says, "but she believes you were the one who spray-painted her house."

"Then she was wrong."

"There's another report from four days later. Mrs. Smith's car was set on fire. You don't remember that?"

He thinks back, but there's nothing there—no neighbor, no car, no fire. "No."

Tim taps the pen against the table. "Okay, here's the way I see it. Do you watch the news?"

"Sometimes."

"And read the newspapers?"

"Sometimes."

"Good. We're going to get the detectives back in here now and we're going to tell them what we think is going on."

"Which is?"

"Which is not only do you confuse your books with the real world, but also news reports too. You have an overactive imagination. You can't switch it off. We're going to tell the police you have confused the news story with your own reality the same way you confuse your fiction with your reality. We're not going to answer any questions because you have no memory of the event and can't help with any answers, and any questions they ask at this point may only end up having you confess to a reality that never happened. We get through this, then we can get you out of here and back home."

"Back home or back to the nursing home?"

"To the nursing home."

He taps the photograph. "I didn't hurt her."

Tim puts his pen and his pad back into his briefcase. "Wait here for me, Jerry, I'm going to go and talk to the detectives alone. I'll be back shortly."

"They were going to bring me a gin and tonic," Jerry says.

"What?"

"The detective asked if I wanted a drink. He said he'd get me one right away."

"Okay, Jerry. Wait here and let me see what I can do," he says, and then he slips out the door and once again Jerry is left waiting in the interrogation room, thirsty and all alone.

DAY FIFTY-ONE

Your name is Jerry Grey and there is nothing, absolutely nothing, wrong with you except for the fact you can't remember spraying a word you shouldn't mention across the house of your neighbor. Here's the thing. The shake. The rub. The lowdown. Future Jerry, you don't know for a fact you did what they think you did. Just because you hid a can of spray-paint in your office doesn't mean you used a can of spray-paint on your neighbor's house. After all, there are kitchen knives in the kitchen, does that mean anybody stabbed over the last twenty years was stabbed by you? The can is a holdover from days of Renovation Past, just as there are other paints stored in the garage. The plan after finding the spray-paint in the hiding spot had been to dump it. That much you remember. Toss it into a dumpster in town somewhere. The problem with that scenario is Sandra took the keys off you so you can't drive anymore. She took them last night. She said you may not realize it, but sadly you're starting to slip a little. She said she's taking them off you for your own safety, and for the safety of others on the roads. It hurt. But you know the truth, you know why she's really taking them. It's to control you. *Don't do this, Jerry. Don't do that*. It's all you hear these days.

The police never came back yesterday, but that doesn't mean they won't. You had to get rid of it, or face life without parole, spending your days breaking rocks in the sun. If you couldn't drive, you could at least walk. Nothing illegal about that. Neighbors weren't going to look out the window and go *Oh, there's Jerry, off to dump incriminating evidence*.

So that's what you did.

At least started to do. Until Captain A became involved.

There's a park three blocks from here, which you thought was far enough away to dump the spray can because the police, after all, weren't looking for a murder weapon, and any radius they searched would probably be within twenty feet of the house. Now, looking back, the whole thing seems silly and there never was any real need to dump the can in the first place. The police were never going to get a search warrant—the crime hadn't made the news and nobody had been hurt. It was, for all intents and purposes, not a big deal.

You left the house with your small gym bag that holds a towel and a water bottle and nothing else, but on that day (that day is still *this* day) it held nothing but the facts, ma'am, and they were facts you needed to dispose of. Across the road you could see Mrs. Smith's house baking in the sun, the letters being burned deeper into the wood, the temporary undercoat to mask the letters thin enough for them to already be bleeding back through.

You reached the park. Often there'd be kids playing there, but not then because it was school hours. You sat on a bench (and do you remember that time you were meeting Sandra and Eva here years ago? It was ninety-something degrees and sweat was pouring off you, you had big sweat rings on your shirt and your forehead was gleaming, and you got here first and while you waited one of the mothers came up to you and asked you to leave, that your type could all rot in hell—and then you said, *What, struggling authors?* She said *No, kiddie fiddlers,* and before you could answer, Sandra showed up). You were feeling exhausted. You'd been awake most of the night, your mind racing with what you may or may not have done. There was a trash bin a few feet away, and you had come here thinking it was a good place to dump the spray can, you were a little sleepy, then you were thinking what if somebody found it, and then . . .

Then you weren't thinking anything. At least not the Jerry Grey you me us we used to be. There had to have been some awareness, though, because you weren't hit by any busses, you didn't take all your clothes off, you still had your wallet and hadn't tried to shoplift bags and bags of cat food, so you were still functioning, just at a different level, at a *Jerry isn't home at the moment so please leave a message* level. A sleepwalking level. Captain A steered you to your parents' old house. You even went as far as trying to open the door before knocking on it. That's what you were told by the woman who now lives there—a woman who wasn't your mother.

You can't remember the conversation, but Henry, the man whose name doesn't appear on the phone bill but does on all the books, can take a pretty good stab at it. Henry?

Jerry was confused. Jerry fucked up. Jerry is as mad as a hatter.

Thanks, Henry.

So there you have it. Thankfully (and ain't that going to be a word we're going to look out for in the future? *Thankfully* it all worked out okay, *thankfully* you didn't really have dementia) the woman who now rents that house you showed up at was a nurse at the Christchurch hospital, and she recognized that you were confused, you were scared, she could see who was really driving, and she took you inside and told you everything was going to be okay, she sat you down and made you a cup of tea. You asked why she was living in your house. She asked who you were, and you were . . . a little unsure, but you had your wallet, it had your driver's license (Sandra in all her *Let's control Jerry* wisdom at least didn't take *that* off you), and once your name was out in the open you became Functioning Jerry, at least a little, and you told her where you lived. She asked if you had your cell phone, and it turned out you did. She called Sandra at work. Sandra said she was on her way. In that time you were plied with biscuits to go along with the tea and a story of the neighborhood, including a murder that happened there a long time ago. Did you remember that? No, what murder? It had happened twenty years ago, maybe even thirty, well before Mae (that was the nurse's name—Nurse Mae) had moved onto the street. In fact Mae had only been living in that house for six months. She was around your age, and you envied how sharp she was.

It's strange that's the house you went to. It's not where you grew up. You lived a few miles away in a similar looking house on a similar street, a different neighborhood, even a different school district. You lived there from the age of three (which you can't remember) to the age of twenty-one (which you can remember), and your parents both lived out their lives in that house. But when you were nineteen a young permit driver was showing off his fast new car to his fast new-car buddy, lost control, and drove that thing through your front yard and into the side of your house. The guy driving the car broke his back, and his friend was on life support for a week before they turned off the machine. Your family was unharmed, but did have to find somewhere else to live while the insurance company searched for a loophole (the house wasn't covered for automobile accidents) before admitting they had to pay, and then the builders . . . well, you know what builders are like. So your family rented this other house for three months that turned into six while the family house was rebuilt, and why you returned to that particular house and not where you grew up is a mystery, but Captain A deals in mysteries, doesn't he?

When Sandra showed up, she thanked Nurse Mae for her time, including a hug, and for a moment you thought Sandra was going to clutch herself to Mae and tell her all that was wrong. Then she thanked God you had wandered into the house of a nurse and not some gang member tweaked on meth.

An hour later you were in your office using work emails to distract you from the fact you'd completely lost time when Sandra came in. She was holding your bag in one hand, which you had left in the car. In the other hand she was holding the can of spray-paint, which you had left in the bag.

You argued about it. Of course you did. You told her the truth, and the truth is you were throwing it out because you knew how it would look if you got found with it, even though it wasn't the *actual* can used. She said you were throwing it out because you had done what Mrs. Smith had accused you of.

I knew it was you, she said, and she walked over to you, crouched in front of you so she could look you in the eyes, and put her hands on your knees. *I didn't want to believe it, and I tried not to believe it, but I knew it. Oh, Jerry, what are we going to do? Things are steadily progressing now.*

I didn't do it, you said, concerned at her use of *steadily progressing. Are you going to tell the police?*

She shook her head. *Of course not. But we have to do something. We can't let Mrs. Smith pay for all that damage when we know you did it.*

I didn't do it.

And we need to look at other options to make sure this doesn't happen again.

Like what?

She gave you a sad smile that told you there's a lot of heartache and heartbreak on the way. *Let's discuss it in the morning,* she said.

So there you go. Tomorrow you'll get to hear what those options are. Good news? There isn't really any good news today.

Bad news? Your parents are dead. You've known this for a while, since they died, actually, but it's probably a good thing for you to know. Dad drowned in the pool, and Mum got the Big C a few years later. That saying how you can never really go back home? It's true, partner. Especially in your case.

✦

They take a fresh sample of his DNA, as if the previous sample could have been corrupted, even though Jerry knows the chances of that are even slimmer than him getting his old life back. They wipe a cotton swab on the inside of his cheek and he feels like a character in one of his novels, the one where the innocent man is accused of murder and his protests just make him look guiltier. He's not asked any more questions because his answers can't be considered relevant. Nothing he says, according to his lawyer, is relevant. This is who he is now, he thinks. Irrelevant Jerry. Nurse Hamilton comes close to having to be restrained when she sees the mark on his face. The detective whose fingers he broke is nowhere to be seen.

Nurse Hamilton sits in the interrogation room with Jerry, the two of them alone while others outside discuss his future.

"It's going to be okay," she says, and she squeezes his hand and they stay that way, waiting to see what happens next.

What happens next is Jerry's lawyer enters the room and tells them they're free to go, and that tomorrow, under his supervision, Jerry will be interviewed by a specialist. The detective whose fingers he didn't break escorts them downstairs without a word. Nurse Hamilton is parked a block away, and the detective walks with them to the car. Jerry climbs in and the detective and Nurse Hamilton chat for a few seconds and he wonders what they're saying and figures it can't be anything positive. At least the drive back will be nicer than the ride here.

When Nurse Hamilton gets into the car she tells Jerry once again that everything is going to be okay, then they're on the road.

"Do you really think I hurt that woman?" he asks her a minute later. They're at a set of lights that are green, but traffic is at a standstill thanks to a family of ducks up ahead crossing the road. Eva used to love seeing sights like that when she was a kid. She'd pin her face and hands to the window and talk to them as they wandered past.

"Honestly, Jerry? I don't know. I just don't know."

"Then why aren't you afraid of me?"

"Look at me, Jerry. Do I look like I've ever been afraid of anyone?"

The ducks clear the road, heading away from the direction of a park and towards a fish-and-chip shop, making Jerry picture a scenario where the ducks are ordering dinner, and a different scenario where they're becoming dinner.

"I wish I could remember back then," he says. "I used to keep a journal. Where is it?"

"Nobody knows what happened to it."

"You mean it's not at the home?"

"Nobody found it. Not even the police. You must have hidden it somewhere."

"Maybe," he says. The movement of the car, the day's events, the silt is still clearing. Something is coming to him. "What happened to my house?"

"It was sold."

"There are people living in there now?"

"I assume so. Why?"

"Because there was a place in my office where I used to hide things," he says, nodding now, the image clear. "Maybe we can go there and look? The journal must be there."

"I'm sure the hiding place was found by the new owners," she says.

He shakes his head. "If the police couldn't find it, the new owners wouldn't have either."

"The police probably didn't know they were looking for it," she says. "But you haven't mentioned this before."

He wonders why that could be. Perhaps he didn't mention it before because he didn't want to know. Perhaps enough of him remembered that it was best he forget. Only now he needs to know. "It was under the floor. If we find it, it might tell us what happened."

"I don't know, Jerry."

"Please?"

"Even if it is there you might not like what you find. I don't want this to sound mean, but perhaps it's best you leave it alone. We should just call the police and let them handle it."

"What if I didn't shoot her?"

"Is that what you think?"

He throws his hands up. "There's one big plot hole in all of this," he says. "If I'm going to start confessing to crimes, why the fictional ones? Why not the real ones? I think it'd be the other way around."

She doesn't have an answer for that.

"What if the journal clears me? Please, when was the last time I was like this?"

"Like what?"

"So aware. So me. This Jerry right now, he wants to know what happened. He's hopeful he's not the monster you all think he is."

"I don't think you're a monster," she says. "And to answer your question, it's been a while since you were this clearheaded. A few months at least."

"My daughter thinks I'm a monster," he says, and it's all making sense now. The distance between them. "That's why she never comes to visit. She hates me."

"She doesn't hate you," Nurse Hamilton says.

"She doesn't even call me *Dad* anymore."

"It's hard for her."

"I need the journal. I deserve those answers," he says, and if he has remembered on previous good days not to mention the journal because it's as bad as what everybody suspects, and can't remember that now, then so be it. "If I can find it, I can apologize for it. It won't mean much to anybody, but I have to start somewhere," he says, and if he can apologize, if he can start down the road of being forgiven and being honest, then maybe the Universe will go about cutting him some slack.

She thinks about it quietly. He can see her going through the options. He wants to add more, but he's frightened anything else may push her back from the decision he needs her to make.

"Okay," she says, and then she pulls out of the flow of traffic to the side of the road to a stop. "Let me call your lawyer first. I want to clear it by him, and I want to make sure I'm not doing anything illegal."

"I'll be okay, I promise."

"Don't get your hopes up, Jerry. There may not be anybody home, and even if there is we don't know they're going to let us in, and even then the journal may not be there."

"I know. I know."

"And if we do find it, the police will want it. They may consider it as evidence. They may not give it back to you."

"I just need to read it. That's all."

"Are you sure about this? I mean really sure?"

"I'm sure," he says. Then adds, "I'll be okay."

"This is the house where Sandra died, Jerry, and you may be about to read your own account of being her killer. I'm going to call Eric to come and help us because I think there's a very good chance that *okay* may be the last thing you're going to be."

DAY FIFTY-THREE

They're installing alarms, Future Jerry. Can you believe that? Jesus, next thing they'll get a giant cat door just for you and you'll have to . . . wait, message from Henry . . . what's that Henry? Oh, that wouldn't be called a *cat* door, it would be called a *door*. Then you'll have to wear a goddamn magnetic collar to make sure the other dementia granddads on the street don't wander in and raid the fridge and shit on the carpet and chew up the arms of the lounge set.

It was actually What's Her Name's idea, the counselor with the big boobs. Sandra rang her this morning and told her you'd gone a-wandering, which was something the counselor said was likely to happen. There's a guy coming around tomorrow to work on the place. Alarms on all the doors that lead in and out of the house, including the garage door. No alarms on the windows, because if you're sane enough to try and escape through the windows as to not trigger an alarm, then you're sane. The alarms are for when Captain A is driving this train wreck. You wandered off ONCE and instead of being sympathetic, Sandra is putting in the boot. Christ, she has NO IDEA how this feels. She isn't THE ONE who is suffering, she isn't THE ONE who is losing her mind. If you can find your car keys, maybe you can buy a tent and drive to the beach and toast some marshmallows and leave your *Let's control Jerry* wife here to do whatever the hell she wants for a few days.

The wedding is now less than three weeks away. You're too scared to look at your credit card bill—which, by the way, you don't get to see anymore. All those things arrive online now, and you can't access any of it because you can't remember the access number or the password, though, to be honest here, Future Jerry, at this stage in the game you're thinking you can remember them and that Sandra has changed them. She wants you to ask her what they are just so she can tell you they're the same as they've always been, but you won't give her the satisfaction.

You spoke to Hans today. He came around to see you. Unlike Sandra, *he* is on your side. He has no idea how it feels, but at least he's sympathetic to the cause. He showed you the new tattoo around the base of his neck, just below the collar line so he had to pull his T-shirt down a little, and there in finger-sized lettering were the words *The Cutting Man*.

It's because I love your books, man, he said. *I'm so proud of you.*

You told him about the alarms and the wandering, and the accusation your neighbor made.

Must be bloody frustrating, mate, he said, and he's the only one of your friends to call you *mate* because you actually hate the term, but Hans does it because it's a Hans thing to do. *Sounds like that lady across the road is crazy.*

Barking mad. She's more demented than I am.

What time are you being neutered?

First thing in the morning. Then I can't open a door without Sandra knowing.

And the police, do they think you spray-painted her house?

Probably.

And how's the wedding coming along?

It must be the social event of the year the way Sandra and Eva are racing around. Tomorrow evening we have to head to a restaurant to sample some desserts, and I have to go with them so I don't run away.

Sounds fun.

Only it won't be fun. You're going to stand there like an idiot, trying foods, being asked what you think is best, then having whatever opinion you do have overruled by one of the girls. *Jerry likes the chocolate? Oh, sorry, Jerry, but everybody else coming to the wedding prefers vanilla.*

Sandra asked what to do about Mrs. Smith. You made the joke about hiring a hit man, but she didn't laugh. Perhaps it really is no laughing matter, but maybe where you are in the future, Jerry, perhaps you can look back and get a chuckle from the whole thing. Sandra has the idea of leaving an envelope full of cash on Mrs. Smith's doorstep, enough to cover the costs of painting. You don't like the idea of paying for something you didn't do, and you're going to need that money if things get worse and you have to get home care. You pointed out to Sandra that

Mrs. Smith was going to know where it came from—after all, who else would feel guilty enough to pay?

Hopefully this is as bad as it's going to get. You have reached the final stage of grief, it seems. Sandra said it the other night when she said things are progressing. Now it's just a matter of preparing for how bad it's going to be. And how quickly it's going to get there. You've reached stage one of stage five—you've accepted you're losing control, but wandering off once in a while isn't the end of the world, and who cares if you forgot the plate?

Ah hell, you've probably forgotten all about the plate. You got hungry this afternoon and heated up a tin of spaghetti. It's not rocket science—use a can opener, pour the contents into a bowl, nuke the bowl in the microwave for two minutes. It's not like you're going to burn the house down. You were halfway through eating when Sandra got home from work, came in, and noticed there was no plate. That's right, Future Jerry, you'd dished the spaghetti straight onto the table. Even when Sandra pointed it out it took a few seconds to register that there actually *was* no plate.

That was the moment you accepted your fate, that there was no way of shaking Captain A free, that he was going to ride you to the grave.

Sadly, Jerry, it's time to accept that this is happening. It's happening quickly too. You'll be okay for the wedding—that's what you've told everybody, and you will be, you have to be, but Christmas isn't looking good. Look on the bright side—at least this year you can't get in trouble for buying the wrong gifts.

Good news. It was really good to talk to Hans again. The wedding plans are coming along nicely and you've never seen Eva so happy. Her smile these days is almost enough to make you cry because you're going to miss it like hell. She looks so much like Sandra back when Sandra was twenty-five. It's spooky. "The Broken Man," the song Eva wrote, is now being played on the radio, and debuted at number twelve. You preferred it when she sang it, but even so, it's such a huge thrill. She has now sold a second song, and says an offer has been made for a third.

Tomorrow night we're sampling some desserts for the wedding, and while we're doing that, Sandra's sister is going to be letting people into your house for Sandra's surprise birthday. It should be fun.

Bad news—there are fork marks in the table from where you swirled and scooped the spaghetti. A year ago if the table had been marked by accident, Sandra would have suggested getting a new one. But not now, which can only mean she's having an affair. It's pretty obvious when you know how to connect the dots, which you're an expert at. Soon she will try and talk you into a care facility. Then she can pick out a new table without you. She can walk hand in hand with her replacement of you into different department stores and they can spend your money together. The table is proof she's already moving on, and at least now you know why she changed your pin number for the online banking and has torn pages from your journal. She doesn't want you to spend what is now their money, and you must have figured this out earlier and written about it, and she found out and tore out the evidence.

It also explains why she has been spending so much time away from home over the last few weeks. You don't want her to know you've figured it out, so mum's the word, Future Jerry. The under-the-couch hiding spot was a pretty stupid place to try and hide the journal. Just goes to show the disease is affecting you more than you'd thought. Time to hide it with the writing backups. You know where that is.

Nurse Hamilton calls the lawyer, whose name Jerry knew half an hour ago but can't remember now. This Swiss cheese of a memory reveals some things and hides others. He listens to the phone call, but only gets one end of it; when she hangs up she fills in the blanks.

"The diary would be considered evidence, especially if it shows a clear intent to shoot Sandra. Your lawyer says we need to be careful," she says. "However, he also said that since it's your personal diary, you have every right to take a look at it. Then he wished us the best of luck and to keep him updated."

"It's not a diary," Jerry says. "It's a journal."

She calls Eric next and instructs him to meet them at the house. It's a short conversation, and Nurse Hamilton nods occasionally during it. When there's a break in traffic, she turns the car. They drive in silence, and the closer they get to his house the more things begin to become familiar. He can't remember the last time he was here, and with that thought comes the dark little add-on that the last time he was here would have been when he killed Sandra. Which he believes is still up for debate. Hopefully the journal will give them some answers.

They park outside. Nurse Hamilton puts her hand on his arm to stop him from climbing out. "Let's wait for Eric. He won't be long."

"We can't wait," he tells her. "I have to know. I *have* to know."

"Just a few more minutes."

He feels like opening the door and making a run for the house, but instead he agrees to wait. To distract himself, he tells her about the house, how he found it all those years ago, how he was driving with Sandra to meet a different real estate agent at a different house when they drove past this one with an *Open House* sign out front, the details as clear in his head as if it were yesterday, making his frustration at forgetting more recent things that much greater. They knew as soon as they walked inside the house they could see themselves living their lives out there.

In a way, they both did, Jerry thinks.

A woman dressed in a light blue dress with matching shoes approaches from across the street, walking apace, suggesting her message to them needs to be delivered urgently. Jerry recognizes her.

"What is *he* doing here?" Mrs. Smith asks, and the *he* makes Jerry sound like he didn't just shoot his wife, but ate her too.

"And you are?" Nurse Hamilton asks.

"I am the neighbor that . . . that *murderer* was harassing before he shot his wife. For all I know I was his intended victim. I'm lucky to be alive," she says, then pauses for a few seconds to let the enormity of that situation sink in. "I've called the police. They're on their way."

"Perhaps you should wait inside for them," Nurse Hamilton says.

"I have every right to stand in my street," Mrs. Smith says, "he should be back in the nuthouse he got sentenced to."

"There's no need for talk like that," Nurse Hamilton says. "Please, I really think it best you wait inside rather than upset Jerry."

"Why you would have a cold-blooded killer in your car? I—"

"Thanks for your time," Nurse Hamilton says, and she winds the window back up.

Mrs. Smith's mouth forms an O shape, which then becomes a *well I never* look. She turns and heads up her driveway but doesn't go inside. She stands by her front door and watches, glancing at her watch every few seconds.

"We should go," Nurse Hamilton says. "We can always come back."

"But we won't come back, will we?"

Before she can answer, Jerry opens the door, and when she grabs his arm this time he shrugs it off. By the time she catches him he has already reached the front door of the house and knocked. He's never knocked on this door as a stranger, only when he's locked himself out getting the mail, or if he's lost his keys. He's never knocked and not known who was going to answer.

They hear footsteps approaching. "Let me do the talking," Nurse Hamilton says.

A guy in his midforties opens the door, a pound overweight for every year of his life. He has bed hair that's black on top but gray along the sides, black bags under bloodshot eyes, a white T-shirt that says *Sneezes for Jesus* under an unbuttoned blue shirt.

"Can I—" the man says, but that's all he says, because then he stops and stares at Jerry. "You're Henry Cutter," he says, and gives a huge smile before thrusting his hand out so fast Jerry almost jumps back. His nose sounds blocked. "Oh my god, Henry Cutter! Or I suppose I should call you Jerry Grey, right?"

"Right," Jerry tells him.

"I'm a huge fan," the man says, pumping Jerry's hand up and down. His grip is sweaty. At the same time a cat appears in the doorway, a longhair tortoiseshell that pushes itself against Jerry's legs before doing the same to Nurse Hamilton. "Your biggest fan even," the man says, before turning away and sneezing into a handkerchief. "Sorry, hay fever," he says. "Name's Terrance Banks, but people call me Terry," Terrance says, talking quickly to get through his sentence before sneezing again. When he's done, he carries on. "I bought this place because it was yours and I thought it might help inspire me. Oh geez, I'm already blabbering! Jerry Grey—on my doorstep!"

"You're a writer?" Jerry asks, wanting the common ground, knowing it will help with why they're here.

"Trying to—" he says, then starts sneezing again, his body hunching over with the first, the second, the third sneeze. "Trying to be. I've got a room full of rejection slips, which I figure puts me halfway there, right? Next step is a room full of books." He laughs then, a self-deprecating laugh that makes Jerry like him. "I guess it must seem kind of weird, right, me buying the place because it was yours, but it was also a great investment, you know? Property normally is."

Jerry figures it is, easy to see the connection between murder, devaluation, time for people to move on, and profit.

"I'm Carol Hamilton," Nurse Hamilton says, and reaches forward to shake Terrance's hand, and Jerry wonders if it's the first time he's heard her first name. "We're hoping you wouldn't mind if Jerry took a look around the place."

"Mind? No, no, of course not! Please, please, come in!"

They head inside and the cat follows. Terrance closes the door and sneezes a couple of more times. "Sorry," he says. "Coffee? Tea?"

"We can't stay long," Nurse Hamilton says. "I'm sure you're aware of Jerry's circumstances?"

"Yeah, yeah, of course. It's awful, really awful," he says, leading them deeper into the house. "It was just so horrible." He shakes his head, looking distressed at the direction of the conversation. "You were right in the prime of your career. Such a voice, such a talent, just gone like that. If there's anything I can do," he says, and lets the sentence hang there as if there really is something he can do.

By now they've stopped walking, Jerry having pulled up outside what used to be his office. The door is closed.

"Actually there is," Nurse Hamilton says, and Terrance's face brightens. "Jerry left something here he was hoping he could have back."

"You want something back? Sure, sure, happy to help. We sold most of the stuff off, but some we kept. It went with the house pretty good."

"I don't know what you mean," Jerry says. "You had my stuff?"

"When we bought the house, it came with all the furniture."

Jerry nods. He is Understanding Jerry. "It's not furniture I'm after. It's something hidden in the office."

"We're hoping you'll let Jerry take a look to see if it's still there," Nurse Hamilton says.

"Of course! Of course," Terrance says. "I hope it's no bother, but . . . but since you're here, would it be okay if you signed my books? It would be an honor, it really would be."

"I'm not so sure we have that much time," Nurse Hamilton says, reminding Jerry that the police have been called. Would there be any urgency? After all, what could Mrs. Smith have said other than he was sitting in a car parked on the street? It seems unlikely the Armed Offenders Squad will be showing up, but it does seem likely he's breaking some violation by being here—he was committed to a nursing home, he shouldn't be out and about. Best to get out of here as soon as they can, but one thing he's never done is say *no* to a fan wanting their books signed, and he's not going to start saying no now.

"I'm sure we can take the extra couple of minutes for Gary," he says.

"It's Terry," Terrance says.

"Terry. I'm sorry."

"It's okay, don't worry about it."

Terrance opens the office door. "This is where the magic happened. I'm hoping some of that will rub off on me," he says, then laughs again in the same self-deprecating way from earlier before the laugh abruptly ends and becomes a sneeze.

Jerry steps into his office, and that's what it is—his office. It's his desk, and his couch, and his framed prints on the wall. It's his office chair, his bookcase, his potted plant on the table, his stereo, his phone, his lamp. The house came with more than just pieces of furniture. The only thing that isn't his is the computer. It feels like he's stepped back in time. That he's home. That Sandra will be somewhere in the house, or at work, or maybe out shopping.

"It's almost just how you left it," Terrance says.

"It's my office," Jerry says, somewhat disturbed Terry would have kept it the same way. Like a shrine. "This is my office."

"Just like you left it," Terrance says.

"My home," Jerry says.

Nurse Hamilton puts a hand on his shoulder. "This isn't your home anymore," she says, and she sounds unhappy with the development. "This isn't your office. I think it might have been a mistake bringing you here. If I had known it still looked like this," she says, but doesn't finish the thought.

Jerry walks over to the bookshelf. All the books he owned, at least they're gone, replaced by books that Terry has bought, including a whole shelf of Henry Cutter bestsellers, some titles he recognizes, some he doesn't. Also on the shelves are trinkets from his life. When he used to travel, he always collected something from every country. There's a miniature Eiffel Tower next to a bracelet he picked up in Turkey next to a small bobblehead Mozart he picked up in Austria.

"My wife thinks it's stupid keeping the office this way," Terrance says, as Jerry picks up a small, plushy King Kong he bought from the Empire State Building. He can remember standing in the queue, and the cold frigid wind eighty-six stories up, his shoulders hunched as he looked over the city with Sandra, a city more alive than any other he's seen. He can remember that, but not what happened to her.

"But I'm such a big fan of the books," Terrance adds, carrying on, "and you must have had so many good ideas in here and . . . and hey, I know it's stupid, and maybe weird, but sometimes stupid works out, right?"

Jerry puts down the toy. He walks over to his desk and runs his fingers along the edge of it. The desk is backing onto the window so the view outside wouldn't distract him. He looks at the couch.

"You once said in an interview the couch was the best thing you ever put into your office and also the worst," Terrance says. "Some of the best ideas came to you on that couch, but you also lost a lot of hours on that thing."

Jerry nods. He feels nostalgic. He feels like lying on the couch and soaking in the memories of this room. On the wall is the line from *Fahrenheit 451*. He walks over and touches the frame holding it. "It took some man a lifetime maybe to put some of his thoughts down, looking around at the world and life, and then I came along in two minutes and boom! It's all over."

"Is that what you wanted?" Terrance asks. "The Ray Bradbury quote?"

Jerry shakes his head. He can remember printing it out and framing it. He can remember the sorrow on Sandra's face when he explained it to her.

"It's about reviewers, right?" Terrance asks. "You pour your life and soul into a novel, and somebody can dissect it in all sorts of cruel ways in such a short time."

"It's not about reviewers," Jerry says, and when he doesn't offer any further explanation, Terrance repeats his offer of getting them a drink.

"We're fine," Nurse Hamilton says. "Where is the floorboard, Jerry?"

"There's a loose floorboard?" Terrance asks.

"It's here," Jerry says, and turns and points to the bottom of the desk. "But we need to slide the desk back and we need something to pry it up. I used to use a screwdriver. There should be one in the desk."

Terrance shakes his head. "The drawers were empty when we moved in, but I have a screwdriver in the kitchen. Wait, wait, is the gun under there?" he asks, pointing at the floor. "Is that what you're looking for?"

Jerry shakes his head. "There's a journal," he says. He didn't know the gun wasn't recovered. Maybe it is under there too. "If it makes you feel any better, I'm happy for you to reach under for it," he says, but then that doesn't make *him* feel any better. He has the image of this guy finding the gun and holding them hostage while forcing Jerry to write the next book for him, then the gun goes back under the floorboards, hidden there along with Carol Hamilton, Nurse, and Jerry Grey, Crime Writer.

"Sure, sure, of course. How about I grab the screwdriver and you sign some books while I'm gone?" Terrance says, sounding hopeful.

"No problem."

"And if there's time, I was wondering, could I bounce some ideas off you? I'm working on—"

"Please, we really are in a hurry," Nurse Hamilton says.

"Of course, of course," Terrance says, looking like a ten-year-old boy just told off for talking loudly in class. "Here, the books are just here," he says, and he strips them away from the top shelf of the bookcase and puts them on the desk, the thirteen of them forming two piles, thirteen plots and thirteen sets of characters Jerry can barely remember, the thirteenth of which he barely wrote. He picks it up. It's called *Fire Time*, which is a title, Jerry remembers, he didn't come up with but the ghostwriter. He can't remember what he wanted to call it. He can remember it was about an arsonist, but has no idea what it's about now. He hasn't read it or, if he has, he can't remember it.

"Just make them out to Terry," Terry says, bringing Jerry back to the moment. "Just sign whatever you feel like signing."

Terrance disappears. Jerry picks up a pen and wonders if it was one of his pens too. He sits behind the desk. He puts his hands on it and closes his eyes, hoping when he opens them he'll be back in time, that coming here has been a doorway into his past not just in memory but in reality. It doesn't work out that way. They can hear Terrance sneezing from the other end of the house. Jerry starts signing the books. Book signings are easy when you're signing just one book per person, he thinks, but complicated when that one person owns many of the novels. He's always felt like he needed to sign a different message in every book. He signs *To Gary, thanks for being a good sport* in the first one. *To Gary, thanks for being a fan. To Gary, I like what you've done with the place.*

He's up to the sixth book and struggling for more ideas when his biggest fan returns. He comes over and looks at the one Jerry's signing and his smile disappears a little.

"What is it?" Jerry asks.

"It's . . . umm . . . nothing, nothing at all. Thanks for signing these. Now let's find that hiding space."

They push the desk aside. Jerry crouches down and works at the floorboard with the screwdriver, digging it in just enough to lift the board and get his fingers under it. A cool draft comes out from under the house that sends Terrance into another sneezing fit.

"Just like in one of your books," Terrance says, getting himself under control.

"Really?"

"The Stranger Below."

"I don't remember it," Jerry tells him.

"Was one of your best, Jerry—but they're all your best. You want me to take a feel around?"

"If you could."

Terrance leans down and gets his arm all the way into the hole, but when he pulls it back out, it isn't the journal he's holding. Or the gun. It's a light blue shirt. He looks at Jerry, then at Nurse Hamilton. The shirt is balled up, but Jerry can see a collar and a cuff and what looks like rust. Terrance hands it to Nurse Hamilton, who shakes it out. It's a long-sleeved shirt, formal looking, except for the rust that isn't rust but blood, of which there isn't a lot, but a significant amount.

Nobody says anything. Jerry keeps staring at the shirt, trying to place it. Terrance looks nervous. He glances at the screwdriver in Jerry's hand. He's just met his idol and his idol is a psychopath who's now armed. Jerry puts it down. Terrance reaches back under the floor. He rotates his body a little as he reaches in every direction, patting the ground first, then patting the underside of the floorboards in case the journal is taped to the back of them. He keeps his head twisted so he can keep his eye on Jerry the whole time.

"Nothing else," he says. "Are you sure it's here?"

"It has to be," Jerry tells him.

"Let me get a flashlight."

He disappears. Jerry picks up the pen. He carries on signing the books.

"Jerry," Nurse Hamilton says. "This is your shirt."

"We don't know that," he says, not wanting to look at her. "I'm a shorts and a T-shirt guy. I only wear them on formal occasions."

"Like Eva's wedding?"

He doesn't answer. He signs *To Gary, best wishes* in the rest of the books simply because he's run out of other things to say. Terrance comes back and uses the flashlight and a combination of angles to see what they can see beneath the house, which turns out to be nothing except dirt and dust and plenty of cobwebs.

"Do you mind if I take a look?" Jerry asks.

"Jerry, we really must be going," Nurse Hamilton says.

"Just a minute, that's all."

The front doorbell rings, both from the hallway and from the receiver in one of the desk drawers. Terrance disappears and Jerry reaches under the floor in all the same directions Terrance reached, and gets all the same results. "It's not here," he says, and he can hear the frustration in his voice. "It should be here, but it's not. It doesn't make sense! It should be here, but it's not!"

"It's okay," Nurse Hamilton says, looking concerned. "It just means you've hidden it somewhere else."

"There is no *somewhere else*," he says, and they can hear voices in the hallway coming back towards them. "She died in here," he says. "Right there on the floor. He said my office was just how I left it, but it's not, because when I left it Sandra was dead right there," he says, pointing at the floor, "and when I look there hard enough I can see her. I can see all the blood," he says, then looks at the shirt. Was shooting Sandra a formal occasion? Did he dress up for it? "I need the journal to know . . . to know I didn't . . ." he says, then he tries to reach deeper into the hole, jamming his shoulder against the floor so hard that it hurts. "I need to know I didn't do this."

"It's okay, Jerry," Nurse Hamilton says, and she rests the shirt on the arm of the couch and walks towards him.

"It's not okay," he tells her, and he can remember sitting in this room writing up a storm, writing up a world of storms, all those words . . . why the hell can't he remember the journal?

He pulls his arm out. He slumps against the desk. Terrance is back, and with him Eric. "How you getting on there, buddy?" Eric asks.

"We need to pull up the rest of the floor," Jerry says, and gets to his feet. Pulling up the floor is exactly what they need to do. The journal will be under there, then he can find out who really killed his wife, because it couldn't have been him. Couldn't have been. Then he and Henry can figure out together what they're going to do to that guy. "Gary, we need more screwdrivers and some pry bars," he says, and when nobody reacts, he stars clapping his hands. "Come on, people, we need to get to work!"

"Umm . . ." Terrance says, and then looks to Nurse Hamilton.

"I used to rip apart houses and put them back together for a living," Jerry says. "This will be a breeze," he says, but nobody moves. What in the hell is wrong with them?

"We need to go," Nurse Hamilton says. "Perhaps Terrance can look after we're gone?"

"Who the hell is Terrance?" Jerry asks.

"I'm Terrance," Terrance says. "Or Terry, for short."

Jerry shakes his head. "You're Gary. Unless . . ." Then it all makes sense. "He's lying! If he's lying about his name, then he's lying about the journal!" he says, shouting now. "He found it already! He wants to be just like me! He found it when he reached under a minute ago and threw it out of range! He's going to steal it!" He understands everything. He is Jerry Grey, a crime writer, a man who can see how things end one third of the way through, and yet he missed this one. "You killed Sandra so you could buy the house cheap!"

"Jerry . . ." Eric says, while Terrance stands still, looking stunned.

"He killed Sandra so he could steal my journal," Jerry shouts, and then he picks up the screwdriver from the desk. He lunges with it towards Terrance, who jumps back. At the same time Eric reaches into his pocket for the gun, and Jerry realizes it's not just Terrance that's in on it, but all these people. They all know what happened here, they all played a part in Sandra's death, and they're trying to trick him into believing he did it. "You all killed her. You wanted my house and you wanted my ideas," he says, and Eric brings his hand out of his pocket and it's not a gun, but a syringe. They are going to poison him and make it look like a heart attack. He turns towards Eric—he has to take out the biggest threat first, and that's when there's a huge weight on his back as his arms are pinned to his side, and he realizes he messed up, that Eric isn't the biggest threat at all. Nurse Hamilton has him in a bear hug. The woman who is afraid of nothing. He tries to shake her loose, but she's too strong. Eric steps in and Jerry can see his reflection in the orderly's glasses. A moment later the needle of the syringe punctures Jerry's arm. Something warm floods his body, making him immediately tired. His body becomes heavy. He drops the screwdriver. It rolls across the floor and falls into the gap left by the missing floorboard.

"I didn't see it coming," he says, and he smiles as the world starts to disappear, and then laughs at the irony of it all. For the first time he couldn't connect the dots. He closes his eyes and he thinks of his body on the autopsy table, the coroner saying there are no signs of poisoning, the world being led to believe that it was Captain A that took him away.

DAY FIFTY-FOUR

And wasn't it exciting?

Here are some fun facts for the future. If somebody offers you a dessert, say yes. You are a dessert guy. There are plenty of guys you are not. You are not a car guy, you are not a dog guy, you are not a hip-hop guy, you're not a sane guy but a dementia guy, and you ARE a dessert guy.

Tonight was the first dessert tasting you've ever been to, and in that demented little head of yours you had imagined it would be like a wine tasting (and haven't you always wanted to go to one, swirl around a glass, and go . . . hmm . . . grape?). You thought you'd hold a cake-loaded fork up to your nose, wave it around a few times, go hmm, a hint of flour, a hint of . . . my, is that cocoa? Is that a dash of cinnamon? A wave, a sniff, then a bite, you let your mouth fill with the taste before spitting it out onto a napkin.

It wasn't like that, of course, and that's not even the most exciting part about the day. You're still feeling some kind of rush from what just happened, but it's time to do that thing you do, Jerry (or should I say Henry?), that you've done to others over the years, and that's get through the boring bit first. Don't worry—it gets better.

You thought it was a restaurant you were meeting Eva and Rick at, but it was a bakery, and the owner was a friend of Rick's aunty, or the uncle of a cousin, or somebody he was abandoned with on an island for a year, and they stayed open late so you could all meet there and gorge on two dozen different types of desserts, which got narrowed down to three for the wedding. The baker was a guy in his midforties, a good-looking guy with great hair and a great laugh who made Sandra laugh a lot, laugh a lot and touch her own hair (which she wore down, something she hasn't done in a long time—and you know what that means, right?), and the way they looked at each other made you think this could be the guy she's going to take table shopping. Because of that, every dessert you tried you said you hated, to the point that Eva told you to *Lighten up, Dad*, and Sandra said you were being rude. The truth is the desserts were fantastic, so fantastic that you would leave Sandra for the baker if you had the chance (actually that's a joke, Jerry—you've already got one Big D in your life and don't need another). You said you weren't being rude, that you're not really a dessert guy, and you didn't understand why they couldn't have left you at home to work out your ideas for the new book.

You know why. That was Sandra's answer.

And you did know why. Because you might rip up somebody's roses. You might go spray-painting. You might eat pasta off the carpet. However, if you did step outside, an alarm would go off. And why? Because day fifty-four started with a knock on the door. Sandra was up, you weren't, but it was the alarm guy. Two of them actually. You wandered down in your robe an hour later and they were standing in the kitchen talking to Sandra, who had just made them coffees, and you didn't like the way they were *looking* at her, but what was worse was the way Sandra *liked* the way they were looking at her. They introduced themselves to you while they had their coffees, then they went back to work while you went and lay on the couch to think about the next book. It took them three hours in the end, and then they showed you and Sandra how everything worked, but you didn't pay much attention because you were in your *Who gives a shit* phase, and why not? These alarms were there to control you, and what forty-nine-year-old man likes to be controlled? Every time an external door gets opened now a signal is sent to a wristband that Sandra is wearing to alert her. At least you're not on a leash. Or are you?

It was not long after they left that Mandy called. She said after much discussion in the office it's been confirmed that a ghostwriter will indeed be taking over. There are two options. One is to have the ghostwriter not actually be a ghost, and to have his name on the cover, sharing the workload, sharing the credit, sharing the royalties almost evenly. Option two is the ghostwriter remains a ghost, only your name goes on the cover and the world won't know you had help. However, option two comes with an even further reduced royalty rate. You don't want a ghostwriter, but if they're going to do it, it's better nobody knows, and you told Mandy that.

Sandra saw it differently—she saw your ego getting in the way of money the family could use, but you really can't face having your name on the cover along with somebody else. She's just upset because mentally she's already spent the money on a holiday with the baker. Sandra may be right about the ego thing, but it *is* your career, all that work, all those years—you can't now say to the world *This is my new book—I couldn't write it by myself.* The surprise was Sandra didn't argue, in fact she hugged you and said of course she understood.

In the afternoon she took you suit shopping. You chose a dark one with pinstripes, and Sandra chose a light blue shirt to go with it. You've been measured up, and the suit will be ready in another week. It'll look great at the wedding, and great in your coffin too. Then came the dessert tasting in the evening and you are, F.J., a dessert guy. You could live on desserts, and why not? Soon you're not going to care how you look.

Okay—you've been patient, you've just had another G&T, which makes three, so let's get down to business. At first you were freaked out, of course you were, because the street was full of flashing sirens and people, there was a fire engine and two cop cars and the first thing you thought was that your house had burned down.

It wasn't your house. It wasn't anybody's house.

It was Mrs. Smith's car, parked up her driveway, smoldering away. You had missed the show as the flames had been put out fifteen minutes earlier. There were updates from the neighbors who were all standing on the street that Mrs. Smith's car had been set aflame. Mrs. Smith was on the front doorstep of her house, the freshly painted walls behind her, running her mouth at a hundred miles an hour to the police officers trying to keep up. She pointed at you when she saw you. You were *The Man Goes Burning* from your ghostwritten book.

Somebody had torched her car.

And not this somebody, because this somebody was being rude and not lightening up to the baker who your wife is banging, so this somebody had an alibi, and fifteen minutes later when a pair of officers (not the same pair as Cunt Thursday) intercepted you as you pulled into the driveway to ask what you had seen, Sandra told them neither of you had been home.

Well somebody is home, the officers said. *The lights have been on and off over the last few minutes.*

I assure you there's nobody home, you said, which you knew wasn't true because Eva and Rick would be there, they'd made better time than you on account of your window-shopping on the way back to the car to give them more time. Along with Eva and Rick there would be many of Sandra's friends and work colleagues and some family. At that moment they would be hiding in the dark behind furniture getting ready to jump out and say *surprise*, which it really would be as Sandra's birthday is tomorrow.

We're going to need to search your house. If you're adamant there's nobody home, then it's possible the person who lit the fire is hiding in there, one of the men says.

It'll be our daughter, you said.

Eva won't be there, Sandra said.

There's no need to search the house, you said. *I'm sure it's just Eva.*

But it won't be, Sandra said. *What if somebody is hiding inside?*

There's not, you said.

Sandra didn't believe you. Sandra offered them her keys, and there was nothing you could think to do as the officers went to the front door. When you tried to go after them, Sandra stopped you. *Did you have* him *do that?* she asked, and she was angry, vein-throbbing angry, not like the time you forgot your anniversary a few years back but closer to the time you forgot her birthday. Which you hadn't forgotten this time, but were somehow in the process of ruining.

What? Who?

You know what and you know who, she said.

I really don't, you said, and you really didn't.

Because you don't remember. You're going to use this . . . this stupid disease as an excuse for everything now, aren't you?

She was frustrated and lashing out, and the counselor had warned that you wouldn't be the only one going through the five stages of grief. In all your wallowing and angst, buddy, you'd forgotten that. Sandra is at anger, coming right off the back of stage one—infidelity.

I have no idea what the hell you're talking about.

Hans set that car on fire to hide the fact you were the one who spray-

painted her house, she said, *and now he's hiding in our house and you know he's in there.*

I did no such thing, you said. *And he's not in there. I promise.*

I don't want you seeing him anymore, are we clear on that?

You weren't up for an argument, so you told her you were clear on that.

Then make sure you write it down in your bloody Madness Diary.

It's a journal.

The police were at the door. Both of you were close enough to the house to hear everybody shout out *surprise* as the lights inside were thrown on as the police walked inside. In hindsight, you were lucky nobody got shot.

Sandra's anger disappeared then. The police backed out and read the situation accurately, gave Sandra a few minutes to acknowledge the occasion, then spent the next hour taking statements as everybody else socialized.

Do me a favor, you asked them as they left.

And what favor would that be, sir?

When you find who set fire to her car, why don't you ask them if they know how to use a can of spray-paint instead of accusing me, huh?

You made a good point, partner.

You went back to the party. Sandra hugged you, and apologized for jumping to the conclusion that Hans was inside, and you forgave her, and wondered if she wasn't right in her assumption he was involved. Eva came over and told you the ruined surprise wasn't your fault, and even though it wasn't, it still somehow feels like it was. Even now you don't know what you could have done or said to stop the officers opening your door, but you suspect that Past Jerry, even one as recent as a month ago, would have known.

Other than that, the party went off well, and the guests, of which there were over thirty of them, all had a good time. Sandra got a lot of fiftieth birthday cards, even though she's only forty-nine, joke messages written on the inside. You stayed sober right until after the last guest left and you started writing in the journal, and even now you feel as sharp as a tack. The police ruining the surprise actually made the evening better somehow, as if everybody there had been in on a great story that they could tell—it made the party unique. For her birthday, you got hold of the original lyrics for "The Broken Man" that Eva wrote on a napkin and had it framed, complete with the doodles Eva had drawn in the corners and the lines that had been crossed out and replaced. She actually cried when you gave it to her. Plus some shoes that Eva helped you pick out. You can't go wrong with shoes, Future Jerry, no matter what the occasion.

Good news—hopefully Mrs. Smith and her pastel wardrobe will move out of the neighborhood.

Good news—everything went well. You've known all along that the birthday party was a rehearsal for the wedding, a test to see what you can and can't do, and you passed. It looks like there's some plain sailing ahead.

Jerry is helped out to the car. The world doesn't disappear, but the lights are turned down. He has one arm around Nurse Hamilton and one arm around Orderly Eric, and they're walking down a pathway that seems familiar, as does the house over the road where the old lady is walking from, and the silt that was stirred up before is settling. It's hiding the past. He can feel Jerry disappearing.

"You're a no-good murderer," the woman says, and he thinks that's not true, that he's actually a good murderer since he's been getting away with it. He misses his wife and he misses his life and he just wants to hit the big reset button and have it all back.

The woman talking isn't done. "I hope you rot in Hell," she adds, and it makes him think, why would he ever have wanted to live here?

They get him to the car. They buckle him into the backseat. "Did we get it? The Madness Journal?"

"No," the nurse says, and the silt has settled over her name, hiding it from view.

"It's going to be okay," the orderly says, and why do people keep insisting on that? What is it they know that he doesn't?

A police car shows up. It parks next to them and the old woman approaches it and starts pointing at Jerry while she talks animatedly. The nurse gets involved and there's a long conversation, a lot of head shaking and nodding and the two officers keep looking over at him, but they don't come over. He closes his eyes. The car starts moving. It's relaxing, and he dozes a little, opening his eyes every now and then to look at the road. When they reach the home he's helped out of the car and into a wheelchair. He's wheeled down a corridor and into a small room with a bed in the middle and a bookcase against the wall and a view onto a garden. Two people help him up onto the bed.

"Do you know where you are, Jerry?" a man asks.

"Where's my shirt?" Jerry asks.

"The police have it," a woman says.

"Are they going to arrest me?"

"Get some rest," the woman says, this bear-sized woman who bear hugged him earlier and abducted him from his home.

Then he's all alone. When he tries to sit up he finds he can't, that he's too tired. There is a way out of this nursing home—he's done it before and he can do it again. He'll find the journal and he'll solve the puzzle and then they'll let him go because he can show them he's not a killer at all, that something else is going on here, and once he shows them they'll have to let him live back in his house and he'll be allowed to have the life back they've taken from him. Captain A isn't going to get away with this.

But for now, sleep.

Then dinner.

Then he's getting the hell out of here.

DAY SIXTY

You know what—it might not be sixty. It might be fifty-eight. Or sixty-two. Who knows, and who really cares?

Actually, Madness Journal, let's start over, shall we?

DAY WHO GIVES A FUCK?

That's better. You've been wanting to make more regular updates, but here's what happened—you lost the Madness Journal. In a way it's a good thing too, because you know Sandra has been looking for it. You've caught her. Henry can explain it better. Of course Henry has never been that great at writing from the female point of view (*You just don't get women, Henry—because you're a chauvinistic asshole*, according to one cat-loving, man-hating blogger), but he's willing, if you are, Future Jerry, to let him give it a shot. Henry?

It was dark outside. Rain hammered the shit out of the roof, it hammered the shit out of the windows. Sandra sat at the window thinking about how, once her husband was gone, she wouldn't have to sneak out to spread her legs for people in the back of cars and in restaurant toilets, because that was all very what her mother would call *un-ladylike*. Soon she could have people stay over, maybe get a bit of a gang bang going on like the one she had the day the alarms got installed. She was looking forward to spending all of Jerry's money—oh, the things she would buy! And poor Jerry, sitting in a nursing home with a feeding tube jammed up his ass because that's the way she asked them to do it—sure, it cost extra, but it was money well spent because it *amused* her, the same way Jerry *amused* her when he got confused or lost. The wedding was approaching, and she was hoping his mind would have reached full collapse by then, not only because she was scared about him forgetting who his daughter was when he gave her away and embarrassing Eva, but because there was going to be a lot of cock at that reception and she was definitely up for her share.

She was curious as to what Jerry was up to. Planning on

sneaking back over the road to Mrs. Smith's house? She wondered what he would do next, and concluded he was going to rape the old lady. It would be such a classic Jerry thing to do. She wouldn't care if Jerry did sneak over there to cut the old lady's tits off; however, she did worry about how that would reflect on her. She would always be *the woman with the rapey husband*, and what country club was going to let her in with that label?

There was a flash of lightning and the night sky lit up, she saw her reflection in the window, her cheating whore face looking back, and she slipped out of her chair and was at the door to Jerry's office when the thunder struck, so loud and so close she held her breath and waited for the pictures to fall off the walls, and when they didn't, she opened the office door, stepped inside, and closed it behind her.

The first place she looked for Jerry's Madness Journal was in his desk drawers. Nothing. She checked the couch where she thought Jerry was spending too much time—behind the cushions, under the couch, then she sighed, pushed the desk aside, used the screwdriver from Jerry's drawer to lift the floorboard, and reached under. Her plan was to read it and rip out some of the pages so he would forget what he had been up to. It *amused* her to screw with him.

She still had her arm under the floor when Jerry walked in.

"What are you doing?"

"I'm worried about you, Jerry," she said, pulling her arm out as though withdrawing it from the mouth of a shark, but what she really meant was *I wish you didn't live here anymore. You may be the best-looking man I've ever seen, but you're holding me back.*

"Are you looking for my journal?"

"I want to make sure you're okay."

"It's my journal!" he said, and he sounded like a whiny little bitch, and God how she was resenting him. "It's like a diary, Sandra, you can't read other people's diaries."

"You said I could."

"When?"

"A few hours ago," she said, but it was a lie. It was one
of the benefits of late. She could say anything now and he
couldn't be sure if she was making it up. She thought about
telling him how she had been bumping uglies with Greg from
yoga class just to break his heart, then put her theory to
the test to prove he wouldn't remember. She wished Greg
was here. That guy knew how to bend a body.

"If that was true, then why are you looking for it?" he
asked. "Why didn't I just hand it to you?"

"Because you couldn't remember where you had put it."

He nodded then, and she realized something—he really
couldn't remember where he had put it.

"I was trying to help you, Jerry."

"How do I know you're not lying to me?" he asked, and he
started to cry again, and seriously, she was one sobbing
fit away from stabbing him in the throat.

"It's the dementia, honey," she said, and by now she had
stood back up. She reached out and Jerry fell into her embrace, and she started rubbing his back, and she knew he
was feeling loved, but really all she was doing was wiping
the cobwebs off her fingers from under the floorboards.
"Would you like me to carry on helping you look for it?"

"No," he said. "It's okay. It'll show up—it always does."

"Shall we head back up to bed? Belinda is coming over
early in the morning."

"Who's Belinda?"

She sighed. She had gone through this already. "Belinda
is the florist."

And . . . . scene.

The irony is at that point you really had lost the journal. You'd
forgotten all about the hiding place, and there was even an entire day
in there (which you spent in bed) that you had forgotten you *have* a
journal.

You did find the journal, obviously—it happened without you even thinking about it. It's where you've been hiding the gin. Problem is you've been out of gin for the last week. Hans came over yesterday. You hadn't invited him because Sandra said you couldn't see him anymore, but he showed up unannounced and Sandra couldn't bring herself to ask him to leave. You sat out on the deck. He was wearing a T-shirt that said *Drugs Not Hugs*. Summer is approaching and the days are getting longer, and you need to enjoy every sunset that you can now because you never know when it will be your last—at least the last one you're conscious of. Hans, by the way, is coming to the wedding. Sandra was against it, but ultimately it was Eva's decision—to her Hans is Uncle Hans. He isn't Prison Hans. When Sandra was somewhere deep inside the house Hans pulled a couple of bottles of gin out of his bag.

Here you go, buddy. I'll always be there for you, you know that, right?

I think Sandra is having an affair.

What, Sandra? No way, buddy, he said.

But—

But nothing, Jerry. Trust me, she loves you man, really loves you. I wish I had somebody in my life who was even a tenth of the woman Sandra is. When it comes to love, buddy, you're the luckiest man in the world.

But—

He put his hand out in a *stop* gesture. He looked annoyed. *Seriously, Jerry, don't piss me off, okay? You don't see it because you're too close, but all of this—it's hard on her too. I know Sandra doesn't like me, but don't go saying stupid shit like that, okay? It's this bloody Alzheimer's of yours, buddy, it's scrambling your brain.*

Did you set fire to the neighbor's car?

He laughed and shook his head. You know Hans really well, but even you couldn't tell if that was a yes or a no.

Good news—you found the journal, and you've got another week's worth of gin.

Bad news—the way Hans defended Sandra, the way she makes herself absent when he's around—it's pretty obvious what's going on here. It's hard to know who to feel more betrayed by, your best friend or your wife.

His name is Jerry Grey and he's a crime writer and none of this is real, none of this is real.

Blood on Jerry's hands.

His name is Henry Cutter and he's a crime writer and none of this is real, and even he's not real, he's a figment off Jerry Grey's imagination. Jerry uses him to make money. Jerry uses him to tell stories.

Blood on Jerry's shirt.

His name is Jerry Henry and he is a dementia patient and this is a dementia dream, a dementia attack, and none of this is real, he's in a nursing home and everything is okay.

This isn't the nursing home. This isn't his house. Nothing is okay.

Jerry Grey. Crime writer. Not real.

The dead girl on the floor is a stranger. She is facing him. There's a knife on the floor next to her, this stabbed girl and he wonders, he wonders . . . who is she?

He wonders . . . why is he here?

He wonders . . . where is here?

He is sitting on a couch in a lounge, just him and the dead girl on the floor, surrounded by nice furniture, nice paintings, all the mod cons of life you can't take with you. The curtains are closed. The girl is naked. Her hair is blond and her skin is pale and her eyes are blue, so open and so blue. There's a bathrobe on the floor a few feet away from her. It's speckled with blood. When he tries to stand he finds that he can't. His legs aren't with him, and, and . . . who is this woman? He looks down at his hands. His left one is curled into a fist. He opens it. Inside is a pair of earrings. Diamond earrings. There is blood on his right hand. He closes his eyes and the woman disappears. He feels tired. He wants to sleep now, he wants the dream to disappear. He sways a little, and then he lies down. He reaches around with his eyes closed and finds a cushion. He tucks it under the side of his face. He curls his legs up and rocks softly back and forth, relaxing.

He opens his eyes.

The girl. The knife. The robe. It's all still here.

He is Jerry Cutter. He is Henry Cutter. He is a crime writer. He is a criminal. He is the Breaking Man who killed his wife.

And this girl?

He gets up off the couch. The room tilts, not much but enough for him to reach out and grab the wall. Music is coming from somewhere in the house, something he doesn't recognize. He peeks beyond the curtain to the outside world. It's daylight out there.

His name is Jerry Grey. He is lost. He is confused. This may look real, it may feel real, but it is not. This is probably Suzan with a z. This is the book he wrote. He is inside the pages and soon somebody will save him.

When he moves, the girl's eyes follow him until he's south of her body. He picks up the robe and covers everything except her face. He crouches next to her and studies her features, this girl, this stranger, who is she?

Her cheek feels warm. She hasn't been dead long, but she is dead—there's no denying that—CPR isn't going to help. The paramedics could be two seconds away and there'd be nothing they could do except stare at all the blood. Death is in her features, in the way she is looking at him, the way her face is sagging, the way she seems to be turning gray in front of him. She must be in her midtwenties, maybe even thirty. She smells like soap. He stands up. He looks around the lounge as though expecting to see an answer, maybe even somebody standing here who can tell him what is going on. He has never been here before, he's sure of it.

Haven't you? Henry asks, and he's had conversations with Henry before. Not in the Before Days, back when things made sense, but the After Days, when the Alzheimer's really began to take hold.

"Did I do this?"

What do you think?

Jerry looks down at his hands. He's still holding the earrings. He tucks them into his pocket. "Is she from one of your books?"

Oh, so it's my books now, is it?

"They've always been your books," Jerry tells him. "So is she?"

He sits back down on the couch as Henry thinks about it. He wonders just how insane he really is. Dementia. Shooting his wife. Confessing to crimes and holding a two-sided conversation with himself. Who is more crazy—him or Henry?

I don't think this is one of your books, Jerry. I'm sorry to be the voice of reason here, but it does all seem very—

"Real," Jerry says. "I need to call the police."

Oh you do, do you? And tell them what? For all you know you wandered away from the nursing home, you got lost and confused and you knocked on a random door and when nobody answered you came inside, and this is what you found. If you call the police, they will come here, they will arrest you, and that's the end of the story. Even if you didn't do this, that's the end of the story.

"So what do we do?"

We quit wasting time and get out of here.

He shakes his head. The girl, the wide open eyes, staring at him, studying him. Blaming him. "I have to call the police."

You said that already. You'll be in jail before you even know what hit you.

"I didn't do this."

I know. I believe you.

"Do you really?"

It could have been a deadbeat boyfriend, or a jealous BFF, or an overly friendly neighbor.

"It could have been anybody," Jerry says. "So what do you suggest I do?"

You're a crime writer, Jerry. If you get arrested, you can't use those crime-writing skills to figure out what happened. You have to run.

"What does that mean?"

If this was a book, what would you do?

"Call the police."

No. Pretend this isn't real life.

"This is real life."

Of course it is, but you're missing my point. Are you deliberately being stupid?

Jerry closes his eyes. He can't stand the dead girl looking at him any longer, but even with his eyes closed he can still feel her gaze. He opens them back up. He looks at the bloody knife on the floor before adjusting the robe to cover the woman's face too. "What is your point?" he asks Henry.

Think of this as your book.

"Okay."

And in the books when people should go to the police, what do they do instead?

"Anything but go to the police."

Exactly.

"So what do you suggest I do then?"

Pour gas over everything and burn the place down then get the hell out.

Jerry shakes his head. "I'm not doing that."

You should.

"No."

Then wipe down everything you touched, including the wall where you steadied yourself a few minutes ago. Find the laundry and grab some bleach and pour it over her body. Take the knife and dump it a few miles from here. Make your way into town. I have an idea—make your way to the library. We'll figure out the rest from there.

"The library?"

Libraries relax you. You used to spend a lot of time there after school, and you used to read book after book, wanting to grow up and be an author. It was those days, those library days, that shaped you into the man you became.

"Sick?"

An author, you idiot.

He walks into the dining room. The music gets louder, and he thinks it's coming from the bedroom. There's a clock on the wall. It's seven fifty in the morning. He finds the laundry and goes through the cupboard and finds a half-gallon container of bleach that is just short of being full. He carries it into the lounge and looks at the dead woman. How can he pour bleach on somebody whose name he doesn't know?

The same way you killed somebody whose name you don't know.

"So I did kill her?"

It's possible. But if you didn't, then staying here is a mistake.

He heads back into the dining room, then into the hallway, and in the corner by the door is an *A Place for Everything* shelf that has keys and sunglasses and a handbag on top. He opens the handbag. Inside is a purse, and inside that is a driver's license. Fiona Clark. Twenty-six years old—the same age as his daughter.

"My name is Jerry Grey and I'm a writer," he says, putting the license back. "My name is Jerry Grey and none of this is real."

But it is real. There's a dead girl in the lounge to prove it.

W MINUS SEVEN

The wedding is one week away. There's no chance of forgetting this, buddy, not with Sandra mentioning it every hour. The wedding has become this big, all-encompassing thing that always seems so close but never actually happens, and of course big, encompassing things often come with problems, the latest of which is with the flowers. Our florist is a very pretty woman by the name of Belinda Something Last Name, who reminds me a little of Sandra Something Last Name (just kidding there—Sandra has your last name, at least for now). Same winning smile, same bubbly personality. She's like Sandra's much younger sister, if Sandra had a much younger sister (does she?). Belinda has been around a few times now to meet with Sandra and Eva, and she's always full of smiles, and she always asks how you are in a tone that makes you believe she really wants to know.

At the moment they're stressing about the flowers. There's been some weird insect outbreak and the sources Belinda uses have had large percentages of their crops ruined, the insects eating half of them and shitting on the rest. Belinda may have to order from somewhere further away, as all florists are, and that means they really need to lock in what flowers they want, as the original ones are hard to get now, creating a shortage on other types too, which means, of course, the prices are all going up. Your crush on Belinda waned a little at that point, but her sad smile at this tragic turn of events won you over. Then you got bored. Then you got thirsty. Then you excused yourself and went into your office. Then you snuck out the window so you wouldn't set one of the alarms off and went for a walk, because you should be able to walk, shouldn't you? And get some fresh air?

You didn't go far. Just far enough to pick up some cigarettes. You walked to the corner store, which is a little short of a mile away, and you bought a pack. Jerry Grey, who can predict how stories end, can probably predict what happened next, right? That's right—when you got outside you put a cigarette into your mouth and before you even lit it you knew you don't smoke. You never have. And right in that moment you remembered that it's Zach Perkins who smokes, the detective from some of your books, and then you remembered that even *he* gave up smoking a few books ago. Right in that moment you also knew that the captain was real, that you were sick, and it was all going to unfold just like the counselor said.

You tossed the cigarettes and walked home. Belinda's car was still parked outside. You climbed through the window and lay down on the couch and thought about what had just happened, and wondered if there would be other times you would think you were one of your characters.

Thank God you didn't think you were the Bag Man!

The Bag Man, in case you've forgotten, stabs women in the chest and then ties a black garbage bag over their heads. He was in book five, and showed up again a few books later.

The Alzheimer's isn't going to let you go, Future Jerry, and it's bringing with it a few quirks, along with the bigger ones of mixing up your character's dirty habits as your own. One quirk is that you talk to yourself now. You've caught yourself doing this a few times. You don't just talk to yourself, but you have conversations with Henry, your favorite writer in residence. Nothing deep and meaningful, but he'll occasionally say something like *You should put that into the journal* or *You deserve another drink*. Henry isn't a real person, and you've never seen him as such, but that hasn't stopped him from making small talk.

The other development is the drinking really has become your best friend, though Sandra would tell you he's the friend that doesn't leave when the night is over. She knows you're drinking—but doesn't *really* know because she can't catch you. All the slurring and unbalanced walking you blame on Captain A. You are planning on cutting back before the wedding—if you're going to forget Eva's name when you're giving her away at the altar, you'd rather it be from dementia than from being a raging drunk.

Good news—your problems don't seem as bad anymore. You're caring less and less about the real world.

Bad news—the bad news is that the good news above really should have been bad news. Not only have you accepted what's happening, but you're ready. Bring it on, Captain A. Do your best. Oh, and in case Future Jerry can't say it, let me say it—fuck you, Captain A, and the disease-ridden whale you rode in on.

Back in the lounge, the girl, Fiona Clark, hasn't moved. She hasn't gotten up and fled his imagination and taken all that blood and violence along with her. Is somebody due home? There are photographs around the room—one on the bookcase, one on the TV stand, a couple hanging on the walls, and in them is a recurring character, a good-looking guy around Fiona's age, embraces and kisses and laughter. A recurring character who could be at work, or on his way here.

He finds a bathroom. He washes his hands under hot water and scrubs the blood away. The music has been replaced by the low hum of bantering DJs. He can't hear what they're saying. He uses a towel to dab at the blood on his shirt, but only manages to darken and smear it. He uses the towel to wipe down the taps and the basin, then wraps the towel over his hand and uses it to open the wardrobe door in the bedroom. There are only women's clothes in here, so the guy in the photographs doesn't live here, but then he finds a jacket that is big enough to fit him that the guy could have left behind, or belongs to an ex-boyfriend, or the father, or even the victim herself. He puts it on to cover his bloody shirt.

He wipes down other surfaces in the house, including the container of bleach that he doesn't use, nor can he even remember for sure if the bleach would have helped. He can't bring himself to set fire to the place. When he's done he crouches next to Fiona and searches for something to say, but what is there? *Sorry? Sorry I stabbed you in the chest?* He cleans the knife in the kitchen sink then wraps it in the towel. He heads for the front door. There are ads on the radio now. Jingles. He pats down his pockets to see what he has on him. He doesn't own a cell phone, so he grabs Fiona's, and while he's at it, he takes all the cash from her purse, which turns out to be ninety dollars. When he reaches for his own wallet, he finds a neatly folded black plastic garbage bag tucked into his back pocket. He has no idea why he has it.

Don't you? Henry asks.

He takes the SIM card out of the phone and wipes his prints off and has one foot out the door when the song his daughter wrote comes on the radio. He recognizes it immediately. When she finds out what he's done, it will destroy her.

Then make sure she doesn't find out.

He tosses the SIM card in the garden as he leaves. The towel with the knife wrapped inside is tucked under his arm. He's not sure what street this is, let alone what neighborhood he's in. Everything looks middle class, nothing too run down, most of the cars parked on the street or up driveways are Japanese imports, most of them around seven or eight years old. He walks to the end of the block. The street signs don't mean anything to him.

He needs to dump the towel. He keeps his head down as he walks. Soon an intersection has to make sense. He reaches a park two blocks later. There's a bunch of playground equipment in the middle but, thankfully, no kids, which means he can sit on the bench and not have anybody rush over to call him a child molester while he's collecting his thoughts. There's a trash bin twenty yards away. He figures it's a good dumping spot, then figures it's actually a really bad one, that the police will end up looking here. They're going to look in every trash can and dumpster within a five-mile radius. Looking at the trash bin and thinking about dumping the evidence gives him a sense of déjà vu. Has he done this before? Or was it one of his characters?

Honestly, I couldn't tell you. I couldn't even tell you what today is.

He needs to bury the knife. Or throw it into a river. Dump it in the ocean or send it into space. He takes the plastic bag out of his pocket and shakes it out, then puts the towel and the knife inside and rolls it all up. If he really had killed that woman, he's sure he would know it. He would feel it somehow.

Like Sandra?

Sandra, dead because of him. He should do the world a favor and take the knife back out of the bag and become Henry Cutter and cut, cut, cut his way into oblivion. There is no mystery here—he killed his wife, he killed the woman he found on the lounge floor, and quite possibly the woman the police were asking him about.

He starts to shake. He can't catch his breath. He's a fool, a silly fool for wanting to escape the nursing home to prove his innocence because all he's done is hurt somebody else. He is Jerry Grey, a crime writer, but really he's nothing more than a confused old man who isn't even old, but made old by the Big A. Jerry Grey, creator of worlds, killer of women, confused madman.

He's a monster.

He's the Breaking Man.

He doesn't know what to do.

God help him, he doesn't know what to do.

W MINUS FIVE

You saw Doctor Goodstory yesterday and again this morning. He said Captain A is going to make this a pretty quick journey because you are now in the advanced club, all the way baby, from zero to a hundred in just a matter of months. Aside from being tired a lot more often, you told him you don't really feel a lot different. Sure, you feel muddled sometimes, but otherwise very much yourself. When you got home, you printed out the Ray Bradbury quote you like so much, and put it into a frame where you can see it from your desk. Things really do feel like they're all over now, just like the quote says.

Sandra and Eva are still running around like the sky is falling. You spent this afternoon with them at the church Eva is getting married in, Saint Something or Rather. It's a really pretty stone church with lots of beautiful gardens out the front and a cemetery out the back, a horseshoe ring of poplars and oak trees separating the two. You can't deny there's a creep factor to the place, what, with all those bodies in the ground only a minute away from where Eva and Rick are going to exchange their I dos. Of course that's the old horror writer in you thinking that. You've probably forgotten this by now, Jerry, but your first few manuscripts were about vampires, and zombies, and shape-shifters. Back then if you knew the real horror was waking up at three in the morning confused while taking a piss against the bedroom wall, that the real horror was stepping out your back door and stepping through a memory wormhole, then you'd have written a successful horror novel years ago. Eva getting married at a church by a graveyard—the failed-to-be horror author can't help but see the timing of all of this coinciding with the timing of the zombie uprising, the zombies choosing your little girl's big day for a little big day of their own. You feel bad Eva's marrying her hip-hop-loving boyfriend in a place like this, but they're doing it because of you, because

Captain A
Is taking you away,
Yo.

After the church visit, you all headed out to the winery where the reception is being held. Eva and Rick were lucky there, because there was a cancellation, so everything worked out. It's out in the country a little, mountains in the far distance, vineyards in all directions, a lake, a beautiful building, all of it stunning, stunning, stunning. And expensive. If there is a zombie uprising on the day, just hope nobody tells them it's an open bar.

The last few days have been full of meeting people and ticking i's and dotting t's—the priest, the florist, the band, the caterers, picking up your suit, and you had to go back into town and see the dessert baker again. You had to stand there and nod and pretend you had no idea what was going on between him and Sandra, who again wore her hair down. Henry keeps saying you have to take care of that situation, and you will, after the wedding. There's the rehearsal in a few nights' time, where you'll be shown how to walk in a straight line with Eva on your arm, how to shake Rick's hand, then how to sit down in the front row next to Sandra. Everybody is worried you're going to mess it up, that you're going to make it halfway down the aisle, shit yourself, and trip over the priest.

Oh, another thing, you got the notes today that your ghostwriter has written up. There are some changes he's planning on making, but none make any sense. He's even suggested a name change to the novel. They're going with *Burn Time*. You emailed Mandy and told her to go ahead, that everything looked fine, because it's easier just to let it all happen now. Since you can no longer have the title you wanted, you've written *The Captain Goes Burning* on the spine of the Madness Journal so, if you're wondering why it's there, well now you know.

Hans came over again today. He brought more gin. You hid it away in the office after he was gone, but you're not going to touch it, not till after the wedding, then you're going to drink as much of it as regularly as you can. You've always wondered if the difference between being an okay writer and a great writer was sobriety. All the greats—they've spent time coked out of their minds or starting the day with a morning Scotch. Future Jerry, there are more days in your past than your future—that has been true for some time now, but even more true now. Spending your days in a nursing home staring out the window while a nurse wipes the drool off your face isn't the future for you. When the wedding is over you're going to drink yourself to death. You should get to decide how you want to go out, and that seems like a pretty good way. It does mean this journal doesn't really have much of a purpose anymore, except maybe as a coaster.

You were out on the deck with Hans when the florist came over to see Eva. She smiled at you through the window of the French doors and you smiled back, and Hans grinned and slowly shook his head.

Got yourself a little crush there, have you?

No, you said, and shook your head.

I hear ya, mate. If things get to the point where you have to go into a care facility, and I'm sure they won't, but if they do I'll make sure there are some nurses in there who look like her.

Of course there's no way he can do that, but the sentiment made you both laugh, and you can't deny to yourself that if the nurses looked like the florist, then the nursing home can't be all bad. You told Hans you'd started talking to yourself, and he said everybody does that sometimes, but he thought you meant you were saying things like *Hmm, now where did I put the phone?* You told him about the conversations with Henry.

Is he asking you to do things? Hans asked.

Like what?

Like hurting people.

You shook your head while you answered. *No, it's more normal than that. Like the conversation any old two friends would have.*

He the one who told you to spray-paint the neighbor's house?

It was a good question, and one you couldn't answer. If you did spray-paint her house, was it on the suggestion of somebody who doesn't exist?

At least you can't leave the house without the alarms going off, right? Hans pointed out.

I can sneak out the windows.

Just don't let Henry talk you into sneaking out to visit your florist, huh?

He laughed then, and you laughed too, and why not? Everything is funny in Batshit County.

Good news—the weather report is good for the weekend. It's plain sailing ahead.

Bad news—you're going to Rick's bachelor's party later this week. You don't want to go, but Rick's dad has promised to look after you. You're only staying for the dinner part of the evening. Could be fun. Or it could be a nightmare. Things will be better when this is all over. Not just the wedding.

❧

It turns out Jerry does know what to do. Of course he does. It's why he took Fiona Clark's cell phone and searched her purse for cash. It's like he was telling himself (or Henry was telling him) back in the house: he has to think of this like one of his books. What would the Bag Man do if he were innocent?

He wasn't.

He starts walking again. The streets are different but look the same—same houses, same cars, same atmosphere, but then he finds a street that gets a little busier, and he follows it, like following narrow streams to bigger ones until you find the sea, and that's what happens here, a sea of traffic, of people, a main road he can identify. The good thing about Christchurch is you can't drive for ten minutes in a straight line without passing within a mile of a mall, and he figures he's about a thirty-minute walk from the nearest one now. He must be used to walking, because the nursing home is a good distance out of town. He wonders how long it took him to walk from there. A long time. Maybe all night. It takes him forty minutes to reach the mall. He hates malls. Yet he's always thought that if you took the malls away, society would fall apart. It would be like watching the world if the wheel had never been invented. He dismisses the idea of dumping the knife in one of the bins there. Whoever empties them could find it.

He walks past an electronics store with half a dozen TVs pointing at him, some displaying TV shows he doesn't recognize, and some display-ing him as he walks past them, a camera sending back a live feed. He walks past bookstores, shoe stores, a bank, a confectionary shop, jewelry stores, a sports store, stationary stores, a toy store with a giant stuffed pig in a tuxedo on display in the window. He reaches a supermarket with aisles full of sugary foods and bored-looking people. He buys a bottle of water and a sandwich and a SIM card. The girl at the checkout asks if he's having a good day, and rather than telling her the truth he tells her it's going well, then asks how her day is going. She tells him it's also going fine, and he guesses it is for her because he didn't wake up in her house earlier. When he heads back to the mall exit he passes the shops in the reverse order, the only difference is the TVs on display are now showing the news, and on the news is a picture of him, Jerry Grey. . . .

You are Jerry Grey.

"The author who wrote under the pseudonym Henry Cutter . . ."

You are Henry Cutter.

". . . has disappeared from the nursing home . . ."

You live in a nursing home.

". . . he was committed to after the murder of Sandra Grey, his wife . . ."

You murdered your wife.

". . . last year. Grey is suffering from Alzheimer's and is likely to be lost and in a very confused state, and if spotted the police should be called immediately."

He heads to the sporting store he passed a minute earlier. He spends half of his remaining cash on an overpriced rugby cap (go All Blacks!) and tugs it tightly over his head and tucks the front of it down a little. From there he heads to the bathrooms and finds an empty stall and locks the door and sits inside. On the back of the door somebody has written at the top *Damien is awesome*, and below that people have written other things, reminding Jerry of the comment sections online, a long list starting with *That's because Damien has a vagina* and ending with *Fuck the world*. He opens the packet with the SIM card and slots the card into Fiona Clark's phone. He starts to call Hans and straightaway there's a problem. He has no idea what Hans's number is. Why would he? He hasn't remembered anybody's number in a while now, and not because of the dementia, but because his smartphone has remembered everything for him for several years now. He's lost the habit of committing numbers to memory, and maybe that's where all of this started. Is this what he's done the other times he's escaped the nursing home? Found his way to a phone not knowing how to call for help?

In this day and age there has to be a way, doesn't there? A goddamn way of calling somebody! How difficult can it be? He bangs the palm of his hand into the side of his head. Come on! Those numbers are in there somewhere!

Calm down, Jerry. The voice of reason. The voice of Henry Cutter, who wrote the most unreasonable things until a ghost had to start writing them for him. *The numbers may not be in there, but what about emails?*

He's right. Jerry hasn't used email in a long time, but if he can access his account then he can email Hans. He uses the phone to go online, and he has to concentrate, really concentrate to remember his own email address so he can log in, letting his fingers roam over the phone, being guided by muscle memory, which he manages to do, the address coming to him, and back in the day—the day of Sane Jerry—he used the same password for everything. In the password field he types *Frankenstein.* Five seconds later he has access to his account. There are over eleven hundred unread emails. He doesn't read any, and is about to compose one of his own to Hans when he remembers that not only does he have access to his emails, but also to an online address book. Hans's number is there.

He makes the call. The whole bathroom smells like wet dog and bleach. Hans doesn't answer. He leaves a message. He thinks about what other options he has. He looks back through his contacts and Eva's number is in there. Could he call her? He decides to give it a few minutes in case Hans calls back, which is exactly what happens. He answers the call.

"It's me," Hans says. "Sorry I didn't answer, but I never do if I don't recognize the number."

"I'm in trouble," Jerry says, the words falling out of him, the sense of relief almost overwhelming. Suddenly he is no longer alone in this.

"I know," Hans says.

"No," Jerry says, "you have no idea."

"Eva called me earlier, plus now it's on the news and—"

"It's worse than that," Jerry says. "Can you come and get me? Please? I really need help. I'm at a mall."

"Which one?"

"It's . . ." he says, and he knows the name of the mall, it's on the tip of his tongue. "I can't think straight."

"Go and find a security guard, or the mall management office and tell them who you are. You can wait there while—"

"I can't do that," Jerry says, shaking his head.

A pause for a few seconds from Hans's end of the phone, and then, "What is it you're not telling me?"

Jerry stares down at the bag with the sandwich and the bottle of water he bought earlier. "I'll tell you when you get here. I'll go out front and see what mall it is and I'll call you back."

"What's happened, Jerry?"

"I'll tell you when you get here. I'll call you back."

"Just stay on the line, Jerry."

He stays on the line. He walks out of the bathroom and into the river of people carrying books and DVDs and clothes, some pushing strollers, some pushing shopping carts, and he walks to the same entrance he came through earlier. When he's outside he turns around and there in big letters is the name, and he feels stupid for having forgotten it. He tells Hans, and Hans tells him to stay exactly where he is, and that he'll be there in ten minutes.

Jerry hangs up and tucks the phone into his pocket. He opens up the bottle of water and drinks a quarter of it while staring out at the cars, all while staying exactly where he said he would stay. He's opening the sandwich packet when it hits him.

He's left the bag with the towel and the knife back in the bathroom.

He is desperate to start running, but restrains himself as to not draw attention. There are so many shops, so many ways to turn, so many people around him as he walks. He can't figure out how to get back to the bathroom, not right away, and by the time he does his ten minutes are up and Hans is ringing him. He opens the bathroom door and goes to the stall where he sat earlier. It's empty. He looks at the back of the door to make sure it's the same stall. *Fuck the world.* The bag with the towel and the knife has gone.

W MINUS THREE

You went wandering again today, and because of that Sandra considered keeping you in tonight and not sending you on the bachelor's party. You didn't really care one way or the other, but in the end she decided she wanted you to go. Probably so she could get you out of the house for obvious reasons. You went along and spoke when spoken to and didn't cause any kind of scene. No doubt the party became more raucous once the old-timers had gone, that Rick and his friends drunk their way along to a strip joint, but for you it was just dinner and no wine but water, some overcooked chicken, and a soggy salad. You sat there pretending not to notice the whispered comments and not-so-subtle nods in your direction. You were the guy with Alzheimer's, and to them that made you a joke. It made you a joke because they would never be like you, the same way you used to think you would never be like this, and what could be funnier than your mate's father-in-law losing his mind at forty-nine and occasionally going off to Batshit County for long walks in Batshit Park? You were home by ten and are keeping your promise to ride the sober train all the way to Eva's wedding.

So. The wandering. That's what you want to know about, right? What tips can that sieve of a brain of yours hold? Well, there are a couple of things. If you're going to wander, take a wallet with you. It's good if you can identify yourself, and even better if you can pay for a taxi or a bus. Money is good—so keep it on you. Just as good is a phone. Try to take your phone with you. A bottle of water would be good too—helps with the dehydration, and who knows how far you can walk?

Today you snuck out the window to avoid the house alarms, and the thing is, you have no memory of doing it. You have no idea if the intent was there to go for a walk on your own, or to go and buy flowers, or to do any number of possible things a man will do once he leaves his home with barely enough cash to buy a hamburger combo. You don't know which version of Jerry made that decision, or which version of Jerry showed up at the florist where Belinda works. The florist is in town, right between the two main drags of Manchester and Colombo. And how did you get there? A true magician never reveals his tricks, Jerry, and Captain A is nothing but the master of slight of hand. Look over here while he wipes Jerry's mind!

Belinda asked if you were okay, and you told her you were, because you really were okay, Future Jerry, you were on a mission, one so top secret even you didn't know the agenda. She knew about the Big A (it seems everybody does), and she sat you down in the office and made you a cup of tea and rang Sandra and told her she would drive you home. By this time Captain A was releasing the reins a little, and you were becoming equally aware and embarrassed of the situation. Belinda kept smiling at you, and told you not to worry, that her grandmother has Alzheimer's and she's used to it, which actually upset you because it made you feel so *old*.

She swung past her house on the way to pick up something for Eva that she would have been dropping off later in the day anyway, which is why she was happy to drop you home. She asked if you would be okay waiting in the car, and you said yes, and that bit you remember, but then Captain A tightened the reins a little and Belinda found you sitting on the back doorstep talking to her cat a few minutes later.

Sandra was worried sick by the time you got back to the house. She'd been getting ready to call the police just before Belinda phoned her. The net result is alarms are being put on all the windows. If that doesn't work, then perhaps the next step is to have a GPS chip sewn into your back where you can't reach it.

Good news—the wedding is close now. There's the rehearsal in a few hours, and remember—practice, practice, practice. Bad news—Sandra said earlier, *I can't wait for all of this to be over.*

When you asked what she meant by that, she sighed, and said, *What do you think, Jerry?* before storming off.

Honestly? You don't think she's just referring to the wedding. She probably has some pamphlets somewhere, the way people do when they're thinking of shipping their folks off to a home, the final step before they visit the big home in the sky.

✦

Jerry's cell phone is still ringing. It echoes around the bathroom. He stares at the stall where a few minutes ago he was sitting, as if by looking longer and harder the bag with the towel and knife will reappear. He heads into the corridor and answers the phone.

"Where are you?" Hans asks.

"The bathroom."

"I told you to wait outside."

"I'm heading there now."

He hangs up. He almost drops the phone when he puts it into his pocket because his hands are shaking so much. He takes the same route back outside. Hans isn't there, not right away, but then ten seconds later he is, pulling up in a dark blue SUV. Hans leans over and opens the door and Jerry climbs in. He drops the supermarket bag on the floor between his feet. He wipes his sweaty hands on his jacket.

"Jesus, Jerry, you look terrible."

"Drive," Jerry tells him, and that little gem has come right from the Henry Cutter playbook, along with *Follow that car* and *It's quiet. Too quiet.*

Hans doesn't need to be told twice. They move smoothly through the parking lot past other cars, turning into and out of parking spaces.

"You got a destination in mind? The nursing home?" Hans asks.

Jerry stares at his friend while thinking of an answer. He has put on more weight than the Hans he remembers. Some of that is muscle and some of that is the accumulation of pounds you see on out-of-shape bouncers, the slab weight that enables them to pop a punching bag off its chain but would have them puffing to pick it back up. It looks like he has a few more tattoos poking out from beneath his collar too. This Hans has evolved so much from the one he first met in university.

"Not the nursing home," Jerry says. "Just away from here."

"Tell me what happened," Hans says.

Jerry leans back. His legs are jittering, his knees popping up and down. They exit the parking lot. "I'm not . . . I'm not entirely sure," he says, which sums up his life these days pretty well, he thinks. "I escaped the nursing home."

"You've done that a few times now."

"They keep you updated?"

"Eva keeps me updated on your progress," Hans says.

"It's not progress," Jerry says. "It's the exact opposite of progress. It's . . . is there a word for that?"

"*Un*progress," Hans says. "You want to tell me what happened, or do you just want me to drive around aimlessly?"

"Let's put the air-conditioning on," Jerry says, and he starts fiddling with the controls but to no avail. His hands are still sweaty. "It's a hundred and fifty degrees in here."

"It's seventy," Hans says, then flicks a switch. Cool air comes through the vents and Jerry holds his hands in front of them. "Maybe if you took your jacket off you'd feel better. Jerry?"

Jerry reaches into the bag for his water.

"Jerry?"

He gets the lid off. He gulps down a mouthful, then another, so quickly his throat hurts.

"Jerry?"

He wipes his hand across his mouth. He looks at his friend. "It's possible I killed somebody," he says.

Hans looks over at him. "What? Jesus, Jerry, what?"

Jerry turns the air-conditioning off. He suddenly feels cold. "I woke up in a house I've never been in before, and there was a woman there." His words start to speed up. "She was naked and lying on the lounge floor. She'd been stabbed."

"Oh thank God," Hans says, and he smiles, and looks genuinely relieved, and that reaction is completely opposite to what Jerry was expecting. Is this all some kind of joke to him? "Trust me, everything is going to be okay."

"I found her that way, but I didn't do it. Somebody is trying to set me up, but I don't know why."

"Calm down," Hans says, and he checks his mirror, he indicates, and then he turns the corner and parks on the side of a quieter street.

in the shade. He takes his seat belt off and twists in his seat so he can face Jerry. "You didn't kill anybody. You know what you used to do for a living, right?"

"Of course I know, but that isn't about this."

"You wrote crime novels," Hans says.

Jerry is shaking his head. "I know. But like I said, this—"

"Very good ones too," Hans says, interrupting him. "People were always saying how real they felt. So if they felt real to other people, Jerry, how do you think they felt to you?"

"This isn't like those other times."

"You've been confessing to crimes that were in your books. These are all—"

"You're not listening to me," Jerry says, fighting the frustration.

"I am listening."

"No you're not," he says, and he opens the jacket to reveal his bloody shirt. "I didn't do it. I was there, but I didn't do it."

Hans says nothing. He drums his fingers on the steering wheel while he stares at the blood, and after a while he stares out the windshield. Jerry lets him think. He can't remember this morning, but he can remember that Hans likes to really think things through. He takes another mouthful of water then puts the bottle back into the bag. Finally Hans looks at him. "Are you sure about this?"

"Very," Jerry says. "Somebody is going to find her soon and the police are going to think it was me."

Hans shakes his head. "Listen to me, trust me, this is all some plot out of one of your—"

Jerry shakes his head. "You're still not listening. They already think I killed somebody, and I'm not talking about Sandra."

"You know about Sandra?"

"That she's dead? Yes. That I killed her? No. It wasn't me, but that's not who I'm talking about. Yesterday I had to go to the police station," Jerry says, and of course he doesn't really know it was yesterday—maybe it was last week. Or last month. "This other woman the police questioned me about, she was the florist for Eva's wedding."

"Oh shit," Hans says.

"What?"

"They're asking you about Belinda Murray," Hans says, and here comes the concern Jerry expected from him two minutes ago.

"You know her? Wait, wait, did I know her?"

Hans doesn't look just concerned but worried too. He starts drumming his fingers faster. He checks over his shoulder as if looking for somebody watching them. "You took . . . well, you took quite a liking to her. You wandered out of your house once and went to see her at work."

Jerry shakes his head. "You're making that up," he says, trying to figure out a reason why Hans would, and coming to the conclusion he wouldn't. "Even if you're not, visiting her at work isn't the same as killing her."

"You're right, it's not the same," Hans says, and he looks away. He stops drumming his fingers.

"What?" Jerry asks.

"Nothing."

"Come on, there's clearly something you're not telling me."

Hans turns back towards him. "It's like you said, Jerry, it's not the same."

Jerry shakes his head. "Just tell me."

Hans shrugs, then sighs, then runs his hand over his smooth head. "Well, the thing is, Jerry, you also visited her at home."

"What do you mean I visited her at home?"

"I mean exactly how that sounds. It was when you went to see her at work. She gave you a lift back to your house, but she swung by her house too. So you knew where she lived."

Jerry keeps shaking his head. It can't be true. However, there are so many things happening that seem impossible, yet he knows they aren't. Things like waking up this morning in the home of a dead woman, to finding a bloody shirt under the floorboards of his house.

"They never found her killer," Hans says.

"You think I did it?"

"I'm not saying that," Hans says.

"What are you saying?"

Hans looks out the windshield a moment. He does that Hans thing that Jerry has seen so many times before; he can almost see the gears turning inside his head. Finally his friend looks back at him.

"The night she was killed you rang me. You were lost and confused, and I picked you up on the street and you had blood all over your shirt. Just like now. I asked what had happened, and you said you didn't know. I drove you home. I helped you back through your window. I sat with you on the couch and you remained quiet for some time, then you begged me not to call the police, and when I asked you what you had done that required the police to be called, you refused to answer. I . . . for some reason, for some stupid reason, I didn't call them. Because you were my friend, and what was done was done, and I didn't call them when I should have."

For a few moments Jerry's mind is blank. Absolutely blank. It's sensory overload. Too much information all in one hit, and he and Henry and even Captain A are all switched off into darkness, but then one simple piece of information sneaks in and reboots his system: he is Jerry Grey and he is a monster.

"Jerry?"

"It's Henry's fault," he says.

"What do you mean?"

"Henry wrote those books and it made me crazy. I became one of the monsters he kept writing about. I really did it? I really hurt these people?"

"I can't make the same mistake again, Jerry. I'm sorry, but I have to take you to the police. We have to let them figure out what's going on, and most of all we have to make sure you can never hurt anybody else again."

W MINUS TWO

The rehearsal last night went well. You may be a sandwich short of a picnic in the upstairs department, as your grandfather was always keen to say (before it became *a picnic short of a barbecue*, then *a picnic short of the Pope shitting in the woods*—that was a red flag there), but everything went off without a hitch.

The church—boy, you've been there so many times this week you might need to start paying rent. Father Jacob is a priest hovering somewhere between sixty and old age, a down-to-earth guy who seems to have never laughed at anything in his life. He's pretty okay for a priest, but you've never really been a priest guy. Add that to your list. You're not a car guy, a priest guy, a jeans guy, or a religion guy. You're a dessert guy. You're a running-out-of-sandwiches guy. Every time you step into that church here comes Henry Cutter, the failed horror writer to darken your mood by playing the *Something bad is right around the corner* game, probably because right around the corner is the graveyard. Horror Hack Henry, would you like to take over?

"I do," Eva said, and the crowd was smiling and some, like Eva's mother, were weeping. Weddings had always made her weep.

"I now pronounce you man and wife," Father Jacob said, then smiled and looked at Rick. "You may now kiss the bride."

Rick kissed his bride and the crowd started to clap. Everything had gone off without a hitch—even Jerry had walked his daughter down the aisle perfectly, the right pacing, the right smile, the right amount of pressure on her arm as hers interlocked his. It was a long kiss between the new husband and bride, and people started to laugh, and then the happy couple turned towards the crowd and they smiled.

Soon the wedding party was moving down the aisle, people throwing confetti into the air, an usher waiting at the
door, and that's when it happened, the front doors busting
open as the zombies piled in, the doors hitting the walls
so hard that wood splintered everywhere. Dozens of zombies who had just clawed their way out from the graveyard
behind were coming into the church.

"I do love a good wedding," the first zombie said.

"Brains," said the second one.

"Good point," replied the first one. "Brains." Then another said it too, and another, and the word was catching,
because soon it was on the lips of all the dead people. The
other things on their lips were the living as the zombies
tore into them, and within seconds Eva and Rick were running for their lives. . . .

Thanks, Henry, that's enough. Don't give up your day job!

You don't really think that's what is waiting for everybody on Saturday, but you can't shake the feeling *something bad* is going to happen
because it's been a year of bad feelings, hasn't it? Both Sandra and Eva
are being extremely encouraging, and seem to have a lot more confi-
dence in you than you have. In the church Sandra keeps squeezing your
hand and telling you everything is going to go great, and she seems so
happy, which makes you happy. Being in the church with your hand
in Sandra's, and your arm around Eva, watching them smile, watching
them laugh, it gives you a sense of completion. This is the way life is
meant to be. Yes, things are going to change, but right now, right in
this moment, your family is happy and that's all that matters. In fact,
this week's episode of you sneaking out and getting confused is a good
thing. If you think of the Big A as a pressure cooker, then letting out
some steam to walk into town means it's not going to blow anytime
soon.

The rehearsal went well. More instructions. *Jerry, stand here. Dad,
walk there. Jerry, hold Eva like this.* You will do nothing if not follow
orders. As for the speech—you don't get to give one. Of course not,
because Pressure Cooker Jerry needs to be contained, and even though

that makes you sad, you can understand it. It is, sadly, just the way things are now.

Oh, by the way, speaking of the way things are now, guess what happens on Monday? That's right, alarms are being put on the windows. It's official—soon you're going to be a prisoner in your own home.

Good news—the alarms mean Sandra isn't planning on putting you into a care facility right away.

Bad news—your world is getting smaller. You don't really need the alarms now because you don't even want to go outside. You just want to curl up on the couch and drink. You used to think the difference between being a good author and a great author was . . . ah, hell, you've said that already.

❦

They pull out from the side of the road. Jerry plays with the radio until he finds a news channel. Hans makes the next left to take them towards the center of town. Jerry plays with the label on the water bottle. His legs are still jittering.

"It's tough, you know? Thinking of myself that way," Jerry says. "Thinking of myself as a killer. It doesn't feel right. No matter how I try to see it, no matter what angle I come at it from, I can't get the label to fit."

"What happens in your books, Jerry, when people are hoping for the best?"

"They get the worst."

"I'm sorry, buddy, but that's what this is."

Jerry nods. His friend couldn't have summed it up any better. Still . . . "It's not right. I know what you're saying makes sense, that there's a certain kind of logic to it, but it just feels too convenient that I can remember some things but not others. Why can't I remember any of this morning?"

"The doctors say that you blocked out what happened with Sandra, that it's too difficult for you to accept. Stands to reason you'd be doing the same thing now."

"I'm not that guy, Hans. I've never been that guy. I shouldn't have wiped down the knife. If I'd left it alone, then the real killer's prints would have been found on it."

"It sounds like you were trying to get away with it," Hans says.

The words annoy him. "It's not that. I just knew how things looked. That's why I took the knife to the mall with me."

"What?"

"I wasn't going to dump it there. I just went there to get food and a SIM card. I was going to dump it later."

"You should have called the police."

"No," Jerry says. "I called you because you can help. Because you've

always been there for me. Because you're the only person who will believe me. When I came out to meet you I realized I'd left the bag with
the knife and towel behind in the bathroom."

"Jesus, Jerry, are you kidding me? Or just yourself? You called me
because you think I can help you get away with murder. Just like you
did last time. Only this time I'm not helping you."

Jerry shakes his head. "That's not true. Somebody wants me to think
I'm the Bag Man."

"What?"

"The Bag Man. From the books."

Hans shakes his head. "I know who the Bag Man is, Jerry, and you're
not him."

"I didn't say I was. I said somebody wants me to think I am."

"Was the woman this morning killed the way the Bag Man kills?"

Jerry thinks about the woman on the lounge floor, the bruises and
the blood. He thinks about her eyes open and staring at him. He tries
to remember the Bag Man. He can't remember the *who* or the *why*,
but he can remember the *how*. The Bag Man stabbed his victims and
when they were dead he tied a plastic garbage bag over their head. He
was impersonalizing them. "She was stabbed in the chest. I even had a
black garbage bag on me."

"Jesus, Jerry . . ."

His heart is hammering. "But I didn't do it. I would know if I had."

"Because you trust yourself."

"You have to help me."

"Help you how, Jerry? By stealing a detective's badge and walking
around the crime scene asking questions? Chasing down leads and
bending the rules? Pulling a mobile DNA testing kit out of my ass?"

"No. Well, yes. I don't know. Not exactly. But we can figure it out."

They drive in silence again. The lunchtime traffic is fading as people
return to work. He sees a boy of two or three accidently drop his ice
cream on the pavement then start crying, his mother trying fruitlessly
to console him. Behind them a bus comes through early on a red light
and almost hits a cyclist. Jerry keeps rewinding the clock, going further
back into the morning, but continually comes to a stop the moment
he came to on that woman's couch. As far as he can tell, time before

that moment didn't exist. His heart beats harder the closer they get to the police station. When they are two blocks away he's sweating again.

"Can we pull over?"

"We're almost there," Hans says.

"Please. Just for a few minutes. Please, hear me out. As my friend, listen to me."

Hans looks over at him, then indicates and pulls in against the side of the road. "Talk," he says. "But you've only got a minute."

"I didn't do this," Jerry says. "My DNA is on record. If they'd found my DNA at Belinda's house, they'd have made the connection. But none was there."

"You're a crime writer, Jerry. You know how to commit a crime and get away with it."

He remembers Mayor suggesting something very similar on the ride into the police station. "That's not what happened," he says.

"Then you have nothing to worry about. The police will figure it out."

"No, they won't. It'll be worse than that," Jerry says, and he can connect the dots ahead of him, he just can't connect the ones behind. He's not the man he used to be, but he certainly hasn't gone from crime writing to crime committing. "If I go in there and tell them about today, and we tell them about the florist, then it's going to be like writing a blank check."

"What are you talking about?"

"They're going to take every unsolved homicide over the last few years and they're going to pin them on me. They'll probably go back further too. They're going to say I got sick five years ago. Or ten. Every open homicide is going to close with my name in the whodunit box."

Hans shakes his head. He looks lost in thought. "That's stupid."

"Is it? You really think so?"

"They're not going to take . . ." Hans says, then stops talking.

"What?"

Hans doesn't look at him. Just keeps looking ahead. A truck passes close enough to the car to make it sway on the axles.

"What?" Jerry repeats.

"Nothing."

"There's something. Tell me."

"It's nothing," Hans says.

"Tell me."

Hans breathes out heavily. He sounds like a man who's cutting wires and hoping a bomb isn't about to explode. "Let me think for a few seconds," he says.

"Tell me!"

"Goddamn it, Jerry, I said let me think."

He thinks. And Jerry lets him think. And they stay parked on the side of the road two blocks from the police station, and Jerry stares out the window while his palms sweat and while Hans thinks some more. Hans tilts his head back and covers his face with his hands. He keeps them there, so the words are muffled when he talks. "There was another killing last week," he says, then drags his fingers down to his chin, stretching out the skin on his face and tugging down the bottom of his eyes. "It's still unsolved. A woman by the name of Laura Hunt."

"I think I've seen it in the papers."

"You can remember that but not this morning? I see what you mean about it all seeming convenient."

"It's the exact opposite."

"Laura Hunt was twenty-five. She has the same sort of description as Belinda Murray. Eva told me that you wandered last week. It was the same day Laura Hunt was killed."

Jerry doesn't know what to say, not at first, but then reverts to what he knows is the absolute truth. "I didn't kill her," he says.

"Jerry—"

"They found me in the library in town," he says. "If there had been blood on me, I'd have been arrested, but instead the police called Eva and told her to take me back to the nursing home. I didn't hurt anybody, I promise you. If you take me to the police, I'll become the ultimate scapegoat."

"Can you even hear what you're saying?"

"You're supposed to be my friend. You're supposed to believe me."

"What's wrong with your arm?" Hans asks.

"What?"

"You keep scratching it."

Jerry looks down to see his fingers digging into the side of his arm. If he can scratch an itch on his arm without knowing it, what else is he capable of doing? "Nothing's wrong with it."

"The cops are going to look at the knife and think somebody was planning on hurting somebody at the mall then changed their mind," Hans says. "They'll find blood on it."

"I washed it pretty good."

"They can always find blood on those things," Hans says. "It has a way of getting into nooks and crannies you don't even know are there. What about the bag, Jerry? Are your prints on the bag?"

"What bag?"

"The plastic bag you put the knife and towel in."

Jerry's hands start shaking and he looks out the side window. "They'll be on it."

"It's only a matter of time before they come for you anyway," Hans says. "The longer you try and avoid them, the harder it's going to go when they find you."

"Then help me. Don't let them pin every unsolved homicide over the last twenty years on me."

"I'm sorry, Jerry. We have to go to the police."

"You think I'm guilty."

Hans doesn't answer for a few seconds, then he looks down at his hands. "I'm sorry."

"If you think I'm guilty, then you owe me, because you killed Sandra."

Hans says nothing. He gives Jerry a cold, hard stare.

"You killed Sandra," Jerry repeats. "If I'm guilty, then you're guilty too."

"Don't go there, Jerry."

"The night the florist died, if I killed her, then you should have gone to the police. But you didn't. And because you didn't, I was able to kill Sandra. If you'd taken me to the police then Sandra would still be alive. But you didn't. And she's dead. And that makes you an accomplice."

"Jerry—"

"You can't have it both ways," Jerry says. "I don't think I did any of it, but if I did, then Sandra's blood is on your hands for not doing the right thing. You have to live with that. The only way to clear your conscience is to help me prove I'm innocent of everything."

"You don't think that every single day I'm aware how my decision to help out my best friend led to her dying? Huh?" He punches the steering wheel. "You stupid moron."

Without any warning Jerry twists towards Hans and swings with his left arm. He punches his friend as hard as he can in the mouth, but the angles and the geometry of the enclosed car don't give him as much leverage as he would like, making the punch less effective than he'd hoped. Hans's head snaps to the side. Before he can get a second shot in, Hans gets his arm inside of Jerry's and hits him in the throat, not hard, but hard enough to struggle for his next breath and to start coughing.

"What the hell, Jerry?" he asks.

"It's," he says, gasping for breath, "your fault. It's. Your. Fault."

"Shut up," Hans says.

"If you—"

This time Hans reaches across and punches him in the arm. "I said shut up. I wish to God I had turned you in that night."

Jerry wishes the same thing. Sandra, Hans, Eva—they were meant to protect him. They were his guardians, and now people are dead because of him.

If it's true.

Which it can't be.

"Help me," Jerry says. "I would never hurt anybody."

"You have to realize it's not your fault," Hans says. "None of it is. It's this damn disease. You're not the same guy any of us used to know. You're a good guy, you're not a killer. You're not the Bag Man or even the bad man you think you are. I get you're scared, I get you don't want to go to the police. I understand what you're saying, about the blank check, but—"

The cell phone Jerry took from the dead woman starts to ring. He gets it out of his pocket and stares at it.

"Who is it?" Hans asks.

"I don't know. You're the only one who has the number," Jerry says.

"Where did you get the phone?" Hans says.

"From the dead woman. But the SIM card is new, I got that from the mall. Should I answer it?"

"Give it to me."

Jerry hands him the phone. Hans answers the call and says hello then just listens. Jerry can hear talking on the other end but not enough to understand what is being said. After fifteen seconds Hans hangs up without saying anything. He hands the phone back.

"Who was it?" Jerry asks.

"Guy's name doesn't matter, buddy. Probably wasn't his real name. Said he worked at lost and found at the mall. Said he found a package that he was pretty sure belonged to you."

"Then why didn't he call the police?"

"That was the police, you idiot," Hans says, then takes a deep breath. "Sorry, I shouldn't have said that. But it wasn't lost and found, it was the police trying to get you to go back."

"But how? How did they get my number?"

"I don't know. Wait . . . wait . . . you said you went into the bathroom to put the SIM card in, right?"

"Right."

"Because you just bought a new one," Hans says.

"Right."

"SIM cards come with the phone numbers written on the sides of the packet. Where's the packet, Jerry? Do you have it or did you leave it there?"

Jerry pats down his pockets and then searches the supermarket bag. "I must have left it in the bathroom."

"Then that's it. They're already tightening the noose, Jerry. But there's another option," Hans says. "An option I can give you because you're my friend."

"What option?"

"Take out the SIM card and switch off the phone."

Jerry does as he's told. Then he wipes the phone down with his shirt and tosses it out the window.

"You didn't need to do that."

"Well it's done. Now what?" Jerry asks.

"Now they're going to run the surveillance footage of the mall look-ing for the guy who carried a package into the bathroom and left it there. Then they're going to follow you out and watch you climb into my car. Thankfully it's a mall, not a bank—the footage of you climbing into the car is going to look like the kind of footage you see of Bigfoot. The prints will give them your name, only they're not going to know where you are, but when they figure it out they'll send an Armed Of-fenders Unit after us."

"All that for a knife that got left behind?"

"No, Jerry," he says, and he turns up the volume on the radio. "All this because the woman you don't think you killed has just been found."

WMD

That list of yours, the *I can't believe it* list, well, here's something juicy to add. You ruined the wedding, J-Man. Of course you did—you were always going to, weren't you? It was a self-fulfilling prophecy, the wedding ruined for no other reason than because everybody, including yourself, believed you were going to ruin it. Really, what you should be doing is making an *I can believe it* list, and put this one on the top.

It is still the day of the WMD. The Wedding of Mass Destruction. The day your family went from a mixture of pitying you / being slightly put out by you / being somewhat amused by you, to straight out hating you. *Hate* is a strong word, but not strong enough. Thank God Sandra doesn't know about the gun, otherwise right now you'd be bleeding from a dozen holes. At the moment you are hibernating in your office too scared to face her, and you've watched the footage from today over and over just like hundreds of other people have because Rick's best man, let's call him Prick, has posted it online. All the bloggers who hated you in the past now love you because you've given them one more reason to hate you. The video was posted online less than an hour ago and has already had over a thousand hits. The wedding itself went okay, but that's because all the *Stand here, Don't stand here, Walk like this* practicing got you through it. It was at the reception where things went downhill—and downhill is really understating it, partner. It's a tough decision to put this into the journal for you, because in the future whatever little bit of your brain that hasn't turned to soup is better off not knowing what happened. That's what Alzheimer's is, really—it's a defense mechanism—it stops you from knowing how bad things are getting / have gotten. And for you, Jerry, things just got a whole lot worse.

But you know what? This journal is all about being honest. Best to write down all the details, and of course you can always go online and search *Jerry Grey Wedding Speech* if you want to see the moment it all happened, if you want to see your family watching in horror as what's left of your dignity plummets.

Context. That's what you need. There is some good news because the ceremony itself went off without a hitch, so let's start there, huh? Your wife disappeared in the morning to be with Eva and the brides-maids to go *ooh* and *ahh* as they had their hair done, to relax the nerves with a glass of champagne, to have their makeup expertly applied, and to just generally enjoy the morning. Hans came to look after you, and you sat out on the deck like always and you had a beer and since no-body else was around, he lit up a joint just like he used to. The morning was hot. It's not even summer yet, but if today is anything to go by, then the city is going to blister and burn.

The wedding was scheduled for two o'clock. Around twelve you put on the new suit and it looked sharp, really sharp, and you can count the times in your life on one hand that you've worn one. You actually liked the feel of it, liked the way it made you look grown-up. All these years hanging out at home in a T-shirt and a pair of shorts always did make you feel like a kid. In a suit you looked like somebody to be taken seriously, and that's something else you've always thought—nobody ever took you seriously. Why not? You were just a crime writer, and do you remember that time you were detained flying back into New Zealand because you wrote *Makeup* on your immigration form as your occupation? The woman at passport control didn't find it funny and you were detained, but only for fifteen minutes during which you were given a stern telling off and a reminder that immigration was not a joke. But the fact of the matter is you *are* a makeup artist. Technically. Or were—because now you have a ghost makeup artist tapping those keys on your behalf.

Hans drove you to the church and you got there thirty minutes early and things were still being set up. Belinda was there with her assistant carrying flowers out of the back of the van and loading them into the church, and you chatted for a minute with her before she had to disap-pear to the winery half an hour away to unload some more.

Guests started to arrive. They hung out in the parking lot in the sun. It was too nice a day to spend in the cool church. Some of them smoked, some laughed, chitchat filling the air. Rick and Prick and the groomsmen showed up in a black limousine, and it was pretty obvious they'd had a few drinks to calm their nerves, then a few more just for the fun of it. Rick had the same look in his eye hundred-meter sprinters have just before the firing gun goes off. He came over and you introduced him to Hans, and Hans took his hand and applied a little too much pressure and said *If you ever hurt her, if you ever cheat on her, Jerry here may not be around to protect his little girl, but I will be. You step out of line, buddy, and I will punish you,* and the way he said it—well, he wasn't bluffing and Rick knew it.

I would never hurt her, sir, Rick said.

Then we don't have a problem, do we?

No. There was no problem.

The problem was still to come.

More people were showing up, and Rick and his entourage went into the church and you stayed outside with Hans. There were family members you hadn't seen in a while, mostly from Sandra's side, her sister the gossip who has been married herself three times, a couple of cousins and an aunt and uncle you couldn't remember from your side, a lot of Rick's friends and family you'd never met, and a lot of Eva's friends, some you've known since she was a kid. You shook a lot of hands, said *How have you been* a few dozen times, *Nice to see you again* a few dozen more, people who were strangers, people from your life you couldn't remember, here was Jerry with his Alzheimer's, Jerry to be pitied, Jerry who everybody was worried was going to mess up, and isn't that just the setup to the world's greatest punch line? Isn't that what they wanted? People go to car races hoping to see a good crash, don't they?

When the cars with the bridal party pulled up all murmurs coming from inside the church came to a stop. You could hear the pews groaning as everybody shifted to look back towards the door. Eva climbed out of a dark blue fifty-year-old Jaguar, and she looked so much like Sandra on your wedding day that your heart froze and for a moment you were scared, actually scared you were having what Mrs. Smith would sum up as *an episode.* But it wasn't an episode—it was Eva looking stunning, looking beautiful, the smile on her face so large she looked as though she owned the world, and your heart melted. You were changing, but you had done your job. You had helped raise this amazing woman, and no matter what the future had in store, nobody could take that away from you.

You took her hand and hugged her, and told her she looked beautiful, and her smile widened and she hugged you back, and she was happy, she was filled with so much joy you actually felt like crying. You hugged Sandra and her smile was almost as big as Eva's, and she also looked like she was going to cry, and in that moment, Jerry, you forgave her for everything. Sandra had given you the best years of your life, and she still had a future ahead of her. Her body was warm and comforting and she smelled amazing, her hair smelled great, she felt fantastic against you, and in that moment you embraced your future. You had reached the top of the grief pyramid, your name was Jerry Alzheimer, and you were going to let Sandra put you into full-time care if that was her desire.

Sandra went inside to sit in the front row. There was already music playing in the church, but now it changed to a different piece that was your cue to start moving. The flower girls, who were related to Rick in some way, wandered down the aisle first, everybody in the church going *They're so cute, they're so cute, they're so adorable*, and they were adorable, of course they were, these little kids that didn't have Alzheimer's. The bridesmaids went next—two of them, friends of Eva's since primary school—and then you led Eva, people in the crowd almost breaking their necks to get a better view, Eva beaming the whole way, little nods and extra smiles for certain people in the crowd, and you did what you had been told to do, nothing more, nothing less, step after step all the way to the front, and Jerry falls over and the crowd goes wild! No, that's not what happened, but it's what they expected. You got Eva to the front, gave her a hug, and then shook Rick's hand. You said *It's over to you, now, son*, before glancing at Hans. Rick glanced at Hans too and you were all on the same page.

You sat next to Sandra and held her hand and the ceremony began. You watched Eva get married. There were tears and there was laughter and there were no zombies as far as the eye could see. Rice was thrown at the end and people clapped as the happy couple walked back down the aisle, arms linked, lives linked. Outside the photographer started putting the bridal party to work, *Stand here, Smile, Now you, Now you and you, Now just the family*. If that was it, then it would have been a perfect day. But of course Captain A had something else in mind, didn't he? Look at this hand while he fools you with the other. That's the magic of it all.

The wedding party disappeared to other locations for more pictures, and everybody else had two hours to kill. The crowd slowly departed, breaking up into mostly groups of two or three and getting into the cars to drive to the winery. Father Jacob stood outside shaking hands and making chitchat, and you had this weird image of him sticking business cards under all the windshield wipers, with little *Ten percent off your next confession* coupons attached, or *Absolve two sins for the price of one*.

Hans drove you to the winery, and Sandra went there with her parents. You sat at a table under a sun shade chatting with Hans as others slowly arrived, and it was like the church all over, everybody outside killing time and mingling, only the difference here was they were all holding glasses of wine or beer. You were drinking water even though Hans had smuggled in two hip flasks full of gin and tonic for you, to which you told him *thanks but no thanks*, then *thanks* and had a drink anyway. The nerves were gone because there was nothing left to do except listen to the speeches, eat dinner, and maybe hit the dance floor.

You only had the one drink, and were back to water when the speeches began, and you hated that you didn't get to say anything, that Sandra was muzzling you for the occasion, and you thought . . . this is what you thought: *Hey, that's my daughter too, everybody else gets to say something so why not me?*

Why not you?

The answer became obvious once one speech ended and you interrupted the emcee while he was introducing the next speaker, because you had something you wanted to say. Some words of wisdom.

And the crowd went wild, didn't they?

The video online has now had 3,981 hits. It's going viral. And there you are, walking up to the stage. Jerry Grey in his wedding suit and his funeral suit, but it's not Jerry Grey at the wheel, it's his magician buddy, Captain A. It's all there for the world to see, 4,112 hits now, and the human race, well now, they sure do love a good show, don't they? Especially when it's at the cost of somebody else.

Let me describe it for you. Jerry Grey. At the stage and to his right the wedding table, and at the table are the wedding party, Rick and Prick and the groomsmen, Eva and her bridesmaids, glasses of wine and plates and flowers, and to Jerry's left the band, and next to Jerry the emcee with the smile on his face, the kind of guy who was just going with the flow, the kind of guy who looked like he'd still be emceeing while the ship went down—and that is what happened, isn't it? So that's the scene. Jerry on stage and the room goes quiet. What's he going to say? What's he going to do? Well step on up, Future Jerry, and catch yourself a tale.

Hi everybody. My name is Jerry Grey, and for those of you who don't know me, I'm the father of the bride, Jerry says, and he turns towards the wedding table and smiles at his daughter, and she's smiling, or trying to, and off to the side people are standing near Jerry trying to figure out a way to get him to sit down. To contain him. They're hoping for the best.

But Jerry doesn't want to be contained.

As the father of the bride, I want to start out by thanking you all for coming along on what has been, and I'm sure my lovely wife will back me up here, one of the best days of our lives. To see our little baby girl all grown up, to have become this beautiful, charming, and caring woman, well, I don't need to tell you all what an honor and a pleasure it has been along the way as we've gotten to know her. And Rick, Jerry said, turning his attention to the groom, *we are looking forward to getting to know you, and I want to welcome you to our family.*

Pause for clapping.

But please, can you stop coming around to the house with that hip-hop music of yours cranked up? It frightens all the neighbors.

Pause for laughter . . . It's there, it's polite, it's enough to make Jerry feel confident.

Now, some of you may know that I'm a crime writer, and that's a very different beast from being a stand-up comic, which means I may not be able to make everybody laugh, but, Eva, what I can do if you ever need it is give you the perfect alibi.

Another pause. More laughter this time. Jerry is feeling good, feeling good, he's looking comfortable on stage.

Why couldn't you have sat down then, F.J.? But you didn't, because Captain A was the master manipulator and had something he wanted you to say.

As the father of the bride, having been where you're sitting now twenty-five years ago, it reminds me of what my own dad said to me back then, a piece of advice I wish I had taken. He said, Jerry, run!

Laughter. Genuine laughter, especially from the older folks in the crowd who all can relate to what Jerry is saying.

But seriously, folks, as any parent will do when they're seeing their child getting married, you think back to when it was your own time, you think back and you wonder how the years have gone by so quickly, there are always ups and downs in a relationship, and the older you are the more you've been through, and the more you've been through the more advice you can give. Of course everybody has advice, a lot of us say My advice is don't take anybody's advice, make your own way, and thankfully, folks, that's not the chestnut of wisdom I'm here to impart. Rick, I'm hoping I can come to think of you like a son one day, and I want to tell you that you are a very, very lucky man marrying my daughter.

Ooh. Ahh. The crowd is lapping it up.

I envy you. You're not making the mistake I made by marrying a whore.

There is a pause in the crowd as people try to interpret what Jerry just said. They heard the words—at least they think they did, because surely he didn't just call his wife a whore, did he? And if he did, then surely it was a joke, wasn't it?

Jerry carries on.

Had I mentioned that my lovely wife is a whore?

Lots of gasping as people realize he's not joking. Everybody inhales at the same time and the air in the room goes thin, but Jerry hardly seems to notice. He's still looking at Rick and he's smiling.

I didn't know it when I married her, but I do now, and isn't that always the way, people?

Pause for laugher. None. Jerry looks confused.

Isn't it?

Hans has come up to the stage and is reaching for Jerry, but Jerry shrugs away from him. *Sandra has been fucking people. Lots and lots of people, including my good friend Hans who's right here, everybody, Jerry* says, and points at his friend. *She wants to put me into a home so she can go table shopping with the baker. She's a—*

And that's as far Jerry gets, because then Hans is dragging him off stage, actually dragging him from the collar of his funeral suit, the back of Jerry's feet sliding over the floor, and people are standing up, and somebody says in a high-pitched voice, *holy shit, holy shit, holleee shit*, and there's Sandra, storming off, and Rick hugging his new wife, and Jerry still ranting away, *bitch, slut, whore*, all of it coming from his mouth.

Over six thousand hits now. It's speeding up.

Good news—at least the ceremony went okay.

Bad news—it's all bad news, partner.

✤

Hearing it coming over the radio is a confirmation Jerry doesn't want. He looks towards the police station. The top few floors are looming over the surrounding buildings. He can picture cops staring out the windows at him, binoculars finding him, a sniper rifle narrowing in on his head. He can picture a tactical team already in the elevators making their way to the ground floor.

"They're going to make the connection between the knife and the crime scene quickly," Hans says. "My guess is that evidence is already on its way back to the station and in about fifteen minutes they're going to be fingerprinting everything and about fifteen minutes after that they're going to have your name. You agree so far?"

He nods. The crime writer inside of him agrees.

"Surveillance from the mall is going to find you going into the bathroom, and they're going to run the footage in both directions and find out where you came from and where you went. They're going to find you buying the hat and buying the SIM card, and that's going to tell them they're dealing with somebody who knows what they're doing. It's going to tell them that Jerry Grey committed a murder and had the sound mind to try and get away with it, which means when they come for you, they may be trigger-happy. If I take you in now, that can be avoided."

"You said before there was another option," Jerry says. "I want to know what it is."

"Whether you did this or not," Hans says, "you look guilty. Nobody is going to see it any differently. Even I don't see it any differently. If they don't shoot you when they find you, then there'll be a trial, one that Eva will have to sit through and learn all the awful things you've done, and then they're going to make a big show out of executing you, because that's what they're going to do, Jerry."

"Execute? What the hell are you talking about?"

"The death penalty, Jerry. It got voted back in last year. There was a referendum."

"What?"

"It was a big thing. The crime rate in this country, hell, you know it better than anybody. The people wanted to be heard. It was a big talking point in what was an election year, and the result of that is it's been voted back in, and the government agreed to do the will of the people. It hasn't been enforced yet, but you trying to get away with this today, people are going to think you're of sound mind and, therefore, you're going to be a pretty good candidate for the noose. The country will finally get to see the results of their voting put into action."

"But I didn't hurt anybody," Jerry says.

"I love you like a brother, I really do, but that's your future. So the way I see it you have three options."

"We run," Jerry says.

"That's not one of them," Hans says. "You can't run. I won't let you run. So option one is you let me take you into the police station right now and you avoid the possibility of getting put down in the street like a rabid dog. Option two is I take you to a strip joint and I can give you a thousand bucks to blow on strippers and drink and you can have the last, best, final day of freedom before I call the police."

"And three?"

"Three is you go out on your own terms. We go and find a sunset somewhere, we have a few drinks, we reminisce about old times, and we both drink a little too much and you take some pills and you—"

"No."

"You die with your dignity and with your best friend by your side."

"Jesus, how can you—"

"Because you killed those girls, Jerry. You killed Belinda Murray and Laura Hunt and the woman this morning, and you killed Sandra. That's how I can suggest it. And if you were thinking straight, you'd suggest the same damn thing."

"But I'm innocent."

"Is that really what you think?" Hans asks. "You think somebody set you up? That somebody framed you?"

"It's possible," Jerry says.

"Yeah? Is that Henry Cutter or Jerry Grey saying that?"

"Both."

"Look, Jerry, you could have taken a flight to Mars last week and you wouldn't even know it. And if somebody set you up, how? They give you Alzheimer's too?"

"I didn't do this," Jerry says.

"I know you didn't. It was Captain A."

Jerry shakes his head. "This wasn't the disease. It wasn't me. Somebody is doing this to me."

"Like in one of your books."

"Exactly!"

"You don't think it's more likely you snuck out of the nursing home and made your way to this woman's house?" Hans asks.

Jerry feels like screaming. He feels like punching a hole in the world. Why won't his friend listen to him? "Please, you have to trust me."

"Trust you? Tell me about Suzan with a *z*," Hans says.

Jerry doesn't answer him.

"Tell me about her."

"She was different," Jerry says.

"Different how?"

"Because her I remember killing. I'm sorry, and I wish—"

Hans puts up his hand to stop him. "She's different, Jerry, because she doesn't exist. She never existed."

Jerry doesn't answer him, not right away, but then the brain chemistry does that little trick it sometimes does, it washes over and clears another memory, and he wonders at what expense, at what other fact or person he's just forgotten. "She's from the books, isn't she."

"Yes. So don't you think it's possible that if you can remember killing a woman who never existed that you may not be able to remember killing one who does?"

It makes sense. Perfect sense.

"We need to find the journal," Jerry says.

"What journal?"

"The one I couldn't find yesterday."

"What are you talking about?"

"You don't know?" Jerry asks.

"Know what?" Hans asks.

"About my Madness Journal?"

"What in the hell are you talking about, Jerry?"

"I've been keeping a journal since the day I was diagnosed with Alzheimer's. I was calling it a Madness Journal. I thought you knew."

A few seconds of silence. Jerry can see his friend's mind racing.

"What was in it?" Hans asks.

"Everything," Jerry says. "Everything I could remember back then that I can't remember now. I wasn't writing in it every day, but I wrote in it plenty. It was a way of reminding my future self of who I was. That future self is me, I guess, but without it I can't remember what I wrote."

"Did you write in it when Sandra died?"

"I don't know, but I imagine I would have."

"How do you know the police didn't find it?"

Jerry shakes his head. "They didn't. Nobody knows where it is," Jerry says. "There's a hiding place in my house—"

"It's no longer your house, Jerry."

"I know that, Christ, I know that, okay?" Jerry says, throwing his hands into the air. "I remember thinking last night I needed to find the journal, and that I had to find a way to escape so I could go and find it."

Hans runs both his hands over the top of his head. "Ah, geez, Jerry . . . really?"

"That journal might prove I'm innocent."

"Or it might prove the opposite."

"Then at least I'd know, right? But there's a problem."

"Because there's a new owner," Hans says.

"We went there yesterday—"

"We?"

"Me and Nurse Hamilton. Gary let us—"

"Gary?"

"The new owner. He let us inside and I found the hiding spot, but there was nothing there, only I think it was there and Gary found it and is hiding it, the journal and the gun."

Hans frowns. "The gun?"

"Yeah," he says, getting frustrated at all the interruptions. "The police never found that either, but maybe it's not there because I didn't shoot Sandra?"

"Is that also what your nurse thought? That the new owner was hiding the journal?"

"I don't know," Jerry says. "I remember thinking they were all in on it."

"All?"

The way Hans asks that, it makes Jerry realize how crazy he's sounding. *They're all in on it.* That's also right from the Henry Cutter playbook. "There was an orderly there too. They had to sedate me. But the journal has to be there, right? Maybe that's—"

"They had to sedate you?"

"Jesus, will you just let me finish?"

"There are too many blanks, Jerry."

"They had to sedate me because the shirt made them think the worst, and they wouldn't believe me about the journal, and the journal is the key to all of this. That's why—"

"What shirt?"

"There was a shirt under the floor," Jerry says, wishing his friend could keep up.

"Was it blue? Was it covered in blood?"

"Yes."

"That's the shirt you wore to the wedding. You were wearing it that night when I picked you up."

"Don't you see?" Jerry asks. For the first time he feels like he's on track. "We have to go back there and convince Gary to give the journal to us. That has to be why I left the nursing home. That must be where I was trying to go. If I can find the journal and prove I didn't do any of this, then Eva will want to be in my life again. She'll call me *Dad.* She'll come to visit. You have no idea how it feels to have a child who wants nothing to do with you."

"You're sure it exists, this journal of yours."

"Absolutely."

"Okay," Hans says. "So let's say it does. What's your plan? We go and make Gary tell us where it is? We don't even know he took it and, I hate to burst your bubble here, Jerry, but to me it sounds like he didn't take it at all. Either somebody else found it, or you hid it elsewhere. Where else could you have hidden it?"

"I don't know. What I do know is that I need your help. Please. Will you help me?"

Hans says nothing for a while. He just stares at Jerry, and Jerry can see Hans's mind unlocking the problem, the way he always has.

"Okay," Hans says. "Let's head back to my house and work on a plan."

"Why don't we go straight to my old house?"

"Because we have to think about it, Jerry. It's foolish to rush into something without a plan."

"But—"

"Trust me. Going in without one is a surefire way of failure. I wish you'd chosen the stripper option," he adds, and he checks for traffic and then does a U-turn. "It sure would have been a hell of a lot more fun."

WMD

It's now one a.m., which makes this Sunday, which actually means this is no longer the day of the WMD. Time to start over.

WMD PLUS ONE HOUR

The online video has now had more than twelve thousand hits. If only your books could sell as quickly. There are also over a hundred comments. The Internet gives everybody a voice, and it seems those who can't spell are the first to take advantage of that.

Ha funny.

Guys a genious. Bet his wife really is a whore.

Guys a hack. His books r shit.

Guy's a fag. FAG! No wonder his wive screws round.

God loves everybody—but even he thinks this shmuck is an asswhole.

These kinds of comments have always made you fearful of where the world is going. You worry one day people will have the courage to say in the real world what they can now only say anonymously through social media.

Since writing those comments down in the Madness Journal (no cutting and pasting here, Jerry), the hit count has gone up another thousand. At this rate every single living person in the world will have seen it by Christmas, unless some celebrity kills somebody or flashes their junk to the media. Hard to know whether it's crashing what's left of my career or helping it. What's that old chestnut? *All publicity is good publicity?* This will put that to the test.

Sandra came into the study earlier. It really has been a day for good ol' chestnuts, because she pulled out the words that follow, and here's how it all began. . . .

We need to talk, she said.

I'm really sorry, Sandra. I feel so ashamed and—

How could you, Jerry? And I don't just mean how could you say those things, but how could you think them?

She was crying. Tears are what Henry used to think of as emotional blackmail. Many of his female characters used them to get their way (you really are a chauvinistic pig, Henry), and all you could do was tell her how sorry you were, over and over, but being sorry wasn't going to fix it. You were forming a plan—Henry can tell you.

Jerry was going to get his gun. Jerry was going to shoot the son of a bitch who put that video up online. Then Jerry was going to shoot himself too.

Thanks, Henry.

Do you really think those things? Sandra asked.

You wanted to say *no*. The word even formed in your mind, this little word so big and powerful, too big it got stuck, too big it was crushed under its own weight. *Yes,* you said. *And I don't blame you, I really don't.*

You did nothing to avoid the slap you knew was coming. It echoed around the room. If this had been a book or a movie Sandra would have realized what she had done and gasped and apologized, and in the end you'd have made up. It would have been the ultimate rom-com: you being put through the wringer, your relationship being pulled apart from every direction near the end of the second act, but all would have been saved late in the third. If only.

She slapped you again, this time much harder. Act three was going to be tough work to come back from this, and you realized this is why rom-com writers don't throw a hilarious dose of Alzheimer's into the rom-com mix.

You think I'm a whore.

No, it's not that—

Then what? she asked.

I know you've been sleeping with the baker.

What?

And the guys who put in the alarms. You're always disappearing for wedding stuff, and I know, you said, and tapped the side of your head because that's where the proof was baby, pure and simple, *you've been sneaking off to be with other men. Including Hans.*

Anybody else I'm screwing? she asked.

The cops who came to the door after the car got set on fire. And probably even a few people from the wedding, you said, because honesty is the best policy, isn't it?

You must really hate me to think that way, she said. *Have you always thought these things?*

Only since you started sleeping around, you said.

It's this . . . this . . . disease, she said, spitting out the words. *It gives you carte blanche, doesn't it? You can say what you want and you don't have to own it because it's not Jerry, it's his bloody Alzheimer's, but you have to own this one because half the world has already seen it. You became a laughingstock tonight, Jerry, you embarrassed yourself and you humiliated me and you ruined Eva's wedding. I know you're sick, I know things aren't the same, but how am I supposed to forgive you for this?*

That's when you went ahead and made things even worse. *It's your fault.*

Now she was the one who looked like she had been slapped. *My fault?*

If you hadn't been cheating on me none of this would have happened.

She burst into tears and ran out of the room.

Good news—there is none.

Bad news—you're probably in your final few days at home now. Your wife can't handle the truth (what movie is that from?), and the hit count of you ruining Eva's wedding just topped thirty thousand.

Good news. You have two unopened bottles of gin with your name on them.

✦

Hans's house is twenty years old, a single-story brick home with a neat and tidy yard on a neat and tidy street, a pleasant-looking area in which Jerry can't imagine Hans fitting in too well. His tattoos alone must make him stand out. But then again he's never been one for company. Hans has had a few girlfriends come into his life, girls with sultry smiles and big tattoos. But just as easily they'd drift away and move on to bigger or lesser things, drugs or booze or a different bad boy on the path to aging fast. Hans has always been one to move on as well, literally moving to a different house every two or three years.

Hans pulls the car into the garage and uses the remote to close the door behind them, putting them into darkness. The garage windows have been covered with pieces of cardboard taped into place.

"Nosy neighbors," Hans says.

"The rest of the place the same way?"

"Not all of it, no," Hans says, opening the car door. The interior light comes on.

"Have I been here before?"

"Not here, no. I only moved in six months ago."

They get out of the car. Jerry grabs his plastic bag and Hans flicks on the garage light so Jerry can follow without walking into a lawn mower or shelf. They head into the house. It's neat and tidy and there isn't a lot in the way of furniture.

"You've been here six months and you don't have a dining table?" Jerry asks.

"You want to discuss the way I live, or what we're going to do about your situation?"

"Fair point," Jerry says.

They head into the lounge. There's a TV and a couch and nothing else, no coffee table, no bookcase, no pictures on the walls. He imagines Hans sitting in here watching TV while his dinner plate rests on his legs. No wonder he hasn't had a girlfriend stick around longer than two months. Jerry sits on the couch and Hans disappears then comes back thirty seconds later carrying a wooden stool. He places it opposite Jerry and sits down. Jerry starts to work on the sandwich. He can't remember the last time he ate. It's chicken and ham with tomato. He picks out the tomato and offers it to Hans who shakes his head. He dumps it back into the bag. Hans switches on the TV to a news channel and puts it on mute.

"When the police come knocking on my door," Hans says, "and they will, I'm going to—"

"I thought you said they wouldn't be able to make out the license plate of the car?"

"They're going to cross-reference people you know with vehicles they own, but this address isn't the same address my car is registered to. So that gives us time. My guess is we have a couple of hours then we have to hit the road. You have two hours to figure out where this journal of yours is."

"I already know where it is," Jerry says, and he's been thinking about it the entire drive here. "The new owner has it. He found it under the floor and for some reason he wants to keep it."

"And what reason would that be?" Hans asks.

"I haven't figured that bit out yet."

"Okay, so let's keep that as a possibility. But I want you to consider something else. I want you to think about where else you could have hidden it. If we go in there and it turns out this guy really doesn't have it, then where do we look? That's what you need to figure out now, Jerry. Where else can we look?"

"Okay," Jerry says.

"And once we find it, we read it, and we go to the police no matter what it says, okay?"

"Gary has it."

"Okay, Jerry?"

"Yes, fine, okay."

"Think about where else you could have hidden it."

Jerry takes another bite from the sandwich. "Fine, I'll think about that, but we also need to figure out who would want to frame me," he says, talking with a mouth half full.

Hans shakes his head. Then he sighs. Then he looks at his watch and then he shifts a little on the stool. Then he says, "Fine. Then let's think about that. Do you have any suggestions?"

Jerry puts the last bit of sandwich into his mouth. He hits a piece of tomato he'd missed on his earlier pass through. He perseveres and chews on, and he thinks about who would want to frame him, and then he lets Henry Cutter think about it too. In fact he lets Henry do all the thinking because Henry's got the better mind for it and, sure enough, Henry comes up with an answer.

It's the guy, Henry says. *Gary is the one framing you.*

"It's Gary," Jerry says.

"What?"

"He found the journal, and I've obviously written enough in there for him to realize I can't remember things, so now he's killing women and leaving me at the scene. The shirt under the floorboards was probably one of his."

"Jesus, Jerry, can you even hear how ridiculous that sounds?"

Yeah, my bad, Jerry. That was a bit of a stretch.

"Forgetting about the fact that I dropped you off at home that night, and I saw you wearing that bloody shirt, how does he do it?" Hans asks, carrying on. "He waits outside the nursing home every night in a van hoping you're going to escape? Then, the times you do, he picks you up, kills somebody in front of you, you take a nap and wake up and forget where you are? Then conveniently forget everything leading up to it?"

Jerry doesn't answer him.

"Do you have any idea how that sounds?" Hans asks.

Again Jerry doesn't answer him.

"Okay, so let's say some version of that is true, then why?"

"Because he can't fake it," Jerry says.

"What?"

"He's trying to be a writer. He wants to be like me. Only so far all he has is a room full of rejection slips."

"You're still not making any sense."

Jerry looks at the TV. There's footage of bags of tightly wrapped cannabis and a bunch of police officers talking to people, footage of officers searching a house, of people being put into cuffs. The cops have put a dent in the nightlife of partygoers across the city, forcing the teenagers heading into town to damage their livers on alcohol now that all that weed has been confiscated. He remembers he once wrote a book about a gang who sold meth to high school kids. It didn't end well for any of the characters. Is that where he's heading now? To one of Henry Cutter's bad endings?

"The biggest piece of advice I give people is write what you know, and fake the rest. There's only so much research you can do. There's only so far you can get into somebody else's head."

"I remember," Hans says.

"Gary is killing these women so he knows how it feels, what they feel, what the whole thing looks like. It's research. He can make his fictional world believable."

"There are a million crime writers out there, buddy. If what you were saying had any merit, the good ones would all be killing people. Look, Jerry, let me be honest here—what you're saying just doesn't add up."

Jerry knows it doesn't. Of course he knows that. But throw a drowning man a brick and tell him it'll float and he'll pray to God you're right.

"And the blood on your clothes today?" Hans asks.

"He put it there."

"And the plastic bag in your pocket?"

"Okay, fine, so it's not him," Jerry concedes. "But it's somebody, right? Because I'm not that guy. I can't be that guy you see on the front page of the paper, the sick, twisted pervert who hurts women. I can't be that guy, and if you don't trust me, then trust Sandra. She would never have married somebody who *could* become that guy."

Hans rubs his hand back over his scalp. "You do make a good point," he says, "and I have to give you marks for trying. But everything you say can be contradicted by the fact you have Alzheimer's. It's a wild card. I know you want to think differently, but it does make you a different person."

"But it doesn't make me a killer. People don't just wake up one day wanting to kill people. There has to be something wrong with them, something fundamentally wrong in their past. The guy who bought my house, maybe he's innocent in all of this, but I still think he has my journal. We need to make him talk."

"And how are you going to do that? You going to torture some poor guy on the hunch of a man who five days a week wakes up forgetting his own name?"

Jerry doesn't answer him.

"And this guy, does he have a wife?"

"I think so."

"You want to tie her up too so she can't go for help? Threaten to kill her in front of her husband? Cut her fingers off until he tells you where the diary is? Kill him if you have to, even though you're not a killer?"

"It's a *journal* not a *diary*, and it won't come to that."

"Okay," Hans says, "okay. Look, you said you can't be a killer, because if you were there'd be something fundamentally wrong in your past, right?" Hans asks.

"Right."

"What about Suzan with a *z*?"

"She's not real," Jerry says.

Hans shakes his head. "She is real, mate."

"Don't say that," Jerry says. "It's not funny."

"No, it's not funny at all, and the last thing I wanted to do was tell you this, but you're really leaving me no choice here. Suzan with a *z* existed. She lived a few doors down from the house you lived in for six months when your other place was being fixed up. Her real name was Julia Barnes and I think you killed her."

WMD PLUS TWO HOURS

It's been an hour since the argument. Ten minutes since your last drink. The online video now has over a hundred thousand hits. You've been called ten different types of gay and ten different types of asshole, and a hundred types of everything else. The office door is slightly ajar, which means you can hear other sounds from around the house, the last of which was the bedroom door softly shutting when Sandra went up to bed. You'll be sleeping on the couch tonight, though you won't have to get too used to it—you'll be sentenced to the nursing home very soon.

This may be one of your last free moments in the office, so you're feeling nostalgic. Some details are fuzzy, others are clear. You can remember the time Eva got stung by a bee when she was nine years old, which led to her throwing out a plushy bee toy she'd had since she was a baby, plus every one of her children's books that had pictures of bees in them. You can remember the day your mother called with news dad had died. You can remember teaching Eva to fly a kite, how the string broke, how it disappeared on the wind and you convinced her it was going to head into space, and how every night for the following few weeks she would ask where the kite was now, and you would say it was near Mars, near Jupiter, how it was stuck on the rings of Saturn but working its way free, and she asked how you knew all this and you said NASA would call every night because they were tracking it with one of their giant telescopes. For the last few hours you've let multiple memories flood your brain, enjoying the process, very well aware that soon they will be walled off by the changing landscape of neurological pathways.

The video has now had more than a hundred and ten thousand hits. Hard not to wonder what it will max out at, or wonder if your publishers know about the speech, or what tomorrow will bring. So many people you know will have seen that video, from your editor to your doctor to your lawyer to the florist. Hard not to wonder what these people are all thinking of you right now.

All this wondering . . . you need a walk. You need some time apart from the Madness Journal. It's time to sneak out the window, maybe find a bar somewhere and just . . . sit. Kind of like your dad used to do instead of coming home to the life that was making him unhappy. Maybe take a nap first.

Good news—let's see . . . you're still alive.

Bad news—you're still alive.

❧

Jerry stays on the couch while Hans goes into another room. He sips at his bottle of water while he watches the news. The story has something to do with gas prices going up, and he realizes that's one thing he'll never have to worry about again, and with that thought comes another one—it's also something that Fiona Clark won't have to worry about. A sense of recognition quickly follows, and he realizes he's done this before—not kill somebody, that he has never done—but watched the news only to see a dead woman on the television screen, his imagination on overdrive as it fills in the blanks. Sometimes the imagination of a crime writer is a powerful thing. In fact he'd go as far as to say it's a curse. It's one reason he used to try and avoid the news—when he sees somebody murdered, his mind goes to the event, he pictures their last few moments, what they went through, the fear, the begging, the desperation to survive. It's the five stages of grief on an escalated scale. His mind takes him there, but it also takes him to the moments before, those choices made on the way home when the victim could have turned left instead of right, made that green light before it turned red, if they hadn't skipped their coffee—decisions and processes bringing them closer to death. His imagination runs the other direction too, moving forward after the crime, a mother collapsing at the news, a husband punching a wall, children confused and scared, a boyfriend begging the police to have five minutes alone with whoever did this, people being sedated the same way he had to be sedated yesterday. He scratches at his arm, the needle prick still itching from the injection.

Hans comes back with a laptop and sits next to him on the couch. He sets the laptop on the stool and drags it closer.

"I don't think I can handle one more nail in the coffin," Jerry says.

"We can still go to a strip bar," Hans says.

"Let's just get this over with."

Within a minute Hans is pulling up stories, and there is Suzan with a *z*, only she isn't Suzan with a *z* but Julia with a *J* and with a face Jerry can remember, a face he can picture when he thinks of the book he put her in, this is the woman he thinks about when he confesses to murder. Julia without a z, whose backyard he stood in thirty years ago while embracing the darkness. Blond hair and big blue eyes, athletic, his neighbor, the woman he would see jogging in the mornings, her ponytail bouncing up and down, this girl not much older than Eva is now. They read the articles. Julia had broken up with her boyfriend six weeks earlier, a guy by the name of Kyle Robinson. According to her friends, he was harassing her. He was phoning her all the time, showing up at her work, showing up at her home, he would send her flowers and, on one occasion, he placed a dozen dead roses on her doorstep. Her friends told her to contact the police, to get a restraining order, but she defended him. She said he wasn't really that bad, even though he had hit her a few months before they broke up, just the once, if you don't include the other time he'd pushed her hard into the wall. She thought reporting him would aggravate the situation. Then her body was found, and the boyfriend was suspect number one. It was a label he couldn't shake, and within forty-eight hours he was arrested and charged with her murder, and a year later he was found guilty and sentenced to fourteen years in jail. Eleven years into his sentence another inmate stabbed him in the throat and the boyfriend left the prison system three years early in a body bag.

"There's nothing here to suggest anything other than the boyfriend killing her," Jerry says.

"He always said he was innocent," Hans says, leaning back into the couch.

"But we wouldn't be having this conversation if you didn't think I killed her," Jerry says.

"You used to talk about her a lot. From the day you moved onto that street, you used to talk about how hot the girl was that lived opposite you. Talked about her all the time, right up until she died. It was not long before you met Sandra. For those few days after she was found, and before the ex was arrested, you were as nervous as hell. I figured, you know, it was just because somebody you liked was murdered and that it upset you, but I also remember wondering if she'd still be alive if I hadn't shown you how to pick a lock."

Jerry can't remember any of that, then suddenly he's talking with Sandra, they're talking about going to the movies on a date, he's telling her he's a closet Trekkie and she's asking him what else he was keeping in his closet. What did he tell her? He told her he was keeping the body of his ex-girlfriend in there. Jesus, was it more than just a joke? If he can remember that, then surely he should be able to remember Julia. Only he can't.

"When the boyfriend was arrested, my suspicions about you disappeared, but then over the last year you started confessing to Suzan with a *z* and, well, I guess I've always figured Suzan could have been her."

"And you said nothing."

"Of course I said nothing. It was thirty years ago, she's dead, the boyfriend is dead, you were in a home flicking between the real world and wherever it is your mind goes when you're no longer in control. It's a closed book, mate."

"And a year ago when you found me covered in blood?"

Hans nods. "Yeah, I thought about her that night too. Of course I did. It made me wonder."

Hans closes the lid on the laptop. The news on the TV shows cop cars and reporters and rubberneckers all standing outside a house where police tape is strung across the front. It's the house from this morning. Hans uses the remote to turn up the volume. The police aren't releasing the dead girl's name. They watch the report, neither of them talking, but Jerry knows both of them are thinking the same thing—that he killed her. That he killed Julia with a *J*. His wife with an *S*. The florist with a capital *B*. He killed them all. Even the boyfriend who died in jail, when you think about. He killed them, and his mind, to protect him, is hiding the memories.

"How many others?" Jerry asks.

Hans doesn't answer. He just stares ahead at the television screen where the news isn't getting any better.

Jerry carries on. "Both solved and unsolved, solved where they got the wrong guy. It's been thirty years since Julia Barnes, and if it's true and all this time I've been writing what I know, then how many others? Five? Ten? A hundred?"

"I don't know, Jerry. Maybe there aren't any others."

Jerry slowly shakes his head. He is about to tell his friend he couldn't have done any of this, but finds he can't say the words. Not only could he have done these things, but most likely he did. "Hans?"

"I'm sorry, buddy. We need to go to the police. I've indulged you long enough, but it's time to go. Any more thoughts on the journal?"

"The police are going to pin as many unsolved homicides on me as they can, and I'm not going to know whether to believe them or not."

"It'll bring closure to lots of people."

"But it could be false closure. The people who committed those crimes are going to get away with them if they're pinned on me. They're going to call me the Butcher of Christchurch. No, it'll be the Cutter. They're going to start calling me the Cutting Man."

"They already do."

"The meaning will be different this time."

"We need to take you to the police station, but first you need to try and relax and think about where your journal is."

"Did I do these things? Tell me, Hans, tell me, did I do these things?"

"Yes."

"And there's no doubt in your mind?"

"None."

"Okay," Jerry says, finally accepting he has no other choice. "Then what does the journal matter? Let's just go to the police," he says. "Let's just get this over with."

WMD PLUS ONE DAY

What do you want to hear about first, Future Jerry? The blood? The shirt? Would you rather hear about the knife? How about the phone call to Hans? Or would you rather hear it from the beginning? Yes? The beginning? As you wish.

The Wedding of Mass Destruction made the news, as things can do if they go viral. The news piece was about Jerry Grey, Alzheimer's sufferer, whose unfortunate lapse of Alzheimer's judgment was caught on video and has now been viewed by over one million people. Porn and providing a place to rub salt into the wounds of others at their lowest moments—those are the Internet's two biggest contributions to the world.

The last thing you remember from yesterday is writing in your journal, hiding it away, and then having a few drinks with the plan of sneaking out the window to find somewhere to have a few more. You can remember breathing in the fresh air as you crawled out. It was so crisp it was like it was being swung by the tail and smacked into your face. You were drunk, the perfect amount of buzz where it wasn't going to worry you how far you had to walk, or how much a drink was going to cost, or what kind of bar you ended up in. Only if any of that happened, you don't know. What you do know is that Captain A took over sometime after you wrote in your journal, and when he let go of the controls it was six in the morning and you were sitting on the couch. Your joints were stiff and your feet were sore, and you felt like you'd walked a few miles. You were naked from the waist up. You didn't even notice the blood at first. You made your way into the bathroom, and that's when you saw yourself in the mirror. Jerry Grey looking very pale and tired. Jerry Grey with crows-feet around his eyes and mouth. Jerry Grey naked from the waist up but with smears of blood on his chest and arms and face.

Want to take a stab at what was going on, Henry?

```
Jerry was in the off position. Jerry had no clue what was
going on. Jerry's world was going to get much worse later
that day, but he didn't know it then.
```

You rushed upstairs and you were scared, J-Man, as scared as you'd ever been. You opened the bedroom door, and the world was swaying, and you knew if you found Sandra in there with blood all over the walls, you would scream until your throat tore, until your ears popped, you would scream yourself to death. But there was no blood. You stood for a minute watching her sleep before going back down to the office. You couldn't find your shirt. It wasn't in the laundry, wasn't in the bathroom, then you thought . . . if Captain A had steered you into trouble, perhaps he had tried to cover it up? Perhaps he had hidden the evidence. You moved your desk, used the screwdriver on the floor, and found your shirt under there. It wasn't a wedding shirt anymore, but a funeral shirt, made to look that way by the blood on it. You left it under the floor and put everything back into place. You went and closed the office window that was still open, the window you had climbed out of as Jerry Grey, but by the time you climbed back in you were somebody else. You were Captain A, but Captain A has another name, doesn't he. He goes by Henry Cutter. And that shirt made it obvious that Henry likes to write what he knows.

You went online. You searched news websites for stories that could be connected to your night. There was nothing. You washed the blood off your face and chest at the bathroom sink. You popped a pair of antidepressants and lay on the couch with no idea what to do next. Then you ended up popping a couple more and falling asleep. Right through until noon. You woke up with a dry mouth and the sense that everything was okay, then you remembered it wasn't. You checked your body for cuts, for bruises, for more signs of blood, but there was nothing.

It's the knife, right? That's what you want to know about. Of course you do. At that point it was still hidden in your jacket, just waiting to change everything, and if you had found it then you could have hidden it with the shirt, but you didn't find it—that little surprise was for Sandra. You went out to the lounge where she was sitting on a couch in the sun reading a book.

Isn't there a lunch we're supposed to go to? you asked, and your voice was croaky sounding.

There was, she said. *Eva and Rick were around this morning to check in on me,* she said, and it was *me,* not *us. I told them we wouldn't be attending.*

Why?

Why do you think, Jerry?

You told her you were sorry.

I know you are, she said, *but it doesn't change anything.*

Sandra—

You stink of alcohol and sweat. Go and take a shower and I'll make you some lunch.

You thought about telling her, but how could you? What could you say? You went and showered and put on some fresh clothes and came back downstairs. Sandra was in the office. There was a sandwich on your desk. She was tidying up, she was picking the jacket up, and while she was picking it up she was asking where your shirt was. Before you could lie and tell her you didn't know, she hung the jacket over her arm. She paused. The weight told her something was in there.

Since you're a *Let's guess what happens a third of the way through* guy, then you already know it was the knife she found in there. It was loose in the pocket, blade pointing up, and she was lucky not to have cut herself. She pulled it out and held it away, the same way she does sometimes when she's holding hair she just pulled out of the shower drain. You could both see it wasn't one of your kitchen knives and you could both see the blood on it and you could both see the horror on each other's face. This knife with a blade no longer than six inches, its dark wooden handle, its serrated edge, this little knife that was the biggest knife in the world.

What the hell is this, Jerry?

Seeing that knife told you that as bad as the WMD had been, you had managed to top it. It put the bloody shirt into a different context.

Jerry?

I don't know.

You don't know?

You were standing in the doorway with hair dripping wet even though you had gotten dressed, and then you realized all of you was dripping wet. At first you thought it was sweat, but then you realized you hadn't dried yourself after the shower, that you had just put your clothes straight on. *I don't know.*

Stop saying you don't know. Please, Jerry, think. You need to think. This has blood on it, she said. *It's blood!*

We don't know that, you said, hoping it might be something else. Maybe sauce. Maybe paint. Whatever was on the knife was probably the same stuff you got on your shirt. Something that looked like blood but certainly wasn't.

It's blood, she said.

I don't know, you said, and you said it a few times, over and over.

While you said it Sandra had her own words that she said over and over, and hers were, *What have you done, Jerry, what have you done?*

What have you done?

Sandra wants to call the police. You've begged her not to, after all, nothing was certain, everything was unknown. She called Eva instead and asked her how her lunch went, and asked if anybody else hadn't shown up. Everybody was accounted for. Even Rick's best man who had put the video online, and if you were going to stab anybody to death it would have been him.

It should have been him.

Sandra agreed she wouldn't call the police. Not at that stage. But she would, if anything showed up on her radar.

You called Hans. You told him everything about the shirt, the knife, the blood. He said you probably just found the knife somewhere. It was actually a really simple explanation. He said the blood could be from anywhere, from a cow, a dog, or maybe it wasn't even blood.

There's no point in worrying about something you can't know about, he said. *Worry if you learn more, but until then, just try to act normal,* he said, and you could picture him using his fingers to make quotation marks around the *normal* part, the same way people will be doing at your trial during their *Jerry used to be normal* cross-examinations.

I don't remember any of it.

There's nothing to remember, he said, or words to that effect. You don't know whether he was being vague, or whether he feared the worst.

Is it possible you just found the knife somewhere, like he said?

Good news—really? You think there's good news?

Bad news—the bloody shirt, the bloody knife, is it possible you're more than just a dessert guy?

♣

Jerry is getting off the couch when a photograph of him is shown on the TV, his name beneath it. The reporter says, "Jerry Grey, who became an Internet sensation last year with video of him giving a speech at his daughter's wedding, has been linked to the crime scene by an anonymous source." Then Internet Sensation Jerry Grey shows up on the TV calling his wife a whore, his daughter and her new husband looking shocked in the background of the slightly shaky footage, and the hit counter keeps ticking over.

Jerry Grey. Shot to fame.

Jerry Grey. Shot his wife.

Somebody will write a song or a TV movie about him.

He sits back down as the wedding footage ends and then it's back to today's crime scene, cops moving around in the background, somebody in a suit carrying a fat metal briefcase, somebody with a camera hanging around their neck while they reach into a bag for a different lens. Today's field reporter has the look of a working-class man, sleeves rolled up and no tie, and that makes the news far more real, so jaw-droppingly urgent this man didn't have time to put on a jacket or a tie or even shave. He looks into the camera and carries on talking.

"Details are sketchy, but what appears to be a murder weapon has been located, and evidence at this stage suggests a connection to the former crime writer, which in itself suggests that Grey may now be living inside one of the realities he used to create. Furthermore, a bloody shirt found yesterday at the last residence of Jerry Grey connects him to the homicide of Belinda Murray, a Christchurch florist who was murdered last year, two days before Grey went on to kill his wife. An anonymous source has stated—"

Hans switches off the TV.

Jerry gets to his feet. "Let's go."

"We can't go to the police until we find your journal," Hans says.

"It doesn't matter anymore," Jerry says.

"Of course it does. If there's a chance—"

"Fine, then let's not go to the police. Let's go for option number three. I want a nice view, some good gin, and I want it to be painless. I just want to escape everything. Can we do that?"

Hans says nothing for a few seconds, then slowly nods. "Do you know what you're saying?"

"I know exactly what I'm saying. Will you help me?"

"If that's what you want."

"I want to talk to Eva first," Jerry says.

"You can't tell her."

"I know. I just want to hear her voice. I want to tell her I'm sorry."

"Okay."

Hans dials Eva's number as they walk back through the house. Jerry remembers that Hans has always been good with numbers. If Hans ever gets his own Captain A, numbers will be the last thing to go. Eva answers the phone and Hans tells her that he's with Jerry, and that Jerry is okay. Then he says *yes* and *no* a few times as she fires some questions at him, then he says nothing as she gives him an update of her own, by which point they're leaning against the car in the garage.

"Okay," Hans tells her, and then he hands Jerry the phone. He looks like he's just heard some news that has made all of this even worse. He leaves Jerry by the car and disappears back into the house.

Jerry puts the phone up to his ear. "Eva?"

"Are you okay, Jerry?"

Despite everything, it's good to hear her voice. "I'm sorry about your mom," he tells her.

"I know you are," she says, "and we can talk about that later. I'll meet you at the police station with your lawyer, okay?"

"Sounds good," he says, and he pictures her sitting there waiting, waiting, and he never shows up. The nice view, the sun on his face, pills and booze—that's where he'll be. There are worse ways to go.

"Jerry . . . there's something you need to know."

He breaks out in a cold sweat and almost drops the phone. Nothing good ever comes after those words.

"The shirt found yesterday, it was—"

"I know," he tells her. "I saw it on the news."

"What wasn't on the news is that the police have been searching your room at the nursing home." Hans comes back into the garage. He's carrying two bottles of gin and has a bottle of tonic tucked under his arm. He has a sad look on his face. He climbs into the car. "They found a small envelope with jewelry in it," Eva says, carrying on.

"Your mother's?" he asks, and it's Henry that answers first, using his indoor voice.

Not Sandra's, no. Remember what you had in your hand when you switched on earlier? He reaches into his pocket and the earrings are still there.

"No, not Mom's," Eva says. "But they seem to think . . . it's . . ." she says, but then she starts crying.

"Eva—"

"I can't do this. I love you, Jerry, but I can't do this, I'm so sorry," she says, and then she's gone, the line is dead, and Jerry stares at the phone willing her to return, willing for things to be different. He climbs into the car and hands the phone to Hans, who slips it into his pocket.

"She hung up on me."

"I'm sorry, buddy."

"The police have been searching my room and they found something."

"She told me," Hans says. "The pieces belong to three women, all of whom were killed on days you were found wandering in town. I'm sorry, buddy, but it really . . . well . . . I'm not sure what to say."

Jerry closes his eyes. How many have there been?

Hans uses the remote to open the garage door. He starts the car and they back down the driveway.

"There's more," Hans says.

"I don't want to hear it."

"One of the orderlies says you told him last night you killed Laura Hunt. She was killed last week in her own home. He said he dismissed what you were saying, that he thought you'd probably seen it on the news and you got mixed up the way you've been doing lately. Now, of course, he sees it differently. As do the police. It was the day you were found in the library."

If people had listened to his confession, they could have stopped the monster. But all they heard was Captain A making shit up.

"You promise you'll stay with me till the end, right? You'll make sure everything goes okay?"

"I promise," Hans says.

Jerry thinks of his Eva, and the pain he is sparing her.

"The journal," Hans says. "Are you sure about it? Are you absolutely sure you had one?"

"Without a doubt."

"Where else could you have hidden it?"

Jerry closes his eyes. He pictures his office. He can see the floor, he can see himself prying up one of the boards with a screwdriver. "There was nowhere else."

"If I were to sneak in there later tonight to look for it, where would I start?"

"You'd do that for me? You'd hide it if there are bad things in there?"

"I'd destroy it. But where would I look, Jerry?"

"I don't know."

"It's important," Hans says.

"I know," Jerry says, scratching at his arm harder now.

"What's wrong with your arm?" Hans asks.

Jerry looks down to see his nails dragging across his skin. He's been doing that a lot lately. He rolls up the sleeve of his shirt, exposing the needle mark that looks raw and inflamed. "Everything is wrong with me," he answers. "Come on, let's go before we miss the sunset."

"Show me your arm," Hans says.

"Why?"

"Because I asked."

Jerry shows him his arm.

"They've been injecting you?" he asks, and they're still in the drive-way.

"Just yesterday, when we went to look for the journal. They had to give me a shot to calm me down. I told you that already. I guess my skin is a little irritated."

"You've got a few other marks there," he says.

"I don't remember the other time."

"They look like they're faded injection points. They make a habit of injecting the people at the nursing home?"

"I don't think so. Like I said, they did it yesterday because we were at the house, and—"

Hans shakes his head before interrupting him. "Let me think a moment," he says, his voice hardening.

"Why?"

"Just shut up. Let me think."

Jerry shuts up. He lets his friend think. He starts drumming his fingers against the steering wheel. Over and over. Thirty seconds pass. A minute. He stops drumming his fingers. He looks at Jerry.

"There is something that has been bothering me about this all along," he says. "The nursing home is a long way out of the city. It's a good fifteen miles. Just how do you think you covered that distance? You didn't drive, right?"

"I don't know for sure. I think I walked."

"It's a long walk."

"It's the only explanation."

"Do you remember walking?"

"No."

"So let's say you did walk. In which case you walked aimlessly all that way to the house of somebody you had never met," he says. "With your neighbor when you were young, and with the florist, you knew them. Why would you kill people you don't know? How did you choose them?"

"At random," Jerry says, because it's the only senseless answer that makes any kind of sense.

"If it was random, why somewhere close to town? Why not somewhere on the outskirts of town? If you walked, you would have passed through dozens and dozens of other streets. A thousand homes. Two thousand. Why walk fifteen miles to the edge of town, then another five miles to the victim's house, especially when it's somebody completely random?"

"I don't make those decisions," Jerry says. "That's Captain A."

"It doesn't make sense," Hans says.

"Captain A seldom does."

Hans starts drumming his fingers again. "All that walking, and then you go up to the door of a house you've never seen before, and a woman you don't know lets you in. You choose the house of a woman who somehow you know is alone. That's what we're saying here, right?" Before Jerry can answer, Hans carries on. "Twenty miles between where that woman died and the nursing home, and you've got injection marks on your arms. You can remember everything after but nothing before."

"What are you saying?"

Hans uses the remote control to open the garage door back up. They drive inside. He unclips his seat belt and looks over at Jerry. "I'm saying there's a reason why it seems so convenient you can't remember killing any of these women, or breaking into their houses. I'm saying maybe you didn't do this after all."

JERRY IS DEAD

Dear Future Jerry. It is now two days past the WMD. It's hard to say exactly when to call your time of death, but the doctor wiped his forearm across his head, shook his head at the nurse, and walked out of the operating room sometime the night before last, knowing there was nothing more that could be done. That was the night you became a monster. The Jerry you used to be, the Jerry I used to be, he's gone. All that's left is this sick, twisted fuck who later today is going to blow his sick, twisted-fuck brains all over the wall. Damn you, Doctor Goodstory for not being able to fix me. Damn you, Past Jerry, for letting go, for giving up, for allowing yourself to become this way. It was your job! Your goddamn job to save us! Where was the fight? Past Jerry from day one and day four and five, you got yourself into this mess. You could have done it, you know. You could have done the world and that poor young girl a favor and put that gun into your mouth back when Doctor Goodstory gave you the news. But no, Past Jerry thought he knew best. For a guy who's supposed to be able to see where things are going, you really made a mess of this.

People say suicide is a selfish act. They say it's cowardly. People say these things because they don't understand. It's actually the opposite. It's not cowardly, in fact it takes incredible courage. To stare Death in the face and tell him you're ready . . . that's a brave thing. A selfish act would be to hang on to life as you're dragged through the media and the courts, your family dragged with you. Some will say escaping that is where the selfishness comes in, but that's not true. Your death right now is like pulling off a Band-Aid—quick pain for your family that will fade. You owe them at least that. Journal. Suicide notes. Drink. Gun. That's the schedule, partner.

Where to begin. Well, you know the beginning. The Big F taking you right past when you should have shot yourself, right into the heart of the WMD. The speech (two million hits now) and then the knife, and you and Sandra fought about that knife. You convinced her not to go to the police because, after all, what had you done? Perhaps nothing. Perhaps you had found it. Or stabbed a giant rat—and the world wouldn't miss a giant rat now, would it?

After finding the knife, you and Sandra spent most of the afternoon watching the news. You said very little to each other. You just watched the news and waited for the call. You didn't know who the call would come from, just that it would. Mrs. Smith was still alive, because Sandra had found an excuse to go over and check on her, and it wasn't anybody from the wedding party, but that still left nearly four hundred thousand other people in the city. The call didn't come. The rat scenario was building some strength. The idea had learned to walk. It was wobbly, but with enough time it would have a life of its own.

The idea died this morning. It died when Eva called and asked if we had heard. *Heard what?* Sandra asked. *Heard about Belinda*, Eva said. *What about Belinda?*, Sandra asked, though no doubt her mind was a little train, chugging its way through different scenarios, pulling into the *My husband killed her* station, and yes, that's exactly where she disembarked. Belinda was dead. Somebody had stabbed her to death in her own home. Eva was crying on the phone, and Sandra was too, and even you cried, J-Man. You cried for Belinda, you cried for Sandra and Eva, and you cried for Past Jerry and for yourself.

The world is an awful place. Who would do this? Eva's voice was coming through the phone, saying these things over and over. Sandra just kept saying she didn't know, she didn't know, but she did know. Her skin had gone so white she looked as though she had been stored in the fridge for the last two months. They spoke for ten minutes. You sat in the dining room while Sandra sat at the kitchen bar, her back to you for most of the call, and you watched the clock. It was ticking away the amount of time Belinda had been dead. It was ticking away the final moments of your life too. You knew it then, just as you'd suspected it the night before— you knew if you had hurt somebody, you would pay the ultimate price. You clock-watched while your mind constructed the final scenario. You would use the gun. It would be quick.

When Sandra got off the phone she continued to sit at the breakfast bar. She wouldn't turn to face you. She was crying. Her body was shaking softly as she tried to contain it. You so desperately wanted to go to her, to put your arms around her, to hold her as she cried, but she would never allow it. And what would you say even if she would? If you touched her, she would scream. Or die. You just knew it. She was already on the edge. So you stayed sitting at the table, tracing your finger around the marks you had scarred into it with the fork.

What do we do now?

They were her words, her back still to you. She was like cracked glass, one slight knock and she would shatter.

I didn't kill her, you said. *I couldn't have.*

You were attracted to her. It was as clear as day, she said. It was only clear because she had been reading the journal. She wasn't done. *You have the gall to accuse me of having an affair, where you're the one all this time who was obsessed with somebody half your age. I knew it, I knew it because you couldn't take your eyes off her, and you even went to see her at work, Jerry! At work! And . . . oh my god,* she said, and she spun the bar stool so she could face you, and you knew what was coming—it was another piece of the puzzle slotting into place. *That day she brought you back home, she went to her house first! You knew where she lived!*

Sandra—

Don't, she said, and put her hand up in a stopping gesture. *There is nothing you can say, Jerry, nothing,* she said, and she was right.

She stormed out of the room. You didn't call after her. You couldn't. What could you have said? Even now she's upstairs either having just called the police, or still building up the nerve to do so.

Future Jerry, you feel like a character in one of your books. You've done this. You own this.

So this is it. You've still got two suicide notes to write, one to Eva and one to Sandra. This journal will end up being nothing but the ramblings of a madman. Soon to be a dead man. Then it's time to dig the gun out from its hiding place. Sandra will have to face the horror of running downstairs and discovering you, but at this stage it seems she'll see that more as a relief than anything.

Good-bye, Future Jerry. If there's another life waiting for you, hope-fully you can do better in the rewrite.

❖

The garage door closes behind them. They both stay sitting in the car in the dark.

"Last year you told me you were starting to talk to yourself," Hans says. "You were holding conversations between you and Henry Cutter. Do you still do that?"

A year ago that would have embarrassed him. Now it's just an everyday thing. "Sometimes. Why?"

"Henry is the one with all the big ideas, right? The one with the book ideas, the one who can put a plot together."

"It doesn't really work that way," Jerry says. "He's just a name, it's like I put my author hat on when I go to work, but it's still me who comes up with the ideas. Henry isn't a different personality," he says, but sometimes he isn't so sure. Henry has been helping him today, and aren't there times he suspects that Henry is just another name for Captain A?

"So put your author hat on now," Hans says, "because that's what we're doing. We're going to go to work."

"Work?"

"I need to know if it's possible."

"If what's possible?"

Hans opens his car door. The interior light comes on. Jerry can see tools hanging on the walls, some gardening equipment, some rope and a shovel and rolls of duct tape that are the go-to tools of Henry's trade.

"I want you to think like an author while I pitch you this idea. Can you do that?" Hans asks.

"I can try."

"You need to do more than try," Hans says. "Okay?"

"Okay."

"Good. So this is a story about a crime writer who's in a nursing home. He has dementia. He keeps confessing to crimes he thinks he did, but he didn't do them, he just wrote about them. There are crimes he has done—for example he shot his wife and he killed a girl just after his daughter was married, and there's a chance he killed another girl when he was young, so he's not an innocent person, but he doesn't deserve to be punished for crimes he hasn't committed. Today he wakes up in the middle of a crime scene, and he has no memory of how he got there or what he's done."

"Is there a point to this recap?" Jerry asks.

"The entire time he questions why he can remember some things but not others. The Alzheimer's, of course, hides things from him. And he's repressed painful things from his past. But he can't remember walking into town, can't remember these women, can't remember any of it. He finds that he's been drugged, and recently too. Nobody has ever figured out how he escapes from the nursing home, or how he makes his way into town." Hans pauses and stares at him. "Come on, Jerry, keep thinking of it as a novel."

"But it's not a novel."

"Get Henry to think of it. Goddamn it, Jerry, work with me here. Close your eyes and pretend you're back in your office and you've got your author hat on, and you're letting Henry do all the work. You and Henry are writing your next big seller."

Jerry closes his eyes. He thinks about his office. He can remember the smell of the room, can feel the desk beneath his fingers, the jade plant on his desk he bought ten years ago that was still on that desk when he was there yesterday. He can remember the way the sun fell into the room, the angle fractionally different every day, the way it would hit and fade the framed *King Kong Escapes* poster on the wall. Only he wouldn't see it fade, it faded the same way you don't notice a child growing every day, but you know it's happening. In *King Kong Escapes*, King Kong was pitted against his exact robot duplicate, a battle of the titans, and boy how he loved those B movie posters from half a century ago and how much Sandra hated them, how she wouldn't let him hang them anywhere else in the house. He would sit in his office and he would use Henry Cutter as an alias, but he didn't *think* he was Henry Cutter. He was Jerry Grey, the author, whose exact author duplicate built a life on creating fiction. He wrote during the day, and at night he watched stories other people created for TV. He would read books by other writers, go to movies. Fiction was his life. Henry Cutter was only a name and, like earlier today, he needs Henry's help.

I'm here, Jerry. All you had to do was ask.

"Are you thinking of this as a novel?" Hans asks.

They think about it as a novel, Jerry and Henry together again, the dream team, and that's always been how they've done their best work. "Yes."

"Everything I just told you, if it were a book, what would be happening?"

"It's easy," they tell him, and it is easy. Henry and Jerry—they've always been the master of solving a mystery. How many times has Sandra told them to shut up when they've been at the movies, or watching something on TV, because they were unable to stop sharing their predictions? And this is the mystery to top all of them, and they've always enjoyed a good puzzle.

Jerry pictures it. He puts into words what he and Henry can see. Just how he used to do it, but instead of typing, he's talking. "The crime writer with dementia couldn't find a way to sneak out of a nursing home. Sure, maybe once, perhaps twice, but not more than that. Not when people are trying to keep an eye on him, which means he had help, but then the needle marks suggest he's not being helped but being drugged. He's being sedated and snuck out, then driven into town."

"Why would somebody do that?" Hans asks.

Jerry pictures it. He bounces some ideas back and forth with Henry, and then they settle on one. "He's being snuck into town on the days of the murders. Snuck into town and dumped somewhere. That way there's a pattern. He's not dumped at the first crime scene, because then whoever is doing this can't kill any more women without the perfect scapegoat, because he knows the writer will be caught. He also knows he can't keep doing it forever. He figures he can kill four women. The first three, he dumps the writer at random locations, but on the fourth he leaves him inside the house to wake up and get his prints and DNA all over the place, which is what happens, and the writer thinks he's done it."

There is silence in the car, and he looks over at Hans expecting him to laugh, but Hans doesn't laugh. Instead Hans asks, "So who's the killer?"

"Isn't that obvious?"

"Indulge me."

"Somebody who has access to the nursing home and to the drugs to sedate the patients. Somebody who knows the writer is confessing to crimes. Somebody who hides jewelry in the writer's pockets so the writer will think he took them."

"Somebody from the home," Hans says.

Jerry nods. "Sometimes people say my books are implausible. I remember that."

Hans shrugs. "Most crime novels are. If they weren't, then they'd be no different from real life. People don't want to read about real life."

"This is real life."

"True," Hans says. "But keep thinking of it as a story. Do you remember what Eva told me earlier on the phone?"

"She said one of the orderlies said I'd confessed to him last night that I'd killed somebody."

"Fiona Clark," Hans says. "If somebody is sneaking you out, don't you think it's the same person who says you confessed?"

"Unless I did confess," Jerry says. "I could have confessed because I did it, or I confessed because I saw it in the news and thought I did it."

"In these books of yours," Hans says, "what would be the next step? What would a person in your situation do?"

"Go to the police."

"No he wouldn't," Hans says.

He wouldn't, Henry says. *Come on, be honest here.*

"People never go to the police," Hans says. "They should, but they never do, because if they did then that would be the end of the story, right? It would be wrapped up by chapter three. And anyway, the police would never believe this story. Somebody has been drugging you, Jerry, and I just don't see you walking twenty miles, and I don't see the police worrying about the fact that there are no witnesses who saw you walking all that way. Think about it."

Jerry thinks about it. Both him and Henry. Then they carry on. "In a book the next step would be for the writer to go and see the orderly he confessed to. The same orderly who has access to injections, and who had injected the writer in the past." Jerry remembers something else then. "The same orderly who wants to be a writer."

"Write what you know," Hans says. "How about we reverse that? How about we do what you write and go and pay this guy a visit."

"His name is Eric," Jerry says, "and he might be innocent."

"That's what we'll figure out."

Before they can start to figure it out, a car pulls into the driveway on the other side of the garage door. A moment later two doors are opened and closed. There are footsteps, and then knocking on the door. *If this were a book,* Jerry thinks, *then this would be the police arriving ahead of schedule.*

THE FINAL DAY

Before the gun does its dirty work, there is one more thing to report. This isn't being written down because you think things are going to work out okay, or that Captain A has found a different white whale to chase and doesn't need this vessel anymore, but because when your family looks back at everything, they can understand what it was like. Maybe it can help others. Hard to call it a silver lining, but maybe researchers in the near future might learn something here that can help them map the streets of Batshit County.

You are trying to keep the suicide notes short. One is written and the other is still pending. The written one is full of *I'm sorry* and *I love you*. The person you need to apologize to the most is Belinda Murray.

Sandra came down to the office earlier. She actually knocked before coming in, which is something she always used to do before opening the door, which always made your job feel so *formal* for lack of a better word. She knocked and she came in and sat on the couch. You sat in the office chair with the suicide note hidden beneath the pad you're about to write the second one on. She glanced at the pad then at you.

Have you killed other people? she asked, and she sounded so resigned to the fact there would be more bad news.

No.

But how can you be so sure?

It was a question you've been asking yourself, and you gave her the answer you'd come up with. *Because I'd know.*

So you knew you killed Belinda?

It was a flaw, one you had seen, one you couldn't get around. *No.*

Then how can you sit there and say you've never hurt anybody?

You had no answer, and didn't offer one. Instead you asked a question of your own. *Have you called the police?*

No, she said.

Why?

I'm trying to make a decision. Tell me what you remember.

So you told her. You remembered the speech at the wedding, you remembered coming home and watching it online over and over. Her face tightened into a scowl when you told her you were drinking. You told her about sneaking out the window.

To go and see Belinda, she said.

You shook your head. *Just to go for a walk. To stretch my legs. To find a bar somewhere.*

She looked like she didn't believe that. *And then?*

And then I was back in my office.

Tell me about the shirt, she said.

What?

Your shirt. I checked the laundry and it's not there. I can't find it anywhere. She looked at the floor. *Is it under there?*

You thought about lying, but what was the point? *Yes.*

You hid it, she said.

Yes.

Then why not hide the knife?

Because—

She held her hand up. *I get it. Because you didn't know you'd done it. You found the shirt, but not the knife. That's why I'm not calling the police,* she said, *because I know you weren't in control.*

It was time to ask her the question. *What are you going to do?*

I think the question is what are you going to do?

She stared at you then, and finally you got it. She wasn't deciding whether or not to call the police, she never had been. Sandra was giving you another option, an option that, under the circumstances, shows just how much she still loves you. It was an option you were already in the process of taking, and perhaps she sensed that. You had humiliated her and ruined Eva's wedding, you murdered a young woman, but Sandra was only thinking of you. She was going to allow you to decide what was coming next. Future Jerry, just know that in that moment you have never loved your wife more.

I just need a little time to figure it out, you said, the words slow and even, their unspoken meaning clear, and you never looked away from her and she never looked away from you. *How about you take a walk to clear your head?*

She said nothing for a few seconds. You're sure she already knew what she was going to say, but the silence was appropriate. It gave the moment the final bit of gravitas it needed. Then she said, *I can do that. How long do you need?*

You needed twenty minutes to write the second note. Most of everything else was in order, it was just going to come down to the semantics. You had to choose what you were going to wear, and what kind of mess you were going to make. You pictured how long it would take to line some plastic trash bags around the floor of the office so you wouldn't ruin the resale value of the house. It will be messy, but your office is where you want to do it. You pictured cutting the bags open, laying them flat, and hanging a couple of them on the wall. You pictured drinking one more gin and tonic, then perhaps a second, sitting in the office chair, the doubts, the belief this was going to happen, more doubts, the stereo off, no sound at all, then one giant sound. You're not sure if you'll be thinking of the girl you killed when you pull the trigger, or your family. You'll know soon. You did some quick addition: twenty minutes to place the trash bags and twenty minutes to sit in your chair drinking your drink and coming to the end.

An hour, you said. *I need an hour.*

She stood up. She wasn't crying, but she was close. Her mouth was shaking a little. You walked over to her, and you felt strong. She put her arms out and you stepped into them and wrapped your own around her and she sobbed into your neck and held you tight, and she felt like she's always felt, warm and comfortable, and before Captain A ruined your life you would hug Sandra like that all the time.

I love you, you told her.

She couldn't bring herself to say the words back. She couldn't say anything. Then she was running out of the office and out of the house, leaving you alone.

Completely. And utterly. Alone.

You will never see another person, Future Jerry. Never talk to another person.

Since then you've been busy. You told Sandra an hour, but that didn't allow for the Madness Journal entry, but thankfully other things haven't taken so long. The suicide note was ten minutes. It took fifteen to tape a couple of trash bags to the wall, and there was a tarpaulin in the garage that you've ended up laying across the floor. The mess should be pretty well contained. You also have a pillowcase to put over your head to contain the splatter. Since then you've been writing and ignoring the phone that keeps ringing, because what could you possibly say to anybody calling? Everything is ready to go now, and these words on this page are now nothing but a stalling tactic. It's time, Future Jerry, to put down the pen and conclude this messy affair. What will the bloggers say? The ending was predictable, maybe. From Jerry Grey's first book it was obvious he would blow his brains out in his office.

Still stalling. Sandra will be back in ten minutes. The gun is on the desk. It's heavier than you remember. It's going to make a hell of a sound, but with the office door closed, nobody is going to hear it.

Still stalling.

It's time.

Jerry stays sitting in the car as Hans makes his way inside. The front door of the house is adjacent to the garage, so when Hans opens it Jerry can hear the conversation through the wall. His instinct that the police have arrived early is proven to be correct. They introduce themselves as Detectives Jacobson and Mayor. He's sure they are the same two men who drove him into the police station. They tell Hans he must know where Jerry Grey is.

"What makes you think I know?" Hans asks.

"Because we ran the number he called from the SIM card he purchased, and that led us to you," one of the men says, and that's why they're here so early. Neither Hans nor himself, nor Henry for that matter, made that connection. Jerry figures he's lucky not to be in the back of a patrol car right now. Then he figures that may still happen depending on what Hans says.

"Yeah, he rang me," Hans says, "and yes I picked him up from the mall. He was confused and lost. I rang his daughter and told her he was safe. I was going to take him back to the home, but then she gave us some news to make me realize we needed to head to the police station."

Jerry's heart sinks at the idea of Hans turning him in. Carefully he opens the door, making no sound. The idea he is innocent is taking hold, and he's not going to let these people take that away from him.

"So he's here at the moment then," one of the detectives says.

Hans laughs. "Sorry, guys, but you've jumped the gun on that one. When I told him I was going to take him to you, he hit me when we were stuck at the next set of lights and jumped out of the car. He ran across the road and by the time I was able to turn the car around I couldn't find him."

Paused at the doorway between the garage and the hall, Jerry considers what he's just heard, then slowly makes his way back into the garage.

"So you let him go? That makes you a bad friend," one of the men says, but Jerry is thinking the opposite. The fact Hans isn't betraying him makes him a good friend. The best friend he could have right now.

"No, it makes me a good friend for not hitting him back."

"You knew he was wanted in connection with multiple homicides, and you didn't feel any civic duty to call us and update us?"

"In other words why didn't I do your job for you? Is that what you're asking?"

"What my partner is asking is why are you bullshitting us? We know he's here."

Hans laughs again. "You guys have more of an imagination than Jerry, and if he was here, and you believed it, then it wouldn't be you here, but an armed unit busting down my door."

"So you won't mind if we come in and take a look around?"

"Of course I mind. My parents always told me not to talk to strangers, and that's what you guys are, right? Plus my lawyer would be against it. He would want you to have a warrant because that's the way he thinks. I tell him he's just being pessimistic, but you know, I've been to jail before because the police took advantage of me being such a trusting guy. I'd hate you to come inside and see something out of context and suddenly think the worst. I'm a by-the-book guy, as should you guys be. Do you have a warrant?"

"This isn't a joking matter," one of them says.

"I'm not joking. I'm telling you he isn't here, and you're standing on my property calling me a liar and asking if I mind having my rights violated. Now, I've told you what happened and I've been friendly about it, but now my patience is wearing thin. So, unless you have a warrant, we're done here."

"With your history, mate, you do know you're playing with fire. Harboring a fugitive will see you back in jail."

"He's not a fugitive, he's a confused man who doesn't know what he's done or what he's doing, and right now he probably doesn't even know where he is. Come back when you get a warrant."

"It won't just be us coming back," one of them says, and then Jerry hears the door close.

There are retreating footsteps as the men head back to their car.

He hears one of them say to the other, "I told you we should have just waited. This has gotten too personal for you."

"The son of a bitch broke two of my fingers," the other guy says. "Of course it's personal."

Jerry can't hear the rest as they move out of range. Hans comes into the garage. He puts his finger over his lips to tell Jerry not to say anything. Then he walks to the garage door and listens, but by now the two cops have gotten into their car. They start it, back out of the driveway, and park on the road.

He heads back into the house, beckoning Jerry to follow him.

"If they're parking outside, then they're getting somebody else to take care of the warrant," he says, keeping his voice low.

"I think people are already on their way," Jerry says. "One of them had his hand in a cast, right?"

"That's right."

"I broke his fingers. I think they came here ahead of the others because they want the arrest."

They walk into the dining room, and Hans unlocks the French doors that lead into the backyard. "In that case they'll be here any minute, and if it's the Armed Offenders Unit, they'll be storming the place. You need to run, and right now."

"You're not coming with me?"

"I have things I need to take care of here." He hands Jerry a cell phone. "Climb the back fence and make your way through the neighbors' house to the street. Turn left and when you get to the end of the block turn right. You got that?"

"I got it."

"Say it back to me."

"Over the fence to the street. Turn left, then right at the next intersection."

"Keep walking in that direction and after two hundred yards there's an alleyway. It leads through to a park. Head down there and stay hidden until I call you, okay?"

"What are you—"

"Just do it. Come on, let's go. And if they find you, don't you dare mention me, okay?"

They move quickly across the backyard, where the lawn is ankle deep and the surrounding garden is overrun with stinging nettle and weeds big enough to have developed inch-thick trunks. Jerry climbs the fence and drops to the other side behind a house that has a small inflatable pool, and a sand pit with cat shit littering the top of it. He thinks, he thinks, how did life get to this point? He makes his way around the side of the house and past a tricycle and a soccer ball to the street, breathing heavily already. He turns left and runs like Hans told him to. At the end of the block he turns right and keeps running and finds the alleyway. He's halfway down it when he hears a car approaching. He turns around to see a patrol car passing by, but it doesn't slow down and nobody in the car looks in his direction.

He reaches the park. One of the greatest things about this city, he remembers, is the number of parks. It's why it's called The Garden City, and not because of the amount of people getting buried in vegetable patches. Of course that's the kind of thing Henry would quip about in one of his books. This park has a few people in it, some kids playing on the swings, another one on a merry-go-round, some teenagers smoking by the toilets with their hoodies shading their faces. Henry would quip about that too back in the day.

There are a bunch of trees lining the north side creating shade. He could go hide in there, but if people see him walking in it'll raise suspicion. Then he sees it—a park bench right where lawn meets tree. He makes his way over and sits down. He feels exhausted. He gets the phone out and stares at the screen. He acts like he's texting or checking the weather, the way people do when they're alone in social situations and have a phone handy. His ankles are sore from the stinging nettle. He scratches at them and the relief is instant before getting worse.

The phone rings. "Hans?"

"You at the park?" Hans asks.

"I'm here."

"Good. Stay calm. When the cops are done here, I'll come and get you. I'll have to drive around for a bit to make sure I'm not being tailed, but hopefully I'll be there in an hour or two. Do nothing. Just stay out of sight until I come for you, okay? Stay at the park, okay?"

"Okay," Jerry says.

"Okay?"

"I said okay. I'll sit here and wait for you."

"Good. Don't wander off, Jerry. In fact, why don't you spend your time thinking about where else you could have hidden that journal? It's important we find it."

They hang up. Jerry stares at the phone and he sits in the shade as alone as ever, the police hunting him as his exhaustion grows deeper. He's thinking about Eric the orderly, he's getting a little sleepy, and he's wondering if it's possible Eric has done these bad things. He covers his mouth as he yawns. He tries to think about where else he could have hidden the journal, and there's something there, a memory like a splinter in his brain that he can't quite get to, but instead of focusing on that, he thinks about Eric. He yawns again, then suddenly snaps awake, unaware he was starting to doze. He sits up a little straighter. All he has to do is stay awake and wait for Hans. Then they'll find Eric. He wonders what exactly it is they're going to do to make Eric confess. He starts to doze again, telling himself to hold on, hold on.

THE REPRIEVE

Today is turning into one of the longest days of your life. This latest development is for you, Future Jerry, because you may not be dying today.

It's hard to make sense of. It only unfolded an hour ago. Henry should be the one to tell it, but Henry's job is to create. Your job, Jerry, is to tell it like it is. And here's how it is. . . .

You completed the second suicide note. This one to Eva. The notes were neatly folded into separate envelopes, each one labeled and left on the desk where they couldn't be missed. The trash bags were all taped in place, and you were moments away from Captain A finally having to abandon ship. You were sitting in the office chair looking at the couch wondering if the couch wouldn't be better for what you had in mind, but it would mean shifting the trash bags and that really was just more stalling. Plus it would ruin the couch. No, the office chair would suffice, and really, what did it matter?

You weren't going to use the pillowcase anymore. The idea of being found that way, of the photograph being leaked somehow, that in a few days it would be all over the Internet—Jerry Grey wearing a pillowcase on his head, look what a fool he has become—that was an idea you couldn't stomach. You put the barrel of the gun into your mouth and your teeth scraped against it and you didn't like that feeling either, so you decided to fire through the side of your head instead, and you were going to do it, then you weren't, and then you were. It was like a switch being flicked on and off. Do it, don't do it, do it. You thought about how some suicides fail, how the bullet changes path and rattles around the skull and makes a lot of damage but doesn't kill. You put the gun back into your mouth.

You were looking at the Halloween photograph on your desk of Eva dressed up as a patrol officer from CHiPs when you pulled the trigger, but it was the bloody shirt, the knife, and the dead girl you were thinking about. It was always going to be about the girl.

Nothing happened.

The safety was on.

You were figuring how to turn it off when Sandra burst into the room. You dropped the gun on the desk and stood so quickly the chair rolled back, got caught in a crease in the tarpaulin, tipped over, and snagged the trash bag hanging on the wall behind it and ripped it down.

Thank God, she said, and her clothes were pasted to her body, sweat was dripping down her face and her cheeks were flushed. She was out of breath.

I just need another minute, you told her.

She marched towards you. She looked at the gun, then she took in the plastic bags and the tarpaulin and the horror of it all struck her and actually brought her to a stop. Her expression changed from one of relief to one of horror. Then she started to shake, and she made it to the couch and fell into it as much as she sat into it. She was no longer flushed. She was now ghostly pale. But she was still sweating, even more so, and panting.

I just need another minute, you said, because in that moment it felt like she was upset you hadn't yet followed through with the plan.

She shook her head. *Please, sit down with me*, she said, and when you didn't move, she held her hand out towards you. *Please, Jerry.*

You moved to the couch and sat, but didn't take her hand. You had a mental connection with the gun because of what you almost went through together, and could feel it back on the desk waiting to be included in the conversation.

I had a phone call, she said. *I've been trying to ring you. It's why I ran back. To stop you. I'm . . . I'm so sorry I . . . I shouldn't have left you like that to do . . . to do what you were going to do*, she said, and she started to cry. You wanted to put your hand on her shoulder, wanted to tell her everything was going to be okay, but you couldn't bring yourself to do it. Things weren't going to be okay, and let's not forget, Future Jerry, that by this point in the game she was already screwing the baker and the alarm guys and who knows who else. Right there in that moment when you thought that, you need to know you also thought about the gun. For a second—not even that, but just a microsecond—two things happened. The first is you saw her pinned beneath the baker as he moved inside her, he was wearing his big baker's white hat and it was ringed with sweat, his big baker's white ass in the air. The second thing you saw was the gun, you on one end of it, the other spitting out bullets into Sandra's chest. Two unpleasant thoughts, not even a microsecond, but there nonetheless.

Do you remember Mae?

From one of the books?

No. A few weeks ago you wandered off and got lost and confused and you knocked on her door. It was the house you lived in for a little bit when you were younger. Mae was—

Nurse Mae, you said, and you remembered her. You couldn't remember the trip to the house, but you could remember being there, the tea and the chatting and then Sandra coming and picking you up. It was the day you were trying to dump the can of spray-paint.

That's her, Sandra said, and she sounded pleased you remembered. Hell, even you were pleased. You allowed yourself a moment, a fantasy really, to imagine that the worst of the Alzheimer's was behind you. Ahead were the five stages of getting better. *She called to see how you were doing.*

Why?

Because you went there on Saturday night.

I . . . wait. What?

I want to see the shirt.

Why?

Because I asked.

You pried up the floorboard and showed her the shirt. She didn't look as unhappy as you'd have thought. You balled the shirt up and put it back, and then she explained everything. You can't remember her words exactly. If Prick had been here with his video camera it would now all be up online to refresh your memory, but you can remember the gist of it.

At around three in the morning, Mae was woken up by a knock on the door. She opened it to find you standing there, and out on the street was a taxi you had arrived in. You had no money, and like the last time you had gone to her house, you were confused. She paid the taxi driver then took you inside. She told Sandra she thought about putting you back into the taxi and telling the driver to take you where he had found you, but the problem was she couldn't know for sure where he had found you, or even that you wouldn't just jump out at a red light and run for the hills. You sat at her kitchen table and drank a cup of tea and when she went to call Sandra, you asked her not to. This, of course, was after she explained you didn't live there anymore, which by then you were figuring out. Your reason for not wanting her to call Sandra was simple—and you were able to show Mae just how simple it was by showing her the video of you ruining the wedding and what was left of your life. She agreed then not to call Sandra, but insisted that she call somebody. You told her about Hans. You had your phone. You made the call, and he didn't answer, which was no surprise since it was in the middle of the night, so you left a message.

Mae sat up with you drinking cups of tea and you made small talk. The weather. Life. Music. She said you were fading in and out of the conversation, sometimes animated, other times you'd just stare ahead as if switched off. If any of this is true, Future Jerry, and there is no reason to doubt it, then it's one of those events that didn't cement itself into your memory banks. You were Functioning Jerry in the *off* position, and even though there were some on moments, none of them stuck. Hans called around five a.m. According to Mae, you insisted on meeting him out in the street.

When Sandra told you all of this, you closed your eyes and tried to picture it, and at first there was nothing, but then that changed and you could see yourself climbing into Hans's car, but whether it happened exactly how you saw it, or whether you could imagine it because you've climbed into cars thousands of times, including his, you don't know. If it's true, you certainly don't remember the drive home.

You were with Mae for several hours, Sandra told you. The news says Belinda was killed around three a.m. That's the same time you were knocking on Mae's door. The police keep saying they want to talk to anybody who saw anything that night, and want to talk to anybody who lived on her street who was awake around that time. Three a.m., Jerry, don't you see what that means? If you had killed her before then, Mae would have seen the blood on your shirt. I asked her what you were wearing, and she said the same clothes from the wedding, from the online video. Then Hans picked you up.

You've spoken to Hans? you asked.

Not yet, she said. *Something must have happened after he dropped you off, but whatever that was, it doesn't involve Belinda. She was already dead by then.*

Then whose blood is it?

Sandra went quiet then, because she didn't have an answer. You were picturing the whole cycle again, watching the news, waiting for the phone call, waiting to see who else was dead.

But then Sandra did have an answer. And it made perfect sense. *You haven't spoken to Hans,* she said.

That's right.

Is it possible it's his blood?

You thought about it, as if it were a memory you could recall, but of course it wasn't. Maybe you'd had an altercation, and he had driven away bleeding and . . . was he even still alive?

Jerry?

I don't know. I guess it's possible.

She looked at the trash bags, the tarpaulin, and she started to cry. *I almost didn't make it back in time. I rang and rang, but you didn't answer, and Mae only rang me because she wanted to check in, she said she regretted not ringing me the other night, and if she hadn't . . . or if she had put it off a little longer, then right now you'd . . . you'd—*

You finally reached out to her, placing one hand on her knee and the other on her arm. *But she did ring you, and you did make it home in time,* you said, and you felt relief, but you also felt scared because there was still the matter of the bloody knife and the shirt. Something had happened.

Let's clean this up, then call Hans, she said.

Cleaning up the room was everything in reverse, and it felt weird because hanging up the trash bags and laying out the tarpaulin, well, never during any of that did you think you'd be putting this stuff away. Sandra wasn't able to get hold of Hans, but left a message. She sounded concerned, yet you know she'd have forgiven you if you had hurt him.

Then she went upstairs to freshen up. To get her emotions under control. To process everything that was going on. To change out of her sweaty clothes. That was when your phone rang. It was Hans.

I'm in trouble. I've humiliated my family and I'm the laughingstock of the world, and I've—

People will get over it, Hans said. *You're only one waterskiing cat away from being forgotten about.*

It's worse than that, you told him, and then you poured yourself a drink. You asked him if it were true that he had picked you up. He said yes. You asked if the two of you had fought, if you had cut him, and he said no. You asked if there was blood on your shirt, and he said nothing then, as if he was the one who was having problems remembering. So you asked him again, and then he said yes, there was blood. He said he had asked you about it at the time, but you had no answer. You asked where the knife came from, but he hadn't seen one.

It doesn't line up with what Nurse Mae told Sandra, but somewhere between all that hearsay, and the gin and tonics, the details have gotten lost. But it will get sorted soon. Hans is on his way over.

Henry is trying to say something, but he can't find the words, which is a shame because it feels important. Hopefully Hans and Henry can work together to help figure it out. You asked Hans to bring over another couple of bottles of gin too. Hans will know what to do. Solving problems—that's such a Hans thing.

❧

Jerry is sitting in a taxi handing money over to the driver when his phone rings.

"You okay, buddy?"

The driver looks concerned. He's a big guy whose chest is hanging on his stomach, and whose arms are as thick as Jerry's legs. He has skin tags tagging his neck and sunspots spotting his scalp. To Jerry he looks like a human baked potato.

"I'm . . . I'm okay."

"You sure you're okay?"

Jerry looks out the window. He's outside his house. The phone is still ringing.

"This is where I live," he says.

"Then good job I brought you here," the taxi driver says. "Are you sure you're okay?"

"Yeah, yeah, I'm okay." The driver hands him his change. Jerry looks at his wrist, but he's not wearing a watch. "What's the time?"

"Just after six."

He climbs out of the car. The day is darkening. It's cool too. He looks down at the phone, but doesn't recognize it. Where has he been? Shopping? Visiting friends? The taxi stays where it is while the driver fiddles with something on the dashboard.

Jerry answers the phone. "Hello?"

"I'm on my way."

"Hans?"

"I've got him," Hans says. "I can't believe I'm doing this, but I got him."

"Got who?"

A pause from Hans, and then, "Are you . . . are you okay?"

Jerry looks at his house. Yes, he's okay. He must have wandered, but where he went he doesn't know. What he does know is that lately he hasn't been well. He's been forgetting things. He pats down his pockets, but can't find his keys. Sometimes he climbs out windows and goes where he shouldn't, and if that's what he's just done, then perhaps he can climb back in. He moves up the pathway and around to his office.

"I'm fine," he tells Hans.

"You're still at the park, right?"

"What park?"

"The park where I told you to wait for me."

"I don't remember any park. I'm back home."

"The nursing home?"

"What nursing home?" Jerry asks, though something about that *feels* familiar, but he can't figure out why. He reaches his office. The window is shut and locked. He can see through the window and though everything looks the way it always looks, there is something a little different. The computer looks newer than he remembers, and things are in slightly different places, but for the most part it's how it should be . . . except off a little. "No, I'm back at my house. What park are you talking about?"

"You're back home? At your house?"

"Pretty much."

"What does that mean?"

He makes his way to the front door. Maybe Sandra will be home from work. She's going to give him a hard time, but if he's lucky by the end of the day he will have forgotten. And if she isn't home, there's a spare key hidden in the backyard. Funny how he can remember where the key is, the day they wrapped it in a small plastic bag and hid it in the garden just under the edge of the deck, but he can't remember the last thirty minutes.

Perhaps *funny* is the wrong word.

"Jerry?"

"It means I'm right outside, about to head inside."

"You've remembered where the journal is?"

"You know about that?"

"Listen, Jerry, you need to listen to me very carefully. I want you to stop walking. I want you to stay on the sidewalk. I'm going to come and pick you up."

He's almost at the front door. He searches his pockets again in case the keys are hidden in there somewhere—how many times has he looked for his wallet or keys or phone in a pocket only to have found them there on the second or third time hunting through? He doesn't see what the big deal is with Hans. He also doesn't find the keys. He does find a pair of Sandra's earrings, which seems a little odd.

"Jerry?"

"Yeah, yeah, I heard you, but you're not making any sense."

"Concentrate, Jerry. What do you remember about today?"

He thinks back over the day. He actually can't remember anything. That happens sometimes. His family is worried he's going to mess up the wedding because of it. He knows they're thinking of putting him into care.

"Jerry?"

"I don't remember much," he admits.

"You don't live in that house anymore, Jerry."

"Yeah, right," he says, and then laughs, and then he starts knocking. Nothing funnier than playing a joke on somebody who is losing their mind.

"Are you knocking?" Hans asks.

"I don't have my key."

"Seriously, Jerry, you don't live there anymore. You need to wait for me on the street."

"But—"

"Are the police around? Do you see them?"

"What? Why would there be police here?"

"You live in a nursing home. You've wandered off. You rang me earlier and I came and picked you up from a shopping mall. You don't remember any of this?"

"None of it," Jerry says, annoyed at Hans for still pushing this silly joke.

"You have to—"

"I don't get it," Jerry says. "I'm missing the joke."

"I'm not joking."

"I can see all my stuff through the office window."

"That's not your stuff."

"Ring me back later when you're making sense," he says, then hangs up.

He knocks again, but there's no answer. Either Sandra isn't home or she's in the shower. The phone starts ringing again, but he ignores it. He makes his way to the side gate, noticing that the shrubs they planted last spring have all been torn up and replaced by different ones, a layer of bark put down, a family of garden gnomes guardians to it all. He reaches through and unlatches the side gate, and when it swings open he's staring at a yard that feels slightly out of whack. It takes him a few moments to figure it out, and that's when he notices the pool has gone. When the hell did that happen? He's used to losing things by the pool, but never has he actually *lost* the pool. The garden is different too, but the deck is the same, as are the pavers surrounding it, and he digs his fingers under one and lifts it. The key is still there. He steps up on the deck and opens the bag and at the same time looks through the windows of the French doors into the house. The world tilts further. He doesn't recognize any of the furniture, and there's a large painting on the lounge wall of horses running along a beach that he doesn't remember ever seeing.

Sandra has finally done it, she's kicked him out and the baker has moved in, all the furniture has been replaced, and she didn't even have the decency to let him know. Maybe this is what Hans meant when he said he doesn't live here anymore. He gets the key out of the bag.

"What are you doing here?"

He turns towards the voice. Mrs. Smith has always reminded him of a generic grandmother he'd throw into one of the books for some bad guy to toss down a flight of stairs. "Look, I appreciate your concern," he says, "but I'm fine. And as you can see we've taken care of the gardens. Thanks for stopping by."

That's when he notices there's one thing about her that he's overlooked. She's holding a hockey stick. She has both hands tightly wrapped around the handle, with the heel pointing in his direction. Is this a mugging?

"I've called the police," she says, so this isn't a mugging, and the words trigger a memory, the same woman saying the same thing, and he was sitting in a car when she said it, he was in the passenger seat and they were parked right there on the road, and who was he sitting next to?

"They're going to lock you away for what you've done, for ripping out my roses and setting fire to my car." She adjusts her grip on the hockey stick. "And for spraying that word on my house."

"What are you talking . . ." he says, then the images all come rushing, so many of them at one time it makes him dizzy, so many he can't make any sense of them. He sits down on the doorstep with Mrs. Smith watching him, looking as though she wants to wind up her arms and let loose with that hockey stick.

"Nobody is buying the Alzheimer's bullshit, Mr. Grey, so stop playing that card. You're a no-good, rotten son of a bitch who murders women for fun, and if you—"

"What?"

"If you think that you can sneak back into your old house and—"

"What?"

"And kill the new owners, well, you take one more step and I'll put this through the side of your head." She changes the angle of the hockey stick to make it look more threatening to prove her point. "I made the national side back in my day, so don't think I don't know how to use it."

The national side? At what? Hockey-stick fencing? "What are you talking about?"

"You're rotten inside, Mr. Grey. Mean to the core."

"There is something wrong with you," he tells her. "What kind of person makes up this shit?" Then he realizes he's the kind of person who makes up this shit. He does it for a living. He's a professional liar. A makeup artist.

"You just stay where you are," she says, and prods the hockey stick at him. "Your wife is dead because of you."

"What?"

"You killed her."

Hearing her say that . . . well now, she shouldn't have said it. Shouldn't. Have. Said it. He grabs the heal of the hockey stick in both hands and then it's a tug-of-war between them as he gets to his feet and pushes forward. He's heavier and stronger and younger and madder and he pushes her easily back down the pathway. Her foot goes into the garden off to the side, she stumbles, holding onto the hockey stick to try and keep her balance, and suddenly he realizes what's about to happen. As annoying as she is, the last thing he wants is her falling over and cracking her head open. He tries to keep his grip on the hockey stick to stop her from falling, but she's too heavy, and the stick comes out of his hands. She loses her balance then and topples over, her ass hitting the ground a second before her back, her head hitting a second later, and as he stands there staring at her, he realizes what she said is true—Sandra is dead.

Your name is Jerry Grey, Henry tells him, and he'd forgotten all about Henry, camping out in the back of his brain, there to offer commentary along the way. *You're a crime writer who doesn't live here anymore, your Alzheimer's tips the world upside down and shakes the hell out of it. The police are coming for you, they're coming for you. Oh, also, you shot Sandra.*

But it's Hans that is coming for him, not the police, Hans coming around the side of the house, Hans coming to a stop where Mrs. Smith is making friends with the lawn. She isn't moving.

"What the hell, Jerry?"

"It . . . it was an accident."

"Is she . . . ?"

"I don't know, I don't know."

Hans leans down and checks for a pulse. He has to move his fingers around for a few seconds and tuck them into a wrinkle that makes his fingers disappear to the first knuckle, but then he nods and he looks relieved. "She's still alive. Help me get her up onto the deck."

They get her upright, each holding one of her arms over their shoulders as they lift her onto the deck. The sun loungers there haven't been cleaned after the winter, they're covered in dead leaves and cobwebs and bird crap, but between them they get her laid down on one. "We can't just leave her like this," Jerry says. "It's too cold."

"Why did you come here?" Hans asks. "You've remembered where the journal is?"

"No," Jerry says. "I don't even know why I came here."

"Do you know where it is?"

Jerry nods. "The guy in there has it. The new owner of the house. Gary Somebody. It's in there somewhere. That must be why I came back."

"Then we need to go in and get it," Hans says.

"She called the police," Jerry says, looking down at Mrs. Smith.

"She said that?"

"Yeah."

"Okay, then we don't need to worry about her getting cold because they'll be on their way." He pulls Jerry back in the direction of the street. "If we have to, we can come back later."

They reach the car. It's not the same car Hans was driving earlier. It isn't until Jerry is sitting down and putting on his seat belt that he realizes they're not alone. Eric the orderly is slumped across the backseat, eyes closed and softly snoring.

I DON'T KNOW I. DON'T KNOW.

You don't know what's going on, but Sandra is dead and Sandra is dead and Sandra. Is. Dead.

You must have fallen asleep and when you woke there was a gun in your hand and why is Sandra dead? What happened? You must have shot her because there's a hole in her chest and her body is cool and it must have been a while ago and—

You don't know.

You don't know.

The Madness Journal, now more important than ever to get your thoughts down. Important to write and remember. But write what? You don't.

Know.

What happened.

Jerry doesn't know. Henry doesn't know. Jerry and Henry are similar sounding names and you don't know if you've ever noticed that before but. You must have, really, and Sandra is dead in your office and. She's lying on the floor and. There's blood all around her, it's leaked. From holes. In her chest and her eyes are open. Open, she's staring at me as you write and you.

Don't know what to do. Since the police aren't here it means she was shot in your office and nobody heard anything, which makes sense because that's where she is, that's where the blood is, and.

Think. Think, Jerry.

Think and remember.

What do you remember?

Nothing, but a quick look back into the Madness Journal tells a sorry story of a man taping trash bags to the walls and sitting in the chair and the safety stopping the gun from going off and then Sandra arriving, but you me us we don't remember what you spoke about but it's there in the journal and you've read it and you called Hans, you called

him six hours ago, and the cat died years ago, but you still tried to buy
cat food for it, which was way before the baker fucked Sandra and you
fucked the wedding and you need to call Hans again to see if he did
come around and if he did you need to ask what you spoke about and
you need to know what made you angry enough to.

Shoot.

Sandra.

With the gun you were supposed to shoot yourself with, the gun that
is on your desk within easy reach right now.

Jerry fucked up. Jerry got confused. Jerry . . .

Shut up, Henry, for the love of God, please. Just. Shut. Up.

Your brain feels like it's bleeding. Like it's swelling. Like it's going to
explode. You need to call Hans. He will know what to do. Somebody
writes *bitch-whore* on your letter box? Then call Jerry. But a dead body
you need to make disappear? Well now, Hans is your guy.

But you don't want to dispose of a dead body. What you want is for
this not to have happened. Since it has happened, all that's left is to go
back to Plan A—to shoot yourself in the head *sans* pillowcase.

Have you done this? Have you done this awful thing?

You don't know. Surely you would know if you had. Wouldn't you?

Jerry messed up. Jerry is a coward.

Shut up, Henry.

You need to call the police. You need to.

You don't know. What to.

Do.

You don't.

Know.

You want to wake up and find none of this has happened.

Bad news—Sandra is dead.

Bad news—Sandra is dead.

❧

"What the hell?" Jerry says.

"I'll explain on the way."

"On the way to where?"

Hans starts the car. They leave Mrs. Smith and her neighborhood—Jerry's old neighborhood—behind, the houses flicking by, houses he used to see every day but can no longer remember.

"What do you remember?" Hans asks.

"Five minutes ago none of it, but now I remember most of it, starting with waking up today in that woman's house. I remember finding the park you told me to go to, and waiting for you. I . . . ah, hell, I think I must have fallen asleep. Then next thing I knew I was at my old house."

"I spoke to you a few times," Hans says. "I thought the police might be tailing me, and I figured it was too risky to come and pick you up right away. I went online. The nursing home has a website because everything has a website, and aside from telling the world what they do, the site also tells the world who is doing it. They have a whole section with the staff there, including brief biographies. There was only one Eric there. I called you back and you were even more determined to question the guy. The way you were explaining it . . . it was making sense. Made sense to at least talk to the guy, right? But it made even more sense to go through his house when he wasn't there, and see what I could find."

"So why is he in the back of the car?"

"Because it didn't work out as planned," Hans says, and does it ever? Certainly not in any of Jerry's books, Jerry thinks. "After getting his name online, a phone book gave me his address. Then I gave a buddy of mine a call. I drove to the mall, and I go in and meet him in the bathroom and give him my car keys, and he gives me his, and two minutes later he's pulling the fire alarm. Everybody ends up moving outside, and in the sea of people I get rid of anybody following me. I head out into the parking lot and then I drive to Eric's in my buddy's car. This, by the way, is Eric's car."

Hans says it all so matter-of-factly, as if this is the norm, and Jerry guesses for Hans maybe it is. He glances back over at Eric. There is duct tape holding his hands behind him, and more duct tape covering his eyes.

"It's not as bad as it looks," Hans says, and Jerry isn't so sure. He's also feeling less sure about the whole idea Eric could be guilty. "I gave him a shot, probably similar to the stuff he's been giving you," Hans says.

"So how did you go from wanting to search his house to having him sedated in the back of his own car? What happened?"

"What happened is I knocked on his door and I figured, you know, if he answers I can ask him some of those questions."

"And he answered?"

"No. Which made me figure he wasn't home."

"You broke in?"

"Of course I did. I go inside, thinking that if he's a writer, he probably has an office, and an office is a good place to start looking. Only he's in there on his computer with a set of headphones on. He hadn't heard me. He sees me, and he recognizes me right away because I've been to see you at the nursing home a number of times, and—"

"You came to see me?"

"Of course I did, buddy. Back to the point, Eric sees me because his desk is facing the door, and he jumps to his feet, and because he knows who I am he does the addition very quickly and figures out why I'm there. Or at least he thinks he knows. He doesn't even say any-thing, but he throws a coffee cup at me, then comes charging at me. He doesn't even get a shot in," Hans says, smiling at Jerry. "Before I knock him onto his ass. He looks up at me, and he looks angry, and worried, and I tell him I'm there because he killed those girls. He tells me he has no idea what I'm talking about. I tell him I know he was framing you, but he shakes his head and tells me I'm making a mistake. He tells me you're a psychopath, so then I kick him in the head. He's out cold and I'm getting ready to tie him up when I notice his wedding ring."

"He's married?"

"Yeah. There are photographs on the walls of his house to prove it. So I figure the best thing to do is get the hell out of there. I tidy up the mess so the wife won't think bad thoughts the moment she gets home, then I drag him through to his car and throw him in the back. I don't want him to wake up, so I head to my car because I have a couple of shots in there—"

"Shots?"

"Shots to make sure he stays asleep."

"Your buddy had them in his car?"

"No. I took them with me. They're there for option number three, remember? One shot puts you to sleep, and that's all I gave Eric. But enough shots . . . well, you go to sleep and you stay asleep. I give Eric one, and I'm on the way to pick you up from the park when I phone you. That's everything. Now we have to go somewhere and question him."

Jerry isn't sure what to say. It all seemed like a good plan back when Hans and Henry were bouncing around ideas the same way Henry would bounce around ideas with his editor. It all seemed possible at the time, but seeing Eric unconscious in the backseat changes the game in a similar way it would if Jerry walked into his publisher's office dragging in a dead prostitute and a serial killer and pitched the plot for his next book. There is a world of difference, Jerry thinks, between making shit up and making shit happen.

"Jerry? Earth to Jerry?"

"Yeah, I'm still here," Jerry says.

"You zoned out."

"I'm okay."

"He's guilty, right?" Hans asks.

"Is he?"

"He's the one who told the police you confessed to him. And somebody drugged you, right? It's either that—or you really did sneak out of the home and walk twenty miles to single out a woman you had never met. Plus he knew. The moment he looked at me, he knew he'd been found out."

"What if he wakes up?"

"He won't," Hans says. "Not yet."

"How can you be so sure?"

"I just know."

"So where are we going?"

"I know a place," Hans says, and of course he does.

The day is getting darker. Even though he doesn't like Mrs. Smith, he hopes somebody has found her already. At the end of the month daylight saving time will kick in and the days will get longer, but right now there isn't much light past six thirty. Hans has to turn on the headlights. Traffic isn't too bad because rush hour was over an hour ago. The quality of the neighborhoods degrades the further they go, until they enter one in which every fence is tagged and the sidewalks have cracks with more weeds pushing through than there is grass on front lawns. They park out front of a two-story house that has no front garden, just a huge slab of concrete taking up the entire yard, patches of oil scattered across it, a hopscotch layout created by duct tape in the center. There's a *For Sale* sign nailed to the fence that must be fresh since there's no graffiti on it, or maybe there's an amnesty on *For Sale* signs. The amnesty doesn't stretch to the rag doll that has been nailed beneath the sign, a roofing nail going through the middle of the doll's face, giving her a metal nose the size of a quarter.

"Wait here," Hans says, and he turns off the headlights before getting out of the car. Then he leans back in. "I mean it, Jerry. I'm only going to be gone a minute, but don't wander off, okay?"

"Is that meant to be a joke?"

"It was meant to be, but halfway through it stopped being funny."

Hans walks up to the front door reaching into his pocket along the way, then he's in the dark and Jerry can't see what he's doing, but he knows his friend is most likely picking the lock, something he's always thought is a cool trick for his characters, but something he'd never be able to do in real life.

You can do it, Henry says, and Jerry decides it's neither here nor there.

A minute later Hans is heading back. He's wearing a pair of thin leather gloves. He glances at the doll on the fence, and Jerry wonders if he's conjuring up the same kind of images that Horror Book Henry would have thought back in the days when fiction and nonfiction were two completely different things. In another universe, that doll could pull the nail out of its own face and carry on doing what it was doing before somebody assaulted it.

It's awkward getting Eric out of the back of the car. He's heavier than Mrs. Smith, and Jerry is sure he'll have a sore back tomorrow from all this lifting. But they get Eric upright, and then they get him up the driveway and past the wide open door and into a hallway. Before lifting him, Jerry took Eric's glasses off and put them into his pocket for safekeeping. It's dark inside and Hans manages to point his cell phone light ahead as they walk, giving Jerry a brief rundown along the way.

"Used to be a drug house," he says. "It was just small-time stuff, mostly just a couple of guys selling weed to partying teenagers, but the guys were informants for the police, so the police let them do their thing as long as their thing didn't go beyond that, but of course it went beyond that because they got into some beef with another couple of guys a few blocks away, and next thing you know the average life expectancy in the neighborhood drops substantially. Nobody wants to buy in this neighborhood, and nobody wants to buy a house where a couple of dealers got themselves nailed to a wall, and the cops never did find their dicks." Jerry looks concerned, and Hans laughs. "Don't worry, I'm kidding. They did find them. Anyway, that shit was months ago, and nobody ever comes by here, and the police have no reason to. Not while it's empty. Come on, let's get this guy upstairs."

There is no furniture in the house, nothing to try and avoid, no rug to trip on. They get to the stairs and it's a tight squeeze and Jerry's not sure what the difference is going to be upstairs compared to downstairs when it comes to questioning somebody, but there must be something significant to be going through all of this. He thought by now they'd have Eric strapped into a chair with a knife to his throat, but there are no chairs and no knives.

Upstairs smells like cat piss and the air is stale. Every wall he looks at he can imagine two men nailed to it. They dump Eric on the landing because they're both too exhausted to drag him further. Jerry starts to wonder if this is one of those moments when he's actually in the *off* position, Functioning Jerry who can't seem to store any memories, Functioning Henry who is calling the shots.

"You okay, buddy?" Hans asks, puffing a little.

"No," Jerry says. "None of this is okay. Now what?"

"Now we get him to talk."

"And just how are we going to mange that?"

"We hang him out the window."

"You're kidding, right?"

"It's the easiest way."

"You've done it before?"

"I've seen it done," Hans says.

"In real life?"

"In movies," Hans says. "It always works."

"But won't he just tell us what we want to hear if we do that? It won't count, right? I'd confess to anything if it'd stop me from getting dropped on my head."

"Then we make him tell us something only the killer would know."

"And what if he isn't the killer? What if I really am?"

"Then if you're a killer, you shouldn't be feeling too bad about this, right?"

Jerry hates how that statement makes perfect sense.

"Look at where we are, Jerry. Look at the situation we're in. You're lucky the taxi driver earlier didn't figure out who you were. You're a wanted man who is running out of time, and if you're to be believed, an innocent man. If you don't want to do this, then fine, we take Eric back home and drop you off with the police and you won't get to look for your journal and you'll plead guilty and Eva will continue to never want to speak to you, and the police will blame you for every unsolved crime over the last thirty years. Or we trust your gut, and we question him."

Jerry doesn't know what to say.

"The clock is ticking," Hans says. "Are we doing this or not?"

Jerry nods. The decision made.

They drag Eric into the nearest bedroom. Houses always look sad when they're empty, Jerry thinks, and this house looks so sad he feels like they ought to put it out of its misery by torching it when they leave. There is wallpaper hanging from the walls and large stains in the carpets and funny-shaped circles of mold on the ceiling. He can't imagine what a real estate agent would say as a selling point—unless they listed it as an *ideal home for the budding pyromaniac*. The bedroom is facing south, over the backyard, where there is very little in the way of light, but just enough to see the backyard has been paved in concrete too. Jerry guesses the previous owner hated gardening. Hans unlocks the window, then has to shoulder it upwards because it's swollen in the damp air. Eric is still unconscious, and he's still wearing his orderly clothes from the home. Seeing him here is so out of context but not enough to jar Jerry back into the world of rational thought, because surely he can't be there now.

"We wake him up, and then we hang him outside," Hans says, and he takes the tape off Eric's eyes, but leaves the one over his mouth. "We let him get a good look around, and then we drag him back in. I'll slap him around a little, and we don't ask questions, what we do is we give him statements. We don't say *Did you kill those girls?* What we say is *We know you killed those girls*. Got it?"

"I got it," Jerry says, his stomach turning at the thought, but not turning as much as Eric's will be.

"Don't drop him," Hans says.

"I won't."

"And I want you to keep thinking about where you hid your journal, okay?"

"I'm trying."

"Then try harder."

"It doesn't work like that," Jerry says.

"You ready?"

"As ready as I'll ever be."

Hans wraps duct tape around Eric's ankles, pinning his feet together. Then from his pocket he pulls out a small vial. "Smelling salts," he says. "Trust me, Jerry, everything is going to be okay," he says, and he opens the top and waves the vial under Eric's nose.

DAY SOMETHING

You need to start trusting yourself. You are Jerry Grey, you are not a killer. Unless you killed your wife. And the florist. And, now that you think about it, just how did your cat die six years ago?

Today is the WMD plus something, and the day of Sandra's death plus one. You spent last night not phoning the police. You spent last night sitting on the floor in Sandra's blood, holding her hand as she got colder and colder. Your clothes soaked up her blood, and you had to shower and change earlier because you couldn't stand it any longer, and when you came back she was exactly where you had left her. You were hoping—well, it's obvious what you were hoping for.

Spending all night watching over Sandra, you thought mostly of how your actions had tainted all the good times you'd had. Your amazing life together, the passion with which you loved her. You poisoned all of that by taking away her future. You wondered what the future without her would be. The answer was simple—it would be empty. And Eva? The news will destroy her. Days after tying the knot, she has to go to her own mother's funeral. She will never talk to you again. You hope her anger towards you doesn't cloud the way she sees the world, that it doesn't darken her music.

And of course you wondered about Hans. About Nurse Mae. The discrepancy between what they told Sandra. There are answers you need, but how can you look for them when you don't even know the right questions?

You need to call the police but not yet. Aside from holding Sandra's hand, you've also been reading the journal. There are things in here you simply can't remember. Not just things when you were in the *off* position, like showing up at the old house or at the florist's, but other things too—like forgetting you had lost the gun, forgetting about asking Doctor Goodstory what else we could do.

Before Sandra died, she asked if you had spoken to Hans, and you said no, but you had spoken to him. You'd called him the day after the wedding. He'd said *There's no point in worrying about something you can't know about.*

Worry if you learn more, but until then, just try to act normal.

You had even forgotten about Counselor Beverly, who spoke to you about the stages of grief.

You haven't forgotten the wedding speech.

You still have no memory of the night after you snuck out your window, but the things that didn't make sense a few entries ago still don't make any sense now.

Where did the knife come from?

Did you have blood on your shirt and Nurse Mae missed it, or was Hans mistaken about that? It doesn't seem like the kind of thing anybody, let alone Hans, would overlook. Either something happened between you walking out the door of Nurse Mae's house and climbing into Hans's car, or . . .

Now there are more questions. Why shoot Sandra? You don't remember shooting her, is it possible you didn't? But you don't remember spray-painting *the* bad word across Mrs. Smith's house, and you obviously did that, so there's no denying the fact you do things and then forget. It's all part of the Alzheimer's package.

The phone rang before and you let the machine get it. It was Eva. *Hi Mom, hope you're doing okay, just checking in before we leave for Tahiti tomorrow. We'll try and head over in the morning to say bye.*

She sounded so happy, like her life was just beginning. She and Rick are going away on their honeymoon tomorrow and you can't let them know what's happened. Not yet. Let them enjoy their week.

It means not calling the police.

You can do that. For Eva.

You'll call her back tonight and say you're busy tomorrow, that Sandra is taking you to check out a couple of nursing homes, and to make sure they call when they get to where they're going.

Good news—it's doubtful there will ever be good news again.

Bad news—Sandra is dead. You can't fix that in the rewrite.

✦

The smelling salts work. Eric opens his eyes and there's a muted sound of coughing that can't quite make it past the duct tape. He looks confused. He squints against the light and twists his head away from the light of the cell phone. He starts to fight the duct tape holding his hands behind his body. He starts squirming on the ground.

Hans punches him in the stomach. Hard. There's a sharp intake of air through Eric's nose. Jerry always thought his friend would be capable of something like this, but seeing it happen makes his own stomach clench.

"Calm down," Hans says, then gives Eric a small slap. "Calm down."

Eric can't calm down, but he manages to stop coughing and he manages to stare at his two captors without struggling. He doesn't manage to hide the fear in his face.

"You know what we want," Hans says. "First there's something we ought to show you."

They get Eric to his feet. The orderly tries to struggle, but the duct tape is keeping the fight to a minimum. They stand him against the window so he can face out, then Jerry realizes Eric probably can't see much at all. He takes the orderly's glasses out of his pocket and puts them on Eric's face.

"You're obviously a bright guy," Hans says. "You've proven that by getting away with murder. Since you're bright, you must be able to figure out what's going to happen if we throw you out the window, which we're willing to do, unless you tell us about the women. First some facts. We're two stories high, and if you survive landing on your head from that height you're going to wish you hadn't. Second, when we take the tape off your mouth, you're going to have the urge to scream. I would advise against that. We're in the kind of neighborhood where people are used to hearing screams. Maybe one of them will call the cops, maybe not. What's doubtful is somebody rushing over to help you. What's doubtful are the cops getting here in the time it takes for you to travel from the window to the patio. Do you understand what you're being told?"

Eric nods. They turn him so his back is to the window. The whole time his eyes are wide, *bugging out of his head* is perhaps how Henry would describe it if Henry was in one of his less original moods, Jerry thinks. Or *as big as saucers* if Henry was being a lazy prick.

"We know you killed the girls," Hans says, and Eric looks confused, or at least is trying to look confused. Jerry studies his face, his features, looking for recognition and understanding, but all he sees is fear and uncertainty.

"We know you injected my friend here," Hans says, and flashes the cell phone light in Jerry's direction for a second. Now Eric looks even more confused. Hans carries on. "We know you snuck him out of the nursing home. Now, I'm going to take the tape off your mouth and you're going to answer me—if you don't tell us what we want to know, we're going to drop you. Okay?"

Eric, who is shaking his head through the last bit of Hans's speech, now starts nodding. Hans removes the tape, and the moment he does Eric draws in a deep breath and starts to cough. A few seconds later he gets himself under control.

"I don't," he says, and then coughs a little bit more. "I don't know what you're talking about."

"Are you sure?" Hans asks.

"I'm positive."

"I mean are you sure that's the way you want to play it? We know you set up Jerry here."

"You injected me," Jerry says.

"Of course I injected you! You were getting out of control. We had to calm you down!"

"You've injected me more than once," Jerry says.

"We often have to inject you."

"Then how does he escape if he's been sedated?" Hans asks.

"I don't know," Eric says, his voice breaking a little. "Nobody knows. But the days he escapes he's not sedated, and last night, well, it must have worn off."

"You hear that?" Hans asks.

"Hear what?" both Eric and Jerry say at the same time.

"A reason to toss you out the window," Hans says. He spins Eric around so he's facing the view outside again.

"But—"

Eric doesn't get to finish the sentence, because right then Hans punches him in the side of the face, a fast, hard jab that rocks Eric's head sideways and knocks his glasses off, the hit echoing through the room, bringing an extra layer of reality to a day that has been unbelievable and way too real for Jerry all at the same time. Blood flows from Eric's nose. Jerry wants to say something, but isn't sure what. He wants his friend to dial it back, but this is the way things get done. This is how you get the facts from bad people, and those who don't stay committed only get lies and half-truths. He crouches down and grabs Eric's glasses and puts them back on for him.

Hans puts the duct tape back over Eric's mouth then pushes his head through the open window. Eric struggles at first, then relaxes as more of his body is pushed through, a struggle at this point only doing him more harm than good. His face bangs against the building as they lower him, his body dragging over the windowsill, bumping and slowing as different body parts grip against it. Then he's all the way out, Hans holding one leg, Jerry the other, both of them straining at the effort required.

"He's facing the wrong damn way," Hans says.

"I'm sure he still gets the point," Jerry says, struggling for breath.

"We should try and turn him."

"How?"

"How about—" Hans says, but it's how about nothing, because Jerry loses his grip on Eric, then with all that extra weight Hans loses his grip too, and then Eric is falling, the distance covered so quickly he reaches the concrete before Jerry is even aware of what's just happened. Eric's sudden fall ended by his sudden stop, and Jerry wonders if this is one more death that will be filed away on his things-to-forget list, whether tomorrow he'll be denying this to himself, perhaps the same way he's been denying everything else.

DAY TWO WITHOUT SANDRA

You slept upstairs last night. It felt like a betrayal leaving Sandra downstairs, but you couldn't spend another night on the floor next to her. You just couldn't. You didn't sleep well, just in fits and starts, and you lost count of how many times you reached across the bed, needing to find Sandra asleep and okay and not being able to. When you went into the office this morning, you went with the hope she wouldn't be there, that she would be cooking breakfast or reading a book. But of course she was there, she's still here. You sat on the floor next to her and spun the chamber in the gun around and around, thinking about putting it to your head and pulling the trigger, but never getting close.

The alarm guys came to the house yesterday. At least you think it was them. There was knocking from the front door a few times that you ignored. They eventually went away. Last night you called Eva and gave her the *We're busy looking at nursing homes* line, and she wished you the best of luck. The moment you call the police you will lose her.

You are in limbo now, just spending the hours imagining your life without Sandra. But that was your future anyway, wasn't it? So here's what's going to happen, Madness Journal. This will be Past Jerry's final entry before being shipped off to jail, his final few lines before calling the police later today. Or tomorrow. The longer the wait, the more time Eva can have thinking the world is okay.

So, what to say to the police? Say nothing. Don't tell them anything. If this is all you remember, Future Jerry, then remember this: don't tell them about Belinda, about the shirt, the knife, about Hans. It's their job to figure out what happened, and if you lay all the evidence out there for them, they won't look beyond it. You'll go from Jerry Grey Crime Writer to Jerry Grey Death Row Inmate. You'll be a scapegoat. They're not going to believe you had nothing to do with Belinda Murray's death, and they'll shape the evidence around Nurse Mae's statement. They'll say the timeline was off, that you were there earlier or Belinda died later. You've written about this world long enough to know how it works.

Say nothing, Future Jerry. Say nothing.

Who knows, in another month or two maybe you'll have forgotten all about this.

Final words?

Stop writing what you know.

And fake the rest.

They run downstairs, each of them stumbling, Jerry tripping into Hans, Hans tripping into Jerry, more good luck than anything else keeping them upright as Hans's cell phone lights the way. When they get to the bottom they don't actually know where to turn. They don't know the layout of the place. Hans makes the decision and Jerry follows. They head into what turns out to be the dining room, then the lounge, no furniture to bang their knees into. From the lounge there's a sliding door to the backyard. Both men are breathing heavily. Neither has said a word. They stick to that tradition as Hans twists the lock and opens the door.

Because Eric's hands were tied behind him, he never had the chance to try to use his arms to break his fall. There is no need to check for a pulse. Jerry can feel something rise up in his stomach.

"Hold it in, Jerry," Hans says.

Jerry takes a deep breath. He tries to hold it in. But he can't. He turns and vomits against the side of the house. He can still hear the sound Eric's head made when it hit the pavement, can feel that sound vibrating around the bones in his body, like biting heavily on a ball bearing and cracking a tooth. He wipes his sleeve over his mouth. His hands are shaking, and then he realizes his legs are shaking. His arms too. Everything is shaking. This is what it is like to have killed a person. If he's done this before, surely he'd recognize the feeling. This is new to him.

"Why the hell did you let him go?" Hans asks.

"Don't put this on me," Jerry says. "It's not like I have experience at this kind of thing. This is why in movies the guys doing the holding look like bodybuilders."

"All you had to do was hold on."

"Well dangling him outside the window was a stupid idea."

"Yeah? You want to carry on doing this alone?" Hans asks. "You think you're better off without me?"

"No, of course not," Jerry says. "I just didn't know we were going to be killing anybody. We just murdered him, Hans."

"Damn it, Jerry, I know that, okay? But before you head to church to confess, just remember what he did. He killed those women and framed you for it."

"But we don't *know* that," Jerry says, "not for a fact, and even if that is true who the hell is going to believe us, huh?"

"Come on, let's go," Hans says.

"And what? Just leave him out here?"

"We need to make use of the time we have," Hans says. "Soon his wife is going to start wondering where he is, then she's going to start phoning around, and in a few hours she'll probably be calling the police. They're going to make the connection pretty quickly since both of you have gone missing," Hans says.

"We can't just leave him like this," Jerry says. "It's not right."

"There's no point in dumping him anywhere," Hans says. "We're going to have to admit to what happened, but once the police figure out the kind of man he really was, then that'll go in our favor. Plus it was an accident."

"I don't mean dumping him anywhere," Jerry says. "But we can't just leave him out here on the patio. It's not right."

"None of this is right," Hans says, then he disappears inside.

Jerry leans up against the house because the ground is swaying. He crouches down and tries to be sick again, but there's nothing, just bile. When Hans comes back he's carrying a shower curtain. They roll Eric into the shower curtain, his body making clicking sounds as broken bones roll over each other. Jerry picks Eric's broken glasses off the ground and puts them in Eric's hand. When they've turned him into a cocoon they try to lift him. The wrapped feet keep slipping out of Jerry's grip and hitting the ground. Somehow the dead man feels heavier than he did five minutes ago. Jerry fills his hands with layers of plastic rather than trying to scoop them under the body. This time they get Eric inside and they lay him gently on the floor, and he doesn't go *oomph* because he can't make those noises anymore. No matter what is real and what isn't, Jerry just killed a man.

Hans uses his phone to light their way back through the house. They don't say anything as they walk out the front. Hans closes the door behind him and the lock latches back into place. They walk casually to the car and climb casually in and then casually drive out of the street—nothing to see here, nothing going on, no sir, no ma'am, just two law-abiding citizens out for a drive after casually dropping somebody to their death.

The tension builds in the car as they drive. Jerry can't tell whether Hans is going to take him right to the police or hang him out a different window all by himself. In fact he has no idea where Hans is going. It's creeping up to eight o'clock and there isn't much to see in the way of life on the streets. They drive for fifteen minutes and Jerry watches the houses and the cars parked out front and the occasional person wandering along, and he craves all of it. He wants to wrap himself up in that life, the normality of thinking about dinner and TV and the onslaught of bills. He wants to be Jerry Grey back before Captain A steered him into the dark.

"We're here," Hans says.

"Where?"

"Eric's house," Hans says, turning the car into the driveway. He presses the button on the remote to open the garage door. "We're committed, buddy, and we've come too far to turn back now."

"You're kidding."

"How long have we known each other?" Hans asks.

"Honestly, I have no idea. I don't even know how old I am," Jerry says, but as soon as the words are out an answer comes to him. He's forty-nine. One year short of the big midlife crisis.

"You're fifty," Hans says, and the news is almost as upsetting as any other he's had today. "In that time, have you ever known me to kid?"

"Honestly, I can't remember that either."

Hans laughs at that. "God I wish that was a joke. Come on, let's start looking around."

"Didn't you say he was married?"

"I did, but look—do you see any lights on? And there's no other car in the garage. Come on."

"Doesn't mean she isn't home."

"The house is empty," Hans says.

"How can you be so sure?"

"I can just tell. It's like a secret power."

"But isn't that what you thought earlier when you first came here only to find Eric inside?"

"It's a secret power that is occasionally wrong. Like I said, Jerry, we're committed."

They drive into the garage. Hans pushes the button to close the door behind them.

"So what's the plan?" Jerry asks.

"The plan is we don't mess things up," Hans says.

"And if the wife is home?" Jerry asks.

"Then that will be a problem," Hans says, "but thankfully we have these," he says, and pops open the glove box and pulls out the leather pouch with the syringes inside.

"Good thing you brought them along."

Hans shakes his head. "These aren't mine. I found them in here earlier. They're Eric's. They're what he sedated you with. No reason for him to have them in his car, right?"

"He had his car yesterday," Jerry says, "when he came to the house."

"And he should have returned them to the nursing home, but he didn't, because they are for his own personal use."

"What if we use one on his wife and she's allergic to it, or we over-dose her?"

"That's not going to happen."

"How can you be so sure?"

"So what do you want to do, Jerry? Nothing? Go to jail and let the world think you killed those women when it was Eric? The chances are she's not even home, and the longer we sit in the car debating it, the closer she's getting. We could have been in and out by now. Come on, we have to go in and prove he did these things."

"And what if he didn't?"

"Then we just killed an innocent man. There's no point in holding back. We're so far down the rabbit hole that it doesn't really matter how much deeper it gets."

They move into the house, the internal door bringing them into a hallway. Hans flicks on a light. Jerry notices his friend is still wearing gloves. "See? I told you it was empty."

"Shouldn't we leave the lights off?"

"Why? Eric was supposed to be home, right? It'd be weird if the lights weren't on."

"Yeah, I guess."

"You go search the study," Hans says. "I'll start elsewhere."

The study is the first room on the left. There's a bookcase on the wall and Jerry's books are there, plus those of others, a bunch of authors Jerry has met and had drinks with at festivals, a bunch of true crime novels, some how-to and tips on writing. There's a desk facing them. It's solid wood with scars and scratches and dents. It looks old, all that character beaten into it over the last hundred years. Behind the desk is an office chair on wheels, and on top of the desk a computer, a printer, a couple of novels, a bottle of water, a phone, and a printed out manuscript. On top of the manuscript is a snow globe a little bigger than a baseball, a castle on the inside of it, the flecks of glitter lying prone on the bottom. The room is carpeted, which makes it unlikely there are any hiding spaces beneath the floorboards, but he still kicks at it anyway, listening for something that might give, but there's nothing.

He sits in Eric's chair. He starts with the drawers. There are some magazines, some office supplies, some bank statements. No jewelry, no strange porn or photographs of neighbors through windows. He picks up the manuscript. It's bulky. It's been many books since he last printed out a manuscript. He used to do all his editing and reading on the computer. He figured he was helping save the environment.

He reads the first few pages.

Are you kidding me? Henry asks, and Jerry is thinking the same thing.

By the time he gets to the end of chapter one, his heart is pounding in his chest. He wants to scream. He wants to go back to where they left Eric and shake him from the collar and ask him why he would do this. He carries the manuscript through the house until he finds Hans in the garage, where he's searching a set of shelves that are home to paint trays and brushes and sandpaper.

"Jesus, you look like somebody just walked all over your grave," Hans says.

Jerry holds up the manuscript. "This opening chapter," he says, struggling to keep his voice even, a struggle he loses, "is about a crime writer who has Alzheimer's." He waits for the appropriate reaction from Hans, which he doesn't get, because he thinks Hans should be throwing things across the garage. He carries on. "This guy, this guy starts confessing to crimes that he thinks he's committed."

"So you inspired him."

"I more than just inspired him!" Jerry says, and starts shaking his head, annoyed Hans is acting like it's no big deal. Dropping Eric on his head doesn't make him feel as bad as it did a few minutes ago. "He's taken all the bad shit that's happening to me and used it to try and get a book contract."

"There anything in there about sneaking into people's houses and framing the author?"

It's a good point. Jerry's anger subsides as he thinks about it, then his heart starts to race with the possibility. There could be some answers in here. "I'll keep reading," he says, then looks at the beginning of chapter two. He reads a couple of paragraphs while leaning against the doorframe. Hans watches him.

"Oh no," Jerry says.

"What?"

"Give me a minute," Jerry says.

"Jerry—"

"A minute."

He reads the chapter. Hans moves to the next shelf along. A few minutes later Jerry turns the manuscript towards his friend. "Look," he says. "Look!"

"What am I looking at?" Hans asks, coming over.

Jerry points to the chapter heading. It says "Day Who Knows." He's looking at a chapter entry set in a nursing home. The entry is in the form of a diary. The main character is keeping a Madness Journal. The main character's name is Gerald Black, and Gerald has no idea how long he's been in the home. However, Gerald's words sound exactly like Jerry's. In fact so much like Jerry's own words that he knows they are his own. He has written them, but he doesn't remember when. The sense of betrayal is so strong he feels like tossing Eric out the window all over again.

Hans takes the manuscript and reads. "This is you," he says.

Jerry starts pacing the garage. "Eric has my journal."

Hans looks up from the pages. "What?"

"Those are my words. I recognize them. Somehow he got hold of my journal, and he's been using it to create that," he says, nodding towards the manuscript.

Hans reads for a few more seconds, then looks back up at Jerry. "Are you sure?"

"It's the ultimate *Write what you know*," Jerry says. "It must be here somewhere." He closes his eyes and puts his fist against his forehead. He taps it lightly a few times. "I must have had the journal all along at the home. I don't know. It doesn't make sense. But those are my words," Jerry says, pointing at the manuscript. "Not all of them, not whatever is stringing the plot together, but some of them. Somehow Eric got hold of it."

"How? If the police couldn't find it, how did he?"

"I don't know. All I know is that he has it."

Hans hands him back the manuscript. "Okay, so the orderly took your journal and used it for his story, and if it's here we need to find it."

"And proof that he's a killer," Jerry says.

"That's what we're looking for. But we really need that journal. If he's taking it back and forth from the nursing home," Hans says, "it could be in his car. I'll give it a thorough search."

Hans opens the car and starts going through it. Jerry heads back down to the study. He sits behind Eric's desk. He switches on the computer. While it's booting up, he goes through the closet where there are some clothes hanging and some boxes on the ground. He starts pulling them out. He hears Hans walking down the hallway back towards him. He opens one of the boxes to find a bunch of bank and mortgage statements.

"Who the hell are you?"

It's a woman's voice, and it startles him, and he turns towards it. He's never seen her before, but he knows it has to be Eric's wife. Before he can answer, Hans steps in behind her and pushes a needle into the side of her neck. She doesn't even have time to struggle. It only takes a couple of seconds, and then she's asleep, Hans lowering her gently to the ground.

"Holy shit," Jerry says, jumping to his feet.

"She'll be fine," Hans says. "But look what I found," he adds, and he tosses a book towards him. Jerry catches it and opens it up. It's a journal, but not his Madness Journal. Only in some ways it is. There are no eyes on the cover.

"It starts from your time in the nursing home," Hans says. "Which means the original is still out there, and we still really need to find it."

DAY WHO KNOWS

Some days I know who I am, I wake up and I know where I am and what's going on, and the nurses here call that a good day. The irony is the good days are full of bad memories. I think I prefer the bad days. When everybody is a stranger, when I forget my family, then I forget what brought me in here. I can forget what I have done.

Today I know. Today is a good day. My name is Jerry Grey and this is my journal. The nursing home, this disease, they are my penance.

There's an orderly here by the name of Eric. He suggested a journal might help with my condition. I have Alzheimer's and it's been advancing quickly. They tell me when I first got here six months ago I would know who I was six days a week and on the seventh my mind would take a rest and all would be lost. Since then the ratios have been changing. They tell me I spend half the week not knowing anything at all now. I spend periods of being Jerry Knows Everything, and equal periods of being Jerry Knows Nothing. Sometimes I'll have an entire good day, sometimes an entire bad day. Because of the Alzheimer's, I can never be sure what is real.

Except there is one thing I am very sure of. I killed my wife. Of all the things to forget, that's the one thing I pray that I can.

The diary came about because I've been writing things down on scrap bits of paper, I've been writing about my days and finally Eric had the idea of giving me a proper diary I could write in. It's going to remind me of the man I used to be, and most of all it will remind me of my loss. Aside from those two things, it's also going to document how crazy I've been and how much more crazy there is to go. I'm going to call it my Crazy Diary. I'm going to write in it when I remember to, which . . .

Wait. Not Crazy Diary. Madness Diary. I've done this before. I was keeping a diary back before . . .

Before I murdered Sandra.

Where that diary is now, who took it, I have no idea.

Eric says keeping the diary will be useful, and that I should put everything in here that I can think of, which is why I'm doing this. He says I should think of it as therapy. He said it might help me get back to where I was, but if the memory of my Sandra lying dead and bloody on my office floor is true, then I don't want to get my life back. Then he said something that encouraged me, something hopeful, and in a place like this hope and encouragement are the only things to stop one from curling up in a corner and waiting to die. He said the way technology advances, it's impossible to know what the future holds. If that's true, if there is a chance of getting better, then I need to do what I can to make that happen. Eva must hate me. She must. And it will be a painful journey getting back to the man I used to be, painful to relive the bad things I've done, but I must do this if there is any chance of saving my relationship with her. Eric also thinks I should jot down other ideas I have for books. He said it's a way of exercising the brain, that I need to keep my mind active. Medical technology might bring the old Jerry back, but it won't bring back Sandra. I will do anything if it will help me reach out to Eva, anything to tell her how sorry I am.

The memory I have of Sandra is as strong as some of the memories I have of my characters. Sometimes the only proof I have she ever existed is the wedding ring on my finger and the photograph I have of her and Eva in my room. Sometimes I get confused between shooting her and having one of my bad guys shooting one of my good guys. I don't remember it, but I have enough imaginative tools to be able to picture the scene. I do remember the blood, and holding her hand. I remember calling the police and asking them to come and help. I remember them arriving and a while later taking her away and me away—Sandra to the morgue, me to the police station. I know there were a number of days between my wife dying and me calling for help, days in which I wanted Eva to have some semblance of a honeymoon, but I don't know how many. Two or three. Maybe four. I don't think there was a trial, but I don't know for sure. I think between the defense and the prosecution a deal was made. I was sick, nobody doubted that, sick and better off in a care facility than a prison.

As the Alzheimer's continues to evolve, I will remember less and less of what happened. This illness is like having a hard drive full of photographs and videos and contacts being deleted. By the end of the year the ratio might be one good day to ten off days. With that in mind, let me get down what I remember and tell you who you were and what's been happening.

Let's start with the nursing home. It's a good distance out of the city, making me feel like me and my fellow patients are all in the *out of sight out of mind* category. It's a pretty big place, two stories and maybe thirty rooms or so, the staff all warm and caring and always wanting the best for everybody here. The grounds are pretty big too, lots of flowers and trees and some of the patients hang about outside pulling weeds or sitting in the sun, while others remain in one of the common areas, watching TV or reading books or chatting. There are a couple of people in cots, aware of nothing, just banging their heads all day long while they soil themselves. Some of us can feed ourselves, and in that small act we can at least take some enjoyment from our food, but others have to be fed, the nurses with barely enough time to feed one patient before moving on to the next, mealtime a chore, and it's heartbreaking. Absolutely heartbreaking, and whatever the staff are being paid here it isn't enough.

I often think about escaping, about finding my way back to Eva and begging her to forgive me—two things I think are impossible. However, I have been stopped on the edge of the grounds a few times, getting ready to wander into the woods. I think that if I could make it back home to where I used to live I would do better there. Surely there I would be able to keep more of myself intact, rather than in this unfamiliar place where my memory is being split into smaller pieces every day, fragments being cast into the great beyond. Surely I could use my crime-writing money to buy my house back and for home care. But the courts . . . the law . . . they won't allow it. That's the man telling me what I can't do. The man frowning on me because I shot Sandra. How much money does the man pump into war, and tourism, and sport, compared to Alzheimer's research?

As far as first entries go, I think that covers it. There's more to explain. If I can remember any of it, I'll carry on later. I'm not sure how to finish a diary entry. My instinct is to finish it on a cliff-hanger, and I guess that's the crime writer in me. Oh, by the way, there is a crime writer living inside me—his name is Henry Cutter. On a good day, Henry is nothing more than a pen name, but on a bad day I sometimes wonder if he's the one who takes over. If so, then it must have been Henry that killed Sandra, because I have no memory of it.

Cliff-hanger time. I'm not so sure Sandra is the only person Henry has killed.

It's a journal, not a diary Jerry thinks, as he puts the journal down after reading the first entry. He can remember it now—not what he wrote, but the act of writing. He can picture himself sitting in his room in the chair by the window and filling the pages. He can even remember the first entry, can remember Eric giving him the journal to write in, Eric's advice about putting in plot ideas to keep his mind active. Of course it was all a lie. Eric was an ideas thief. A stealer of words. There never would be a pill to cure Alzheimer's—not in Jerry's lifetime.

He's sitting in Eric's chair behind Eric's desk with Eric's wife asleep a few rooms away. He and Hans picked her up to make her more comfortable. He's getting used to hauling unconscious people around. Hans suggested laying her down in one of the bedrooms, but in the end they settled for a couch in the lounge, as Jerry didn't want her waking and getting any ideas—such as the fact they killed her husband. She will be asleep for at least a few hours, Hans has assured him. Then she'll wake up and her journey as a widow will begin, from pain and sorrow to disgust after she learns the kind of man her husband really was. A word thief. A killer. This woman would shoot Jerry now if given the chance, but within the week she will be thanking him.

Reading the first entry of this journal sparks his awareness of the original. He can remember sitting at his desk scribbling on the pages while Sandra's body lay on the floor. It's possible he wrote something that would help him understand all of this, which just confirms his theory that he needs to get hold of it, but it also suggests something else. It's possible he wrote about that night in this second journal. The first entry he just read is almost identical to the one Eric pasted into his manuscript. He flicks to the end of the fledgling writer's document, hoping there will be some answers, but there is no end. Eric must have been still working on it. Jerry remembers hitting that brick wall himself over the years, getting ninety percent of the way through and not knowing how to wrap things up, then realizing it was necessary to change that ninety percent in ninety different ways.

He rolls the chair over to the computer. Stuck to the monitor is a Post-it note, the words *Write what you know and fake the rest* have been written on it. He finds the novel on the desktop, along with five others. He double-clicks *Crime Writer Working Title* and then starts scrolling through it. Right away he can see it's longer. In this version Gerald Black, the crime writer in question, has found a way to sneak in and out of the nursing home so he can carry on his killing spree. Gerald sneaks into the back of a laundry truck, as if he's escaping a prison from a 1960s movie. Jerry wonders if that's how he's been sneaking out, but can't recall any laundry trucks.

Gerald, it seems, is replicating the crimes from within his books, but nobody suspects him. The police believe an obsessed fan is responsible. Eddie, the orderly hero, believes Gerald may be responsible, and that Gerald has been faking his illness all along. To what end, Jerry can't fathom. Living in a nursing home isn't living the dream, and if you're that good at faking an illness, then you may as well fake your innocence and find another way to not get caught. It's something Eddie hasn't been able to figure out either—or at least explain. Jerry's diary entries are forced into the narrative, but they don't quite work, because the entries are from a man who is genuinely losing his mind, not from a man making it all up. Seeing his words in these pages makes him feel even more violated and continues to blunt the edges of guilt he might have felt for dropping the orderly to his death.

Jerry picks his journal back up. He reads the second entry and sees that it starts to divert from the entry that Eric has written in his book. Maybe the ratio is going to change the same way it does between his good days and off days.

The third entry starts with the words *Don't trust Hans* scrawled several times across the top of the page. His heart does that hammering thing it's been doing lately, and he can sense Henry's presence, his curiosity piqued. He looks up at the doorway to make sure his friend isn't standing there watching him. He isn't.

Jerry carries on reading.

don't trust Hans, don't trust
Hans, don't trust Hans, don't

DAY ANOTHER SOMETHING

The words at the top of the page here aren't mine. I mean, they are mine, because it's my handwriting, but I didn't write them. I mean, okay, I wrote them, but I don't remember writing them. The words are big and black, written with a marker, like a point being forced, and I can only assume Henry wrote them, Henry who would wear the author's hat, Henry who sometimes occupies my thoughts and takes control of my life. I don't know when he wrote them, or why. I've spent all morning thinking about it, and this is what I've come up with—nothing.

Eric has been asking me questions about the diary, about my past. My life is like a jigsaw puzzle to him, and I'm not sure why he's so interested, but he is. It turns out—and I don't know if this is more sad or funny—that one of the reasons he asked me to keep a diary is because I confessed to a crime that never happened. I don't even remember confessing—but he was telling me I've been getting a little mixed-up between what is real and what is make-believe. When he first told me, I thought it was the setup to some awful joke. The more he insisted, the madder I got at what felt like an accusation. Finally, another of the nurses confirmed it was true. I've been telling people—telling and really insisting—that I kept a woman locked in my basement for two weeks before killing her, which would be a really neat trick since I've never owned a house with a basement. Eric is trying to convince me to write in the diary every day, because he thinks it will help ground me to what is real. He's asked to read it, but I won't let him. I hide it in my drawer when I'm not writing in it. I used to have a couple of hiding places back in what I'm now calling *Jerry's Normal Life*. I remember I had a floorboard under my desk that I could pry up, but I can't remember where the second one is.

Today is a bad day. It's bad because I can remember that Sandra (my wife) is dead, and that Eva (my daughter) never comes to see me. Looking back at the previous entries it seems I only write when I'm having a good day. I should start putting in the date, because I have no idea how long I'm going between entries.

Don't trust Hans.

I don't know why I would have written that. Why Henry would have.

And yet . . . with those words is some kind of recognition, a sense that I have written them before. If I had to guess, then I would say perhaps it was in the original Crazy Diary. This is Version II—Version I was written as Jerry's Normal Life phase entered the Madness phase.

I miss Sandra. I know she's dead, but I don't *know* know, if that makes sense. It's like having somebody come along and tell you the sky is green when it's actually blue. That's how it feels, and the memory of those few days with her lying on the floor are feeling more and more like they belong to somebody else, that they belong to one of the characters I've given life to.

Don't trust Hans.

Really?

I'm off to breakfast now (good news? For some reason I have the urge to say that—but nothing really to say). Oh, and thinking about it, I think I should be calling this a Madness Diary, not a . . . wait, strike that. A Madness Journal. That has a better ring to it.

✦

Once again, Jerry is able to recall writing these journal entries. But he can't remember the actual events described. For all intents and purposes, this is the Madness Journal of a stranger.. The biggest takeaway from the entry is Past Jerry's conviction of a second hiding place. It lines up with what Current Jerry thinks, because that will be where the original journal is hidden.

He reads the next entry and it's more of the same, as is the following one, words that belong to him but are somehow associated with someone else. He puts the journal down. He moves to the doorway and listens for movement. Hans is no longer in the garage but definitely somewhere in the house. He can hear his friend opening and closing drawers.

Don't trust Hans. The earlier entry was clear on that, but didn't provide an explanation. It could have just as easily warned: don't trust Henry. Or don't trust Jerry, because he sure as hell can't trust himself, can he?

If Hans isn't to be trusted, if the author with the Alzheimer's monkey on his back is to be believed, then standing in the doorway isn't the way to go about finding an answer to all this. Nor is confronting his friend. He sits back down behind the desk and picks up the journal. He notices the structure of the entries begins to topple and the prose is too loose on occasion as Jerry starts to lose control of the plot. He suddenly realizes how he's reading these entries, as if they're part of a novel, a story about a fictional character. And in some ways they are, aren't they?

He rolls up his sleeve and looks at the marks on his arm. An idea is coming to him. He looks back at the journal. Chunks of it have been stolen and inserted directly into Eric's manuscript and portrayed as the journal entries of his protagonist. These entries come off as very realistic because they come from a genuine source. They are the ramblings of a madman. Mad, he thinks, because Eric made him that way. He looks back at the marks on his arm, and suddenly he knows. The same way he's able to predict the ending to nearly every movie and TV show he's seen, the same way he knows what's waiting for him on the last page of any novel. He knows that Eric injected him not just on the days he was going out and hurting those women, but also on days he couldn't push his story forward. Eric would inject him just for the purpose of making Jerry's world more miserable than it is, just so Jerry would write about it.

He carries on with the journal. Here's the first instance of being found wandering in town. Past Jerry has no memory of it, and nobody knows how he got there. He reads the entry slowly, looking for the details, but there are none except for a gold locket that Past Jerry finds in his pocket that evening when he's back in the nursing home. He thinks he must have stolen it, so he hides it in the back of one of his drawers.

Current Jerry tilts his head back and closes his eyes and tries to think back to the phone call he had earlier today with Eva. She said the jewelry was found there, jewelry from the women who were killed. Eric must have given those pieces to him.

And if that theory is wrong? What if the next entry is Past Jerry detailing how he escapes, how much he enjoys a good, old-fashioned bloodletting? What if? Only he doesn't think it will. He's not that guy. Like he told Hans earlier, Sandra would never have married that guy.

And like Hans told you, buddy, the Alzheimer's is a wild card.

Following entries find Past Jerry confessing to more crimes from his books: a couple of homicides, a bank robbery, a kidnapping, even to being a drug dealer. He wonders if this was a natural progression, or something Eric orchestrated for his research. Past Jerry is found once again wandering in town, and when he's taken back to the nursing home he finds another piece of jewelry in his pocket, and he has no memory of how he left the home.

"Jerry?" Hans, calling from somewhere in the house. "Jerry, come down here a moment."

Don't trust Hans, Henry says.

But how can he not? After everything Hans has done for him?

He finds Hans in the master bedroom, the bed shoved to one side of the room, the contents of the drawers tipped out, clothes on the floor, jewelry forming a pile on the bed.

"You think some of that belongs to the girls?" Jerry asks, looking at the rings and necklaces and earrings.

"I don't know. Probably his wife's. But that's not why I called you," he says, and he holds up an eight-by-ten envelope. "Check it out," he says, and he tips the envelope up.

Jerry is expecting more rings and necklaces to slide out. He's expecting something that can explain what happened to the woman whose house he woke up in today.

And that's exactly what he gets. Four small ziplocked plastic bags and four photographs that together tell a story. "I found it taped under the bottom drawer," Hans says. "Bloody amateur."

Jerry reaches out to pick up one of the bags.

"Don't touch them," Hans says. "Don't get your prints on them."

"Why not? The police are going to know I was here."

"We don't want them thinking you brought these things with you."

"What are they?" Jerry asks, pulling his hands back.

"It's hair."

"What?"

"Hair," Hans says, and Jerry can see it now, each of the four bags holding a little less hair than you'd find on a toy doll. "Four bags, four victims. He took jewelry to plant on you, and he took hair for himself. He probably found it more personal."

"And the photographs?"

The photographs have all landed facedown. "Well that's the best bit," Hans says, and he flicks them over one at a time, like a blackjack dealer, each image worse than the other, not in terms of quality but quantity. Four photographs virtually the same, each showing four dead women. Except the last one shows Jerry Grey in the background, snoozing on the couch.

The horror at what these girls went through is too much for Jerry, and he finds he can't speak. He moves to the edge of the bed and sits down just as his legs are beginning to give out. "Those poor girls," he says, unable to keep the shock out of his voice.

"You didn't do this," Hans says.

"That doesn't make what happened to them any less painful."

"No, but it means you're not responsible."

"Not directly, no," Jerry says.

"You want to explain that?"

"Eric killed them because I told him he had to write what he knows.

He killed them because he knew he could get away with it by framing me. If I'd never gotten sick, if I were still at home and still had my old life, then I'd have never met Eric. Those girls would still be alive."

"It doesn't work that way. If it did, we'd all be responsible for everybody else's actions all the time. Eric did this, not you. You didn't hurt these girls, Eric did," Hans says.

Together, Jerry thinks, they have just taken care of a serial killer.

"There is one small problem," Hans adds, and any relief Jerry was starting to feel at not being a killer disappears, replaced by a sinking feeling in his stomach.

"What kind of problem?"

"The police are going to think you planted them here."

Jerry doesn't know what to say. Henry, on the other hand, knows. *He's absolutely right, but that doesn't mean you should trust him.* "But the photographs—"

"Could have been taken by you."

"Not the last one."

"Could have been taken with a self-timer."

"The police will figure out when these photographs were printed, and where, and will see it was probably on Eric's computer."

"Which you've had access to," Hans counters.

"Not for long, though."

"They won't know that. The police might think you've been here all day, after leaving the knife at the mall. Look, Jerry, in saying all of that, I think you'll be okay. At the very least it will mean they'll investigate him, right? They're going to look into all the days those girls were killed, and they're going to find a pattern. Maybe they'll rip the place apart and find even more evidence. Maybe they'll find some poor girl buried out in the garden. It could be the wife suspected something too, and she might talk. Could be this jewelry that belongs to the wife originally came from the girls."

"But you believe me, right?"

"Of course I do, but I'm not the one who needs convincing. This guy has been exposed and taken care of because of you, not because of the police, and they're not going to be too thrilled being made to look foolish by a crime writer dealing with Alzheimer's. They're going to look for any angle that could suggest your involvement. The flip side to that is you'll be cleared, and once the media gets hold of the story, you'll be a hero. The country won't like a hero being convicted."

"I'm not a monster," Jerry says, and the relief is back . . . it's back and it's growing, it's spreading its wings.

Hans is staring at him. He has that look he gets when he's trying to figure something out.

"What?" Jerry asks.

"Let's not forget the others," Hans says.

"What others?"

"The others you've killed."

Jerry thinks about Sandra, he remembers the florist, and Suzan with a z, whose real name is lost to him now. He looks down at the photographs, three of them representing women he has killed. Thoughts of his own innocence may have been premature.

"Is it possible I haven't killed anybody?" Jerry asks.

"Two hours ago we dropped a man to his death," Hans says.

"Other than him," Jerry says.

"Possible? Anything is possible," Hans says.

"Anything is possible," Jerry says, letting the words hang in the air for a few seconds before chasing them with the reality. "But you think I did."

"I'm sorry, buddy."

"So now what?"

"Well I can keep looking around while you read the journal. Since he hid these," Hans says, nodding towards the bags of hair and photographs, "then it stands to reason he might have hidden something else. It's not uncommon for people to have more than one hiding space. Ultimately we—"

"That's right! I haven't told you yet, but I wrote in my journal that there is a second hiding place!" Jerry says.

Hans looks excited. "Where?"

"I didn't say."

"Well what did you say?"

"Just that there's somewhere else. I think it's where I used to hide my writing backups."

"Where?"

"I don't know."

"You need to remember, Jerry," Hans says, sounding urgent. "And we need to head to your house and find it."

"I need a drink."

"Seriously?"

"Who knows when I'll get another chance? Plus it might help me think."

Hans slowly nods. "After all you've gone through today, you probably deserve one. Hell, I think we both do."

They head out to the kitchen and Jerry leans against the bench while Hans goes through the cupboards. Hans finds a couple of glasses and sits them on the table, then starts going through the pantry. He finds what he's looking for. Not quite what he's looking for—there's vodka, and no gin, but it will have to do. He grabs some ice from the freezer. There's no tonic anywhere, so he ends up making a couple of vodka and orange drinks. They sit down at the table. All very social, Jerry thinks.

All very mad, Henry thinks.

"Why are you still wearing the gloves?" Jerry asks.

Don't trust Hans.

"What do you mean?"

"With Eric being dead already, the police are going to figure out I'm involved."

"That's right."

"And when they talk to me, they're going to figure out you're involved."

"Not if you don't tell them."

"You don't want them to know?"

"Of course not. I want to help you out, buddy, but I'd also really like to avoid jail too."

"What if I forget that and tell them?"

"If you forget, you forget. But if you remember, and don't drag me into it, then the police never need to know I was here. Look, Jerry, I know it's not right of me to ask this, but I want you to take the fall for what happened to Eric. The police will go easy on you, and if they don't . . ." Hans says, and doesn't finish.

"If they don't what?"

"You're already a killer, mate. I'm just trying to help. I don't want to be punished for trying to help you out."

Jerry looks at his glass, then slowly sips from it. Not as good as a gin and tonic, but better than nothing. He sips a little more. It's a fair point, he thinks, then tells Hans as such.

Hans starts sipping from his own drink. "You remember my dad's funeral?" he asks.

Jerry looks up. He shakes his head. He wonders where Hans is going with this.

"The night before the funeral, you took me into town and we ended up at a bar that had run out of gin. You started bitching at the bartender, asking him what kind of bar it was, and he said the kind of bar where people who complain get their teeth kicked out. We ended up drinking these," he says, taking a sip. "Only time I've ever had them. It's not . . . I don't know the word," he says.

"Not masculine enough?"

Hans nods. "I knew you'd know. You've always been a gin-and-tonic guy, ever since we met."

Jerry finishes his drink. He considers whether he wants a second. "I remember you brought bottles to me when I got sick."

"Sandra wouldn't let you drink, and she took your credit card off you so you couldn't go and buy them. I would bring five of them to you at a time. I have no idea where you hid them, but maybe it's the same place you hid the—"

"In the garage," Jerry says, and he can remember it, can remember a tarpaulin beneath a bench, covering the gap behind the chain saw and the circular saw, and that was where he hid them, behind renovating tools that belonged to a much younger version of Past Jerry, back when Eva was a small girl and his books were still to be given life. He didn't hide all of the bottles there, the rest were under the floor of his office. He can also remember a tarpaulin on his office floor, all laid out ready to catch the mess that a far more recent version of Past Jerry was going to make, one from last year.

"You got through them pretty quickly," Hans says.

Only the bottles weren't under the floor, were they, Jerry? Henry says. *No, under the floor was reserved just for the gun that wasn't there and the journal that also wasn't there. The only thing under there was a shirt you can't remember getting bloody.*

"I'm sorry about what happened to you," Hans says. "You got a bad rap. Not one of the worst I've ever seen, but pretty damn close."

Jerry isn't listening to Hans. Instead he's listening to Henry. He's thinking about the floorboards. About the original journal. How it wasn't under there. The gin wasn't under there either. Nor the gun. Because it's just like he said in Madness Journal 2.0—there's another hiding place.

"Maybe—"

"Stop talking," Jerry says, and he puts his hand out. He's thinking about what he wrote in the journal. He's thinking about those bottles of gin.

"Jerry? Are you okay?"

The writing backups weren't under the floor, but he kept them somewhere safe and secure. Somewhere close. They wouldn't be in the garage, or the kitchen, or a bedroom. Wouldn't be somewhere he'd have to go looking for.

You used to hide them. You were paranoid somebody would come into your house one day and steal your computer, steal everything you worked with, steal your next big idea.

"Were my writing backups found?"

"Backups? I have no idea."

He thinks about his office. Remembers the layout. His mind is becoming warm, the vodka and juice flowing through all the neural pathways in his brain, quickly fogging his thoughts the way it will to somebody who hasn't touched a drop of alcohol in nearly a year, but it's clearing things in other areas as those thoughts link across time, the way alcohol can do that, linking images, dragging out the random, and he's back in his study where he's pouring himself a drink, and those bottles of gin . . . well now, they weren't hidden under the floorboards, were they . . .

"The backups were hidden. I always hid that stuff," Jerry says.

"Under the floor maybe?"

"There was nothing under the floor."

"Then where? Think, Jerry, come on, you're almost there, you're—"

"Shut up," Jerry says.

It has to be somewhere else big enough to fit a few bottles of gin. Where? Not the bookcase. Not the desk. Nothing hidden in the wall. Nothing in the roof. Nothing under or inside the couch.

Wait . . . nothing hidden in the wall? Are you sure about that?

"I almost have it," he says.

Hans says nothing.

"Just let me think," he says, closing his eyes, and there he is, it's a workday and every day was a workday back when he used to write, weekends and weekdays were all the same. He'd work on his birthday. He'd even let Henry Cutter out of the bottle for an hour or two on Christmas Day to get those thoughts down. That was the life of a writer—keep writing, keep moving forward, stay ahead of the crowd because if you don't get that story written down then somebody else would. He's in his office, he's building the word count, and he's wrapping up for the day and he needs to make a backup, needs to get those words secure, because to lose a few thousand of them, let alone an entire manuscript . . . that was one part of being a writer he could avoid. His office, his desk, he's putting a flash drive into his computer, copy, paste, then he's taking the flash drive back out. Then what? What does he do next?

Getting out of his chair. Past the couch and to the wardrobe. He opens the wardrobe door and—

"Jerry—"

Crouches down. There's a box that holds half a dozen reams of paper there. He pushes it aside then—

"You have to focus, Jerry."

Presses the bottom corner of the wall. An opposite corner juts out. It's a false wall, no taller than his forearm but the width of the wardrobe. He pulls it away, and there's the gin, there are the flash drives, one for each novel, there's the gun and there's—

"I know where the journal is," he says, and he stands up so quickly he bangs against the table. The glass slides towards Hans, who catches it before it can fall.

"At the house?"

"In my office," Jerry says.

"Then let's go."

"Let me grab my second journal," Jerry says, and he's already moving back towards the study. "I want to read it on the way."

DAY ONE MILLION

Okay, so it's not really day one million, and I'm not sure how liberal I was with exaggerations in the books. Derek (it's actually Eric, but I've come to think of him as a Derek) told me this morning it's been eight months since I checked in. Which, by my calculations, is nine hundred and ninety-nine thousand days and change short of a million. Still, it feels like I've been here forever.

> Today is a Jerry is Jerry day.
> Jerry has Alzheimer's—check.
> Jerry used to be a crime writer—check.
> Jerry knows he shouldn't trust Derek—check.
> Or Eric—check.
> Jerry is making a checklist—check.

I've been flicking through the journal and seeing I've been piling crazy on top of crazy, and among some of those entries is evidence that Henry has been coming out to play. I've been having conversations with him. Henry and me shooting the breeze. There are two points here, Future Me, that I want to make. It's two-for Tuesday. The first is to stop trusting Eric. Let me put that in big capital letters. DON'T TRUST ERIC. I came into my room earlier and found him elbows deep in my drawer. I think he was looking for my journal. For what reason, I don't know. I asked him what he was doing. He said he was tidying up. Henry thinks he's lying. Henry thinks there's an ulterior motive for Eric wanting you to write in the journal, and Henry does, after all, deal in ulterior motives (most of the characters he creates have one). In this case the motive is Eric stealing my ideas because he wants to be a writer. One thing I can remember clearly from my life of crime (writing) is the amount of people who tell me they want to write a book. It's one of those professions everybody thinks they can do, and I always wanted to say to a lawyer *I've been thinking about trying a case* or to a surgeon *I've been thinking about performing a heart transplant*, as if their job is no more challenging than mine. And the reason, according to them, they haven't written that book yet? Time. It's always that they don't have time, but they'll make it. How hard can it be? Eric is writing a book—and at least Eric is putting in the time, he's said he writes a few hours every night, making it a passion as well as a hobby, and that's something I always respect, and for that I wish him all the best. However, he has once committed what I've always thought of as the cardinal sin, and that's to ask *Where do you get your ideas?*, as if I order a box online every year and have an assistant weed out the bad ones. I've told him *Write what you know*, because there is nothing truer when it comes to the job of making stuff up, but Eric wants to write what *I* know. That's why he's looking for my journal. Sometimes on the days I remember who I am, I wonder if it's the writing that made me this way—all those crazy people running around inside my head—some of that crazy was bound to rub off on me, wasn't it? If Eric wants to be a writer, then let his own crazy do to him what mine did to me.

On the subject of Eric . . . I had this very strange dream a few days ago. He was taking me somewhere. I don't know where, and dreams are like that—just random images taken from random moments of your life. Only, if I'm to be honest, and Madness Journal Version 2.0 demands nothing but honesty, it feels more like a memory than a dream, because dreams are something that disappear even while you're fumbling around, trying to hold the pieces together. But what the hell would I know? Jerry Version 2.0 has faulty software. It was a messy upgrade that's been slowly wiping the original operating system. Whether dream or memory, it was me in the passenger seat, my head leaning against the side window, and we were somewhere in the city and the streetlights were burning bright, hotels and office buildings lit up like Christmas trees against a black sky. I would close my eyes and when I opened them again everything would be different: different snapshots of time, traffic lights, a convenience store, a couple of drunk people staggering along the sidewalk. Then there was a house, and that house didn't move by, it wasn't a snapshot of a moment, it was solid, it was real, and we were parked in front of that house for a while, and there were no lights on inside, there were no lights anywhere other than streetlights. Only it wasn't we, it was just me. Just me waiting and doing nothing, unable to move, as if the signals to all my nerves and muscles and tendons had been severed. I drifted off again then, returning a while later to a world that had moved on, the house no longer there, instead I was in a park somewhere lying on the grass.

If it was a dream, it was the most boring dream I've ever had.

But the thing is . . . I've been wandering. I see I've previously written in my journal I've been caught on the edge of the grounds, on what, in hindsight, may have been escape attempts. When I went wandering I made it into the city. It was some kids who found me on their way to school. They found me lying down on the ground in a park (like the park in the dream, I guess). One of them poked me with a stick, the way kids do a dead insect. But I was alive, and I don't know what I said to them, but they called the police. I wandered again, trying to figure out where I was even as I was trying to determine where I wanted to go. The police found me three blocks away. I was sitting down on the pavement, leaning against a fence. I was trying to collect my thoughts, but my thoughts were a jumble. I was disoriented. I can remember there was a cat that was keeping me company, head butting my elbow over and over. That bit I remember. I remember the kids too. But the rest I don't know. How I got there is a mystery.

Since then, I've learned that it's not the first time I've wandered. In fact, it's the second. And, right now as I write this, I'm staring at a pair of earrings that are on the table next to me. I found them in my pocket earlier. Either I held up a jewelry store or it's the first indicator that I'm about to start cross-dressing. I'll check later to see if I've hidden any high heels in the wardrobe.

I asked Eric whether he'd driven me anywhere. Of course I did. He laughed, and said it was my crime-writer imagination making connections that aren't there. He said he'd have no reason to drive me anywhere, and both Henry and me agree with him. What would be the point? Eric asked if I had any memory of the other time I escaped, and I don't. In fact, I can't even find any mention of it in my journal.

So now for the second point of two-for Tuesday.

Hans came to see me today. I wish he hadn't. I actually had no idea who it was when I first saw him. He had to tell me a few times, and one of the nurses told me that he actually comes to see me quite a lot, that he spends time with me out in the gardens if it's a nice day, walking the grounds and updating me on the outside world. I never remember these talks, and I think that's because when I'm with him I'm not Remembering Jerry, I'm the Jerry that functions in the off position.

I saw earlier that I scribbled in my journal not to trust Hans.

Now I know why.

It's because he tells me things I don't want to hear. He tells me why I'm here. I should respect that at least somebody is willing to level with me, but respecting him doesn't mean I can't hate him. It's always easy to shoot the messenger.

Today we sat down outside. It was cold out, but the sun was shining and provided just enough warmth to make sitting outside bearable.

Why am I here? I asked. *Why can't I go back home?*

How much do you remember? Hans asked, and it was Henry that answered for me, but before he answered he gave me a warning. He said *Something isn't right here, J-Man. Let me get this for you.*

Henry isn't real, I know he isn't real and Henry would be the first to agree, yet I was willing to let him take the lead. I didn't want to listen to Hans. I think even then, as we sat outside, I knew why I didn't want to listen to him, and yet I did anyway.

Do you remember shooting your wife?

I didn't remember that, no, but once the words were out there I did. I knew Sandra was dead. I knew I had killed her, but pulling the trigger—that was something I didn't remember and never wanted to. The news was shocking, it hurt, and for a while I was inconsolable.

Why? I asked, because I had to know. *Why did I shoot her?*

You don't want to know. That's what Henry was saying. Henry, who would observe, who would study, who would connect the unconnectable dots. *You really don't want to know. Don't listen to him, J-Man. It's all bad news.*

But I did want to know.

Hans looked away. He drew in a deep breath. Then he looked at me. Then he asked, *Do you really want to know?*

Yes, I said, and Henry was still telling me no.

I think that she thought you killed somebody else.

What?

There was blood, he said. *Blood on your shirt.*

What shirt? I asked.

And a knife.

What knife?

Let me ask you again, Jerry. Are you sure you want to know?

I told him that I did. That I wanted to know everything. And here's what he told me.

He told me that last year, the night of Eva's wedding, I sat in my office watching a video of myself that had been posted online (that video, that speech, that's something I still haven't forgotten). After watching it several times, I decided to go out. I phoned him hours later, needing a lift. He said there was blood on my shirt, and when he asked me about it, I told him I didn't know. He said over the following days he came to believe the blood belonged to the florist at Eva's wedding, and that I had killed her, and that Sandra had figured it out.

Hans thinks those suspicions made Sandra threaten to call the police.

He thinks I did what I had to do to make sure Sandra couldn't make that call.

Then he reminded me that it wasn't my fault. Killing the florist, killing my wife, he reminded me that it wasn't me, that it was a different version of me, a darker version whose morals and ethics have been stripped away by the disease.

Of course none of that changes the fact that Sandra is dead. Or the florist.

Don't trust Hans. I got it wrong. What I should have said was don't believe Hans. Or, more accurately, don't listen to him. Next time I see him, I'm going to ask him to stop coming to see me. After all, who the hell wants to be reminded of the fact they're a bad man? I just want to become Forgetful Jerry again. Maybe it's time to stop writing in the journal. Maybe it's time just to let nature take its course.

Let nature take the pain and the anger and the memories away.

They're driving back to Jerry's house at a steady pace, Hans behind the wheel, Jerry with his eyes scanning over the final entry in the journal, the entry ending with him wanting nature to take the pain and the memories away. He can't remember writing these words. Jerry feels dissatisfied. Instead of the journal offering closure, it has been like reading a book with no ending.

"First thing we need to do," Hans says, snapping Jerry back into the moment, "is make sure the police aren't going to be there."

"Be where?"

"At your old house."

"They weren't there earlier," Jerry says.

"True. But since then you showed up, you assaulted your—"

"I didn't assault her," Jerry says. "She just fell over."

"You think she's going to remember it that way?" Hans asks.

"She'll probably tell them I tried to kill her. But that was hours ago, right? The police will have been and gone."

"Maybe," Hans says. "Or maybe they're still there and keeping an eye on the place, hoping you'll return."

"Or maybe they think I wouldn't be stupid enough to return."

"But you are returning," Hans says.

"So what do we do?"

"You ring the nursing home," Hans says.

"What?"

"You ring them, and you tell them everything that's happened. You tell them about Eric, that he's dead, and that you're at his house and you've found proof of everything he's done. You tell them you're still there and you want them to come and pick you up."

"Why would I tell them that?"

"Because then they'll call the police. They have to. And the police will head to Eric's house to get you. If there is anybody waiting for you at the old house, this should draw them away. We can't call the police ourselves because we don't want them to triangulate the call."

"And what if it doesn't work?"

"You just have to hope that it does," Hans says, and he pulls the car over at the end of the block, about a hundred yards from the house.

"I don't even know the number," Jerry says.

"I do," Hans says, and quotes it from memory.

Jerry makes the call. He asks for Nurse Hamilton. He can feel his heart racing at the prospect of talking to her, of lying, and he's thinking this is why he used to be an author and not an actor, but then he realizes it doesn't matter because either way Nurse Hamilton is going to call the police, either way she's going to tell them where he said he was, and she isn't going to editorialize the call and say *Well, even though he said all that, I really think he was making everything up, so you should keep an eye out on all the other places you're keeping an eye on.*

Nurse Hamilton's voice comes on the line. She tells him that she's worried about him, that they all are, and in return he tells her everything Hans told him to say. When he's finished all he hears is silence. Jerry thinks this must be the first time in Nurse Hamilton's life she's ever been speechless. But the silence doesn't last long.

"You must be confusing the day with one of your books again," she tells him, and he can hear hope that what she is saying is true, that this is nothing more than one of Jerry's Days of Confusion. He can also hear her doubt. What she knows for a fact is that the police are hunting him because they believe he's a killer.

"There are photographs of the women Eric killed. And he was keeping locks of their hair."

"Listen to me, Jerry, you're not yourself right now," she says.

"I'm very much myself right now," he tells her.

"Eric is really dead?"

"It was an accident."

"Are you by yourself?" she asks.

He looks at Hans. He remembers what Hans asked of him earlier. "Yes."

"You figured all of this out on your own."

"That's what I'm telling you."

"Don't you see, Jerry? You've gotten confused again. You've—"

"This whole time everybody thought I was sick, but it was just Eric all along."

"Eric didn't make you sick, Jerry."

"That's not what I mean."

"Then what do you mean?"

"Just lately. All the bad stuff lately is because of him."

"Jerry—"

"Come to Eric's house and take a look at what I've seen," he says, "and then tell me I'm making things up."

"Jerry—"

"I have to go now," he says, and then he hangs up. When all of this is over, he'll explain everything. He switches off the phone because it seems the thing to do.

"So now what?" he asks.

"Now we give it two minutes," Hans says.

They give it two minutes, in which there are no signs of movement, in which neither of the two men talk. Without discussing it, they give it two more minutes.

"Either they're not moving," Hans says, "or they were never there to begin with. But we need to get in there. We have to get that journal. We can't exactly go up and knock on the front door, because your bloody neighbor will call the police. We can knock on the back door, and if they're home, then—"

"They're not going to let us in," Jerry says. "The owner yesterday thought I was crazy, and today he thinks I'm a killer."

"Then we break in," Hans says. "I have my lock picks with me."

Jerry reaches into his pocket. He shows Hans the key. "We won't need them."

"You remember which house is the one behind yours?"

"No," Jerry says, and shakes his head. Then he nods. "Yes. Maybe. Why?"

Hans starts the car. He takes the next right and comes down the street running parallel with Jerry's. He starts slowing up halfway down the block. "Well?"

"They all look the same," Jerry says, "and I only ever saw it from the back."

Hans gets his phone out. He uses the GPS function and gets a location on where they are. He brings the car to a stop when the blue dot on the screen is in line with Jerry's house, only with one house between.

"That's the one," Jerry says.

"You sure?"

"As sure as I can be."

Hans kills the engine. "We climb the fence. We try to figure out if anybody is home. If not, then we go in. If the lights are on, we wait until they've gone to bed, then sneak in. You're sure you know where the journal is?"

"I'm positive."

"Then let's go."

The house they're parked outside is a two-story house with a concrete tile roof and a flower bed jammed full of roses that catch at Jerry's clothes as he passes them. They move quietly across the front yard and to the gate that enters the back. It opens quietly, and a few seconds later they're at the fence line. Hans boosts himself up and confirms it's the right house while Jerry continues to look at the house they've just snuck past. He can see the glow of a TV set, the glow of lights, but nothing to suggest they've been heard.

"This is it," Hans whispers, then drops to the other side. Jerry climbs over, landing in a backyard that still feels as though it's his. Up ahead is where the pool used to be, but now it's a paved area with a long wooden barbecue table and a pair of outdoor gas heaters. There are no lights on inside the house.

They reach the deck and the sun lounger where they had left Mrs. Smith. Jerry half expects to see her still lying there, but it also won't surprise him if she comes storming through the gate waving her hockey stick any second. A cat sits outside the door—it stares at him, then shifts its attention to Hans before running away. Jerry reaches into his pocket for the key. A moment later he has it in the door.

"What if it has an alarm?" Jerry asks, keeping his voice low.

"Then we run," Hans says. "Just stay quiet. I can't tell if they're not home or if they're asleep."

"I thought you could tell these things."

"Just open the door."

He is expecting the key not to work, expecting one more problem in a day full of them. The key won't work and the lock picks won't work either, but it turns effortlessly. He slowly opens the door. He knows this house. He spent most of his adult life in this house. He knows every shape, every flaw, he knows where the floorboards creak, what doors squeak, and he knows where the secrets are buried. Or, in this case, the wall they are hidden behind. His heart is already hammering, but when he steps across the threshold into the house it hammers even more, so loud that if there are people asleep upstairs it'll be his heart that wakes them.

They close the door behind them and pause and listen, Jerry's heart louder now, his breathing heavy. There is no beeping keypad. No alarm. His hands are sweating. He left the key in the lock, otherwise right now it'd most likely be sliding from his fingers onto the floor. In his mind he can see Eva upstairs in her bedroom doing her homework, or talking on the phone to one of her school friends. Sandra is in the lounge reading a book, or working on her next court case. Jerry can see himself behind the desk of his office, plugging away at the word count. He tries to draw in a deep breath, but it catches in his throat, and then it's like swallowing a golf ball. Hans puts a hand on his shoulder and he almost jumps.

"Calm down, Jerry," he says, keeping his voice low. "The sooner we get the diary, the sooner we can get out of here."

"It's a journal," Jerry whispers back. His eyes have adjusted somewhat to the dark. "Step where I step," he says, and then he starts to walk.

Hans steps where Jerry steps. The furniture makes black holes in the living room. When they reach the hall, he remembers the boards around the door can complain sometimes, so he makes a big show of stepping over them, then a big show of walking down the side of the hallway and not the middle, and the door to the office—his office—is open. They get inside and they close the door, shutting them off from the outside world, Jerry more relieved than ever to have had the room soundproofed.

"Well? Do you think there's anybody home?" Jerry asks.

"I don't know. I don't think so. Let's just get this done," Hans says, and he takes his cell phone out and uses the light to look around the room. For a few moments the office is Jerry's again. His desk, his couch, his bookcase, his framed *King Kong Escapes* poster on the wall. Then he sees all the subtle differences. The books are different. The computer is different. Different knickknacks on the bookcase mixed in with some of his own, different stationary on the desk, a different monitor, the belongings of a different man, belonging to a different life. He wonders why the police didn't tear up the floors and pull the walls down in search of evidence. But perhaps they thought the case looked pretty clear cut.

He makes his way past the desk and to the cupboard in the corner of the room. He opens it. Inside are boxes that, if Gary is anything like him, will be full of receipts and bank statements and all the other joys of being taxed in multiple countries that people don't think about when it comes to being a writer. There's a set of small plastic drawers full of stationary, a set of headphones hanging from a hook in the wall, a pile of magazines, some reams of paper. He starts dragging everything out, hoping he's going to find the hidden space, hoping it's not just something from one of his books, like that time, he suddenly remembers, when he went and bought cigarettes. His heart rate is heading back from extremely elevated into the more comfortable zone of very elevated. It only takes a second for muscle memory to kick in—once the cupboard is empty he lowers his hand and presses his finger into the corner. Out pops the opposite corner. He pulls the board away and hands it to Hans, and then . . .

And then he does nothing. He stares at the cavity, suddenly too frightened as to what may be in there. Or what may not.

You have to look, Henry says. *Looking back is the only way to be able to move forward. You didn't come all this way not to.*

He looks.

The first thing he sees is a bottle of gin. He gets it out. It's half-empty. He unscrews the lid and breaths in the aroma, the smell a brief visit to his old life.

"There's time for that later," Hans says, taking the bottle off him and putting it on the desk.

Jerry reaches back into the hole and the second thing he pulls out is the gun. He holds it loosely from the base of the handle, the way someone would handle it if they were surrendering to an Armed Offenders

Unit. It's a revolver. For a moment he can remember sitting on the floor next to Sandra. He's spinning the chamber of the gun like they do when playing Russian roulette. He flicks the latch with his thumb and the cylinder opens out to the left. Each of the holes are full, but one of the bullets is only a casing, the contents of that casing having ended up inside his wife. Hans reaches over his shoulder and takes the gun off him.

Don't trust Hans.

Probably worried Jerry is going to turn it on himself.

"Keep looking," Hans says.

He keeps looking. This time his fingers close on the journal. He looks at the cover, at the smiley face Eva drew, the eyes glued to the cover, one of them foggy, one of them clear. *Dad's coolest ideas* is written neatly above the face, *The Captain Goes Burning* on the spine. He opens the cover, and there are his words, words from another life filling the pages.

"It's really here," he says.

"Let me take a look," Hans says, and reaches back over.

But Jerry doesn't hand it over. Instead he clutches it to his chest. When he looks back at Hans he sees his friend looking annoyed, and for a moment, the briefest of moments, there is something in Hans's face, something that reminds Jerry that Hans always seemed to know the dark side even better than his darkest characters. Then Hans smiles. Jerry realizes he's being silly, and that everything is okay.

"Please, Jerry," Hans says. "I think it's better if I look. You're too close to it. Too emotional. I can give you the truth in a nicer way."

Jerry decides that Hans is right, that he won't try to twist the journal into the best possible nonguilty narrative the way Jerry would. Hans carries the journal over to the couch and sits down, the phone going with him, not leaving a lot of light for Jerry. Jerry reaches back into the cavity and finds the flash drives. Then his hand touches something long and cold, and he adjusts his grip and puts his fingers around it. It's a knife, no doubt the one used to kill the florist. An image flashes through his mind, of Sandra picking up his jacket and finding the blade in the pocket. It begs the question—if there is going to be a tactile link to a memory, why one that pales in significance to him being a murderer? Why does picking up the knife remind him of Sandra finding it, when picking up the gun reminds him of nothing?

There's a reason why you've always conveniently forgotten those things.

Eric was drugging him to cover up the murders he committed. But what about Suzan with a *z*, Sandra, and the florist? The doctors would say he's been repressing the horrible things he's done, but is that really what's going on here?

No. There's more going on here, Henry says. *Keep looking. You've found your journal, but mine is still in there.*

Was Henry keeping a journal too?

He puts the knife on the edge of the desk and goes back to the hole. He closes his hand around some loose pages.

The missing pages from his journal.

You always thought Sandra was stealing them, Henry says.

But it wasn't Sandra, it was his alter ego, the man who makes bad things happen.

That's what they pay me for.

He sits in the office chair. He turns on the desk lamp, not caring if anybody sees the light from outside, and Hans doesn't seem to care either because he doesn't say anything. He seems too engrossed with the Madness Journal.

Jerry begins to read.

It may be his handwriting, but they are definitely not his words.

They are the words of Henry Cutter.

DAY THIRTY-EIGHT

It's day thirty-eight and you feel great. You taught Mrs. Busybody across the road a lesson today, Future Henry. She wandered over here in her pastel-colored outfit recently to tell you how you were ruining the whole neighborhood, and no doubt she'll wander her way back within the next few hours to come and see you again after what you've done. The way I see it, you were presented with two options. Option one was to tidy up your garden and make her happy, to mow the lawns and pull the weeds and conform like everybody else on the street. Or there was option two. Which is what you went with. Option two was to go over to her house and make her garden look worse than yours. It's funny how she got under your skin so much, but she did, and not only have you helped her with her own garden, but you've put her into book number thirteen. You wanted to give her a real *Hansel and Gretel* vibe, make her the crazy old witch that tries turning children into casseroles, but since you don't write fairy tales you've given her a cameo instead as the local cat lady who chews her fingernails down to the nub as she stares out her kitchen window watching life pass her by before being raped by a clown. Cameos are things you give people who upset you. Somebody ducked into the parking space you were waiting for? Fuck you—you're dead on page twenty-six. Somebody give you a bad review? Fuck you—you're the local pedophile on page ten. Doctor Badstory told you you have dementia? Fuck you.

Writing about her wasn't enough, which is why you went over and ripped out every single rose in her garden, roses she was so proud of. She was there every day checking on them, her husband ten years in the grave and all things considered, that made him one lucky bastard.

Another neighbor—some old tart who turned a hundred years old the same year the Titanic sank—saw you, and you thought . . . well . . . you thought why not do what Henry Cutter always does? And kill people off? But tearing out roses is a long way from tearing out throats, and killing people is only for the books—but you'd be lying to yourself if you didn't admit there was a moment, albeit a very brief one, where you imagined her bleeding to death on the ground, her face riddled with confusion and pain. But that didn't happen, and no doubt she'll tell Mrs. Smith that she saw you, but the thing is you don't really care. What's the worst that can happen? You already have Alzheimer's. Who cares if she calls the police and you have to pay a fine. It'll be worth every penny.

When Mrs. Smith comes over later, just smile at her, and tell her how much fun you had ruining her pride and joy. Then laugh at her, because the one thing people hate in life is being laughed at.

So there you go, Madness Journal. Another bullshit day out of the way on this road to . . . hell, I don't know.

Jerry places the journal entry down. His first thought is that he has no recollection of having ever written it, certainly not from Henry's POV. His second is that Henry is a complete asshole. Was Henry more than just a pen name? Did he actually *become* Henry when he sat at the keyboard? Jerry begins to understand his critics a little better but is baffled by how he ended up becoming an internationally bestselling author. Not with this guy at the wheel.

He hopes Henry wasn't actually at the wheel.

Surely not. Sandra would never have lived with him.

The same way she never would have married a killer?

Well, that's what they are here to prove.

Or disprove. I don't like that you think of me as an asshole, especially when all I'm doing is trying to help you.

Jerry looks back at the pages. Henry never existed, not in the beginning, but perhaps the Alzheimer's gave birth to him. Perhaps Henry grew enough to occasionally take control. There's no other way to explain the journal.

"Can I have the journal?" he asks Hans.

Hans doesn't look up as he keeps on reading it. "I'm not done with it."

"Just for a minute. I want to check something."

Now Hans looks over. "About the day Sandra died?"

"Something in the beginning."

Hans seems to think about it, and Jerry is suddenly sure his friend is about to say no, but then he relents and tosses it over. "Make it quick," he says.

Jerry flicks through to day thirty-eight, but there is no day thirty-eight. There's a day forty. Before day forty are the torn edges in the margin where pages have been removed. His concern about being Henry becomes concern for the other things he's done, the ultimate concern being Henry is the one who killed Sandra. He flicks back to the first page. He can actually remember sitting at his desk writing some of this stuff. Day one. *Your name is Jerry Grey, and you are scared. . . . You lost your phone yesterday, and last week you lost your car, and recently you forgot Sandra's name.* Day four. *You won't be able to hold Sandra's hand and watch her smile. You won't be able to chase Eva and pretend you're a grizzly bear.* Day twenty. *People often think that crime writers know how to get away with murder, but you've always thought if anybody could, it'd be Hans.* Day thirty. *There's a couch in the office. The Thinking Couch. You'll lie there sometimes and come up with ideas for the books, work on solutions, lie there and listen to Springsteen cranked so loud the pens will roll off the desk.* Then day forty, and here Past Jerry has no memory at all of what he's done to Mrs. Smith's roses, and that's because it wasn't Past Jerry who tore them out, but Past Henry. He used to think Sandra was tearing the pages out, but no, it was him. Or Henry. One of them was tearing them out to protect him, to keep the bad things he was doing a secret.

He scans through more pages. The truth is in there, other bad things, and suddenly he knows without a doubt that he didn't kill Sandra. It was Henry. Henry Cutter, writer of words, destroyer of lives.

He tosses the journal back to Hans.

"What is it you're reading there?" Hans asks.

"Just some notes," Jerry says, and he goes back to the loose pages, of which there are another dozen or so. There are more things he has done here as Henry. The whole thing with the spray-paint—that was Henry. He wrote about it before doing it. He had the can of spray-paint on his desk when he was writing the entry. He was getting ready to walk out the door and sneak across the street, and oh how he was looking forward to it. He knew Mrs. Smith would suspect him, but he didn't care. He would deny it. He would suggest she leave the neighborhood because somebody seemed to have it in for her.

That's what Henry wrote.

And where the hell was Jerry then?

He carries on reading. Henry develops a crush on the florist. A few days before the wedding he decides to sneak out the window to go and see her. Jerry remembers that day. Not sneaking out the window, but he remembers being at the flower shop, the woman who helped him, who drove him home, the woman who died the night of the wedding.

It's looking like Henry isn't a dessert guy, but a rape and murder guy.

There are more pages. The truth is so powerful it hurts, his head feels tight, the horror and the anger at what he has done is swelling inside him, his brain feels like it's going to pop. Here's an entry titled *WMD Plus a Bunch of Hours Plus Don't Trust Hans Plus a Bunch of Other Shit*. It starts with Henry waking up on the couch with blood all over his shirt. He checks his body for cuts, he counts his fingers and toes, and comes to the conclusion the blood isn't his. He suspects it might have been from his neighbor, he says *My first thought is the silly old trout from over the road, that she's come over and asked me to trim back the hedges and instead I've trimmed back her arms and legs, sculpting her body back to a limbless blob*.

He checks on Sandra. She's fine. Then he hides the shirt under the floorboards *where spiders and mice can eat it over the next hundred years*. Henry can remember speaking to Nurse Mae earlier in the evening, but not what they spoke about. He says it's like looking through fog.

Something is hinky, according to Henry. Out of whack. And not just Alzheimer's hinky. Only Henry can't figure it out.

The entry ends there. Jerry can't help but be impressed. Henry Cutter has performed his most famous trick: he's driven the story into the unknown. It's been his job for years to make up scenarios, to string facts together in a weird and wonderful way. He is Henry Cutter, he is the master of making a coincidence work, of turning a cliché on it's head, of disappointing a few bloggers and being a chauvinistic asshole.

He is Jerry Grey, he is Henry Cutter, and together they have always been able to connect the dots. What now?

Jerry looks across the room at his friend, who is back to reading the Madness Journal. He looks at the gun resting on the arm of the couch and then at the knife on the desk. He thinks about what he just saw when he flicked through the diary. Day twenty. *People often think that crime writers know how to get away with murder, but you've always thought if anybody could, it'd be Hans*. He looks down again at Henry's loose pages and begins to read.

Don't Trust Hans
A short story by Henry Cutter

Hans could feel his heart hammering in his chest. So hard
it made his hands shake as he worked at the lock. Picking locks was one of his things. Shaky hands was not. He
was excited, not nervous. You learn to pick a lock . . .
well now, it's like having a key to the world. He once told
his friend Jerry that a long time ago. The problem is you
don't get the same feel when you're wearing gloves—that
millimeter of latex numbing the senses and making the tum-
blers feel half the size they really are. But he knew what
he was doing, and it was only a matter of time. Less than
two minutes later there was a soft click and something in
the lock went slack, then tightened again. His key to the
world had worked.

He breathed deep. Nobody could see him. It was a clear
night and there was a half-moon hanging right above him,
eliminating the need for a flashlight. He could see a million stars, and looking out at them made the night feel
timeless, it made him feel tiny. He could taste the air. He
opened the door, the interior a black hole the light from
the moon couldn't penetrate. Ever since he saw the girl at
Jerry's house a week ago he knew he had to have her. Knew
he had to have some up close and personal time with her.
Poor Jerry. He really messed up that wedding. Hans would
rather die than go through what his friend was experienc-
ing. Not that he will go through it. That said, there were
two things he knew for certain in this world—the first
was if you wore new sneakers, people always had to point
it out. They can't help themselves. The second was nobody
thinks they're going to get Alzheimer's. Alzheimer's is for
grandparents.

It was a modern home made of brick, the kind of home
designed to keep out the wolves, but the smart wolves would

always find a way in. That was nature. That was evolution. He stepped inside and closed the door behind him and embraced the darkness. He didn't know the layout, but there were only so many options. He used the display on his cell phone to light the way. He had it on mute in case somebody rang, but who would ring in the middle of the night?

The kitchen was full of modern appliances paid for by love. He had never considered that florists earn the big bucks, but maybe they did. Maybe each Valentine's Day paid for the next big thing, people getting second mortgages on their houses to be able to afford a dozen roses. There was a knife block on the bench. He had his choice. He could do plenty of damage with any of them. He knew bigger was better when it came to telling women what to do, but he also knew in the right hands it wasn't the size that mattered. He chose a knife with a six-inch blade. Half the size of his cock, he wanted to say, but there was no one to listen.

Hans carried the knife into the hallway. He stood motionless. He'd always had the ability to tell if a house was empty, and if it wasn't he could get a sense of where the occupants were. This occupant was in the bedroom. He made his way there. The door was open. The only light was coming from a digital alarm clock. He stood in the doorway and listened to her breathing. His hands were still shaking. He was the wolf.

The wolf did what he went there to do, all the close up and personal stuff that left the girl with her eyes lifelessly open and her body temperature dropping. When he was done, he made his way out of the house and into the backyard. He was smiling. The moment he had shared with the florist would be something he would never forget—not like his loser friend Jerry, who could have a hundred moments like this and not remember one of them. What a waste. He had felt his phone vibrate a few times over the last couple of hours, and he checked it now and hell, speak of the devil, he had a voice mail from Jerry waiting for him.

Three messages, in fact. Jerry had done that wandering thing again where he gets confused and lost, and this time he had gone back to the house he used to live in thirty years ago. He needed help, and he wasn't going to get that from his wife, not after what he had said about her at the wedding. He wanted Hans to come and get him.

Hans thought about it as he made his way back to the car. And the more he thought about it, the more he began to see an opportunity. He had been careful not to leave any evidence behind—he knew how to clean up a crime scene, but of course sometimes you just got unlucky. If the police had a solid suspect that wasn't him . . . well now, wouldn't that be a wonderful thing. He rang Jerry back.

Jerry was happy to hear from him. He told Jerry he would be there soon, and to meet him outside once he pulled up. The key was to be subtle. He had learned that from Jerry's books. The key was to make Jerry come to the conclusion he himself was a killer. The key was to make Jerry try to hide the evidence, which would only serve to make him look guiltier. Hans still had the knife. It didn't have his prints on it. The plan had been to dump it into a deep hole forever, but now the plan was changing. Evolving. It was survival of the fittest, and Jerry's days were over. What did it matter if the world thought he was a killer?

He drove to the house where Jerry was waiting. Not much had changed in the thirty years since he was last here, or maybe it had and he just didn't give a shit. He parked outside the old house and Jerry came walking down the pathway to the car with that stupid dopey look Jerry has these days. The *I'm confused and don't know what the hell is going on* look. There was an overweight woman watching from the doorway and that was a loose end, but not one he felt needed taking care of immediately. He would see where things went.

Jerry climbed into the car, thanked him, and then . . . then nothing. His friend was switching off again, wasn't he?

"Jerry? Hey, Jerry, are you with me?"

Jerry wasn't with him. Jerry was walking the fields and shitting in the woods of Batshit County, population: Jerry.

He drove the rest of the way to Jerry's house, but pulled up twenty yards short. He didn't want to risk waking Sandra. He climbed out of the car and came around to Jerry's side. His friend was in a state somewhere between consciousness and sleep. He allowed Hans to lead him to the house. Hans could feel Jerry switch into some kind of automatic mode. He climbed through the office window and sat on the couch. At that point Hans could do anything he wanted, so what he did was sit down and think things through. He went out to the car and brought in the murder weapon. Jerry was asleep. He wiped blood from the knife onto Jerry's shirt, then dropped the knife into the pocket of Jerry's jacket after putting Jerry's prints all over it.

Then he left. He felt sure Sandra would be calling the police by the end of the day. She would see Jerry's shirt covered in blood. She would find the knife. She would turn in her husband. Hell, maybe Jerry would kill his wife too, and that'd be the icing on the cake because the bitch never has liked Hans. It was about time Jerry was useful for something.

❖

Useful Jerry. That's who he is now. He flicks back through the story, a story he can't remember writing, a story Henry went and penned all by himself. His heart is hammering again, it hammers hard then skips a few beats and then hammers some more. He feels light-headed.

It's a story, he thinks. Just a story, prefaced with the words *A short story*. It doesn't say *A short essay*. It doesn't say *A witness statement*. It says *short story*, because it's fiction, because it's made up, because that's what he and Henry do—they are makeup artists. And in this case, one of those makeup artists has gotten carried away with things, but that's Henry's thing, the same way Hans's thing is picking locks (maybe) and killing women (maybe) and how Jerry is a dessert guy (definitely). But it's also Henry's thing to find the truth in a lie. It could have gone that way. Jerry could have woken, found himself wearing the shirt Hans had bloodied, then hidden it before going back to sleep. Or none of it happened. He killed the florist and he killed his wife and the Alzheimer's is trying to protect him from the truth.

Don't trust Hans. Should he?

"You okay, buddy?" Hans asks.

Jerry looks over at his friend. Hans is staring at him, a hardened look on his face. There's a shift in mood in the room, a darker tone that makes him feel cold. He gets the sense Hans has been watching him for a while now.

Be careful.

"I'm fine," he says, but he's not fine. It's all coming together now. Don't trust Hans, because Hans is a psychopath.

"What are you reading?"

"Nothing much," Jerry says, and he flicks his gaze to the arm of the couch where the gun he found earlier is resting. It's the quickest of glances, but Hans must notice it too.

"Ah hell," Hans says, and he picks up the gun. "Those pages, they fit into here, don't they." He points the gun at Jerry and shakes the journal with his other hand. "You were bound to figure it out sooner or later. Either way, it all ends here, buddy. I just needed the journal."

"You killed Sandra," Jerry says. "You killed the florist too."

"You were close to figuring it out in here," Hans says, still holding the journal, "but what I don't understand is why you tore out those pages. What do they say?"

"You killed Sandra," Jerry says, ignoring the question. He starts to get up from the desk. "Jesus, the girl from all those years ago! Suzan with a *z*. That was you as well?"

"She was the first. Don't move any further, Jerry."

Jerry shakes his head. He feels sick. This man has been his friend for thirty years. They've studied together, commiserated together, celebrated together, drunk and laughed and partied and talked all kinds of shit in all kinds of states together. His friend. His goddamn friend. "How many have there been?" he asks.

"What does it matter?" Hans asks.

"You're insane."

Hans shrugs. "Really? All those things you write about, and now with the Alzheimer's messing with you, you're calling me the insane one?"

"You're not going to get away with this."

Hans laughs. "Jesus, you really know how to pull out the clichés, even in the end."

"I don't understand," Jerry says. "Why were you even helping me today?"

"I wasn't planning on it," Hans says. "I wanted to take you to the police."

"But you changed your mind."

"I had to, once you'd mentioned the journal. I couldn't take the risk you'd written something in there that would come to bite me in the ass if it was ever found. And good thing too, because you had."

Jerry thinks back to earlier this afternoon. They were only a few blocks from the police station when everything changed. That must have been when he told Hans about the journal. Everything since then has been in the pursuit of Jerry remembering where he'd hidden it.

"What about Eric? What was all that about? Did he really do those things?"

"Eric? Of course he did. He was one of your bad guys in the flesh, Jerry. A real whack job."

Jerry looks at the gun. Then he thinks about the knife on the desk and has to make a conscious effort not to look in its direction. If he can just get to it . . .

And what? Outrun a bullet?

"So now what? You're framing me for the bad things you've done too? Just like he did?"

"Hey, it was a good plan," Hans says. "Seems a shame to waste it just because it didn't work for him."

"You shot Sandra."

"I did."

"Why can't I remember that?"

"I drugged you," he says. "I came over that day after you called me, and injected you when we were in the office. I had to. I knew eventually you'd figure it out. Hell, I should have known the blood on the shirt was a mistake. That's where I messed up."

Jerry tries to picture the moment, but there's nothing. This man who was supposed to look out for him betrayed him. Just like Eric. "There's no way you can get away with this," Jerry says.

I think he's doing just that.

Why couldn't Henry have warned him? Doesn't he always connect the dots?

You're not the only one the Alzheimer's is affecting, buddy. And I did try to warn you.

He did. But it was a little late.

"What are you going to do? Shoot me in here? Then what? The police are going to come here and they'll figure it out."

Hans smiles again. "All these years you kept coming to me for advice. You kept wanting to know how things work. You made shitloads of money off the help I gave you, and what did I get in return? Huh? A mention in the acknowledgments. But how about a fucking royalty check, huh? You owe me, Jerry. Think of this as me collecting, and think of this as you getting to live one of the scenarios you often gave your characters."

"What are you talking about?"

"Your characters. You've put them through hell. Absolute hell. Some of the decisions they've had to make . . . they're impossible . . . even for me. And now you're going to get a taste of that. You know what your problem is, buddy? You think about yourself too much. You must think the whole universe centers on you, that you pull all the strings. But you don't seem to pay any mind to how your actions affect anyone. Your amazing wife, your talented and beautiful daughter, your loyal friend, always at your disposal. You'd think we were all created by you. That we only exist when you're in the room."

Jerry thinks for second, wonders if these words could possibly be true.

"What the hell does that even mean?"

"It means your life has been over since the diagnosis, Jerry, but I've still got a lot of living left to do. Good living. Let's wrap things up on good terms, huh? Good terms is a win-win for us. I get to carry on with my life, and this shitty existence of yours gets to come to an end. We end things on good terms and I don't have to hurt Eva. Or I shoot you right now and drive to her house."

"You son of—"

"Don't," Hans says, when Jerry starts to get out of the chair. "Just don't. Not until you've heard me out."

Jerry stops moving. "Don't hurt her."

"Then don't make me. You write a confession, you take the easy way out, and I don't go and—"

"Don't say it," Jerry says, and the images are already there, Eva crying, Eva bleeding, Eva naked and begging for her life.

"I'll make sure she knows you're the reason I have to hurt her. But you can save her, Jerry. Right here, right now."

"You won't get away with it. The police will know you did it."

"Maybe they'll figure it out, maybe they won't. What is certain is Eva will be dead. You have nothing left, Jerry. But you can do this for her. You can save her."

Jerry begins to say something then realizes he doesn't know what. His mouth is dry. His heart is hammering again, and soon it won't be able to hammer anymore. "You want me to shoot myself," he says.

"It's as simple as it sounds," Hans says.

"I—"

"You confess to a few things on my behalf," Hans says, "and I promise I'll never see Eva again. You have my word. You don't do this, and I'm going to kill her, and I'm going to have myself some fun while doing it, just like I did with the florist."

"Have I ever killed anybody?"

"You really are a chump, Jerry. No, you haven't, but you will be killing Eva if you don't do what I ask."

It doesn't require any thought. In fact, from the moment Hans mentioned Eva's name he knew where this was going. There is no choice. It's what any parent would do. Die to protect their child. It comes with the territory. "What do you want me to say?"

"You're the writer, I'm sure you can come up with something. Think of it as your greatest work of fiction."

Jerry starts to nod. "Okay," he says. "First I need to know what happened. That day with Sandra. I need you to tell me."

"Why? It won't do you any good to hear it."

"Please. I have to know."

Hans shrugs, like it's no big deal. "She figured it out," he says, "and looking through those final few pages, you almost figured it out too. In fact I think you did. That's what's in those loose pages, isn't it? They're from the diary, aren't they?"

"It's a journal," Jerry says, "and yes."

"Why did you rip them out?" When Jerry doesn't answer, Hans starts to smile. He carries on. "You don't remember ripping them out, do you?"

"I think Henry tore them out."

"What?"

Jerry doesn't feel like explaining it. But he thinks Henry was tearing them out because Henry was just as crazy as Jerry, and when you're the king of Mount Crazy, you do things that don't make sense. Maybe Henry was trying to protect him somehow. Maybe Henry tore them out because he knew the journal would end up in the wrong hands. He had to save what he thought was important. Whatever the reason, Jerry thinks it doesn't really matter. Not now. Not when there's a loaded gun pointing at him.

Instead of answering Hans, he asks again what happened with Sandra.

"We were in your office," Hans says. "The gun was still on your desk.

You asked me again about the blood on the shirt. You told me Sandra had spoken to the nurse. You and Sandra were confused because the events didn't line up. The nurse hadn't seen blood on your shirt, and the time of death for the florist suggested you were innocent. You went to the office door to call to Sandra, and as soon as your back was to me I injected you in the neck. A few seconds later you were out cold. I laid you on the couch, then just waited until Sandra came in. She rushed over to you and I closed the door behind her. She looked up at me and I could tell she had figured it out. She had that same look on her face you had a few minutes ago."

"You asked her what she knew?"

"There was no point. I knew that she knew, and she knew that I knew that she knew. One shot to the chest, that's all it took. Sound-proofing really is a wonderful thing, Jerry."

Jerry can feel himself coming apart at the seams. All of this started that night at the party when he said *this is my wife* . . . and couldn't remember Sandra's name. That image is as clear as it was the day it happened. It means that right now he's having the worst good day he's had since being diagnosed. The disease allowed him to forget Sandra's name, it allowed Hans and Eric to take advantage of him. Sandra, dead because of an illness for which there is no cure. All of this because the Universe is punishing him. But what for? If not for killing, then for what? The answer comes to him quickly. It's because he did the one thing he swore he would never do—he based a character on a real person. Suzan with a *z*. She was a real person with a real family and real feelings, and he betrayed that. He turned what happened to her into a story. He wrote about it for entertainment.

"You're a monster," Jerry says.

The knife. Go for the knife.

But if he goes for it, and fails, then Eva is the one who pays.

"Maybe," Hans says. "But hey, we did have a good time today, right? We did get a killer off the street."

"Is that why we hung him out the window? Because you wanted to kill him?"

"We had to, buddy. He'd seen my face. Despite everything, Jerry, I really was trying to help you there."

"Why? Because you didn't want somebody else framing me for their crimes? Was this some sort of twisted contest?"

"Partly," he says. "Well, mostly. And before you ask about his wife, she's not going to remember anything, clearly. But Nurse Mae, well, that's one loose end I'm going to have to tie up."

"You don't have to hurt her."

"We'll see."

"All that stuff about the police going easy on us, that was bullshit," Jerry says.

"Just write the note, Jerry. And don't mention Suzan. We don't want to complicate the issue. Now hurry up before I change my mind and decide to go and pay Eva a visit. And make sure you sell it. You're not writing to save your own life, you're writing to save your daughter's."

My Confession
By Jerry Grey

My name is Jerry Grey. I'm a crime writer, I'm a killer, I'm
a deeply flawed individual. This is my confession.

There are so many things I want to say. First and fore-
most, I want to apologize to my family. I wish I could tell
Sandra how sorry I am, but what's done is done, it was
done by me, and there's no going back. I shot you, Sandra, because you found out what kind of man I really am.
If you're somewhere now in the afterlife, I imagine I will
be in a much different version.

The truth is, my entire life I have had needs I've been
able to keep in check, only occasionally letting my true
self out to play, hurting women on those occasions. But when
the Alzheimer's came along, it wiped my impulse control.
Those women over the last few weeks, they didn't die at my
hands. Eric murdered them and there is enough evidence at
his house to prove that. I killed him, and in a way I hope
it helps balance the scales for the others.

Last year, on the night of Eva's wedding, I snuck out
of my house and I walked to Belinda Murray's house. From
the moment I first saw her I became infatuated. There was
something about her. Something that made me feel alive.
I walked to her house, and I picked the lock on her back
door. Picking locks and covering up crime scenes, these are
things I've learned from reading and research and writing.
But I don't want to cover up crime scenes anymore. I just
want the world to know what happened because I'm tired of
lying, and soon I won't be able to lie anyway. I killed Belinda Murray because I wanted to, because I knew it would
feel good, and it did.

I've come back to the place where it all started. I guess
it's here where Passenger A first climbed on board, just
catching a lift until finally being promoted to captain.

It's here where I raised Eva, had a life with Sandra, it's here where the books were written, where Sandra died, and where I will die. I've come back to look for my Madness Journal, but it isn't here, and I remember now, I remember destroying it after I killed Sandra. I had confessed in there what I had done, so I tore out the pages and I tore them into shreds and I flushed them away. Back then I was confused.

Now I'm more clearheaded than I've been in a long time. This isn't just a confession. This is also my suicide note.

I'm not killing myself because I'm a bad man. I'm not killing myself because I'm a monster. I'm killing myself because I'm already forgetting the people I've hurt. The fantasy, thinking about Belinda, about shooting Sandra, that's what gets me through the days. Without those thoughts, I have nothing. I would rather die than forget how it feels to kill.

So that's what I'm going to do.

Jerry slides the pages across the desk. Hans grabs them and sits back on the couch. He reads through it, glancing up every few seconds to make sure Jerry isn't making a break for it. When he's done he moves back to the desk and hands the pages back.

"You can do better," Hans says.

"It's good enough," Jerry says.

"You don't even apologize to your family. You don't tell them that you love them. Add that and sign it and maybe then we're done."

Jerry picks up the pen. *Everybody is a critic*, he thinks, but then realizes Hans has a point. He can remember writing similar letters in the past. One to Sandra, one to Eva, letters he wrote from the heart when he thought he was a killer and he thought saying good-bye was doing them a favor. But he can't capture that mood now. At the bottom he writes

```
I wish I could turn back the clock. Despite all my actions,
I love my family. I love my wife, I love my daughter, and
I would do anything to have them back. Anything. Eva, I'm
so sorry. I love you so much. I wish there was some way to
ask for your forgiveness.
```

He wishes there was something else he could write, some kind of code to let the police know he's innocent, but there's nothing. Jerry signs the confession and slides it back across the desk. While making the addition, Hans has set fire to the short story Henry wrote. The ashes are still drifting onto the carpet. Hans picks it up and reads it. Jerry glances at the knife then looks away. Even if he can get to it, a knife against a gun isn't much of a battle. He now has the ultimate role as a parent, and that's to protect his daughter.

"There's no emotion in here," Hans says.

"It's the best I can do."

Hans nods. He puts down the note. "Here's what I want you to do for me. I want you to focus, really focus on what I'm going to do to Eva if you try anything other than what we've spoken about. You understand me?"

"I understand you."

"Put your palms flat on the desk," Hans says.

Jerry does as he's asked. He knows where this is going. He is, after all, the master of connecting the dots. In twenty seconds he'll be dead. By tomorrow he will be a confessed killer, and Eva will live with that shame, but at least she will get to live. The Alzheimer's has taken his life, and Sandra's, and the women that Eric killed, but he won't let it take Eva's.

Hans moves around behind him, coming to a stop behind the chair.

"Keep your left hand on the desk," he says, "and bring your right hand up to your head. Pretend your fingers are a gun and you're going to shoot yourself."

Jerry does as he's asked. He brings his right hand up, turns his fingers into a barrel and points them against his skull. His hands are shaking. He's thinking he should have gone for the knife. Should have done something. With everything he's lost, all those times he thought about killing himself, he's surprised at how afraid he is to die. Perhaps, if the circumstances were different—

But they're not different, Henry says.

And final words of advice?

You're on your own here, buddy.

"You try messing with me and this will go very badly for both you and Eva."

"I know."

Hans puts the gun into Jerry's hand, and at the same time jams the barrel into the side of Jerry's head. He has both hands wrapped around Jerry's hand, forcing him to maintain the aim. He closes his eyes. He can feel his finger being forced into the trigger guard. He's doing the right thing. For Eva. But before he can do anything else, the wireless doorbell starts ringing.

"Somebody is here," Jerry says, searching again for a way out of this. "If there are others inside sleeping they're going to wake up. You can't get away with it."

"Shut up," Hans says, and he takes the gun out of Jerry's hand but keeps it pointing at him.

The doorbell keeps ringing.

"It's probably the police," Jerry says. "Somebody saw us break in. Maybe the owners heard us."

The ringing stops. There is silence for ten seconds. Then there is tapping at the office window.

"You shoot me now," Jerry says, "and it only makes things worse for you."

"Shut up," Hans says, then he moves over to the curtain. There is more tapping, which is then followed by more silence. Hans peers around the corner of the curtain, careful to keep the gun pointing in Jerry's direction. "It's your nosy neighbor," he says. "She's got a flashlight and that bloody hockey stick she had earlier. Okay, she's leaving. Wait . . . she's moving to the back of the house."

"She's going to come inside, and I bet she's called the police. You should go."

"She won't be coming inside."

"I left the key in the back door. She might."

Hans moves back behind the chair. He points the gun at the door. They wait.

"Don't shoot her," Jerry says.

"What do you care? You hated her anyway."

"Please."

"Don't worry, as soon as I'm done you can add a PS, *I just shot the neighbor* to the bottom of your confession."

The handle on the office door starts to turn. The door opens, and there she is. Mrs. Smith, standing in the doorway wielding the hockey stick. She takes two steps forward, and Jerry has no idea what kind of scenario she was expecting to walk in on, but it certainly couldn't have been this one. To her credit, it only takes her a second to sum up the situation.

"Oh," she says, and she must really like the sound of it because she says it again. Any other person would be caught between fleeing and running, Jerry thinks, but not Mrs. Smith, the woman whose garden he vandalized, whose house he graffitied. Mrs. Smith who has been a constant pain in his ass since the day he moved in. Where others might flee, or be paralyzed by shock, she comes forward, perhaps thinking she can cover the distance quick enough, perhaps thinking the man with the tattoos won't really open fire on a woman older than the sun, perhaps thinking the very idea of a wrongdoing is so offensive she must challenge it.

Hans pulls the trigger.

The gunshot is instant. It's loud, a booming in the room that makes Jerry's ears ring so painfully that instinct takes over and he puts both palms over his ears. Mrs. Smith doesn't do that. Instead she takes two steps forward as if refusing to believe she's been shot before coming to a stop. She looks down at her body where there is no sign at all of any damage, as if the bullet has gone through without harming her, or perhaps it completely missed. But then blood appears just below her chest. She drops to her knees, her face scrunches up into a tight ball, and she uses the hockey stick to prop herself up. She tries to get back onto her feet.

"How dare you," she says.

Hans pulls the trigger again.

And the gun goes *click*.

"What the fuck?" Hans says, and Jerry knows exactly what's happened, that when he kept spinning the chamber all those months ago as he sat next to Sandra, the bullets got out of sequence. Right now the firing pin has landed on the empty shell, the one that used to contain the bullet that killed his wife. Hans turns the gun to the side so he can look at it, as if the problem will be visible, and as he does this Henry speaks up. *Now*, he screams, the word inside Jerry's head almost as loud as the gunshot, so loud, in fact, that Jerry knows he too is shouting out the word.

He throws his elbow back into Hans, getting him in the base of his stomach, just as Hans pulls the trigger. The shot is wide and hits the wall. Jerry turns in the chair and now the fight is on, and this is the way it should be done, he thinks, a fighting chance, and isn't that the best way to end things? A good old-fashioned fistfight to the death? It would be, except for the fact fighting is a Hans thing to do, and therefore he knows how to do it. Then there's the slight fact that Hans still has the gun. A gun he now turns towards Jerry. There is another explosion of sound, and suddenly there's a burning in his stomach and he feels like his kidneys are on fire. The room darkens as his legs weaken. He's able to get his hands onto Hans's hand and push the gun so it's pointing away. One bullet for his wife a year ago, one into Mrs. Smith, one into the wall, one into his stomach. That leaves two.

The knife, Henry says. *Do it. For the love of God, stop stalling!* It's on the desk. He can see it, but he can't reach it. Hans is turning the gun back towards him. It's happening in slow motion. It's pointing at the wall, at the chair, at Jerry's shoulder, then at his chest, and as the gun gets into position the expression on Hans's face changes too, first one of anger, then frustration, then he smiles. A big *Fuck you* smile. An *I win* smile. "Eva is next," Hans says.

The hockey stick, one end still being held tightly by Mrs. Smith, swings through the air and hits Hans in the forearm, not enough power to break bone, Jerry thinks, but enough to make the gun hit the floor. Hans reaches for it, and Jerry goes for the knife. He has a vision of knocking it off the desk, of it skidding over the floor, but no, his hand wraps tight around the handle. He doesn't hesitate. He swings it towards the man who killed his wife. He swings it as hard as he can, swings it for Sandra, for the florist, he swings it for Suzan with a *z*, he swings it for Eva, for everybody this man has hurt, for all of those that have had their lives ruined by their own Captain A. Most of all he swings it for himself. He conjures up all the anger he has and swings it as hard as he can.

It finds Hans's neck.

It goes in the side, the entire blade, slicing in on an angle so the tip comes out the front. Jerry puts all his strength into it, pulling forward, trying to cut all the way through to the front, but it won't move any further. Not that it matters. Hans stops going for the gun and puts his hand to his neck, blood shooting out like a fountain, a gurgling sound coming from deep inside his throat. He straightens up, both hands on the wound now, trying to stem the flow, but it's no good. Already the light starts to fade from his eyes. He stumbles and leans against the wall, the knife still buried all the way into his neck. Jerry reaches down for the gun. He points it at Hans.

"This is for Sandra," he says, but before he can pull the trigger, the hockey stick comes back into view. It comes swinging into his field of vision, held by a woman too stubborn to die. It hits Jerry in the forehead and all the lights in the world switch off.

DEAR DIARY

Dear Diary, dear Future Jerry, dear Anybody Else who is reading this, my name is Jerry Grey and I have a story. I am a father, a husband, a crime writer, a gunshot survivor, I have Alzheimer's, and I am a convicted killer. I murdered my wife. I don't remember killing her, and I don't know whether to be grateful for Captain A hiding that from me or not. I live in a psychiatric facility with bars on the windows and locks on the doors and gray walls in every direction. Sometimes I have questions, and sometimes the doctors answer them, and sometimes I don't believe what I'm hearing, and sometimes to prove their point they'll show me a copy of the confession note I wrote. Other times they'll show me the newspaper articles too. On days when they don't have time to answer my questions, they just medicate me. It's easier that way. For them, and for me.

They tell me I've been here a year now.

This is day one of keeping a diary, which I'm doing in an attempt to keep my sanity, of which there is very little left. Though, really, I think it's more of an attempt to preserve some of the man I used to be. It wasn't my idea, but the idea of one of the doctors. He thinks it may help.

Sadly, the man I used to be is a monster. I killed a lot of people. I killed my wife. I killed a florist who worked on my daughter's wedding. I killed my best friend, Hans, I killed a woman who used to be my neighbor, and I also killed an orderly at the nursing home where I used to live. There are diaries, I've been told, that I've kept in the past, but the police have them now. Some days I think those diaries might tell me I'm innocent, other days I think they just confirm what I wrote in the confession. It means all the things I don't want to be true are, indeed, true. Yet the only person I can remember killing is Suzan. Suzan with a *z*.

When I try to think of these people, their names and faces all fade into a murky past, but not hers. I remember quite clearly standing in the backyard of her house, the moon bright and full, I remember embracing the night and feeling the blood pulse through my body as the need took me over. I had wanted Suzan from the moment I first saw her. I wanted to know how she felt.

So, Diary, I'm going to tell you all about it. But first . . . I don't really like the name *Diary*. I've been thinking of *Madness Diary*, but that doesn't quite fit. I'll think about it and see what else I can come up with.

Future Jerry, let me tell you about Suzan.

Madness Diary, let me tell you how my life as a killer began. . . .

ACKNOWLEDGMENTS

Out of the nine novels I've written so far, this one has been the most fun for me, and perhaps the most personal. In the book, Jerry keeps saying "write what you know," and for the first time I've gotten to do that. There is plenty in Jerry's life that is similar to my own—and of course there is plenty that isn't. For a start, he's older (though that'll obviously change one day) and, Alzheimer's aside, he's in better shape than I am. He went to university, I didn't. He has a wife and a daughter, I don't. We are both closet trekkies, both drink G&Ts, and we have the same artwork hanging in our offices—the *King Kong Escapes* print hangs near my desk, and of course there's the music. Each of the books I've written has a soundtrack—a very loud soundtrack that blasts throughout the house and half the neighborhood. Why so loud? Because I don't want to hear myself sing. Nobody wants that. *The Laughterhouse* was written to The Doors, *Cemetery Lake* to Pink Floyd, *Joe Victim* to Bruce Springsteen. Others have had The Killers, The Rolling Stones, The Beatles . . . the line in the book about the music Jerry listens to being immortal—that's truly what I believe. This book was actually written to the tunes of David Gray—he's always been one of my favorites, and I've pretty much been binge listening to him for the last year or so. In fact, I started learning guitar recently, and it's David Gray songs that I practice with.

The last few books were written in a variety of countries, but this one was all New Zealand. Half in the summer and half in the winter. Like I say, this one was a lot of fun for me. It feels like I've been living with Jerry for a long time now—and I get the feeling I'll be living with him for some time yet.

Like all the books, *Trust No One* only exists because of the wonderful and dedicated team at Atria Books in New York. There's my super fantastic editor, Sarah Branham, who always guides me in the right direction, pointing out what I can't see until all the pieces fall into place. Judith Curr, David Brown, Hillary Tisman, Janice Fryer, Lisa Keim, Emily Bestler, Anne Badman, Isolde Sauer, Leora Bernstein, and all the others—thank you for giving my books a home. And of course thanks to Stephanie Glencross, my editor at Gregory & Company in the UK, who once again nailed things on the head, sending me down the necessary path of many rewrites.

Let me sign off once again by thanking you, the reader. Thanks again for the messages, for heading along to festivals to say hi—it's always inspiring to see people passionate about books. Like always, you guys are who I write for. You guys are the reason I like to make bad things happen . . .

Paul Cleave
April 2015
Christchurch, New Zealand